THE
THINGS
I DO
FOR YOU

Books by Mary Carter

SHE'LL TAKE IT

ACCIDENTALLY ENGAGED

SUNNYSIDE BLUES

MY SISTER'S VOICE

THE PUB ACROSS THE POND

THE THINGS I DO FOR YOU

Published by Kensington Publishing Corporation

THE THINGS I DO FOR YOU

MARY CARTER

KENSINGTON BOOKS
www.kensingtonbooks.com

I'd like to dedicate this book to lighthouse keepers and conservancy groups dedicated to preserving them everywhere. Thank you for leaving the lights on for us.

ACKNOWLEDGMENTS

I would like to thank my editor, John Scognamiglio, and my agent, Evan Marshall, for their ongoing encouragement and support. Thanks to my lighthouse experts—Jim Spencer, President of Friends of Doubling Point Light; Patrick Landewe, the Keeper at Saugerties Lighthouse; Scott and Martine Holman, Keepers at Granite Island Light Station; Don and Nandy Town, Keepers at Braddock Point Lighthouse; and Gary Kohs, owner of the Mendota Lighthouse—for their willingness to entertain my questions and suppositions about everything lighthouse and/or bed-and-breakfast related. I would also like to thank Danny Hanlon and Corina Galvin for support for a previous book—sorry I forgot to mention you—thanks to both of you.

I would like to give a special shout-out to my family: Carl Carter for always reading and supporting my work; Melissa Carter-Newman, who is always there to bounce story ideas off of; and Pat Carter, who loves lighthouses even more than I do.

Chapter 1

Bailey Jordan couldn't believe she was going to get away with it. Were they insane? Was she wrong to take advantage of their crippled mental states? If they all survived a plane crash but were stranded on a snow-covered mountaintop without so much as a bag of chips, would she eat them? Could she eat them? She kept waiting for them to tell her it was all a big joke. But they didn't. They kept walking. This was how people got ahead in the world, they bulldozed over friends and family the second they let down their guard. So she would do it. She would not only cross the finish line, she would sprint past it. She would show them. She could not blow this. Because the real reason they were letting her do this, the only reason they were letting her do this, was because they didn't believe she could actually do it.

I could eat you, she repeated to herself. *Wouldn't want to—but could. I could eat you, I could eat you, I could eat you.*

She was on her way to show an exclusive penthouse overlooking Central Park. It didn't seem real. Yet here she was, strolling down Fifth Avenue. She should be taking deep breaths, visualizing the sale, and soaking up the faint scent of tulips swaying in the warm May breeze. Instead, she was obsessing on eating her mentors. That couldn't be good. She should focus on something else, anything else. How about shadows? There were the shadows of the trees looming over the sidewalk, her long shadow striking out ahead of her, and of course, the two elongated shadows tailing her.

Shadow one, her aunt Faye, owner of Penthouses on Parade. Shadow two, Jason Biggs, an ironically small man and the second in command at the high-paced, high-profile agency. Jason was being a good sport. If Bailey were him, she would hate her. Faye was only letting Bailey do this because she was family. Jason was the one who should be showing the penthouse. He had the experience, and the seniority. Bailey had only had her real estate license less than a year. She didn't deserve this opportunity; she knew it, and everyone else knew it. Losing herself in shadows was the only thing keeping Bailey from shrinking into a ball of nerves and rolling down Fifth Avenue with the rest of the midday traffic. Faye's high heels clicking on the sidewalk and Jason's cell phone constantly beeping were driving her crazy. If only she could figure out how to remain classy, yet firmly kick both of them to the curb.

Instead, she focused on putting one foot in front of the other. She crossed Fifth Avenue, snapped pictures of The Frick Collection (a gorgeous small art museum where her prospective clients had recently married) with her cell phone, and peeked in her purse to make sure the chocolate-chip-scented candle was still in one piece. Then, because Faye and Jason were lagging behind, she stopped and fussed with her hair in the window of an off-duty taxi parked at the curb. Was it her imagination, or had the lovely May breeze just turned into a kite-flying wind? When they finally caught up, Jason's look said it all. It took hours for her stylist to straighten her frizz-prone chestnut hair, still hanging slightly below her breasts despite her stylist's desire to hack it to chin level, but only seconds for the great outdoors to whip it into a frenzy. This afternoon Mother Nature was acting more like Mommie Dearest.

Bailey pulled her hair back, secured it with a rubber band, and practiced the spiel she hoped would cinch the sale of the Fifth Avenue penthouse.

"Imagine, if you lived here, you'd pass the Frick museum every day on your way to work—"

"Don't mention work," Faye interrupted. "You never want them to associate work with home."

"Oh," Bailey said. "Of course." How could she make such a rookie mistake? Because that's what she was, an amateur. She was hardly a cannibal, a disappointment to the tribe. Sweat pooled underneath her armpits, and her new high heels carved blisters into her feet. Why didn't she bring deodorant, or perfume, or Band-Aids, or tequila? "Imagine. If you lived here you'd pass the Frick museum every Saturday on your way to the park for a leisurely afternoon stroll—"

"Rich people don't stroll," Faye said.

"Or go to the park," Jason said.

"They're too busy," Faye said.

"Too busy to stroll or go to the park?" Bailey asked.

"Both," Faye said. "They walk briskly—"

"And gaze at the park from their balconies, marveling at all the tiny people below them," Jason said. He touched his Bluetooth and turned his head. "Penthouses on Parade, Jason Biggs speaking." Two ticks for poverty, Bailey thought. She couldn't imagine a life without strolls through the park. She took a deep breath and started her spiel all over again.

"Imagine, you'll pass the Frick museum every day in your limo and remember where you first made your love legal," Bailey said. She could already see Faye shaking her head.

"That makes it sound like their affair was something illicit," Faye said.

"It kind of was," Bailey said. "But you're right. I won't say it." She took a second deep breath and gestured in the direction of the Frick. "Remember where you first took your holy vows."

"They got married in a museum next to a floor full of koi," Jason said. "How holy could it have been?" Bailey wanted to rip

the Bluetooth out of his ear. How could he navigate two conversations at once? Bailey felt her stomach cramp, and she
prayed they didn't notice her grimace.

"Relive where you first fell in love," Bailey said. Still not right.
Their famous clients, Allissa and Greg, fell in love at first sight
on the subway. She was a fashion model who fainted on the up-
town four, he the financial mogul who caught her in his arms as
she went down. It was Fashion Week in New York, and Allissa
hadn't eaten in four days. Neither of them had ever ridden the
subway before. She was doing it for a reality television show au-
dition; his Lexus had been hit by a bus. As he cradled her in his
arms, his overpowering cologne woke her up. The cameras following Allissa for the reality show had captured it all. It wasn't
long before the video went viral, even overtaking the one of the
rat on the train, climbing up the arm of a sleeping homeless
man. Turns out New Yorkers were softies after all.

The fashionista and the financier. Their day of transit slum-
ming led to a whirlwind romance, nonstop media attention,
and marriage. New Yorkers had dubbed them "the Fairytalers"
and couldn't get enough of the dynamic duo. And Bailey was
the lucky Realtor showing them a penthouse. And not just any
penthouse. It was the most beautiful two-bedroom, two-bath
Bailey had ever seen. She would die to live in it herself. She
couldn't imagine anyone saying no to it. And oh yes, it was just
down the block from the Frick museum where the couple got
married. It was like winning the lottery.

The opportunity of a lifetime. One she had no intention of
squandering. One that would not only skyrocket her reputation
and pay handsomely, but a sale that would give Bailey the one
thing she wanted more than anything else in the world. A baby.

She was thirty-six; they had to start trying. But her husband,
Brad, having grown up with a mother who spent money on gin
and cocaine first and incidentals like food, heat, and electricity
second, third, and fourth, insisted they not start their family
until they were financially secure. And he was talking New York
City financially secure, a whole different ballgame than, say,

middle-of-nowhere Midwest financially secure. He wanted their child to grow up loved, and fed, and clothed, and educated. So did she.

But so far they slightly disagreed, couldn't quite put their fingers on an amount guaranteeing security. The commission from this sale would definitely do it. She could already feel their baby in her arms, see the two of them strolling through the park. For despite what Jason claimed, when rich, they would still stroll through the park. And play on the playgrounds, and visit the animals in the zoo, and picnic in the meadow, and ride the carousel, and eat hot dogs and ice cream in moderation, and take turns carrying him or her on their shoulders, and watch Little League games, and share a quiet smile when their exhausted but happy child fell asleep on the way home. She could see their entire family life unfolding in the park. She hoped their baby had her olive skin and Brad's dimples, her loyalty and Brad's charm. But, of course, first and foremost, they just wanted a healthy and happy baby.

Seize the day! She'd been repeating it to herself ad nauseam, trying to psych herself up, build up a little momentum. Unfortunately, that wasn't the only thing building up in her. Gas. Big mistake, having Mexican for lunch. It was all Brad's fault. He just had to call her and rave about the Taco Truck. How he'd seen it on a cooking show, how it was winning all sorts of awards, and how fortuitous it was that today only it would be parked near Faye's office on the Upper East Side. Brad made her swear she'd try it today and report back to him. It was starting to feel like her report was going to be nonverbal: silent but deadly. She was going to kill him. She couldn't lose this sale to flatulence. If she felt something coming on, she was going to have to find an excuse to run out to the balcony. If all else failed, she could always throw herself off it. Death by Taco Truck. Bailey laughed at the thought. Faye shot her a look. Bailey relaxed her lips and donned a more professional expression. The only person she would have shared her crazy thoughts with was Brad.

For the first time in their wild love story, Brad was the one out of work, waiting at home for her. And if she didn't pull off this sale, he would be there to comfort her. He had two bottles of champagne waiting in the fridge. The expensive one in case they were celebrating, and a cheaper one in case they were just drowning their sorrows. It was Brad's idea, and Bailey loved it. Of course she still prayed they'd be popping open the Dom, but knowing they were going to drink champagne either way eased her anxiety. And she had a surprise for him. A silver rattle. It was exquisite. So soft, and slightly heavy, and so comforting cradled in the palm of her hand. It had been expensive, but well worth it. The perfect way to announce it was time. After toasting with the bottle of Dom, he would say, "Speech, speech!" and she would pull out the rattle and clink it on her glass and shake it with a come-hither look. He'd probably rip her clothes off right then and there. Her stomach gurgled. Jason glanced at her and then exchanged a look with Faye. Oh yes, she could eat him. *Beano. Why didn't I buy Beano?*

"I will do this," Bailey said as they neared the building. "I will make this sale." Faye reached out and grabbed Bailey's arm. For such a tall, slim woman, she had a grip like a linebacker.

"Darling," she said. "You have to know the Fairytalers have no hope in h-e-double-hockey-sticks of ever making up their minds. This is practice. Nothing more."

Faye and Jason had already shown the couple hundreds of hot properties in Manhattan, and they'd snubbed every one of them.

"They're a fairy-tale couple all right," Jason said. "Goldilocks and the Bear. This one's too small. This one's too big. This one's too old." As he prattled on, Faye grabbed Bailey's hands and held them up for inspection.

"I thought you were going to do something about this!" she cried. Bailey yanked her nail-bitten hands away.

"I got my hair done instead," she said. She'd done her best, and clearly, it still wasn't enough. Salon-straightened hair and a new outfit: a pencil-thin gray skirt, matching jacket with just a touch of her black camisole peeking out, classy pearls, barely

black hose, and her new black stilettos. Brad had gone with her
to pick out the outfit, and even bought himself a new pair of
shoes. It tugged on her heartstrings, how happy Brad was with a
new pair of shoes. Everything from his childhood was pre-
owned. She hated that he'd had such a tough time as a kid, but
she loved the appreciation he had for the things most people
took for granted. Who was she kidding? All these years and she
was still insanely in love, bordering on obsessed with her husband. Thus, the Taco Truck. One of these days she was going to
have to learn how to say no to Brad Jordan.

"Are you limping?" Faye said. "You look like you're limping."

"New shoes," Bailey said.

"Rookie mistake," Jason said. Bailey ignored them. Despite
the pain in her feet and the rumble in her gut, she felt sexy and
sophisticated. And afterward, she figured the outfit could do
double duty and she'd seduce her handsome husband with her
new, sleek self. But she'd forgotten to take into account the
wind, both outside and inside. And she hadn't had time to get
her nails done. Besides, she didn't want fake nails, and there
was nothing she could do but wait for them to grow out, or finally grow up and stop biting them. She certainly didn't expect
Faye to examine her so closely. At least she'd removed the silver
coyote-head ring she always wore on her middle finger.

"Whatever you do, don't let them see those gnawed-on
mitts," Faye said.

"Do you have gloves?" Jason said. He mimed putting on long
pairs of gloves like an opera diva.

"Certainly," Bailey said. "And rope, and a stun gun, and duct
tape. Everything I need to ensure a sale. Real Estate 101, my
friend."

Jason rolled his eyes. "Hold your hands behind your back,"
he said, demonstrating. "And smile." Bailey smiled. She looked
at Jason and stopped. How many condescending expressions
did the man have? "That was way too much," he said. "You want
to look friendly, but not happy."

"Why wouldn't I want to look happy?"

"Because they're not happy."

"They're not?"

"Of course not. Nobody's happy. So if you look too happy, it's going to depress them."

"So why don't I just not smile?"

"Because you have to pretend to be happy. Just a lot less happy than they are. You want them to think you're secretly miserable but pretending to be happy because you're so jealous of their 'genuine' happiness. My God, Faye, have you taught her nothing?"

"She's stubborn. She gets it from my sister."

Jason shook his head and clicked on his Bluetooth. "Andrew Jackson, assistant to Jason Biggs."

Bailey turned to Faye and raised her eyebrows. Faye smiled and pointed to herself.

I taught him that, she mouthed.

"Sorry, he's not in right now. No, the two-bedroom sold, but there's a lovely loft in Soho that he's just dying to show you. No, there's not, but there's certainly room for one. Of course not! In fact, Jason showed me the place just last night and I thought to myself, what this place needs is a full-sized carousel. I can't believe how you read my mind. Uh-huh. No outdoor space, but the fire escape fits at least six. Pets are a no-go in Soho. A python? I don't know. Does he come when you call him? Then it's probably a pet. Sorry, that's my other line." Jason clicked off. His head began to swivel right and left.

"What's that smell?" he said.

"It must be garbage," Bailey said, clenching her stomach.

As they approached the entrance to the beautiful limestone building where their penthouse awaited, Bailey's attention was arrested by a patch of bright yellow tulips shimmering in the dredges of the afternoon sun. Bailey loved the month of May, littering the city with her favorite color. How simple happiness was sometimes; how free. The color yellow made Bailey happy. It was one of the things Brad loved about her, how much she loved the color yellow.

"Because of you," Brad had said, "I'll never think of yellow the same way again. No matter what." She was twenty-one when he said that to her. First she obsessed on how romantic that was, then she switched to analyzing the "No matter what."

What did he mean by that? Was he already forecasting a future breakup? She'd forever changed his relationship to the color yellow. Was that supposed to be a consolation prize? And if so, was that enough?

"Bails," he said when she complained to him. "Name all the things you can that are yellow. Go."

The sun, flowers, signs, school buses, traffic lights, lemons, plastic squeeze containers of mustard, not to mention the mustard itself, urine—

"Urine?" Brad said. "Urine?!"

Gross maybe, but it still counted, and since he drank a lot of water, always carried around whatever new magic water was on the market, it was a logical choice.

For the rest of his life, simple, everyday and sometimes mundane, ugly objects or disgusting bodily fluids would remind him of her. And she supposed that was good enough.

If, each time he saw the color yellow, some semblance of a thought of her ran through him, yes, that would definitely be of some consolation. Although there was no court of law, no law-abiding-yellow rule that would force him to follow it, still it was out there, as energy, his proclamation. They were forever bound by the color yellow till-death-do-they-part. It would have to be enough.

Was that what love was? Forever changing you in the tiniest of ways, so that *no matter what,* you'd never be the same again? She had a million little references like that with Brad as well, probably way more than he had with her, but it was enough, knowing he would never look at yellow the same way ever again. And they were still together. She'd never faced "No matter what." At their wedding he gave her a hundred yellow roses.

If Faye and Jason weren't watching her every move, she'd love to cut a few of the tulips to bring up to the penthouse. Not that she'd ever really do such a thing. There were a million things Bailey thought about doing, and very few she ever actually did. Brad was the risk taker, the kite soaring for the clouds; Bailey was the one with her feet on the ground, holding the string, poised to tug him back to earth whenever he'd gone too far. So, no stolen tulips for her clients today, but at least she had the chocolate-chip-scented candle in her purse. If only she'd had the time to actually bake chocolate-chip cookies. Imagine a New Yorker having that kind of time! She paused for one more look at the glorious bulbs and soothed her rule-following self with the thought that, once cut, the tulips would have lost most of their brilliance anyway. After all, it was the targeted ray of sunshine making them glitter, and even a wild child couldn't cut down the sun.

"Hands behind back," Bailey said. "Smile, but not too much."

"I just don't get it," Jason said. "How come I can smell the garbage but I can't see it?"

Bailey dug the candle out of her purse and held it up. "Maybe I should light this now," she said.

Chapter 2

Brad Jordan saw the whole thing. There was a man lying on the sidewalk in a pile of glass. Sharp little pieces that glittered in the sun. There was a Cadillac sticking out of an electronics store, smashed like an accordion. The sign above the store read EDDIE'S ELECTRONICS. There were people, so many people. They rushed out of their shops, and apartments, and emerged from subway stops. They pulled over on their bicycles, and cars, and skateboards. So eager to see what was going on. They gathered around the accordion-car and the electronics store, they circled the man, shouted for help, knelt down on the sharp glass.

"Hey," Brad wanted to shout. "Don't hurt yourself." It was strange, he no longer had a voice. People whipped out cell phones and pointed—Brad had never realized how important pointing was in a crisis, but obviously the arm and the index finger were essential—they pointed and they cried out, and they all yelled for somebody else to do something. There were a lot of people leading but nobody following.

They ignored Brad's offer to assist, and rolled the man onto his back. A river of red filled the bed of glass. "It's too late," Brad said. "He's dead." Nobody paid any attention to him. He was surprised that he felt no sympathy for the good-looking dead man, although he had to say, he very much liked his shoes. Would it be wrong to take the shoes off the dead man's feet? Somehow he knew it was wrong, yet he really wanted to do it. Somehow he knew they were really comfortable shoes. And the dead dude certainly didn't need them anymore.

Dude. He hadn't said "dude" since college. How could that be? He didn't go to college, did he? He didn't have the money, and his strung-out mother certainly didn't care what he did with his life. Somebody he knew went to college and he used to visit that someone, and her hair smelled like strawberries, her lips were always shiny and wet with gloss, and she liked the color yellow, and she let him sleep in her dorm room, and read her textbooks, and use her food card in the cafeteria, and he used to say "dude" all the time. Maybe he should have gone to college. Maybe if he had gone to college he wouldn't have wasted so many years saying the word "dude." Maybe he could go to college right now. Right this very moment he knew he could fly over any college in the world. He didn't even need to buy a ticket or go through security, although he already had his shoes off.

He could fly over Columbia, Yale, Princeton, Harvard, even Cambridge! But he didn't want to. He still wasn't a very good student.

Brad laughed. He looked around to see if anyone else was laughing, but they were still so obsessed with the lifeless man. Someone was even kneeling over him, kissing him on the lips. An older woman. It was a harsh city for dating—how desperate did you have to be to make out with a dead man? "Open your eyes!" he wanted to shout at her. "There are live men all around you!" But she didn't listen. She was unbuttoning his shirt, practically ripping it off. And, my God! He could not believe what he was seeing. She actually brought her own lie detector with her. She was hooking him up to it, attaching it to his chest. Now that was a jaded woman.

Good God. She must've hated his answers, she was shocking him. What was next? Was she going to waterboard him in broad daylight? Shouldn't someone stop her? Brad was so lucky he was out of the dating world.

Maybe she should kiss the owner of the electronics store instead. Was that Eddie, in the flesh? He was standing in the doorway of his shop looking like his dog just died. Poor dude. "Kiss him!" Brad wanted to yell. He pointed at the electronics store's owner. He didn't know how he knew he was Eddie, the owner, but he did. He was Eddie, and he'd opened his shop twenty minutes late and that's why when the Cadillac came crashing through he was in the back making coffee instead of standing right in the path of destruction. "Dude, it was a good day to be late!" But once again, Brad had no voice, and now the desperate older woman was pounding on the dead man's chest. Trying to get his heart to beat just for her. *He's just not that into you,* Brad thought. He couldn't remember where he'd heard that one, but he thought it was really funny. Once again, he was the only one who laughed.

Brad quickly grew bored of hovering above the lifeless body. Even the glittering glass shimmering in a pool of shiny red rubies couldn't keep his attention. Rubies. Shoes. Rubies. Shoes. Rubies. *There's no place like home.* And with that, he swirled around and noticed the most remarkable bright light.

Chapter 3

"Imagine. If you lived here, you would be able to sip champagne on your balcony, gaze out at the Frick museum, and relive the moment where you began the most important journey of your lives—your journey as husband and wife." Bailey finished her speech and waited, breath held in, fingers clenched, for her mentors to say something. Really. Anything. Any little thing. They were standing in the living room of the penthouse, on Brazilian cherrywood floors, glittering underneath hundreds of faceted crystals from the magnificent chandelier hanging above them, facing three floor-to-ceiling oval windows, interspersed with a towering stone fireplace and built-in bookcases, topped off with ornate crown molding, and a sweeping balcony with panoramic views of Fifth Avenue and Central Park. The Fairytalers would have to be criminally insane not to fall in love with this place. Still, she'd best keep that out of her pitch. Bailey couldn't stop drinking in all the splendid details of the penthouse, but Faye and Jason could only stare at her.

"That's actually not bad," Faye finally said as if someone had to drag the words out of her mouth with horses and rope.

"It has a whiff of promise," Jason said. Bailey glanced at the glowing candle and laptop she'd propped up on the fireplace mantel. The scent of chocolate-chip cookies filled the air, and the laptop scrolled through pictures of the intimate art museum at both sunrise and sunset. Bailey smiled. But not too much, and folded her hands behind her back. Something lurched inside her.

"Excuse me," Bailey said. She fled to the balcony, cozied up to the railing, and pretended to look at the view. Wow, it was wild being so high above everything. She looked down and marveled at the tiny little trees, tiny little cars, tiny little people with tiny little baby strollers. Tiny little shopping cart. She didn't realize she was talking out loud until Faye interrupted her.

"Shopping cart?" Faye said.

"Carlos," Jason and Faye said at the same time. In sync, they turned and flew out of the penthouse. After a few much-needed seconds alone on the balcony, Bailey followed.

Carlos was a homeless man with a bullhorn and a cardboard sign. He paced back and forth in front of his overflowing shopping cart parked directly on the street in front of the building. His sign read:

ARE YOU PREPARED FOR THE END OF THE WORD?

Didn't he know this neighborhood? It was Fifth Avenue in the Seventies. The only thing the people living on this block were prepared for was Woody Allen playing his clarinet at Café Carlyle on a Monday night. Bailey was all for freedom of speech. Just not now, not tonight. This was hardly the picture of romance and serenity that she wanted to paint for her clients. She looked around for the doorman as Faye and Jason tried to plead with him.

"Fires, and floods, and earthquakes—" His voice raised to the heavens, and he threw his arms up in the air with each proclamation of horror. He locked eyes with Bailey and jabbed at her with his finger. She pointed at his sign, and interrupted his tirade.

"You're missing an 'L.' "

"The earth will open up and—what? I'm missing what?" He followed the trajectory of Bailey's finger.

"You've got clients arriving in twenty minutes," Jason said, poking Bailey in the back. "We don't have time for *Wheel of Fortune.*"

"Are you prepared for the end of the *word*," Bailey read. "I think you're missing an 'L.' "

"Damnation," he said. "Where's my marker?" He dove into his shopping cart, pulled items out of it, and threw them to the ground. A coat, a hat, a coffeemaker, an Etch A Sketch. Bailey took a step closer and tried to peek at the Etch A Sketch to see if he could draw. Unfortunately, there was nothing but squiggly lines. "Where is it? It's gone. Who stole it? It's gone. Who stole it?"

Bailey wanted to point out that he was hardly prepared for the end of the world himself, given his overblown reaction to losing a marker. Besides, wasn't the only potential good thing about the end of the world the fact that no preparation was necessary? Sort of a "Come what may"? She would say "Come Hell or High Water," but he already had that covered.

"Would you like to borrow my pen?" Bailey said. His head shot up out of his cart and he eyed her suspiciously.

"It's not one of those exploding pens, is it?"

"I highly doubt it," she said.

"What about a Sharpie? You got a Sharpie?"

"No."

"Carlos," Faye said. "You promised not to patrol this block anymore."

"So sue me," Carlos said. His clothes were streaked with dirt. His fingernails were black. His shopping cart had old shoes, and rotting food, and wet newspapers. He lifted his head and sniffed. "What's that smell?" he said.

I'm going to kill Brad, Bailey thought, backing away. *Champagne or not, I'm going to freaking kill him.*

* * *

Brad bathed in the light, entranced within its glow. It was a warm blanket, cocooning him. It was a disco light that made him want to dance. It was a shooting star he couldn't look away from. It was a roaring campfire by the beach. It was drawing him in. Yet he held back. He couldn't help feeling he was forgetting something. That was strange, it was his wife who was always forgetting things, running back in to check her straightening iron—

His wife. Brad held his hands up, as if to protect the memory from the light. His wife. The Cadillac. The squeal of tires, the scream rising in his chest, his body flying through the windshield. His beautiful, brand-new shoes. The dead man on the ground. Oh, no.

But the light. My God, the light. It was incredible. You could stare directly at it and it didn't hurt your eyes. He didn't want to leave. He floated higher. He felt filled with love. Had he ever felt such peace? Nobody in their right mind would want to leave this place. He picked up speed and soon he was flying. My God, what a rush! Wait until he posted about this on his Facebook page. He assumed he was heading for a tunnel, but he was in no rush to get there. Although if he could see the light, did it mean he'd already gone through a tunnel? He didn't remember one, and he didn't really care. He was free. He was totally free.

It was the best drug he'd ever taken, the best roller coaster he'd ever ridden, the most popular he'd ever felt even though he was utterly alone. He no longer cared about anything below him. He no longer cared about the Cadillac, or the fact that he'd never gone to college, or his drunk mother, or global warming, or cable bills, or softening bellies, or the deli running out of his favorite beer, or failed businesses, or smelly feet, or terrorism, or condescending want ads, or missing the end of a Yankees game because his wife found some urgent errand for them to run, or finding gray hairs where no gray hairs should ever, ever be found. None of it mattered anymore.

And even though he knew she was still down there, even though he could still somewhat feel her long brown hair falling over his face, and see her nail-bitten fingers, and high cheekbones, and the silver coyote ring on her middle finger, and she was washed in the color yellow—he just couldn't go back.

Actually, that was the problem. He could go back. It was his choice. A voice speaking to him from inside his head said so. *It's your choice. It's up to you.* He didn't even have to think about it. He didn't want to go back. He never wanted to go back. Forward was the only way to go. *I'm sorry,* he thought. *I'm not going back. Not even for my shoes.*

"Are you all right?" the doorman said. Bailey froze in the entranceway of the building. She was hit with a horrible feeling, a sinking sensation of dread, like she'd forgotten something vital. Was it the candle in the penthouse? She never should have left it unattended. Had it tipped over, was the palace burning down?

No, that wasn't it. It was something else.

A few feet away, Faye and Jason were holding cash out to Carlos, like drug addicts trying to close a deal.

"Someone just walked over my grave," Bailey said. The words shocked her. She'd never said anything like that before. She'd certainly never felt anything like that before.

"Oh," the doorman said. "You look pale. Do you want to sit down?"

"My husband. I want my husband."

"Save your soul from the burning flames of hell!"

"Your husband?"

Bailey couldn't think. Not with that bullhorn in her ear. And she had to think. What was she forgetting? Why did it feel like life or death? Maybe the taco plate had been poisoned and in addition to extreme gas she was being hit with paranoid delusions. Or maybe she wasn't paranoid at all. Maybe this was a premonition. She was going to die. Why did she have to upgrade to the deluxe lunch? Would they know to do an autopsy? Would strangers watch her being dissected on one of those medical true-life shows? Would the autopsy reveal that the guacamole had been laced? Or was it something else?

Would the coroner stand near her exposed toes, slowly shake

his or her head, look at the camera, and say, "If only she hadn't eaten the refried beans"?

"They won awards," Bailey said. "Brad said they won so many awards." Maybe she'd gone to the wrong taco truck. It was possible. It could have been another, poisonous, non-award-winning taco truck parked in the vicinity, hoping to lure clueless, hungry victims to their death. Bailey was surprised she could even stand. She stumbled and clutched onto the doorman's lapels.

"Tell Brad I love him," she said. "I've always loved him. And tell him not to blame himself. Even though he was the one who made me eat from the Taco Truck. Things I didn't even want to eat. A few things that I didn't even know what they were. How could I be so stupid? Have you ever done anything stupid? Stupid for love?"

"Please, if you're going to be sick, could you just step outside?"

"Promise me," Bailey said. "He'll blame himself because it was all his fault. Promise me you'll tell him."

"Armageddon!" Carlos shouted. "Armageddon is here. Armageddon is real. Armageddon is now!"

"I don't even like refried beans," Bailey said. "But I ate them anyway. I ate them for Brad." The doorman was trying to remove her hands from his chest and maneuver her outside at the same time. "Because that's what you do when you love someone," Bailey said. "You eat all sorts of things you hate for someone you love."

Bailey's cell phone came to life, blasting out "I Got You Babe." It was her ring tone for Brad.

Chapter 4

It wasn't Brad's voice on the phone, and the news washed over her in sound bites. Accident. Lenox Hill Hospital. Brad Jordan, did she know a Brad Jordan? Of course she did, he was her husband.

Accident, Lenox Hill Hospital, Brad. He was clinically dead, the voice said. But they got him back. The man sounded very excited. Bailey was afraid of dropping the phone, so she clung to it while her purse fell to the ground, and her lipstick, and her keys, and her wallet all tumbled out and began rolling toward the patch of tulips. She noticed, but didn't move to stop them, nor did she answer the doorman, who, sounding cries of alarm, went chasing after her things.

Things aren't important, she wanted to scream at him, people are, my husband is. Clinically dead? A sharp panic rose in her, threatening to turn her into someone she didn't recognize, someone who couldn't handle the news.

"It's coming!" Carlos shouted. "The end is coming!"

"He's okay?" she pleaded into the phone, as if the voice on

the other end was a hostage taker who had complete control over her husband's fate. "He's alive?" *Of course he's alive, he's my husband, I had breakfast with him this morning, dead men don't eat hash browns.*

"He's in critical condition," the voice said. "But he's alive."

"What happened?"

"I was just standing in the emergency room when he came in," the man said. "I broke my arm," he added, but he must have quickly realized Bailey didn't care, for he spared her the details and moved on. "A paramedic handed me your husband's phone and asked me to call you. You were under 'Wife' with a smiley face. He's at Lenox Hill Hospital, in critical care."

Bailey didn't know if he hung up, or she hung up, or the phone went clinically dead. The connection was severed. Bailey stared at the phone for a second, as if it would tell her what to do, how to handle this. The doorman thrust her purse at her, the contents all stuffed safely back inside.

"Taxi," she said. "I need a taxi." She ran to the curb and flung out her arm. The doorman was right behind her.

"Are you all right?" he said. He stepped into the street and held up his arm. They looked like schoolchildren competing to get called on.

"Bailey!" Faye said from behind her. "What's going on? Where do you think you're going?" As a taxi pulled up, the news came out of Bailey in a rush. Bailey heard herself coaching Faye and Jason—*relive where they fell in love*—but in her rush to explain it, she knew she got it all wrong.

"We'll cancel the showing," Faye said. "We're coming with you." Bailey wanted to scream no. Faye never canceled appointments. If she canceled, then something was seriously wrong. If she canceled, it meant she thought Brad could die.

"You stay, Jason," Bailey said. "I have a feeling about this sale." Of all the looks Jason had ever given her, this one she'd never seen before. He looked upset for her. If he sold the condo, then he'd get a cut and Faye would get a cut, and Bailey would get zip. What choice did she have? Besides, Bailey couldn't think straight because the words "clinically dead" were flashing through her mind like a neon sign that wouldn't shut off even after you'd pulled the plug—pulled the plug, Bailey shouldn't think such things—

"Settle your debts before you burn in hell!"

"Carlos," Jason said. "Not now."

"Lenox Hill Hospital," Bailey said to the driver as she and Faye climbed in the back. "Hurry." The cab started pulling out. "Stop," Bailey yelled. "Stop." The cab driver slammed on the brakes. He glanced at her through the rearview mirror. She didn't know where he was from, somewhere in the Middle East. Now was not the time to try and show interest in his culture, and she overrode the voice in her head that said he'd already pegged her as a bossy, snooty American.

"One second," Bailey said. "Do not leave." Abandoning her purse on the seat, she threw open the door, climbed over Faye, and rushed back to the apartment building. Seconds later she returned, panting, and slammed the door. She didn't dare look back at the building because she knew the doorman and Jason were staring at her, mouths agape. Even Carlos stopped ranting for a few seconds before lifting the bullhorn again.

"Inappropriate!" he yelled.

"Lenox Hill Hospital," she said again. She tried to convey "Step on it" with her tone. This time, the cab driver met Faye's eyes in the rearview mirror. He probably thought she was crazy, but Bailey didn't care. He'd probably seen atrocities in his country that she couldn't even imagine. He probably thought she was clueless about what life was really like for some people, and he would be right. All she knew was her life. And half of that life was in a hospital bed across town in critical care.

She clung to the tulips in her hands, at least a half a dozen, ripped from the ground, roots dripping dirt onto the cardboard sign announcing the end of the word, and tried not to cry. Cars and people were passing by, walking their dogs, talking on their phones, buying newspapers, as if that's where the news could really be found. Nobody seemed to know, or care, that her husband had been clinically dead. She clutched the tulips and squeezed her eyes shut. It was entirely appropriate to bring flowers when someone you love had come back from the dead.

At the hospital she cornered a nurse coming out of Brad's room. "I'll give anything," Bailey said. "Blood, hair, nails." The nurse glanced at Bailey's fingers, bitten to the nub. "Okay, nails are a no if you need them today, but I'll grow them, I swear. What else can I give? What does he need?"

The nurse, a middle-aged woman with full, soft cheeks and fawn eyes, repeatedly patted Bailey on the arm. "I'm sure your love will be enough."

How could she be so sure? The nurse was being so kind, so nurturing. Yet Bailey still wanted to scream. Love was enough? For Brad? Had it ever been?

It had certainly been enough for Bailey. In fact, it was everything. That was the problem. Sometimes she was afraid her love was too much for him. Like a plant that grew and grew and grew until it strangled all the pretty little plants around it, blocking out their sun. That's why they had to have a baby. Bailey had too much love to give, too much for one person to handle. Imagine, a child made by the two of them. Brad, Bailey, and baby. B&B&B! Oh, how easy it would be to add another "B."

She had to calm down. Now was probably not the right time to be fantasizing about having a baby. She was just nervous. She wished she smoked. What did nonsmokers do in serious times of stress? "Please," Bailey shouted down the hall after the nurse. "Will you take my blood just in case?" But the nurse didn't even turn around. Bailey steeled herself, then entered Brad's room.

He was hooked up to machines and covered in tubes; his beautiful soft brown curls were all gone, head shaved bald as a baby. His tall body took over the little bed, and his feet hung off the end. Where were his shoes? He swore he'd never take them off. She'd teased him for being like a woman, a ribbing Brad took easily since he was one of the most manly men she knew. Bailey felt a strange pang of panic. As if he wouldn't make it if he didn't have his shoes. She would have to ask a nurse if he'd been wearing them. Good god, why was she obsessing on his shoes?

Brad and Bailey. He was six foot two; she was five foot eleven. Two tall, handsome people, Brad often said. Bailey didn't mind that he called her handsome. She knew he was teasing, she knew he thought she was beautiful. She wasn't perfect by any means. She had a strong face: a broad forehead and a large nose. Prominent cheekbones and full lips, and freakishly long eyelashes, and clear olive skin, and, as Brad often told her, the most remarkable light blue eyes with hints of green. She bit her nails to the nub and wore a silver coyote ring on her middle finger.

Bailey had a Native American slash Mediterranean look about her, although her parents insisted they were Dutch and French and nothing else.

Brad had brown eyes and always liked to sing to her: "Don't you make my brown eyes blue." She never failed to roll her eyes, and he never failed to laugh.

He was in an induced coma due to brain swelling, but the doctor and nurse both assured her they were optimistically hopeful. Those were the words they used. Did they mean to say cautiously optimistic? If they messed up common English this badly, should she worry about their doctoring and nursing skills? Should she throw a fit, ask for their credentials? What a ridiculous phrase that was. They could be either hopeful, or optimistic, but they couldn't be both!

She felt like throwing something. A bad habit from her younger years. She had a coursing temper and when she really got going she would have to throw something, or several somethings, across the room. The louder the crash, the calmer she felt. Brad always teased that she was secretly a passionate Latina or a hot-blooded Italian.

"French," she would say as she hurled a vase against the wall. "Or Dutch," she added after it smashed into pieces. "And nothing more." Where did it come from, then? Her parents didn't have tempers—they were calm professor types. Maybe it was a middle-child syndrome or maybe there was indeed some genetic hot blood lingering in her DNA, or maybe it was just a chemical imbalance. All Bailey knew for sure was that until years of meditation helped her get it under control, she was a thrower.

Maybe she should do it, maybe it would make her feel better. She scanned the room but couldn't decide what to throw. A pitcher of water, a plastic cup, a bedpan? The bedpan, she decided. It was empty and would make the biggest clang. Throwing a plastic cup would hardly be satisfying, and she couldn't take the chance that the water from the pitcher would splash onto the beeping machines, causing them to malfunction and kill her just-back-from-the-dead husband all over again.

She wondered if it was shock making her think all these things, dredging up bad habits, or if her true nature was coming out, and her true nature was so cold of heart that even though her husband's brain was swelling a mere few feet from her, all she could do was pick on the English of those who held his health in their hands, and mentally throw bedpans.

She was not, she realized, as optimistically hopeful as they were. She was terrified. She wanted them to reassure her. She wanted Brad to wake up so *he* could reassure her, which solidified it for Bailey, she was the most selfish person on the planet. She couldn't help it. She had never felt so helpless, and in all her years with him, she had never seen Brad so frail. Which was why she could not fall apart, she must be strong for him. Thank God he couldn't see her right now. The look of panic on her face, her unruly hair, tulips dripping dirt at her feet. She dropped the flowers in the pitcher of water, and instead of throwing it, kicked the bedpan across the room. Hardly satisfying.

Thirteen minutes. The doctor told her Brad's heart stopped for thirteen minutes. She didn't want to hear it. It was as if, besides being the unlucky number thirteen, the news held some puzzle which she must unravel.

Bailey searched Brad's swollen face for traces of the ten-year-old boy she fell madly in love with. Sitting on a rock by a river,

dragging his shoe-and-sock-clad foot through the water, just because he could. That was twenty-six years ago. She followed him
around that summer like he was the last boy on earth. That
summer all she needed was a red rubber ball, gleaming silver
jacks, and Brad Jordan. He was a ball of spirit, a walking mystery. She'd never forget entering his house for the first time.
Brad didn't show an ounce of embarrassment. He flung open
the door and expected her to follow. Dishes piled in the sink.
Television blaring. Two aging black cats sprawled on top of the
kitchen table. He led her into the living room.

"That's my mom." The two of them, standing over the couch.
Elizabeth Jordan, passed out. Arms flung over her head, legs
splayed out, one bare foot hanging over the couch, the other
propped up on the armrest. Gin bottle near her cheek.

"Hello," Bailey actually said. Brad laughed and laughed. His
laugh made her feel like she had magical powers. But it was
what he did next that cemented him in her heart forever, made
her love him even more than the baby bird in her shoe box
back at home, the one she saved when it fell from the nest, and
to Bailey's horror, the mother simply flew away. Brad gently removed the bottle of gin, fixed his mother's pillow, then
smoothed back the hair from her forehead.

"She looks happy," he said. Bailey wondered how he could
tell. But from the slight strain in his voice, she knew it mattered to him. His own happiness was totally invested in his
mother being happy. She didn't know what it was at the time,
but Bailey could feel the force of Brad's fear hammering in
her own chest, his brave front, his desperation. He wanted to
ask someone to save him, to help him, but he didn't know
how. And that was it. Bailey's heart had been plucked straight
from her chest.

"She does," Bailey said. "She looks totally relaxed. You should
see my mom. She's probably screaming at my brother right now
to take off his dirty shoes." Bailey laughed. She felt a slice of
guilt roll through her for making fun of her mother. Even if she
was yelling at her brother, she was also awake and not drunk,
and making dinner, and most likely wondering where Bailey

was. But it was worth it. Brad's jaw unclenched and his shoulders relaxed, and he smiled.

Afterward they played jacks on his kitchen floor. He won. Then they ate Doritos straight out of the bag, and drank Coke he kept pouring into shot glasses, and inhaled chocolate doughnuts that they slipped on their fingers like giant rings. Bailey knew she was doing things she shouldn't. Her mother didn't allow junk food in the house. Or cats on the kitchen table. Or dishes in the sink. Or gin bottles on the couch. It felt dangerous and exciting. And normally, Bailey was the type of child who minded her parents' every word. But there was something about this boy that made Bailey want to break all the rules. By the time Bailey left and returned to her clean home with sober parents, and feline-free dining table, and lemon chicken with rice and salad for dinner, she was in love.

It took several years of stalking for Brad to catch up. But he did, eventually he did. It was twenty-six years later, and they'd been married for seven years. Bailey pulled her chair up to Brad's hospital bed, gently took his left hand in hers, and wrapped it into a little hand sandwich.

"You know," she said. "Most people don't go to such extremes over the seven-year itch." Her laugh sounded hollow in the little room. "You're going to be all right," she said. "You're going to be just fine." She wanted to add, "I'm hopefully optimistic," already projecting a day where the phrase would be a private joke between them—but she couldn't get the words over the lump in her throat, and just in case he was listening, she didn't want him to hear her crying. She leaned over and kissed him ever so gently on the lips, hoping to wake him like a reverse Snow White, wondering if he could hear her, smell her, feel her hair brushing against his collarbone. "I love you," she said. "I love you more than anything in the whole wide world." She laid her head on his chest. His heart was beating, he was still here, he was clinically alive.

Bailey could smell and hear Aunt Faye coming down the hall, returning from the cafeteria. Obsession, and high heels. The pitch of her voice rising higher and higher as she stopped to talk to someone.

"I'm Faye Edgers, Penthouses on Parade, if any of the doctors are ever in the market. I've got places near every hospital. They can roll out of bed and right into surgery."

Then Faye was back in the doorway. Bailey looked up, meaning to smile, but not too much. Instead, she watched Faye take in the sight of Brad, bald and swelling on the bed. Faye opened her mouth. Then closed it. Then she looked at Bailey.

"I can talk to a nurse," Faye said. "Try to get him moved to a bigger room with a view."

"He's fine," Bailey said.

"Oh, darling," Faye said. She opened her arms. Tears came to Bailey's eyes. She wiped them away and sniffed loudly. She looked at Brad, half expecting him to laugh.

"He's fine," she said again.

"Oh, darling," Faye said.

"Aunt Faye," Bailey said. "If you say that again, I'm going to beat the living daylights out of you." Faye sat on an empty chair facing Bailey. She crossed her arms and her legs.

"You remind me of me," she said.

"God help us both," Bailey said. She glanced at Brad, then pointed to the bed as she addressed the ceiling. "But help him first," she added.

Five hours passed in a blur. Faye reluctantly agreed to go home, Bailey reluctantly agreed to get some rest. After she left, Bailey looked at the cup of coffee in her hand and the sandwich in her lap and wondered how they got there. She wondered if the Fairytalers liked the penthouse, the candle, the pictures on her laptop, wondered if Jason remembered the spiel. She would have nailed the sale; she knew she would have nailed it.

She snuck a glance at Brad, feeling guilty for even thinking about the sale at a time like this.

Three more nurses entered. There was no shortage of them

here. So much busywork. Paperwork to fill out, way too much. Updates on Brad's condition, way too brief. Each one left as soon as their message was delivered, but the last nurse lingered. Bailey stared at her, waiting for her to speak.

"I'm afraid I have terrible news," she said. Bailey's head jerked toward Brad.

"Not him," the nurse said quickly. "The driver."

"The driver?" Bailey said. "Of the other car?"

Was he dead? The man who ran into her husband, whoever he was? Was it a drunk driver, or a self-absorbed businessman on his cell phone?

"No," the nurse said. "There was only one car. Your husband wasn't driving, a woman was." The look on Bailey's face must have confirmed the fear of every aging wife, for the nurse quickly resumed speaking. "No," she said. "Nothing to fear. She was an elderly woman—"

"Olivia," Bailey said. She'd completely forgotten. How could she have forgotten? Brad told her over breakfast, he was spending the afternoon with his aunt Olivia. Unlike Faye, who was a vibrant woman only in her late fifties, Brad's Aunt Olivia was eighty-eight years old. "Olivia was driving?" Bailey said. She glanced at Brad. He knew better. Even though technically Olivia's license hadn't been revoked, it should have been. But she always worked Brad like a child, conniving to get her way, and Brad always gave in. This time, it had cost him thirteen minutes of his life.

"Where is she?" Bailey said, taking a deep breath, already talking herself into going easy on Olivia. How dare the nurse not tell her sooner. What would Olivia think? Bailey had been here for over five hours, and she hadn't even bothered to check on her? Which would be worse, that she didn't know Olivia was here, or that she didn't remember they were spending the afternoon together and didn't think to ask?

"I'm so sorry," the nurse said. "She didn't make it. And we need you to identify the body."

*   *   *

It felt so surreal. A cold hospital morgue. A steel gurney. Olivia's body covered in a big sheet. The nurse who accompanied her relayed the details of the accident as she knew them. Olivia ran a red light. Accelerated, then tried to brake too fast at the sight of stalled traffic ahead. She swerved onto the sidewalk, and smashed her Cadillac head-on into Eddie's Electronics. Miraculously, except for a glass storefront and slew of flat-screen televisions, nothing or nobody outside the car suffered any damage. Olivia was dead on impact, and Brad went through the windshield and landed on the sidewalk. He'd been sitting in the backseat. He loved to sit in the backseat and pretend Olivia was his chauffeur.

Bailey shut her eyes, wincing at the thought of her husband's body flying through glass and landing on the sidewalk. It was a miracle he survived. When he recovered, she was going to kill him for not wearing his seat belt.

"Were you two close?" the nurse asked politely.

"She was my husband's aunt," Bailey said. Was that enough of a response? Should she say something else, something kind? After a moment, the nurse gently covered Olivia with the sheet. Bailey stood awkwardly, not knowing what to do. Say a little prayer? She and Brad weren't religious. They considered themselves to be spiritual, though, so Bailey felt as if she should say something. Yet, nothing came except "You shouldn't have been driving," and what was the use of saying that now? Bailey touched the edge of the sheet.

"She hated me," Bailey blurted out.

The nurse looked startled, but quickly recovered. "I'm sure she didn't."

"Oh, she did," Bailey said. "But she loved Brad. So for that I loved her, you know?" Oh God, she was going to cry. But that was good, right? It meant her heart wasn't made of stone. "I love Brad more than anything in the world."

"I'm sure you do."

"And I'm so glad it's her lying there and not him!" Bailey slapped her hand over her mouth and stared wide-eyed at the nurse. "Oh God. You must think—"

"It's been a very emotional day for you," the nurse said. Bailey nodded. That was true.

"Olivia was . . . old," Bailey said. "She had a gentle way of life."

"That's nice."

"Yes," Bailey said. It was a lie. The truth was, Olivia Jordan was one of the most generic people Bailey had ever met. She didn't know how else to describe Olivia, she was just *there*, like a mass-market, bland version of the woman she could have been. And it didn't have anything to do with age necessarily, although Bailey had never known Olivia young, exactly—Bailey just had this theory that people really didn't change. Bailey didn't feel any different at thirty-six than she had at six. She was a little smarter, maybe, and she didn't carry her Easy-Bake Oven everywhere she went anymore, but otherwise she was basically the same. She still ate peanut butter with a spoon, and loved the color yellow, and twirled her hair when she was bored or nervous, and bit her nails to the nub, and she still laughed too loud at all the wrong times, in all the wrong places.

So, yes, older and wiser, but still, the same person she'd always been. Bailey had seen a picture of Olivia when she was around six years of age and she had that same vacant stare, the one that always made Bailey look eerily over her shoulder, as if an unseen spirit behind her and to the left had swiped Olivia's personality out from under her.

"She lived in the Bronx," Bailey said. "Riverdale."

"How nice," the nurse said.

"Yes," Bailey said. The times Bailey spent at Olivia Jordan's apartment were some of the most excruciating moments of her life. Filled with stale sugar cookies, and the sounds of her kitchen clock ticking, and the click click click of the burner when Olivia went to make tea because she no longer had the coordination to light it, but wouldn't let anybody else near the stove. Bailey couldn't make a move in that apartment without Olivia eyeing her. It was like IEDs were planted throughout and Olivia was just waiting for Bailey to step on one and blow them all to smithereens. Everything in her place made Bailey feel heavy and sad, from the doilies on her entrance table, to the brown rings in her chipped teacups, to the new year's calendar hanging on her wall where a generic landscape shrouded in fog stared at you and all the little white boxes were empty.

"She liked sugar cookies, and tea, and she never ever let me touch the stove or the calendar on her wall." Once Bailey brought a black felt-tip pen, and in the little white box designated for the day they visited she wrote *Brad and Bailey were here!!* Then Bailey grinned at Olivia and added a smiley face in the box. Olivia just stared at Bailey and blinked very slowly. Bailey stepped out of the kitchen to use the restroom, and when she returned, the calendar had been dumped in the trash. A new one hung in its place, identical to the old, and the white empty boxes stared at Bailey reproachfully as she listened to the burner click click click.

Olivia kept the windows shut and the curtains drawn, and the bulbs in her lamps were way too bright, illuminating every sparse corner, and every chip, and every stain, and Bailey couldn't breathe when she was there. There was nothing to distract herself with, not even razors in the bathtub. Olivia's television only got one station, and that was if Brad could get the rabbit ears to work. It was where he spent most of his time when he was there, clutching and stretching the wire antennas while bending his body into strange angles like some kind of amateur contortionist.

When he would finally get the picture in, he'd shout at Bailey and Olivia. "Hurry! Hurry! Watch! Watch!" Those were the only times Bailey ever saw Olivia come to life. Like whoever reached the couch first had Brad's undying love. It was a sight to see, Olivia, in tall white gym socks and worn brown sandals, sprinting for the living room. By the time Bailey arrived she'd be sitting up straight on the plastic-encased flowery couch, hands on knees, chin up and proud, smiling at Brad as if he'd just cured cancer.

So Bailey had to sit there next to Olivia and pretend to be interested in the program, more often than not involving God, weight loss, or fishing. Once they sat through an infomercial on Lubricant for Her, how to make your woman wet and wild in bed. Aunt Olivia slurped her tea and blinked very slowly like she was watching a manatee behind glass and not a half-naked vixen writhing on a king-sized bed, moaning for more. Bailey sat and stared, open-mouthed, at Brad, but he was too proud of the quality of the television reception to even notice that she was sitting next to his eighty-something-year-old aunt watching another woman have multiple orgasms. Bailey wanted to lift the plastic off the couch, crawl underneath it, and suffocate.

After that Bailey offered to get Olivia set up with cable and even foot the bill, but Olivia refused, adamantly stating that cable gave you brain cancer. Bailey figured Olivia was mixing cable up with cell phones, another technological advancement she neither owned nor wanted.

And try as they might to take her out to a nice restaurant, or a movie, or even a walk around the block, Aunt Olivia insisted on having a "nice evening at home." As far as Bailey knew, Olivia didn't have any friends, and Brad was her only remaining family. Besides them, she didn't have visitors, or even a cat, and if she played bingo, or knitted, or joined a book club, Bailey never caught wind of it. It was ironic, then, that Olivia ended her life by crashing into an electronics store.

"We should go now," the nurse said.

"I'm sorry, Olivia," Bailey said. "Brad loved you." She could have said "We loved you," but if there was an afterlife, Olivia would know she was lying.

"She would have made a fine grandmother," Bailey said. She absentmindedly rubbed her stomach.

"Are you?" the nurse said.

"Not yet," Bailey said. "But we're going to start trying. As soon as he comes out of the coma. Well, not like the minute he comes out. Unless he wants to. And if the doctor says it's okay. I certainly didn't mean we'd start trying before he comes out of the coma. Unless the doctor thinks it would help him come around?" Oh God, what was she saying? She was talking a mile a minute, and the nurse looked as if she wanted to join Olivia on the table.

"Good-bye, Olivia," Bailey said. The nurse gently took Bailey by the arm and guided her out of the room before she could say another word.

Chapter 5

"It's all my fault," Brad said. Bailey took his hands in hers and gently squeezed. Survivor's guilt. It was astounding, the grip it had on him. Her husband was a changed man; a tortured one. So, following the silent agreement of every happy marriage, what tormented Brad, tormented Bailey. She thought they'd be over it by now, but no. It wasn't like Brad to stay stuck. But besides his mother, whom he hadn't spoken to in five years, Olivia had been his closest living relative.

"It's not your fault," Bailey reminded him again. "She wanted to drive." More like insisted on it, begged Brad to let her cruise around in that Cadillac. Wifely anger surged up in Bailey, but she shoved it down.

"I shouldn't have let her. You said so yourself, you always said it. She wasn't fit to drive."

"Accidents don't discriminate," Bailey said. "They happen every day, whether people are fit or not. Baby, please. Look at me. It wasn't your fault. She would say it herself if she were here. And at least she died doing something she loved—with the person she loved more than anything."

"She hadn't taken the car out all year," Brad said. "She only did it because I was with her."

It had been a month since the accident. Brad had been in a coma for two weeks, then spent another week in the hospital, and finally, this past week he was back in their two-bedroom condo on the Upper West Side. Secured by a down payment from Bailey's first and only sale, it was a modest apartment, but it was theirs. It had a nice-sized kitchen and living room, arched entrances, dark wood floors, and crown molding. It was old-school Upper West Side, and Bailey absolutely loved it. So much so that she could ignore the tiny bedrooms.

But Bailey's favorite thing about the condo was the working fireplace. It brought the feel of a cabin to Manhattan, and she made Brad promise they would use it every year. Nothing spelled home more than the smell and sound and sight of a crackling fire. When she was a kid, some of her fondest memories were building fires with her father. Gathering wood and kindling, bunching up newspapers, helping him light it. Then sitting in front of it for hours, roasting marshmallows or seeing who could sit the closest to it the longest, or simply sitting back and staring into it, mesmerized by its magic. Fire, Bailey told Brad, was as primitive as you could get. Something about a roaring fire made her feel connected to the entire human race.

The mantel was from the fireplace in her childhood home. When her parents moved into a new house a few years ago, her father took the mantel with them and stored it. Then, as a surprise, he and Brad installed it in the condo. It was a beautiful dark oak, with decorative etchings along the side and top. Bailey couldn't imagine anything more special. And although she didn't dare say it out loud, it just felt wrong to set Aunt Olivia's urn on top of it. Brad couldn't stop staring at it. Bailey was the one who'd made the decision to have Olivia cremated.

A colossal mistake. Brad was beside himself. Supposedly Olivia made him promise once that she would "never be fried." Bailey didn't know; how was she to know? Neither did she know how long Brad's recovery was going to take, so of course she decided cremation was the best option. She and Brad wanted to be cremated, have their ashes spread somewhere beautiful. But Brad was staring at the urn as if Bailey had murdered Olivia in her sleep.

"She had nightmares about that," Brad said, pointing to the urn. He sounded accusatory, and angry. Would it help if she told him she put a lot of thought into picking out the urn? It was a deep blue cloisonné urn with copper inlay, and six flying doves etched into the highly polished ceramic. It stood on a hand-carved wooden base and it was called "Flying Home." Looped around the neck of the urn was a gold chain with a metal heart. Olivia's name and birth and death dates were etched into the heart. Underneath, it read BELOVED AUNT. She really thought Brad would see how much thought she'd put into it.

It hadn't been cheap either, although Bailey certainly wasn't tacky enough to mention that. It was probably the most decadent and beautiful thing she had ever associated with Olivia. She was secretly proud of herself for finding exactly the right thing. But Brad didn't seem to notice or appreciate its exquisite beauty.

Patience, Bailey reminded herself. The doctor warned Bailey that Brad might be on edge. Brain injuries were mysterious things. He told Bailey that her husband might not ever be exactly the same man he was before the accident. Luckily, the only changes Bailey noticed, besides his survivor's guilt, was that he was a little quicker to say hurtful things—as if he no longer had a filter between his thoughts and his mouth. Childlike at times. She wasn't going to take it personally.

"I'm sorry. I didn't know," Bailey said. She slid down to the floor and put her head in Brad's lap. After a few seconds, he began to stroke her hair. "Olivia's executor called again this morning," Bailey said. "He wants to meet with you for a reading of the will."

"I know," Brad said. That was hours ago. Brad hadn't gone near his phone.

"Do you want me to call him back?"

"No," Brad said.

"Is there any reason you don't want to call him back?"

Brad sighed. "The Cadillac is totaled, and her apartment was a rental," he said. "Besides her furniture, what's there to discuss?"

"Social Security? Teacher's pension?" Bailey guessed.

"God. It's so, so sad."

"I know." Bailey squeezed Brad's hands again and tried not to take it personally when he pulled them away. She got up from the floor and looked around for something to tidy. Everything was neat and clean, so she headed for the kitchen. She stopped in the doorway and leaned against the frame. Personally she loved the fact that their place was so small that she could talk to him from any room. If they had a bigger place, she would just be some crazy lady shouting down a hallway. "She loved you, Brad. You were her only family."

"I wouldn't have been if my mother hadn't flipped out on us."

"I know."

"I tried to call her, you know. She hasn't even bothered to call back."

Ah, that's why he was mad at the phone. "I know."

"Her only sister is dead and she doesn't call."

Not to mention her only son had been thrown from the car, died, come back to life, and had been in a coma. But even now, it wasn't himself Brad was feeling sorry for. "I know," Bailey said. "I'm sorry."

"I should leave her another message. Hint that Olivia left her millions. See how fast the phone rings then."

Bailey wanted to tell Brad to calm down, but that would just upset him even more. As much as Olivia Jordan's life had saddened Bailey, Elizabeth Jordan's infuriated her. How could such an amazing man come from such an awful mother? Beautiful, and selfish, a drug addict, alcoholic, and magnet for abusive men, including Brad's father—*that* was Brad's mother. Brad's entire childhood revolved around trying to keep his mother safe, and Bailey hated the woman for it. Bailey hated to admit it, but she saw some of the same impulsiveness and self-ishness in Brad. Had he not spent his entire childhood taking care of her, maybe he wouldn't be so afraid to settle down and have a family. Instead, they were always on the move, always scouting out the next "adventure." At least now they were finally in a stable home.

"Speaking of Olivia," Bailey said, "the landlord also called. He wants to know if we'll be clearing her stuff out or paying for another month."

Brad threw his hands up in the air. "I don't want any of her stuff," he said. "And I know you don't."

I want the calendar, Bailey thought. *I'm going to write all over it.* "Don't worry," she said. "We'll donate it. I can contact Goodwill and go over and pack her things. She might have some pictures or something you might want to keep."

"I hate lying around," Brad said. "I want to help." And that was another reason Brad was so irritable. He was a man on the move. Whereas Bailey would have convalesced with a jar of peanut butter, chocolate, paperback thrillers, and a constant stream of shows off Netflix, Brad hated lounging around.

"You need rest. Doctor's orders. Jesse said she'd help me." Jesse was Bailey's closest New York friend. They met in a book club. It still thrilled Bailey that she actually had been in a place long enough to make a friend. Before that they'd always been on the move as Brad tried one start-up business after another.

Surfs Up in Santa Monica, Sweaters in Seattle, and the Coffee Clutch in Colorado, where Brad spent their entire three-month stint whistling "Rocky Mountain High." All of his business ventures failed. It didn't stop until Bailey put her foot down, said that's it—they both had aunts in New York City, and Faye had offered to train her in real estate. Bailey said they were moving to Manhattan, and she didn't know about Brad, but Bailey for one wasn't moving again for at least a decade. To her enormous relief, Brad agreed. He still hadn't found a job, but Bailey was making enough to support them both. They were settled. They were happy. At least, they were before the accident. Weren't they?

"There's something I haven't told you," Brad said. "About the day I died." Bailey took a seat across from Brad so that he would know he had her full attention.

"Tell me," she said.

"I had this experience. I was floating above my body. I didn't even realize it was me! I thought—who is this dead guy lying on the sidewalk and why am I floating over him? Then I saw this light, Bails. I know—it's so clichéd—but it happened—I can't even describe it to you—only that I wanted to stay in it so bad."

"Oh, honey," Bailey said. She left her chair and settled on the floor next to Brad once again. "I'm so glad you didn't," she said. She hadn't brought up having a baby yet, she'd been waiting for the right time. Maybe it was now.

"You believe me, then?"

"Of course I believe you." Well. She believed that he believed it. And who was she to say what the mind experienced when you went through that kind of trauma? She certainly wasn't going to cast any doubt on it, not in his condition.

"I'm so relieved," Brad said. "I didn't think you'd believe me."

"Then what happened?"

"I remembered you," Brad said.

"Me?" Bailey said. "You remembered me?"

"I was just about to go into the light, and I felt like I was forgetting something—like you with your straightening iron—that's when it hit me—I had a wife—I was that dead guy on the sidewalk!"

"Oh my God."

"And the next thing I knew I woke up in the hospital." Bailey clutched onto Brad's hand, then leaned up and kissed him.

"I'm so happy you came back," Bailey said. She ran her hands up and down Brad's arm. "I love this body. I never want to lose it." Brad smiled, but it didn't reach his eyes. "What's wrong, babe?" Bailey said softly.

"I didn't see Olivia in the light," Brad said. "I don't think she made it to the light."

"Oh, babe." She could tell, by the way he turned from her, that she'd said the wrong thing. She hated seeing him like this. Her vibrant husband, broken. A lost child. She wanted Brad back even if it meant he wanted to uproot them and start a dude ranch in Utah. Bailey tried again. "Maybe—it was just too bright to see her."

"It wasn't a blinding light, Bails. I could still see. It was . . . bright. And so warm." He wrapped his arms around himself. For a brief second his face shone. He looked like a man who had just fallen in love.

"Maybe every individual goes into the light alone," Bailey said.

"Maybe," Brad said. He didn't sound convinced. She still felt as if he wanted her to say something, but she didn't know what it was. It was as if her reaction had disappointed him somehow. Whatever he experienced was a result of trauma. Clinically dead, her ass. He'd been alive, and the experience he'd just described had been a dream. All of it was one horrible dream. But it was over now. They had been given a second chance. A miracle. *Let's make a little miracle of our own,* she wanted to say. But there was no use bringing up babies now, not when he was so out of it.

"You should lie down and take a nap," Bailey said. "The doctor said you need a lot of rest." Brad nodded, and this time, he didn't argue. He simply followed her to the bedroom, and by the time she had finished tucking him in, he was fast asleep and gently snoring.

Three months passed before they knew it. Brad's recovery forced them into a quiet summer. Bailey gave up all the secret plans she had for them—getaways to the Hamptons, free concerts in Central Park, movies in Bryant Park. Instead, she allowed Brad time to heal. Which really just meant he sat and stared at things a lot. But fall was here, a time of changing leaves, tangerine skies, sweaters, and back to school. And Bailey was more than ready for a new start. She hoped Brad was too; he needed to embrace life. Hopefully, this would do for a start,

Bailey thought, taking in the martini bar from their perches at the head of the bar. It was crowded, and dark, and noisy. In other words, it was hip. Brad rested his hand on his heart and for a moment, Bailey felt hers tighten up in sympathy. Was he having an attack? He leaned forward.

"Are you okay?" Bailey had to shout to be heard.

"I met with Auntie Olivia's lawyer today," Brad said. Bailey waited, but for a moment he didn't add anything else.

Physically, Brad was back to his old self. Bailey wished she could say the same thing about his mental state. He'd been so secretive lately, including keeping all the details of Olivia's will to himself. Not that she minded. It wasn't like she had any claim to any of Olivia's things. And Olivia had been such a sore subject between them that Bailey usually made a point of keeping quiet about it. But that wasn't why she wasn't responding now.

Not once, in the twenty-six years since she'd known him, had she ever heard Brad utter the word "auntie." To add to the absurdity, his right hand was still placed over his heart like a Victorian woman in need of a fainting couch. But the real reason Bailey didn't respond right away, *couldn't* respond right away, was because she had just stuffed, not one, not even two (which in the court of her mind could still be argued as reasonable), but three giant green olives into her mouth, and, at the very second he dropped the news, was trying to simultaneously suck out the triple pimientos without choking to death. It was a meaningless but strangely satisfying game she'd come up with to dull the pain. There was a reason they were at Jason's favorite hipster martini bar—he was celebrating the sale of the Fifth Avenue penthouse to the Fairytalers.

The closing took forever due to all the stipulations and renovations and requests put in by the Fairytalers. But it was done: signed, sealed, and delivered. They would be moving, starting their glamorous new life. Allissa and Greg (as Jason was now calling them as if they were the best of friends) loved the chocolate-chip-scented candle. And the fact that they would pass the Frick museum every day on their way to work and relive where they began their journey as husband and wife. When Jason put it to them that way, they said, it had just cinched the sale! Jason, only twenty-six, had just made a fortune. Bailey was trying to keep it together. Brad was alive, that was all that mattered. Bailey prayed that if she repeated this enough to herself, she would be able to get through the evening without getting too tipsy and letting the little hipster have it. It wasn't Jason's fault. She was the one who'd told him to stay and show the penthouse. So he'd stayed. And used her sales pitch to woo them, and didn't give her an ounce of credit. That's all. Business was business. What did she expect him to do, split the commission?

Yes, yes, yes, yes, yes, yes, yes . . .

Of course not.

What Jason called "hip," Bailey called "hip-breaker" because the place was so cave-dark you needed a flashlight to see the menu. When she relayed this to Brad, he said their thirties was way too young to talk like that, but Bailey argued that they were in their *late* thirties, and how could you not resent a place that had you stumbling before you'd even taken the first salty sip of your Triple X martini? She would have lodged a formal complaint, but if Martinis on Madison had comment cards, she couldn't see well enough to spot them.

"Did you hear what I just said?" Brad said. Bailey held her finger up and pointed to her mouth, a private code that only a husband could know meant, "I've got a three-olive-pimiento-sucking-situation going on here," then she carefully chewed while he stared at her. She was glad he was alive and feeling better, but Brad was still off. Impatient, quick to snap at her. Daydreamy, withdrawn, obsessed about his Near Death Experience. He was constantly online, Googling other people who had "crossed over." It was as if she was married to John Edward, the psychic. Every time Bailey tried to point out someone's adorable, drooling baby with chubby little cheeks and kissable fat baby legs, Brad would zone out, then somehow bring the conversation back to the light.

Just as Bailey swallowed her olives and was about to ask how the meeting with the lawyer went, Faye popped up in front of them.

"How are you holding up?" You would think she was talking to Brad, but her question was directed at Bailey.

"I think I'm faking it quite well," Bailey said. "Do I look as green as I feel?"

"I don't know," Faye said. "I can't see a thing in this dungeon."

Bailey laughed. "Me neither."

"I know how difficult this must be," Faye said. "And Jason is acting the fool, taking credit for your idea. But don't you worry, I'm going to start setting you up with my bigger clients. You really came through for me. Our talent must be genetic."

"Thank you." That did make Bailey feel better. Was Brad listening to this? Not that she wanted him to feel bad in any way, but she hadn't dared say much about the thwarted sale, and well, it would be nice if he knew that it was her idea, that she would have sold the condo to the Fairytalers, that it would have been her being interviewed on *Entertainment Tonight* sitting next to the smiling couple, that she would have received the enormous check. Jason hadn't even paid her back for the candle, which had cost her fifteen bucks. But Brad didn't appear to be listening. Bailey put her hand on his knee.

"Do you want to get out of here?" she asked.

"You can't leave now," Faye said. "What will people think?"

"That my husband is recovering from a serious accident?" Bailey said.

"Actually," Brad said. "I really would love to get out of here." Bailey was surprised. The old Brad would have talked her into staying. He was always the last one to leave a party. Poor guy. He must be exhausted.

"Sorry, Faye," Bailey said. "But we're outta here."

"All right, then," Faye said. "I'll cover for you." She put her hand on Bailey's shoulder and gave a slight squeeze. Then she leaned over and kissed Brad full on the lips. Bailey just laughed. Faye adored Brad, everyone did. That Jordan charm.

Faye would probably cut off Brad's foot and wear it on her key-chain if she could. Faye finished the kiss, winked at Bailey, and disappeared into the dark. They were almost out the door when the couple of the moment stepped in front of them. Even in the dark, Bailey could make out Allissa's perfectly white teeth. She held out her hand.

"You're Bailey, right?" she said. "Like the drink?"

"Actually I'm named after my great-grandfather—"

"Your aunt's told me all about you," Allissa said. Bailey shook hands with Allissa and Greg, hoping nobody could see that she was just a little bit starstruck. She was even thinner than she looked in the tabloids.

"This is my husband, Brad," Bailey said.

"You were in an accident, right?" Allissa said. It was impossible to say for sure, but as Allissa turned to Brad, her eyes seemed to glow in the dark.

"I was," Brad said.

"The very night you saw the penthouse," Bailey said. "In fact—I was supposed to handle the showing. Until that awful phone call." Brad glanced at her. Was she laying it on too thick? *The chocolate-chip candle and slideshow of the Frick were my idea! And the romantic spiel—relive where you began the most important journey of your lives—that was me too!*

But Allissa wasn't listening to Bailey. She was fixated on Brad. "Can I ask you a personal question?" she asked him. God, she was so pretty. So model perfect. And what was that perfume? No doubt designed in a science lab somewhere, carefully formulated to make every unsuspecting male fall madly, chemically, hormonally, irrevocably in love with her. Was it working? Was Brad in love with her? Bailey squinted but she still couldn't make out much in the dark. Bailey subtly brought her own wrist up to her nose and sniffed. Peanuts. Salted.

"Hit me," Brad said. *Hit me?* Since when did he say things like hit me? What happened to "Auntie" and hand on heart? Why didn't Brad give her the first shot? She'd be quite happy to hit him.

"I heard you were . . ." Allissa stopped.

"Dead?" Brad said, leaning into her. Allissa squealed and jumped back. Then, everyone laughed. Everyone except Bailey. What was so funny about her husband being dead? She felt her heart clench at the thought, the same clawing fear she'd felt when the stranger on the phone said those two little words: "clinically dead."

"Thirteen minutes," Brad said. "Thirteen minutes that changed my entire worldview." Changed his entire worldview? Now who was being dramatic? And what exactly did that mean? What exactly about his worldview had changed? So far he hadn't shared any of these changes with Bailey.

"So—you had some kind of experience?" Allissa continued in her little-girl voice. Bailey felt a string of conflicting feelings wash over her. She wanted Allissa to like her. She also wanted to pull her hair and slap her until she dropped the little-girl act. Bailey felt someone's eyes on her and lifted her gaze to find Greg studying her. For some reason, it made her blush. For once she was thankful for the dark.

"You'll have to excuse my wife," Greg said. "She's into angels and trumpets and all that stuff."

Rich, and beautiful, and saintly, Bailey thought. How nice for her. "We actually have to go," she said, reaching in her purse for her phone. "I'll call a cab."

"Why don't you use our driver?" Allissa said in an excited voice. Like she'd just found a pile of gold.

"No need," said Brad. "We've got wheels."

"We do?" Bailey said. "We've got wheels?"

"Say you'll have dinner with us some night," Allissa said. "Our treat." She snuggled close to Brad again. "I'd really love to hear all about your experience. You must have so much to share."

"Sounds like a plan," Brad said. Allissa launched herself into Brad's arms, hugged him, then kissed both his cheeks before pulling back.

Hey, Bailey wanted to shout. *Get your manicured paws off my hus-*

band's cheeks. *Those are my cheeks.* Greg looked at Bailey and smiled. Then Allissa grabbed Bailey's arm and shook it up and down.

"Don't forget. Dinner, the four of us." Bailey was reaching into her purse for a pen to get their phone number, but Allissa was already gone, Greg trailing in her wake.

Chapter 6

Outside, Bailey exhaled all of her jealousy in the New York night. Only then did she start tingling at the possibilities. Imagine, couple friends with the Fairytalers! Maybe that was even better than the sale. She hoped Brad would go along. He'd always hated the "Celebrity Culture." Brad didn't put anyone up on a pedestal. Ironic, because Bailey always held him up on one and he didn't seem to mind that. And, she had to admit, it was Brad that Allissa was interested in, not her. That was life, wasn't it? Here Brad couldn't care less about the Fairytalers, and like cats who fling themselves all over the one animal hater in the room, they'd launched themselves on him. She linked arms with him, still humming with happiness at the prospect of hanging out in the penthouse with their new friends. Maybe she and Allissa would get pregnant at the same time and spend nine months reassuring each other that their asses were not too big.

"What are you thinking about?" Brad said. It startled Bailey. They used to ask each other that every five minutes, when they were first in love. It had been a long time since he'd asked her that.

"My ass," Bailey said.

"What?" Brad laughed, slipped his hand down, and rubbed her butt. "Funny," he said. "Me too."

Bailey laughed and slapped his hand away. She hoped he would put it back. He didn't. "What do you mean we have wheels?" she asked.

"I have Olivia's car," Brad said. Bailey just stared at him. An image of the Cadillac, smashed like an accordion, rose to mind.

"The Cadillac?"

"Of course not. Turns out Olivia had a second car."

"Olivia had a second car?"

"Are you just going to repeat everything I say?" Brad hugged her to him and kissed her cheek. He was alive. He smelled good. He sounded good. He was back. Right? His worldview hadn't really changed. That's just something one said to celebrities at cocktail parties. "Come on," Brad said. "I'll explain everything in the car."

Bailey felt light-headed as she stood and stared at the car. She was giddy. She felt slightly ashamed of herself, but she couldn't help it, she was downright giddy. Aunt Olivia had a second set of wheels all right, a brand-new Jaguar. Well, a five-year-old Jaguar, but from the new-car smell and mileage, it looked as if Olivia had driven it straight off the lot and into her garage, and that was it. Bailey couldn't get over it. Olivia Jordan owned a sleek, black Jaguar. This was the same woman who wore tall white gym socks with her sandals. It just didn't seem possible.

"This is unbelievable," Bailey said.

"There's more," Brad said.

"More cars?"

"No, silly. Not more cars. But Aunt Olivia was loaded," Brad said. Bailey stared at her husband.

"Olivia had a gun?" she said.

"A gun?" Brad threw his head back and laughed. "Moola, baby," he said. "Aunt Olivia had tons of moola."

"She did not."

"She did."

"How?" What, where, when, why? Bailey couldn't get any of the words out of her mouth.

"Ready for this?"

"No," Bailey said. "But hit me."

"Funny you should say that," Brad said. "Turns out Olivia had a secret life."

"Out with it."

"Olivia was a poker shark."

"No."

"She played online, she played in groups, she played in tournaments."

"No."

"And she was good. Very, very good."

"No."

"You can't keep saying that."

"Aunt Olivia. Your aunt Olivia."

"My aunt Olivia."

"And she never told you?"

"I mean, I'd seen a deck of cards about her place, but she would never even have a game with me."

"I wonder why."

"I think she wanted to keep up a role-model image of herself. You know. To make up for Mom."

"Wow." Bailey was ashamed of herself for judging Olivia. Maybe if Bailey had been a little nicer, Olivia would have liked her. She would have invited her to play poker. Why hadn't the old broad ever taken them for a spin in the Jag? They could've been the best of pals.

And why didn't she spend her winnings while she was alive? Because she was from the Rainy Day Generation. Bailey couldn't remember Olivia ever giving them a single gift. She sent cards instead, filled with bookmarks with pictures of kittens, and chimpanzees, and once an overweight possum "Hanging in there."

How much money did she have? So far Brad hadn't exactly spilled all the dirty details. Bailey wanted to drive, but Brad was finally in a better mood and she wasn't going to push it.

Sitting in this sexy car, Bailey began to get a few ideas. They hadn't made love since the accident. Brad hadn't seemed in the mood, and Bailey respected that. But sitting here, as her husband accelerated their new Jag, Bailey started feeling amorous. They used to love having sex in the backseat of cars. The cramped space, the sweat, the rush, the fear of being caught. Some of the best sex of their lives had been in the backseat of a Chevy Nova. What would it be like in this Jag?

Brad must have been thinking the same thing. He too was looking in the backseat. But unlike Bailey, he appeared to be talking to it.

"You ready?" he said.

"For a quickie in the backseat?" Bailey put her hand on Brad's knee and squeezed.

"What?" Brad sounded appalled. "No."

"Oh," Bailey said.

"I'm sorry," Brad said. He glanced in the rearview mirror. "It's just that I was . . . talking to . . . Aunt Olivia."

Bailey whipped her head around to the backseat. There, with its seat belt fastened around it, sat Aunt Olivia's urn. All thoughts of having sex in the backseat evaporated from Bailey's thoughts.

"Have you finally decided?" she asked tentatively. She'd been waiting for him to decide where to scatter the ashes. Maybe once he let go of them, he'd let go of all this near-death stuff.

"Decided?"

"Where to sprinkle her ashes."

"Oh," Brad said. "No."

No, Bailey repeated to herself. No. She tried to keep her voice light, and not at all worried about his sanity. "Okay. Then why is her urn in the backseat?"

"We're taking her for a little drive." Brad broke into a boyish grin.

"Come again?"

"I thought she'd like to drive around the city."

"Pull over," Bailey demanded. "Right now."

"We're in the middle of Fifth Avenue."

"Find a place and pull over. Please, Brad." Brad swung the wheel to the right like a petulant child, and the Jaguar smoothly cut across two lanes and maneuvered along the curb. God, Bailey loved this car. It momentarily distracted her from the backseat.

"What?" Brad said.

"Why are you driving Olivia's urn around?" Bailey asked.

"I just thought it would be nice."

"Okay," Bailey said. "But it's kind of weird too. Don't you think?" *Please say yes. Please, please, say yes.*

Brad sighed, glanced in the backseat again. "She wanted to drive around that day," Brad said. "And we barely went anywhere."

Bailey pressed the unlock button for her door and threw it open. Fifth Avenue smelled like rain and long-forgotten hot dogs.

"Where are you going?" Brad said.

"I just need a little air," Bailey said.

"Why don't you just roll down the window?"

"I thought I might take a little walk."

"Now?"

"I'm sorry. I know you've been through a lot. I just—it's been really stressful for me too, you know. And I don't want to say anything hurtful or anything I'll regret. So I think while you're driving Auntie around, I'll just walk home, get a little fresh air."

"A half a million dollars!"

"What?"

"Aunt Olivia left us a little over a half a mill," Brad said. Bailey shut the door. She stared at Brad for a long time. Cars swished past them. Central Park horses and carriages headed home for the night. Lights twinkled down the length of Fifth Avenue. Slowly, Bailey turned and stared at Olivia's urn. She felt a sudden fondness for the old gal. It was as if in death, Olivia Jordan had finally come to life.

"Let's take her over the Brooklyn Bridge, and then to the Bronx Zoo," Bailey said.

Sudden wealth. They needed time to breathe and comprehend. Half millionaires. Bailey had been called a lot of things in her lifetime, but an "almost millionaire" was not one of them. And surely, with the right investments, they could lose the "almost" and become true millionaires.

Bailey rolled the word around on her tongue, trying to get used to it. They were lying in bed, having made love for the first time since the accident. One of the benefits of Brad coming back to life was that he had decided to appreciate everything, love everything like it was the first time. And it paid off in bed. Brad seemed to adore every inch of her. And even though he still insisted on wearing a condom, Bailey knew it was just a matter of time before they started trying. After all, they had the money now—Brad would be out of excuses. She snuggled next to him, caressed his head, fuzzy with the hair just starting to come back in. Except for Olivia's urn looming over them from the dresser, everything seemed just a little bit perfect.

Brad took Bailey's hand. "I think you're absolutely right," he said. "Relive is much more romantic than remember. Because it emphasizes *living*."

"Uh-huh," Bailey said. She hoped the baby had Brad's dimples and her love of spicy food.

"I think we should learn from this. I think we should start living before it's too late."

"What?" She recognized his tone of voice. It was the tone Brad used before starting every one of his failed business ventures. She sat up in bed. "We do live," she said. "We are living."

"Are we?" Brad said. "Or are we just going through the motions?"

"We're not going through the motions. We're in motion. Motion is good."

"We have choices to make," Brad said. "With money comes great responsibility."

"Exactly," Bailey said. "Wait here." She jumped off the bed and opened the top drawer of her dresser. It was still dark, but she rattled it anyway.

"What's that noise?"

"Hold out your hand." Bailey joined Brad on the bed again and placed the rattle in his hand. "Open." He opened his eyes and stared at it. "A baby," Bailey said when he didn't speak. "We should really start trying." Brad still didn't respond. "What do you think?"

"I'd say we already got our practice in for the day." Brad shook the rattle.

"You used a condom," Bailey said.

"I said practice."

"Well, next time let's practice without a condom, shall we?"

"Are you sure we're ready for that?"

"I can't think of a better time. Can you?"

"I've got a few things I want to do first," Brad said. "My bucket list." He tossed the rattle aside like it was part of a practical joke. Bailey picked it up. *You already kicked the bucket,* Bailey thought. *Isn't it too late to make a list?*

"Like what?" She sounded harsh. She didn't mean to, but her resentment spilled out of her. Brad rolled away from her. Silence stretched and then loomed. "It's not like we have to decide anything tonight," Bailey said. She reached out and touched Brad's back. He rolled over and faced her again. She smiled at him and gently traced his lips with the tip of her finger. He kissed her finger, then took her hand.

"You're right, you're right. Nothing has to be said tonight," Brad said. "But I have some ideas." Bailey nodded, rolled out of his grip, off the bed, and wandered over to the window. If you laid your stomach on the windowsill, stuck your body out far enough, and looked to the left, you could see the Hudson River.

He had some ideas? Brad Jordan and his ideas. The surf shop was the first one. They were so young then. Tan, and happy, and looking good in their swimsuits. They had just moved to sunny California and life was easy. Every head on the beach used to turn when Brad Jordan walked by. But he was looking at the surfboards. He didn't even surf, but he didn't like the design of the boards or the attitudes of the "dudes in the shops."

One day while they were body surfing, catching waves and waiting to see whose swimsuit the rush of water would take down, Brad grabbed her.

"A surf shop!" he said. "B and B Boards!"

Bailey didn't even hesitate. "Oh my God," she said. "I love it." What she really loved was the idea of their initials forever etched into a sign, hanging for all to see on Santa Monica Boulevard.

"Brilliant, right?" Brad said.

"Right!" B&B Boards lasted five months. They were new to all aspects of running a business, and the more experienced shops in town were determined to crush them. It didn't take long before Brad wanted out.

"We're not Californians," he said. "We're intellectuals. We love to read, to debate, to climb mountains."

"We do?" Bailey said. She couldn't remember them ever climbing a mountain.

"We will," he said. "Seattle! Mount Rainier! Coffee shops! Literary types! Sweaters!"

"Sweaters?"

"It's always raining in Seattle. People are chilly all year round. What do all those coffee commercials show?"

"People in bulky sweaters." It was true. All coffee commercials she could remember featured people cocooned in wool, standing outside with steaming mugs of java, mountains towering in the background. That one lasted less than a year. Bailey couldn't stop sneezing, and it was turning off customers.

The Coffee Clutch in Colorado was next. The most depressing failure of all since Bailey actually loved running the place. They made it just shy of five years before they were forced to close the books on that one. Each "idea" had driven them deeper in debt, and Brad deeper into depression. It was a vicious cycle. Get your hopes up; pour yourself into it mind, body, and soul; spend every penny you have; get crushed. She should pounce on him, chase out whatever ideas he had in his head. But she knew better. She had to be calm and rational. If she hated the ideas off the bat, he would be that more passionate about them, it's just how he worked. But if she pretended to consider the ideas, then calmly, slowly, and logically pointed out their many, many flaws, she might be able to talk him down.

Besides, did she really care what he did with the money? As long as he kept his promise that they would stay in New York and agreed to put at least half down on the condo, or into stocks, or *something* (baby fund, baby fund, baby fund!), then he could be free to pursue whatever he was dreaming up next. She would be mature and drop it for the evening. Seriously, whatever ideas he had could wait until morning. After several cups of coffee. Absolutely no good would come from discussing ideas this evening. She pulled her body out of the window, turned, and faced her husband.

"What ideas?" she asked.

Chapter 7

Who wouldn't want to live in a lighthouse? Bailey. Bailey wouldn't want to live in a lighthouse. She didn't even like night-lights when she was a kid. Brad followed Bailey around as she began to pace through the apartment, trying to see if she could physically shake her mounting feelings of dread and déjà vu.

"We'll turn it into a bed-and-breakfast," Brad said. "Isn't that brilliant?"

No. She certainly didn't want to make the beds of total strangers, or clean multiple sinks and toilets, or call them "our lovely guests," or cook breakfast for them at all hours of the morning, or come running like a pair of Pavlovian dogs whenever someone rang the little bell on the counter. No freaking way.

Perhaps she should have taken note of the fact that the love of her life didn't say, who wouldn't want to run a B&B? To him, the glory of living in a lighthouse overshadowed the business side of his latest endeavor. He wanted to live in a lighthouse first, and incidentally invite total strangers to spend every night with them to fund it second. Bailey did her best to humor him.

"Don't you ever watch *MSNBC Investigates*? We'd be stuck on an island, in a lighthouse with potential lunatics. If our lives are in danger, are we supposed to swim for help?"

"There are lights," he said. "And horns. We could have the Coast Guard there in minutes."

"An axe murderer only needs seconds. Seconds."

"You'll love it," he said next, as if he didn't hear her. "We have to do this. We're never going to have another shot like this."

The irony was, being named Bailey and Brad, their close friends had always called them B&B. Was that what this was all about? Had years of auditory conditioning hypnotized her husband into thinking they were destined to operate a B&B?

"I've been doing research," he said. "On the 'inns' and outs of running a B&B. Get it?"

But she didn't get it, she didn't get it at all.

It was a joke. Inns and outs. As in i-n-n-s. He spelled it in the air with his fingers.

It still wasn't funny.

"Can you picture it? Bailey, baby, can you see it calling to us?"

"Drawing us in so we'll crash on the rocks?"

He smiled, but he didn't think she was funny either. His face took on a quiet, serious stillness. "Don't you see it? Don't you want it?"

It had all transpired in less than five minutes. Five minutes in which Bailey could already see the life she thought they were going to live crumbling before her very eyes. Bailey pinched the bridge of her nose with her fingers. It was a calming technique she'd learned in order to distract herself from smashing objects against the wall. But this time, it wasn't the wall she wanted to hurl something at, it was Brad. It was just stress. And fatigue. This is why you never, ever talked about serious subjects before bed. Bailey flopped on the couch in their cozy living room. All chances of getting a wink of sleep had flown out the window. Brad remained standing, hovering actually, which wasn't hard to do given the square footage of their apartment.

"Does this have something to do with your near-death experience?" Bailey said. She had to ask. Brad didn't answer. Bailey continued. "Because buying a lighthouse won't help Olivia find that other light—which I'm sure she already did—"

"It's not that—but it's a wonderful metaphor, don't you think? Our guests will be drawn to the light! I'll be a keeper of the light."

"Brad."

"A lighthouse. We're actually going to live in a lighthouse. It's a dream come true, it's a dream."

"It's not a dream. It's a total nightmare. Wait. Did you say?"

"Did I say what?" Bailey looked at her husband's face. He was trying to look innocent. He had that little-boy expression. But he'd said it all right. Like her, Brad liked language. He knew the nuances. And even as she asked it, Bailey already knew the answer.

"Tell me you didn't already buy a lighthouse!"

He'd gone to an auction. Just to pass time, he insisted, just to pass time. A lighthouse went up for bid. It was quite common these days; GPS systems were making lighthouses obsolete. The Coast Guard was off-loading them as fast as they could. An actual lighthouse with a keeper's house and everything. It was a sign. He had been led to this auction, this was the answer he'd been seeking. A lighthouse B&B. He bid. Others bid. It made him sweat. It made him mad. He bid. Others bid. He bid higher. And of course he won. Brad insisted he won because he was astute and aggressive. Bailey thought he won because no one in his or her right mind wanted a lighthouse on the Hudson River. Bailey didn't even know there were lighthouses on the Hudson River. Back in the day, Brad told her, there were as many as fourteen. Now there were nine.

Perhaps she could have forgiven him if it had been New England. She would have warmed to the idea of a second home in Maine, or Rhode Island. California even. As long as somebody else was running the bed-and-breakfast year-round and they were the rich lazy couple who visited when they wanted to get away from the city. But no. Brad wanted them to move. He wanted their lives to change a hundred and eighty degrees.

"It's perfect. It's upstate," Brad said. "Until you get used to the idea, you can commute."

"I can commute?"

"I'm going to start calling you parrot if you keep doing that."

"You said it's two hours from Manhattan. Do you expect me to commute four hours a day?"

"You could come on the weekends."

Bailey could not believe her husband had just said that to her, could not believe he wanted nothing more than a weekend wife. He didn't even seem to notice how much it hurt her. For a man who'd experienced such a strong spiritual transformation, he was more out of touch than ever. "I see. And how much did you spend on this overblown man cave?"

"Overblown man cave?" He sounded angry. She was using all of her energy to be patient and he was snapping at her at the drop of a hat. It was time to get a little tougher with him.

"See? Sometimes repetition is a necessary evil. It allows your brain to process the incomprehensible."

"Just look at the pictures, Bails." Bailey was back to pacing, but forced herself to remain in the living room since she was dying to get her hands on Olivia's urn and hurl it out the window. Brad handed her a folder. Inside was a sales contract and photocopied pictures of a white stone house with an attached lighthouse rising behind it. Surrounded by water.

"I don't see any roads," Bailey said. "Where are the roads?"

"That's the beauty of it," Brad said. "You can only reach it by boat."

"We don't even have a boat." Brad just looked at her. "You bought a boat too, didn't you?"

"You'll love it. It's a perfect little rowboat." *If he starts to sing "Michael Row the Boat Ashore," I'm going to kill him.* "We'll paint it yellow."

"I can't believe you did this without me." Bailey headed for the kitchen. She ended up in front of the fridge, staring into it, wondering if anything inside could make her feel better.

"There's also a ferry captain." Brad sounded so hopeful, so excited. So freaking childish.

"What?"

"The island has a ferry captain. He's willing to make a couple of runs a day to ferry our guests back and forth. For a small fee, of course."

"Of course." Bailey slammed the fridge door shut. "Can we forget the fairy god-captain for a moment?"

"There's no need to mock." Brad gestured to the freezer. "I bought cookie dough ice cream," he said. "Your favorite." Bailey wasn't going to say thank you, not in the middle of a fight, but she did accept the carton and spoon when he handed them to her. Maybe a rush of sugar would help her calm down.

"Brad! You've made all these life-changing decisions without me." She'd planned on saying more. A lot more. Only suddenly, no thoughts were left in her head. Just a little bit of brain freeze and the unmistakable desire to smash something. Bailey slammed down the ice cream carton and yanked open the fridge again. She grabbed both bottles of champagne, the ones they'd planned on celebrating with the day she was supposed to show the penthouse. Now forever known as the day he died. Brad hadn't even remembered. Not that she expected him to right away. But months had gone by. Every day he'd opened the fridge and seen the bottles of champagne. They had been his idea. Yet he didn't say a word. Well, might as well make use of them. She popped the Dom first and drank straight out of the bottle. She held the cheap one out to Brad. He shook his head.

"I didn't go there intending to bid," he said. "I swear." Bailey took her time drinking the champagne. She lowered the bottle and held up her index finger. She needed to burp.

"Is it too late to get out of this?" she asked after she finally released the air in her lungs. Brad shook his head. Was he shaking his head yes, or was he shaking his head no? She didn't know anything about him anymore. Not a single thing. He soon cleared it up.

"All sales are final." Once again, he was trying to sound contrite. But it was still there, just beneath the surface. He was on cloud nine, high as a space monkey landing on Planet Bananas.

"You didn't even see the property in person, did you?" She took both bottles of champagne with her to the living room. Brad followed. She suddenly wished they had a balcony. If she had made that sale, they could have moved. They could have bought a place with a balcony. Or, if Brad didn't want to go with her, she could have moved. She could have bought her own little place with her own little balcony. Then she could have thrown herself off it.

"I couldn't see it in person," Brad said. "It was an auction."

"Why didn't you just buy a painting, or an antique sword, or a horse!"

"A horse? Don't be ridiculous."

"Right. Because a freaking lighthouse makes much more sense."

"It's an investment. It's a job."

"How much?"

"Don't worry. We won't have to borrow much." Bailey choked on the champagne, which triggered a violent cough. It took a long time for her to stop. Brad didn't even pound her on the back. He just stood and waited with his new, infinite patience.

"Borrow?" she spat out the minute she could breathe again. "As in you spent the entire half a million on this property?"

Brad shoved the picture at her again. "Look how beautiful it is! It probably won't need much work at all. We'll be able to jump right in and start our life."

"We have a life. Here."

"No. You have a life here. You're the one who keeps telling me I need to get a job, right?"

"Don't you dare put this on me."

"Look at me." Brad took out the largest picture of the lighthouse out of the folder and held it against his chest like he was cradling a newborn baby. "I'm so happy about this. I want you to be happy."

Bailey wanted to be happy too. She wanted to be the young

girl in the ocean ecstatic to have their initials etched in wood. But she wasn't. They weren't kids anymore. They were older now, so why wasn't he wiser? Maybe Jason was right. Nobody wanted anybody to be too happy. Nobody was comfortable around anybody happier than them. Because the truth was Bailey hated Brad's newfound happiness. She hated how every time they went outside he found something he wanted her to stop and stare at. The morning light. A leaf. How the sun was glinting off a penny on the sidewalk. The longer they had to stop and stare at something, the more Bailey felt like something was wrong with her for not seeing its innate beauty, for wanting to get where they were going.

It was wearing her down. The more he thought something was beautiful, the more she automatically hated it. And the hours he was spending on the Internet. Who was he talking to? He was spending way more time with strangers than he was with her. Granted, part of it was her fault. She didn't want to hear all these stories about death, and tunnels, and "life reviews." It made her angry. It made her remember what it felt like to almost lose her husband. Bailey could feel all her promises of being patient with Brad drain right out of her.

Because she couldn't help but resent him just a little lately. He was using his "death" as an excuse to cheat her out of the life he'd promised her. The life she'd earned after following him all over the country. The job she finally had, the home they lived in, the children she wanted. He'd promised, he'd promised, he'd promised. Bailey held up her fingers one by one as she started to list off his failures. "Surf's Up Santa Monica (which is what he named it after promising her it would be B&B Boards). Sweaters in Seattle, The Coffee Clutch." Bailey grabbed the picture of the lighthouse out of his hands and held it up. "Hudson River Lighthouse," she said, adding it to the list.

"It used to be the Sage Lighthouse," Brad said. "But I thought we'd call it Olivia's Lighthouse."

"Please," Bailey said. "Please tell me this is some kind of joke." Brad reached out and took Bailey's hands. There was a spark back in his eyes, a dancing excitement she was all too familiar with. She hadn't seen it in a while, and she wasn't sure she wanted to see it ever again.

"Life is an adventure. You have to take risks. This isn't just going to be a business this time. This time it's going to be a home, Bails. Our home." Bailey, horrified with herself even as she was doing it, began to rip up the picture of the lighthouse. She channeled all her frustrations at the piece of paper as she tore into it and let the pieces fall to the ground. Brad simply watched her.

"Our home is right here. Right here, Brad." She crushed the pieces of the picture underneath her shoe, then walked away. Nothing could have made her feel worse than the sight of Brad picking them up, trying to piece them back together.

"We'll figure it out," he said quietly. He sounded so sad, so lost, so dejected. She wasn't going to fall for it.

"Why wasn't my signature required on this sale?"

At least he had the decency to look sheepish. "It was a cash sale. And technically . . ." He stopped, treading carefully over his words.

"Technically what?" Bailey could feel her throat tighten, her words come out in a constricted breath.

"Technically the money was left to me." She couldn't believe how much that hurt. Even if it was true. Even though she knew as she stood staring at him that Olivia Jordan, wherever she was, would be one thousand percent on Brad's side. If he had spent the money on a half a million Pop-Tarts, Olivia would be warming up toasters as they spoke.

"I mean nothing to you. Is that it?"

"You mean everything to me." Brad came over and reached out as if to touch her, but in the end kept his distance. She knew she would have pushed him away, but she was still mad he didn't touch her.

"You didn't even consult me." The urn. She wanted to throw the urn. She wanted to toss the ashes out the window. What would he do? Given his guilt and obsession with Olivia, he would probably go insane. Brad saw she was looking in the direction of the bedroom.

"Do not even think about throwing that," he said. Bailey hated that he knew her so well. He stepped into their bedroom and returned with the urn tucked protectively under his arm.

"Let's take Aunt Olivia and go see our lighthouse. I think once you see it—"

"We are not driving anywhere with those ashes anymore. Do you hear me?"

"Bailey. She won't hurt you."

Bailey swigged out of the champagne again and then took a step closer to Brad. "Do you hear yourself?" Her voice was barely a whisper. "Do you hear how crazy you sound?"

"You think I'm crazy? You think my grief is crazy? You think the fact that I died is crazy? What else? My out-of-body experience?"

Yes, yes, yes, and sorry, but yes. But as angry as she was, that was still a border she wasn't prepared to cross. Not just yet. Instead, she focused her anger on the urn.

"Ashes to ashes," Bailey said. "You know what comes next?"

"Don't start this again."

"Dust to dust, Brad. Dust to dust." She ran her finger along the urn and held it up. "This isn't the dust they were speaking of, Brad. She has to go back into the earth. Where we all go."

"That's my call," Brad said. "And we're not ready." *"We." He used "we." We're not ready.* "You could be a little more supportive," Brad added.

"What am I supposed to do? Make her a cup of tea? Take her shopping? Find a nice strong vase to fix her up with? My God— you're looking for a fight, aren't you? I can commute."

"What?"

"That's what you said about the lighthouse. You'll go live there and 'I can commute.' "

"I told you—"

"Admit it! You want to live in your little lighthouse all by yourself, don't you?"

"My little lighthouse? Do you hear yourself? Sarcasm and resentment oozes out in everything you say."

This had gone too far. Bailey didn't want to see Brad this upset. He had been through a traumatic experience. She had to get a grip on her anger. "Brad."

"I have to do this, Bailey. I think it's what I'm meant to do."

"This is so typical of you! We have a life here. You and me. You promised, Brad, you promised."

"I know, I know. But things happen, Bailey. I had this incredible, mind-blowing experience. Do you know what it was like? Do you have any idea?"

"You went behind my back—"

"It was pure love, Bailey."

"You spent our money—"

"Love like I've never felt before." Bailey froze. She felt as if she'd been turned to stone. *Love like he'd never felt before?* He saw the look on her face. He put the urn down and approached her slowly. "Not romantic love, babe. Just . . . all-encompassing love. And now I want to share that love with you. This is meant to be. You have to believe me. It's our destiny. You and me."

"No, it's not. Our destiny is a baby, and a condo with a terrace, and Central Park. Our life is here. Not some godforsaken little lighthouse."

"I can't speak for your life, Bails. But there's one thing—no, make that two things that I do know. My life is not here." He picked up Olivia's urn and headed for the door. Halfway there he stopped and turned. "And secondly, there is absolutely nothing 'little' about my lighthouse." With that, he and Olivia's ashes stormed out.

Chapter 8

Bailey stood in Olivia's kitchen, packing the contents of her cupboard into boxes marked DONATE, KEEP, and THROW (which to Bailey meant both "throw away" and literally "throw" if things continued to be this stressful) while Jesse sat at the dining room table drinking tea. Jesse was considerably younger than Bailey, at least a decade. Bailey didn't know Jesse's exact age because when she'd asked her, Jesse said, "In my realm, age is meaningless."

When they first met in the book club, Jesse stuck her hand out and said, "I'm Jesse. Spelled like the outlaw."

She was a spunky girl with delicate features. Her black hair was always cut in a new style. Today half was chopped off while the other half hung in a bob obscuring most of the left side of her face. The one eye Bailey could see was heavily made up. She was petite, yet strong. She was a nurse in the emergency ward at a hospital in the Bronx. She absolutely loved her job, thrived on the chaos and absurdity that filled her nights. Bailey could see it. Jesse was always moving, twitching, doing something. At the book club where they'd met, Jesse was the first to

say what Bailey had secretly been thinking about the book se-
lection that month, *Clown Down,* a highly acclaimed literary tale
of a business executive who secretly longed to be a clown.

"I thought it was a load of shit," Jesse said, in a loud, confident voice when it was her turn to speak. Bailey burst out laughing. Couldn't help it, the laughter came tumbling out of her in
a nervous free fall. Bailey had spent the first fifteen minutes of
the discussion trying to figure out how to politely say that she
didn't "connect" with the book, crafting exactly the right
words. Words that would convey she had been an English lit
major in college, and read all the classics, and yet still, for some
reason, just didn't connect with the book. She figured something was wrong with her. Jesse's perspective, that maybe it was
just shit, had never entered her mind. After all, the writer had
gone to Columbia, won awards. The *New York Times* raved about
the book. Jesse grinned at Bailey. "Right?" she asked her. "Wasn't
it just pure bullshit?"

Bailey hadn't even finished it. She couldn't get through the
first four chapters and she hated herself for it. Jesse redeemed
Bailey's ego just a little bit that day. "I couldn't get into it," Bailey admitted in front of Jesse and the group.

There were a few gasps, one cough, and a quite audible "My
God."

"If the asshole wants to be a clown, he should just go be a
clown. Do I really need four hundred pages of clown ambiva-
lence?" Jesse said. Once again, she took the words out of Bailey's mouth.

"He had a reputation, a high-paying job, a family," someone
interjected. Looks were exchanged all around. Clearly, anyone
could see the book was pure genius.

"I was a little confused," Bailey said. "They kept mentioning
his ruddy cheeks and red nose. But they said he never drank alcohol—so were they trying to say he was, like, actually morph-
ing into a clown?"

"You didn't finish the book, did you?" someone in the group
said.

"I used it to prop up my coffee table," Jesse said. Bailey laughed again. She really wanted to stop, but she couldn't.

"This book is not for everyone," the leader of the group said. "I think those who are more literary minded will relate to the angst and metaphors that fill these pages on a deep, human level. It's everyman. It's the death of the American dream."

"No," Jesse said. "This group is the death of the American dream."

"I beg your pardon?" the leader said. She was the librarian type. Glasses hung from a chain tucked in her ears. Her legs were crossed at the ankles; the index finger of her left hand lay across her lips and touched her nose. She had the look of a martyr practicing infinite patience.

"I just don't see how he's fooled everyone into thinking this book is anything other than complete shit," Jesse said. "I want to scream at you people. It's like, hello! The emperor is butt-naked."

An older gentleman with a vest on top of a sweater threw up his hands. "Buck-naked," he said.

"What?" Jesse said.

"The emperor is buck-naked."

"I'm so glad you agree," Jesse said. She crossed her leg, swung it, and smiled.

But the man didn't stop there. "Didn't you get it? He wants to be a clown. He thinks his life would be complete if only he were a clown. But he is already a clown, don't you see? Corporate America is turning him into a clown, which is what he says he longs to be, only he already is, and he can't see it. His curly red hair, his red nose, his red cheeks—how everyone laughs at him! The embodiment of his life is the life of a clown, he already has what he thinks he wants, and yet he still yearns for it. He drives a VW Bug and piles all his friends in it, for God's sakes. I cried when they kept coming out of that car. I laughed, of course, but I cried too! He couldn't see it. He couldn't see that he already had the life of a clown—"

"But the paycheck of an executive," someone else chimed in.

"Exactly! Not to mention the allegory that all those CEO types are also clowns. My God, the levels of meaning. Irony! Brilliant, evocative irony! And the ending, my God, the ending!"

At the mention of the ending, the group broke out in titters, and whispers, and exclamations. Now Bailey wished she'd read the book. What was the ending? Did he finally run off and join the circus? She was afraid to ask. Jesse met Bailey's eyes and grinned.

"Do *you* drink alcohol?" Jesse asked.

"In moderation," Bailey said, because she still wanted the group to like her just a little bit.

"Good," Jesse said. "I could really use a cocktail. Let's go." With the excitement of a schoolgirl making a new best friend on the first day, Bailey followed Jesse out to the nearest bar. It was the beginning of a surprisingly good friendship. Although Bailey was putting it to the test today. Jesse didn't want to drink tea. Jesse didn't even like tea. She didn't have a say in the matter. It was the first cup of tea Bailey had been allowed to make in Olivia's apartment. A perverse part of her hoped wherever Olivia was, she could see Bailey lighting the burner. And then, of course, she felt guilty, and then pissed off. If Olivia had just been nice to her when she was alive, if she had liked her and let her make tea and insisted she borrow the Jag once in a while, they could have been the best of friends. They should have cleaned out Olivia's place months ago; instead, Brad kept putting it off, paying the rent. But it was time.

Bailey whipped out her marker and advanced toward the calendar on the wall. But just when she was poised to strike, the sight before her stopped her dead. It wasn't the same calendar. Gone were the foggy landscape and barren boxes. Instead, this one featured bustling European cities. The current month boasted Amsterdam.

This calendar was filled with little notes. Poker night. Poker night. Poker night. One night she shook it up and played bridge.

"Are you okay?"

"Olivia played poker," Bailey said.

"I know," Jesse said. "Cool."

"You don't understand," Bailey said. "I never knew. I've never seen this calendar before."

Jesse nodded absentmindedly and pushed her teacup far, far away. "At least she had a life, right?" Jesse said.

"Right," Bailey said, hoping she sounded convincing.

"All that money," Jesse said, looking around. "And she lived here." Bailey had been thinking the same thing. Olivia had been loaded, and still chose to rent this humble abode. It was so depressing. Yet beautiful, in a strange way. Few people had such restraint and would've blown the money in seconds. Take Brad, for example. Regardless, there had to be a balance in life. Olivia could have spent some of it on herself. She could have taken a cruise or flown off to Paris. Maybe, if she had, they wouldn't be saddled with a lighthouse right now.

Jesse took her teacup to the sink. The clattering startled Bailey out of her thoughts. "He really said 'keeper of the light'?" Jesse said.

"He did. Keeper of the light." Bailey felt guilty talking about her husband behind his back like this, but Jesse was one of the few women she'd met in her lifetime that she could talk to about anything. Besides, she needed someone to guide her through this maze of insanity Brad had thrust upon them.

"I could never leave Manhattan," Jesse said. "Couldn't trade this island for another. Isn't it sad? Without gunshots, and stabbings, and really stupid self-inflicted wounds, I don't know who I'd be."

Bailey laughed. "It just means you're doing what you love. What you're meant to do." Could Bailey say the same thing? She tried it in her head. *Without showing condos, and filling out closing paperwork, and scouting the next listing, I don't know who I'd be.* It wasn't true. For Aunt Faye definitely, but not for Bailey. But that was just because she was new at it. She liked the job, and she was good at it, and it was great money. That much she did know.

Without Brad, I don't know who I'd be. That one rang true. Even through all the craziness.

"Or," Jesse said, holding up her index fingers, "it means I'm a freak of nature."

"That too," Bailey said. "I don't want to go," she said suddenly. "I don't want to live in a lighthouse."

"Oh, honey," Jesse said. "I'm sorry."

"I might have been able to warm up to Maine or Rhode Island," Bailey mused. "California. Scotland."

"Ooh, Scotland would be nice," Jesse interrupted. "I might leave freakville for Scotland."

"Right? But what do I get? Upstate New York. He wants us to give up Manhattan for upstate New York?"

"Bummer," Jesse said. "But you have to go."

"What?" Bailey said. She expected Jesse of all people to want her to stay, convince her that Brad was making a terrible decision and she shouldn't put up with it. Wouldn't she miss her?

"Being single in New York sucks the big one," Jesse said. "It's *Clown Down* times twelve. My last blind date met me at Subway. The sandwich shop, not the train. He had one of those punch cards for a free sub." Bailey laughed. "That's not the worst part," Jesse continued. "He didn't have enough punches for a free sub yet. So he only paid for his own sub, then asked them to stamp his card for my sub too." Bailey couldn't help it, she was in hysterics. Jesse joined in the laughter, and within a few seconds, the two of them were shrieking like banshees.

"He should've lost you at 'Let's meet at Subway,' " Bailey said. It felt good to laugh until she cried. What a relief after all the stress of late. She almost hated to think of Jesse finding the one, because she would miss all these hideous dating stories. Thank God Jesse loved her job as a nurse.

"Do you think you could come over to the apartment sometime and, I don't know, casually check Brad out for brain damage?" Bailey asked.

"I'm afraid that's outside my realm of expertise. But if you let that cutie-pie walk out of your life, then I'm going to check you out for brain damage."

"But I love it here. I love my job. I love the guys who flirt with me at the pizza place and know I want eggplant and olives on my slice without even asking. I love that you can even get eggplant on pizza here. I love that you can order toilet paper from the deli at two a.m. and I love that the waitress in Mexicano's knows never, ever to remove the chip basket until it's empty."

"She had to learn that the hard way," Jesse said.

"And I'm sorry. I know I'm not helping my fellow man like you are, but I love real estate. And I think I have a flair for it. It was my candle, and my romantic pictures, and my sales pitch that sold that penthouse to the Fairytalers."

"I know. But, Bails. You don't really want to turn out like your aunt Faye, do you?"

"What's wrong with my aunt Faye? She's one of the most successful women I know."

"Don't get me wrong. I like her. But don't you think she's just a little bit obsessed? She can't even walk into a restaurant without calculating the square footage and table with the best view. And I've seen how she hits up your husband. She would give her eyeteeth to have what you have."

"I know. But I've spent my whole life giving in to Brad. It's my turn. We were finally somewhat happy. Settled. I want a baby. He's taking it all away from me, using his NDE as an excuse to completely uproot our life."

"I'm dying to hear the details," Jesse said. She'd been slowly sliding down in her chair, but now she was leaning forward eagerly. "I love hearing about near-death experiences."

"You and everybody else." Bailey tried to keep her voice light and humorous, but she was aware of it cracking. "He floated above his body, saw—this incredible light, I guess—and since then, he's just not been the same." *Love like he's never felt before.* Bailey couldn't bring herself to say that part.

"Thus the keeper of the light," Jesse mused.

"Thus," Bailey confirmed. "But if he's the keeper, who am I? The prisoner?"

"NDEs are very common," Jesse said. "I hear about that kind

of thing a lot. Believe me, if you had a drainpipe piercing your chest—don't ask—you'd be seeing bright lights too."

"I'm sure. But do they all run out and buy lighthouses?"

"Isn't it better than him running off to casinos or strip clubs?"

"I'll have to think about that one."

"Once I had this terminal patient, an elderly man who looked right at the ceiling and said, 'It's so beautiful.' I swear, I still get chills."

"I do too—and I think it's great that Brad saw a light. And he wanted to go into it—but then he remembered me. He said he came back for me."

Jesse put her hand over her heart. "That's so romantic."

"I know, I know," Bailey said. "I felt the same way."

"But," Jesse said.

"But then he starts talking about how he didn't see Olivia in the light, and how he's worried she's still earthbound, and now he goes around talking to her and driving her urn places like he's starring in *Driving Miss Dead-Daisy.* Is it just me, or should I be a little freaked out here?"

Jesse didn't answer. She was laughing. *"Driving Miss Dead Daisy,"* she said.

"Stop laughing," Bailey said, laughing herself. "That urn is starting to really get on my nerves."

"He'll let her go sooner or later," Jesse said. "Definitely wouldn't make it a deal breaker. But if you're still on the fence about your relationship, then take him to Subway and see if he pays for your foot-long."

"You ordered a foot-long?"

"So he could get two punches."

Chapter 9

C'est Moi was one of the best French restaurants in the city. Located in affluent Brooklyn Heights, it was just off the promenade, a walkway along the East River with stunning views of the Manhattan skyline. Now, this was where Bailey would love to buy a condo. Imagine looking at the glittering city every night from your balcony while sipping a glass of wine.

Despite its reputation, Bailey had never been to C'est Moi. Prices started at about six hundred dollars a person. Bailey didn't think she'd spend that much on one meal even if she ever did become extremely wealthy, but from the sounds of it, the Fairytalers were regulars. How quickly life could change. She and Brad were now driving a Jag and eating at C'est Moi. Not that she was able to just let go and enjoy it. It was all slipping away. Once they moved into the lighthouse, this would all be a distant memory, a sliver of the life they once had. They came early and walked the promenade hand in hand. Bailey's new blue silk dress made her feel feminine and pretty, and she'd even had what was left of her nails filed and applied a clear polish. The silver coyote ring was back on her finger—there was only so much she was willing to change for their new friends. To his credit, Brad was no longer complaining about the double date. Bailey wondered if he had a clue as to the prices of the restaurant. Probably not, and she certainly wasn't going to tell him. She had a feeling the Fairytalers would treat. Bailey and Brad would balk, of course, as was customary, then the Fairytalers would insist and slip the waitress their credit card before Brad could even see the bill. Or maybe they just had a running tab. Either way, on the off chance that Bailey and Brad did have to pay their half, they could always sell the Jag.

The restaurant was on the top floor of the tallest building in Brooklyn Heights, and the table offered front row seats of the skyline. The décor was sleek and understated, allowing the food and the view to reign supreme. The seats were so soft you could sink into them. Champagne was brought to the table the second they sat down, along with little plates of appetizers. Crab-stuffed mushrooms, caviar, and pâté. The Fairytalers had a definite standing order.

"Isn't this the cutest," Allissa said after they toasted.

"It's stunning," Bailey said. Seriously. The cutest? The little Mexican restaurant near them where the salt shakers wore sombreros was the cutest.

"I'll betcha you appreciate everything so much more now," Allissa said to Brad.

"I do," Brad said. He leaned forward in his chair, and his voice rose in excitement. "Every day is this incredible gift."

"Wow," Allissa said.

"But the best part is—I'm not afraid of the end anymore either."

"As in—death?" Greg said.

"They should find a new name for it," Brad said. "Death is not it. We do not die."

"Look at this view," Bailey said. Seriously. Wasn't there a law against talking about death at dinner?

"Do you believe in life after death, Bailey?" Greg asked her. It was as if he knew she'd been trying to change the subject, but he preferred to stir things up.

"We've always considered ourselves agnostics," Bailey said with a quick glance at Brad. "We just don't know what's out there." A collage of memories rose to Bailey's mind, conversations she and young Brad had with all the religious folks they'd met during their travels over the years. Always someone, somewhere shoving a brochure at them with pictures of people's faces contorted in rapture or hell, sometimes it was hard to tell which. Acting as if they had all of life's answers, as if everyone else were doomed. Brad and Bailey always listened politely, but held firm in the knowledge that when it came to the existential questions like where did we come from and what happens after we die, they took comfort in the fact that they just didn't know.

"I do," Brad said. "I know."

Bailey wanted to kick him under the table. Her husband was like a rescued kidnapped victim still being loyal to his captors. But fighting at the dinner table in front of their new friends was definitely not kosher. Bailey turned to Greg. "And you?" she asked. "What do you believe?"

Greg also glanced at Brad before answering. "Nothing," he said, throwing out his arms and sloshing a bit of champagne. "Ashes to ashes. Dust to dust."

Allissa threw both hands over her ears and shook her head. "No, no, no, no, no," she said.

Brad leaned forward and put his hand on her knee. "It's not the end," he told her. Bailey suddenly wished it was the end. She wouldn't mind if the building they were in tumbled into the river. She only hoped there would be a few seconds of something before the big nothing just so she could take one last look at Brad and say, "I told you so." She was feeling so stubborn that she'd actually rather eternity be an endless sea of nothing than listen to his sudden assurances of something. He looked like her husband, he smelled like her husband, and he smiled like her husband. But sometimes, when he opened his mouth and spoke, he just wasn't her husband.

And it left Bailey feeling like she had a tiny hole inside her, slowly ripping her apart, or maybe they had a tiny hole between them, the identity you create when you're a couple, there was a tiny hole in *them,* and it was slowly ripping them apart. In less dramatic terms, it felt like she was back in gym class and he wasn't picking her for his team anymore. They used to roll their eyes at each other or play footsies under the table whenever someone started remotely preaching. But his foot was nowhere near hers, she could tell from how he was sitting, leaning away from her, and she longed for it. She longed for his foot to play with hers under the table in solidarity. Since it wasn't, it made her want to take her foot and give him a good kick in the shins. A waiter arrived and Greg ordered for all of them. Bailey didn't care, as long as they kept the champagne coming.

"Tell them your news," Bailey said.

"Our news," Brad said. A tiny bit of relief flooded Bailey. He'd said "our." Maybe their "them" was still intact after all.

"Oh my God," Allissa said. "Are you preggers?" Bailey felt her heart catch. Brad put his hands up.

"Definitely not," he said with a laugh. "Can you imagine?" Bailey focused on the breadbasket. She wanted to throw it at Brad's head. She bit the side of her mouth. She couldn't believe he'd just said it. That tone. As if it would be the worst thing in the world, as if it would ruin his new zest for life. *Definitely not. Can you imagine?* For the first time in her life, Bailey understood why monkeys threw their feces.

"Not yet," Bailey said. "But we're working on it." There. Take that. "But first we have a little lighthouse to deal with." From the look on Brad's face, the word "little" definitely hit its mark. She wouldn't feel guilty; he knew how much she wanted a baby. *Definitely not.* Since when was it so definite?

"A lighthouse?" Greg said. Brad, who seemed to still be stewing over the word "little," didn't say a word. So Bailey filled them in, trying to impart the news with the neutrality of a journalist, sticking to just the facts. Allissa reacted like a cheerleader. She squealed. She clapped her hands. She leaned forward and stared at Brad as if he were the only man in the room.

"You bought her a lighthouse!" She playfully hit Greg. "Greg's only bought me jewelry, and trips, and shoes, and clothes, and cars."

"He didn't buy it for me," Bailey said. *He bought it behind my back. Big difference.*

"I bought it for us," Brad said.

"It's so symbolic!" Allissa cried. Bailey was surprised Allissa even knew the word "symbolic." She felt as if she were back in the book group. If only Jesse were here to commiserate with. Funny, she used to commiserate with Brad. But that was before his angelic take on everything.

"Has anyone read *Clown Down?*" Bailey said, hoping someone would pick up on her sarcasm. But nobody did. Allissa and Brad continued chatting about the lighthouse.

"I take it a lighthouse wasn't your first choice," Greg said, once again addressing Bailey.

"Well," Bailey said. She tried to sound upbeat. "I like the idea of having a getaway. Like a vacation lighthouse. I'm just not so sure about a bed-and-breakfast. I think we should ease into it. Keep our condo as our main residence—"

"No, no, no," Allissa said. "Not if you're starting a business. You have to throw yourselves into it body and soul." Bailey suddenly wanted to throw her. And who cared about the soul, just tossing her skinny body across the room would suffice.

"Exactly," Brad said.

"Like we say in the model biz, every calorie counts!" Allissa grinned and Brad grinned and Bailey was saved by the arrival of dinner. Bailey dug into her meal with gusto. She would make every calorie count all right! She would stuff herself until it hurt, anything to take her mind off this hideous evening. Allissa, she noticed, sniffed everything, but ingested next to nothing.

"We're going to come," Allissa said. "We're going to stay at your lighthouse."

"Really?" Bailey said. From the way they were throwing money around tonight, it was the best idea she'd heard so far.

"Totally," Allissa said. "And we know so many people, don't we, Greggy?"

"Can't argue with that," Greg said.

"We're going to totally pimp your lighthouse," Allissa said.

"Classy," Bailey said. Another look from Brad. Wasn't he the one who said how phony the rich behaved? Why was she getting all the looks?

Dessert was richer than the main course, something Bailey didn't think was possible. Glasses of port were served alongside it.

"I'm going to tell him," Allissa shouted. She sniffed her dessert, then pushed it away. Greg shook his head slightly, but Allissa was already leaning into Brad. "When I was a little girl," she said, "I was touched by an angel."

"Touched?" Bailey said. "Like, fondled?"

"Bailey!" Brad said. It was a joke, but she and Greg were the only ones who laughed. Bailey openly, but Greg tried to hide his by coughing into one of the red linen napkins. Too much champagne had loosened Bailey's tongue. She turned to Brad.

"What's with all the reprimanding you've been doing tonight?" she said. "Am I embarrassing you?"

"Bails," Brad said. "Please." Bailey couldn't believe it. He was embarrassed by her. In the few hours they'd been there, Allissa had shrieked, clapped, sniffed her food like a hound dog, said "preggers" and "pimp" at the top of her voice, and yet Brad was embarrassed by Bailey.

"I'm sorry, Allissa," Bailey said. "Please continue." Nothing like a little angel incest story, she added silently. Now, that one would have deserved a look. Thank God she held her tongue.

"I'm going out on the deck for a smoke," Allissa said. "Would you care to join me? Hear my angel story?" She was looking at Brad, and Brad only. Bailey waited for him to tell Allissa that he couldn't stand being around cigarette smoke.

"Of course," Brad said. "I'd love to." Bailey tried reversing the roles and giving Brad a look, but if he picked up on it, he didn't show it. Allissa put her hands on Bailey's shoulders.

"It's a horrible habit," she said. "You're so lucky you're not under constant pressure to be thin. God, I envy you." Silence fell between Greg and Bailey the minute they were alone.

"I've heard the angel story a million times," Greg said after a while. Bailey nodded.

"I didn't mean to make fun of it," she said.

"You were fine," Greg said. "You certainly have a great sense of humor."

"Thank you." His gaze was so open and steady that she found herself looking at the view while he looked at her. She couldn't even say for sure that he was coming on to her; perhaps having a boatload of money gave you the confidence to just sit and stare at someone like they were a painting or an odd piece of furniture, one you liked but that just didn't quite fit in with the room.

"Tell me the angel story," Bailey said.

Greg looked like he'd rather chew glass, but after a moment he gave her the CliffsNotes. "When she was ten years old she had a high fever. Woke up in the middle of the night and saw a young woman all in white sitting—or hovering, I guess—above her bed."

"Huh," Bailey said.

"I don't think there was any touching involved," he added with a wink. Bailey tried to control herself but ended up in another laughing fit that Greg seemed to thoroughly enjoy. He was more down to earth than she'd imagined him. Suddenly he leaned forward and lowered his voice.

"Can I tell you a secret?" he said. Bailey was aware of him, his scent, his gaze, his good looks. For some reason it made her ache for Brad. The old Brad. She wasn't so sure about the one out on the deck tolerating cigarette smoke just so he could hear what turned out to be, in Bailey's opinion, a very lame angel story.

"Sure," she said.

"*Clown Down* was the worst book I've ever read." Bailey exhaled. For a moment there she thought he had been about to say something a married man shouldn't say. How could she have been so crazy? First of all, he'd only been married for a few months; second, he was married to a model. He winked at her as if he knew this.

"Much ado about nothing," she agreed. "Much ado about nothing." She forced herself to smile, and chat, and pretend she wasn't counting the seconds before her husband came back inside. Maybe moving to the lighthouse wasn't the worst idea. At least there she could keep him away from a model who not only looked like an angel, but believed in them as well, and Allissa's handsome husband, who made her feel more wanted with a few looks this evening than her own husband had in months. When Allissa and Brad returned, Brad was grinning from ear to ear and Allissa was punching him on the arm.

"He slipped the waiter his credit card," Allissa said to Greg.

"What?" Bailey said.

"Our treat," Brad said.

"You shouldn't have," Greg said.

"We really shouldn't," Bailey agreed. When the credit card slip arrived, she was torn between wanting to watch Brad read the total and wanting to flee from the restaurant as if it were on fire. To his credit, only a wife could have seen the look of panic in his eyes when he glanced at the bill. His neck flamed red, and his eyes slowly met Bailey's. She smiled. *Could've bought another lighthouse,* she wanted to say. The fact that she didn't was proof that she was the best wife that had ever lived.

Chapter 10

"They call me Captain Jack. 'Course, that's not my real name," the ferry captain said. Twenty minutes on his small boat, and Bailey felt no closer to shore than when they started out. At first, she had been almost as excited as Brad to see the lighthouse. But the relentless rain was causing the small ferry to lurch up and down, and between that and Captain Jack talking nonstop, she was feeling queasy and trapped. Brad, however, was in high spirits. He threw his head back and laughed at Captain Jack's-not-my-name. Bailey did not, even though the comment, and the ensuing wink, seemed to be directed at her.

"It suits you," Brad said. "Doesn't it, Bails?"

"Bails?" Captain Jack said.

"Bailey," Bailey said.

"I think I'll call you Bails," Captain Jack said.

"Please don't," Bailey said. Brad stuck his arms out as if he could feel the wind blowing him back, even though they were inside the little ferry. Even the storm didn't stop Captain Jack from telling bad jokes or pointing out the "sights," none of which could be seen through the rain. And the less interested Bailey appeared, the more eager Captain Jack seemed to win her over. He was a tall man in his fifties, in good shape, with blue eyes and salt-and-pepper hair. Too bad he was such a talker, otherwise he fit the strong, silent type to a T. Maybe she should fix him up with Jesse.

Captain Jack held up his finger, readying them for yet another joke. Brad leaned in eagerly. Bailey looked around for a sick bag. "A man comes home to the wife. Honey, he says. The good news is—I've bought a lighthouse. The bad news is—I've bought a lighthouse." Brad and Captain Jack laughed as if it was the funniest thing they'd ever heard.

"Are we almost there?" Bailey said.

"Muhheakantuck," Captain Jack said.

"Bless you," Brad said. The two of them laughed again.

"That's what the Algonquin Indians called the Hudson River," Captain Jack said, once again looking at Bailey as he spoke. " 'The River That Cannot Make Up Its Mind.' " Bailey just looked at him and waited. Sure enough, he continued. "Its conflicting tide makes it flow both ways," Captain Jack said. This time when he looked at Bailey, she could have sworn he was trying to insinuate something. Was he comparing her to the conflicted tide? Could he tell she'd yet to make up her mind about this whole lighthouse endeavor? Or were the waves and chatty ferry captain with the looks of a slightly aging cowboy putting her over the edge?

"What can you tell us about the lighthouse?" Bailey asked.

"She's a beauty, all right," Captain Jack said.

"See?" Brad said.

"What do you think of turning it into a bed-and-breakfast?" she asked. Brad shot her a look. Had she just stepped on some macho invisible line?

"Why, it's a mighty fine idea," Captain Jack said. "Wish I would have thought of it myself."

"Right?" Brad said. "She already gets a lot of visitors, doesn't she?"

"She?" Bailey said. The men just looked at her. "It's a light-

house," Bailey said. "If that doesn't suggest using the male pronoun, I don't know what does." This time, when Captain Jack
roared with laughter, Bailey had to smile a little herself. Then
he clapped Brad on the back as if Brad had made the joke.

"I like her," he said to Brad. "She's a keeper."

"And soon we'll both be keepers," Brad said. The laughter
continued. Bailey, for once in her life, thought of her cell
phone and wished she were a Twitterer. Oh, the things she
would be Twittering this very moment, including signals of dis-
tress.

"Seriously," Bailey said. "We're getting close, right?"

"You don't have your sea legs yet, do you?" Captain Jack said.

"You must get a lot of visitors if you offer this ferry service,"
Brad said.

"Well," Captain Jack said, "this isn't my only job by any
means, and it was always a dream of mine to have a boat. So
when this baby went up for auction, I bought her." He leaned
into Bailey. "All right if I use the feminine pronoun this time?
Boats have been traditionally dubbed a 'she.'" He winked
again, then turned back to Brad. "Holds no more than fifty
people. 'Course, I've never had more than ten on her."

"We don't need more than a few people a night to make the
B-and-B work," Brad said.

"How do you know?" Bailey said. "We haven't actually sat
down and looked at the numbers." Brad shot her another look.
She was definitely embarrassing him. She couldn't help it. And
they hadn't figured out any of the numbers.

Suddenly, Captain Jack's arm shot out and he pointed
straight ahead. "There *he* is!" At first all Bailey saw was a sheet of
rain. Then she heard Brad inhale. She leaned closer to the
glass window. Brad moved up behind her and put one arm
around her waist. Then he pointed. She followed his finger,
and there it was, high in the air, a gently pulsing light.

Once onshore, Bailey and Brad stood, hands clasped, staring. It stood in the distance, alone except for the cypress
wooden fence that surrounded it, sturdy and hauntingly beautiful. Set on this little island, shrouded in fog, Bailey imagined

it looked exactly the same as it had when it was built in 1849. Resting on a massive circular stone base, like a tray being held aloft, the Italian white stone keeper's house with attached rectangular tower rising sixty feet in the air infused Bailey with an unexpected sense of excitement. Her nightmare had not come true—it was not a tuna can rising out of a swamp. She was so not *Sorry, Charlie.*

Not that she was thrilled. That would be pushing it. But this was it, this was happening, and she was going to see everything in a positive light—no pun intended, she thought, glancing at the tower. Living near a river wouldn't be so bad, right? And New York City wasn't too far away, just two hours downriver by train. Downriver. She was already talking like a local. What was it the ferry captain said the Algonquin Indians called this river? Muhheakantuck.

Bailey glanced back at the small ferry idling at the dock. The only other access to the island was a three-mile walk through the woods where the land finally met up with a main road. Most of their future guests would be coming out by boat. So would their furniture. Bailey didn't want to think about that. Nor did she want to think about the hassle of going out for a gallon of milk. The nearest store, Island Supplies, was also back in the main town.

A rowboat was her husband's solution. A rowboat. And he swore up and down he'd be the one rowing back and forth for the milk. Bailey felt like a mother listening to her child beg for a puppy. And everyone knew who would eventually be taking care of the puppy, taking it to the vet, and picking up its poop. Why not buy a zippy little motorboat or even a couple of Jet Skis? Didn't her husband know she wasn't a rowboat kind of a woman? Was there any chance they could get FreshDirect to deliver?

The knots were back in her stomach. Maybe she wasn't excited after all, maybe she was just sick. What had they gotten themselves into? They were standing on a boardwalk with nothing more than two suitcases and a half-baked dream. By which she meant his dream—her other half. *Desolate,* Bailey thought.

It seems so desolate. Although it was kind of cool that they actually owned a boardwalk.

Maybe Bailey would become a nature lover. They were certainly surrounded by it. Tall spiky grass, the expanse of the Hudson River, a chorus of birds, and strange ploppings in the water next to them that Bailey could only pray were fish. They'd only just landed, and she already missed the car alarms of Manhattan.

Brad grabbed her hand and squeezed. They walked slowly down the boardwalk toward their new home, neither of them wanting to rush the moment. Bailey was taking it slow because she was afraid of what awaited them, Brad because he was savoring it.

"I can't believe we're here," Brad said. "This is our lighthouse." He was speeding up now, going too fast for Bailey to keep up without slightly running. But even his quick pace didn't stop Brad from schooling Bailey about the light. Technically the light would still belong to the Coast Guard. Access to Optic, they called it. The light was automated, set in a pattern of four pulses of light followed by one second of dark. The light was originally commissioned by Congress to steer ships away from the nearby shallows of this portion of the Hudson River. The lens that was now mounted in the ceiling of the Crow's Nest was the third light to have a home in this lighthouse. The current one was a solar-powered industrial-looking thing—nothing to feast your eyes on, except he heard the effects at night were quite incredible. The first light was a kerosene lamp lit by whale oil and mounted with reflective mirrors. The second was a gorgeous fourth-order Fresnel lens. Fresnel lenses came in six orders, the first being the largest, the sixth, the smallest. Unfortunately, nobody knew what had happened to that lens, which with its brass frame and hundreds of prisms made of green glass and shaped like a beehive was as beautiful to look at as a rare sculpture, and just as valuable. Brad said he'd try and find a picture of one someday to show her just how incredible that lens was.

Bailey could imagine herself back in the 1800s when it was lit by whale oil. What it must have been like to carry heavy buckets

of sloshing whale oil up to the tower. Oh, the marital arguments that little duty would have provoked. One of them would
be curled in bed, trying to sleep in, the other poking their
spouse in the back.

We're out of whale oil.

It's your turn to get it.

Where's my harpoon?

I don't know—where did you stick it last?

Bailey glanced behind them. Captain Not-Jack stood on the
boardwalk, rain pouring down, unmoving.

"Please come in," Bailey said.

"No ma'am," he said. "But if you need anything, just pop
into Island Supplies." She followed his outstretched finger
pointing off across the river. *So not a rowboat kind of woman.*

"Island Supplies," she repeated. "Got it." Brad was already
waving good-bye with one hand while forging to the door with
his feet. Bailey could have sworn Captain Jack was giving her a
funny look, almost as if he wanted to warn her about something. Then again, how could she interpret such a thing
through a sheet of rain? "You'll come again," she said. "When
we're settled?"

"No ma'am," he said. "But I'll be nearby if you need me."
And then he just disappeared, into the rain, off in a westerly
direction.

"Hurry," Brad yelled. For a moment Bailey was thrown back
to Aunt Olivia's home, watching her run in gym socks and sandals so Brad could show off his television reception skills. She
started to run herself; it was a good idea, considering the rain.

No ma'am. He must have misunderstood her. He couldn't
have turned down an invitation to come inside at a later date.
Was there a reason he wouldn't come into the house, something they should know? Bailey didn't have long to worry about
it, Brad was already opening the door to their new home.

They stepped into a small entryway, most likely used as a
mudroom. Here a second door beckoned, also closed. A gray
mat and a tall black umbrella propped in the corner were the
only items in the space. The high ceiling ended in a small oval

skylight. Brad was grinning from ear to ear, water dripping from his rain jacket. Bailey had to shut the main door. Brad hardly seemed to notice the rain coming in.

"This is incredible," he said. Bailey grimaced. Although she was excited to finally see the place, she was a little irritated at his premature enthusiasm. Incredible? It was a mudroom. Who was acting the part of bogus real estate agent now? Everybody knew the lingo. Cozy meant tiny, and spectacular meant adequate, and sweeping view meant leaning out the window and swiveling your head from left to right. But a mudroom could hardly be incredible. "It's a whole new world," Brad said. He rubbed his hands together. Bailey wanted to grab the key out of his hand and poke his eyes out. Incredible or not, new world or not, Bailey was absolutely freezing.

"You should do the honors," she said, gesturing to the door.

"I have the strongest feeling of déjà vu," Brad said. "Do you feel it?"

"I can't feel anything," Bailey said. "Including my fingers and toes."

"We need to savor this moment. This is an important moment."

"Mental picture snapped," Bailey said loudly, hoping volume would make up for lack of enthusiasm. "Open that door!" Brad glanced at her. She'd overdone it, sounded too game-showy. "Brr," she said, in case he still didn't get it. Brad put his arm around her as if to warm her up, but instead just mixed his wetness with hers. She was afraid to push him away. "Did you notice the captain wouldn't come in?"

"Hmm?"

"Captain Not-Jack. It was almost as if he were afraid of this place."

But Brad wasn't listening. He was standing, hands at his sides, head tilted back, staring at the skylight. Bailey nudged him.

"Incredible!" he said.

"Brad," she said. "I'm freezing."

"Sorry." He made a move for the door, inserted the key. He turned and looked at her. She pasted a smile on her face. God, she wanted to kill him. Her good mood was quickly going down the drain. He was ruining this for her, but if she let on, then she would ruin this for him. She couldn't wait until she had her own copy of the key. "I wish we had a drum," Brad said.

Or just the sticks, Bailey thought. *I could beat you with the sticks.* And then, finally, he was opening the door.

They stepped into a second room, only slightly bigger than the first. Bailey thought she was going crazy. It was like one of those Russian nesting dolls. Would they just keep entering larger and larger rooms? This one had a nice wood floor and was about the size of a baby's nursery, but the ceilings were lower and there was no skylight or windows. She was already wondering what they would do with this room. She thought it was weird. She wondered if Brad thought it was weird, but she was too afraid to ask, in case he thought it was incredible. Luckily, instead of another closed door, this simply had an open archway into the next section of the house. Bailey plowed through it, leaving Brad to stare at every nook and cranny. The archway led to a narrow hall. It was like a maze. None of the pictures had shown this strange series of starts and stops. The hallway creaked as Bailey walked through.

"Why are you rushing?" Brad called. "We need to savor this." If he said "savor" one more time she was going to kill him. Justified homicide brought on by the careless repetition of the word "savor." A jury of English majors would exonerate her.

"I'm hoping there's a house in here somewhere," Bailey said. "I'm just trying to find it."

"That's like the pony joke," Brad said. Bailey just looked at him. "You know, where one kid's an optimist, the other a pessimist. They both are confronted with a pile of manure and a shovel? The pessimist throws a tantrum but the optimist starts digging because 'With all the shit in here, there has to be a pony somewhere!' "

"Right on," Bailey said. "I'm just trying to find our pony."

"You never get a second chance to make a first impression," Brad said. As if the house were a person. He lingered behind, running his hand along a chair rail. Bailey kept going. The hallway was dark and bare except for a newspaper article tacked to the wall. Bailey stepped closer.

LOCAL KEEPER DIES

The floor squeaked behind her as Brad entered the hallway. Bailey snatched the newspaper article off the wall and jammed it in her pocket. Who in the world had tacked the obituary to the wall and why? Brad was all about death these days, twenty-four / seven. She didn't want anything else setting him off. Still, it was silly, hiding it this way. But when Brad caught up with her, she didn't say a word.

Together, they stepped into the main room on the ground floor. Finally, Bailey felt like she was in a real house. It was a huge space, overlooking the Hudson River. Since the lighthouse was on a hill, looking out, she almost felt as if they were floating above the river. Two human-sized windows made it feel as if you could step right out onto the water, walk across it. Like Jesus. Given Brad's recent progression into the spiritual, Bailey decided to keep the walking-on-water parable to herself. Her chest expanded like an accordion as she took it all in, in one big breath. Dark wood floors, tall, tall ceilings, the two huge windows, a fireplace, and walls still clinging onto bits of vintage wallpaper. They were in desperate need of painting unless you wanted the aged antique look, which Bailey sort of did.

"It's stunning," she said. Her voice echoed through the room. She felt a slight breeze and wondered if the distinct dampness always clung to the room. But despite the chill, a peaceful stillness washed over her. Maybe this wouldn't be so bad. Compared to the hectic pace of Manhattan, it was kind of nice to be out here in a keeper's house by the river. Her optimism lasted all of a few seconds. The minute her energy slowed down, Brad's skyrocketed. He began to bounce about the room, waving his hands as he put up imaginary partitions.

"This will have to be the front desk, we'll have to build a counter and wall off most of the space so that when you're sitting back there you won't feel claustrophobic—"

"Wait," Bailey said. "Me? When I'm sitting there?"

"And we'll need room for a copy machine, and a cabinet for the keys—"

"It's a bed-and-breakfast, Brad. Not a Holiday Inn. We can't wall off this room, it's the only decent room of its size."

"You don't know that. We haven't seen the rest of the house."

True. But she had a feeling she was right. She gestured to the windows and the river beyond. "Look, it's almost as if we could walk on water. Like Jesus." Bailey watched Brad closely. The religious connotation seemed to stop him. He faced the windows and rocked back on his heels.

"I suppose we don't have to look like a hotel," he said.

"Of course not. This room is too beautiful to touch."

"Except for this hideous wallpaper. We'll have to peel it off and paint."

"Let's check out the rest of the place." Bailey didn't want to talk about the room anymore; she was terrified it would lead to an argument, especially since she felt like pummeling him. Stuck behind a desk? He pictured her stuck behind a desk? She'd rather be a weekend wife.

"Brad," she said, "if we lived in the city and kept this place as a getaway . . ." She kept the sentence vague and unfinished, hoping it would spur him to finish it for her, agree with her.

"We can't run a business like that."

"Exactly. This doesn't have to become a business. It can be a getaway. Our private getaway. We wouldn't even have to paint." Now that would excite her.

Brad must have sensed an argument moving in as well, for he suddenly plastered a large smile on his face and clapped his hands. "Our tour continues, m'lady," he said, gesturing her to be the first up the narrow set of steps in the right-hand corner of the room.

The next floor held one master bedroom and three small ones. It curved around in an L shape. From here a small hallway connected over to the actual lighthouse. Bailey stood at the entrance to the small hall and couldn't decide whether to check out the rooms first or cross over to the lighthouse. Gray carpeting covered what she assumed were also dark wood floors. She couldn't wait to rip it up.

"At least it's carpeted," Brad said. "It will mute the noise."

"Rooms first, or lighthouse?" Bailey asked.

"Definitely rooms," Brad said. "We'll save the lighthouse for last."

"There are only three guest rooms," Bailey said.

"On this floor," Brad said.

"There's another floor?" They both tried to peer around the corner, but if indeed there was another staircase around the bend, they couldn't see it from where they stood.

"We'll see," he said. "Let's take the rooms in order." The first room on their right was the master suite. Bailey just assumed this would be their room, and she wished it were last instead of first. She didn't like the thought of guests passing her room every night. If only she could talk Brad out of the whole B&B part of this adventure.

Bailey stepped into the master bedroom and once again thought about ripping out the carpet. She didn't care whether it muted the noise, she hated carpet. This room had the same view as the main room downstairs. They would have to position the bed to overlook the river. She could see them lying in on Sunday mornings, eating and drinking in bed, gazing out at the ships. They could even get a telescope.

"We could charge a lot for this room," Brad said. "The honeymoon suite."

"And where will we sleep? The old married couple's suite?"

Brad laughed as if she were joking, grabbed her around the waist and pulled her into him. "We haven't seen the third floor yet," he said. "We could make the entire third floor our little apartment."

"Oh," Bailey said. "Maybe." She'd been ready to pounce, fight him on this one, she realized. Was it happening already? Was the profound appreciation for the fact that her husband was alive already waning? She was ashamed of herself for not being capable of maintaining the feeling. She turned toward him, wrapped her arms around his neck, took in his smell, silently told him she loved him, and kissed him.

"What was that for?"

"You're right," she said. "This is exciting." Brad grinned. Instantly he was that precocious little boy that she knew and loved. They were sharing an adventure, like the many other adventures they'd shared. Why had she hidden the obituary on the wall from him? She felt guilty, as if she was shaping his portion of the adventure, shielding him from the truth. If she pulled it out now, would it look funny? Was there any way of getting around it? *Oh, by the way, look what I pulled off the wall downstairs and shoved in my pocket so you couldn't see it.*

Maybe she'd tack it back up somewhere. Put it on another wall for him to discover.

The two smaller rooms needed work. Thick ugly shag carpet that would have to be torn up. The walls just looked cracked as opposed to the vintage look downstairs. They felt a little drafty to Bailey too. But she could see the promise, the dark wood molding, each with a little wood-burning stove. There would be so much to do. Tear up carpeting, refinish the floors, paint, shop for furniture. It would keep Brad busy, that was for sure. Maybe that was a good thing, maybe this all was for the best. And when they finally turned the corner, Brad was right, there was another stairway leading up to a closed door.

"I told you," he said. Bailey smiled; she would have to be the grown-up, even if it killed her.

"You did," she agreed. "Although it could just be a crawl space."

"What crawl space do you know of that has a door?"

"Excuse me, I haven't been in too many lighthouses."

"This isn't a lighthouse, it's the keeper's house."

"Are you looking for a smack?" This used to be a little joke between them. Bailey would say, "Are you looking for a smack?"; then Brad would grab her and kiss her. This time, he simply stared up at the closed door. "No kiss?" she said.

"What?"

"Never mind. Are we going up?"

"I'm just savoring the moment."

"Brad," Bailey said. "Do you think you could retire that word?" Bailey expected Brad to pout. Instead, he laughed.

"I am using it a bit much, aren't I?"

"You are, my love."

"I shall stop."

"Thank you."

"I'm going to *relish* the moment," Brad said.

"Then I shall pickle it," Bailey said. This time Brad didn't laugh. Bailey waited, impatiently, while Brad relished. Finally he headed up the stairs. For a reason she couldn't explain, she felt her heart lurch when he reached for the doorknob. But soon its erratic beat returned to normal. The door was locked.

Chapter 11

Brad put his body against the door and pushed. "You're going to break it," Bailey said.

"I can't believe it's locked."

"We'll have to relish the moment even longer," Bailey said. "Mustard up the strength." Brad gave her a look. He seemed to have lost his sense of humor.

"You're queen of the pun today," Brad said.

"Sorry. I'm just a little tired. And cold."

"But excited, right? You're still excited?"

"Of course," Bailey said. "Let's go look at the lighthouse. We'll call the Realtor in the morning and see if there is a separate key to this floor." Bailey headed back down the stairs, listening to them squeak. It seemed everything in the house made noise. Hopefully, all of their guests would be nice and quiet. She reached the bottom of the stairs. Brad was still standing by the door. She was going to have to call his doctor in the morning. Something was off with him. She'd been half joking with Jesse, but maybe he truly did have brain damage from the accident. "Brad?"

"Right," he said. "Coming." They crossed over the hallway that connected to the lighthouse. Windows on either side brought the outside in, made it feel like a bridge suspended in air. This time Bailey was the first to reach the door, but it too was locked.

"You've got to be kidding me," Brad said. He sounded angry. He brushed Bailey aside and tried the door himself.

"I'll bet we can get into the lighthouse from outside," Bailey said. "Don't we have a key for it?" Brad pulled out his set of keys. None of them looked like they would fit the old wooden door, but he had to see it for himself. Only then, after he tried each and every key, did they go downstairs and out the front door.

The rain was still coming down, obscuring everything but an expanse of darkness. Why hadn't Bailey talked him into waiting for the next trip? Shouldn't they be getting back to the boat? They hadn't thought any of this through. They didn't even have a flashlight. Just as the thought hit Bailey, the tip of the lighthouse lit up and its beam spread across the river. She laughed out loud. If nothing else, at least every few seconds they would be able to see. Brad laughed along with her and pulled her into him. "Isn't she fabulous?" he said.

"He is," Bailey said.

"Right, he," Brad said. "But the house is a she?"

"Well, she's cold, needs a lot of work, and is shutting us out of several rooms, so what exactly are you trying to say?"

"I think she's beautiful and mysterious," Brad said.

"Okay then, we'll call the house a she. Happy now?"

Brad stopped her from moving forward, pulled her into him and kissed her. He kissed like the old Brad, and aside from the rain pelting them, Bailey gave herself to the moment.

"I've never been happier," he said. Bailey was glad for the darkness. She didn't want to put on a fake smile. She was remembering all the other businesses Brad started, and the pattern was the same. He was always happy at first. But after a month, a week, and then only a few days, he'd grow bored, restless, unhappy. Was this going to be just like all the other times, only this time it would cost him his entire fortune? And then what? Would they be able to slip back into their New York City lives, resume where they left off? Bailey hoped so. God, she hoped so.

She wondered what time Captain Jack was picking them up for the ride home. "What time are we going back?" she shouted over the wind and the rain. Brad probably didn't hear her. He certainly didn't answer.

The key fit easily into the outside door leading into the lighthouse. They stepped into a circular room with a cement floor and a spiral iron staircase going up, up, up, higher than it had looked to Bailey from the outside. She was right about one thing: In addition to being damp and freezing, it was extremely dim. She could barely make out the staircase. She decided not to point out the irony. It smelled like wet cement, but even that didn't bother her. They were about to enter a lighthouse. Maybe she'd been way too negative. It was a pretty cool thing.

"We need a flashlight," she said. "We could break our necks on these stairs."

"Nah," Brad said. "We're more likely to break an ankle."

"Comforting," Bailey said. Brad laughed softly, took her hand, and started up the stairs. Bailey soon pulled hers away. She didn't like the feeling of spiraling up, and she didn't want to lose her balance. She gripped the rail and listened to Brad's footsteps as he ascended.

At long last the stairs spilled out into a circular room, almost as large as the living room in the keeper's house. In the middle of the space was a second spiral staircase, leading up to the lighthouse tower. Brad had found a dim light, and he stood bathed in it in the middle of the room. Sometimes she forgot how handsome he was. It often snuck up on her, like now. He almost glowed beneath the light. When he smiled, his dimples creased and his eyes seemed to shine. Her golden man. Brad flung his arms out. "This is called the wick room," he said. "It's where they used to cut the wick for the whale oil lamp."

"Wow," Bailey said, taking in the room. Aside from its circular shape, it was like a hip loft; one big open space with a cement floor and stone walls. People would kill for this space in Manhattan. "This is so cool," Bailey said. Brad laughed and grabbed her around the waist.

"You sound like we did in college," Brad said. "It's, like . . . totally rad."

Bailey laughed. "Um—like *we* did in college?"

Brad feigned hurt feelings. "I took classes," he said.

"You lurked. Tuition free."

"And no degree." He nuzzled her neck. Bailey dropped her head back and allowed his lips to send shivers down her spine.

"I loved that about you," she said quietly. "You really wanted to be there."

"I wanted to be near you."

"Liar. You loved those classes. Although you should have applied for a scholarship." Brad shrugged. It was true, he'd been so smart, he most likely would have been able to attend as a real student and get a degree. It was one of their first big fights. Bailey tried in vain to get him to apply for a scholarship. But even then, Brad Jordan did what Brad Jordan wanted to do. Bailey reached out and gingerly touched his head.

"For such a hard head, you feel soft," she said. She put her arms around his neck. He was here. He was hers. She pulled him close and held him. If anything ever happened to him, that would be it. She would never have another love like this again.

"I love the wick room," Bailey said.

"I love you," Brad said. "And don't worry, baby, I'll light your wick."

Bailey laughed, then clutched onto him like a life raft. "Don't ever leave me," she said. Her voice was hoarse, desperate.

"I'm here," he said.

"I was so scared when you were in the coma," she said.

"I know."

"I'm glad you bought this lighthouse."

"You are?" He pulled away, looked into her eyes. "Really?"

"As long as I have you, I could live anywhere."

Brad hugged her, but it was quick, complete with a pat on

the back and a peck on the cheek before he was back to bouncing around the room. "We could make this our room," he said.

"We could," Bailey said. "But then we wouldn't know what
our guests were up to."

"We could set up cameras," Brad said.

Bailey laughed. "Like some newfangled reality show? I don't
think B-and-B guests are that exciting."

"So then we'll live here."

"The farther away from guests, the better," Bailey said. Brad
smiled at her. God, what she'd done in the past for that smile,
those dimples. All these years and it still worked on her. Brad
gestured to the remaining set of stairs.

"Shall we?" They began the final climb that led to a small
trapdoor in the ceiling. Luckily, it opened. Bailey was afraid
Brad was going to lose it if he encountered one more locked
door. It was a bit of an effort to haul themselves up into the
tower, but the view and excitement were worth the extra sweat.

"Look at this!" Brad exclaimed as they stood side by side. A
circular lookout with windows all around, lording over the
river. There was a small built-in table loaded down with papers,
as if the previous keeper had just gotten up to make himself a
pot of coffee.

"The Crow's Nest," Brad said.

"It's beautiful," Bailey said.

Brad grinned and started touching the papers on the table.
"River charts and weather patterns," he said. "This is so cool."
Catching himself, he looked at Bailey.

"Totally rad," she agreed. They shared a smile. Next, he
found the door to the small outer deck, built so that you could
stand outside the tower and clean the windows. Bailey would
definitely leave that job to Brad. He sprang the door to the
deck open and started to crawl out.

"Be careful," Bailey said. "What if the deck isn't sturdy?"

"I'll find out," he said with a wink. It was the old, devil-may-
care Brad. Maybe this was exactly the adventure he needed.
She popped up next to him and they stood staring out at the
dark depths of the Hudson River. Suddenly, a loud foghorn

blasted through them. It reverberated through Bailey's skull and lit every nerve ending she had on fire. If Brad hadn't caught her in time, she would have tumbled over the railing. She slapped her hands over her ears.

"I didn't know it did that," she screamed. "Scared me to death!" Brad was laughing so hard he was shaking. She wanted to throw him over the railing. She punched his arm instead. "Not funny." Brad whirled her around.

"No," he said. "Funny. Very, very, funny." And then he kissed her for the second time that day, a kiss so good, so filled with longing that Bailey instantly forgave him for everything. If only it could have lasted more than a couple of minutes.

"What do you mean we're spending the night?" They were back in the keeper's house, standing in the small vestibule.

"He's not answering his phone," Brad said. "What do you want me to do?" Bailey grabbed the phone out of Brad's hand and dialed the number herself. Brad left her there and ventured back into the house. Bailey's call went straight to voicemail. It was a robotic voice. Was this really Captain Not-Jack's number?

"Uh—hello?" Bailey said, even though she knew it was impossible to screen your voicemail like a house phone. "This is Bailey. We thought you were taking us back tonight. We don't even have a bed to sleep in over here and we certainly weren't expecting to spend the night. Please call us as soon as you get this—either way." Bailey clicked off, and then sent a text.

Please call Bailey and Brad ASAP. They were too far away from where he docked the boat to even see if it was there. They could trudge all the way out there, but what good would it do? Unless he'd fallen asleep on the boat. Then they'd be able to wake him up and get a ride back to town. They'd never make it to Manhattan tonight, but at least maybe they could find a motel in town. Or a nice bed-and-breakfast. Bailey laughed at the irony.

"Brad?" She didn't even want to go back into the house, as if in doing so, she would seal their fate for the evening, but that was ridiculous, really, all these thoughts about fate and life and death, and she couldn't blame all of them on Brad—most of them were coming from her. Besides, what choice did they have? It was cold and dark and rainy, and trudging all the way out there to find the boat gone, or Jack gone, or both, wouldn't do anything but make her more wet and miserable than she already was. It would be nice if Brad were feeling the same way. Instead, she found him lying on the floor in the main room as if it were the most comfortable spot in the world.

"Aren't you freezing?" she said.

"Come here," Brad said. "Body heat." For once, she agreed with him. She took her wet jacket off and stood dripping over him.

"Is it dangerous for us to fall asleep in wet clothing?" she said.

"Dangerous?"

"Yes. We'll catch colds. Or hypothermia."

"I don't think you catch hypothermia," Brad said. "You succumb to it."

"Is this really a good time to be correcting my English?"

"Sorry." He patted the floor. Bailey ran her hands over her wet clothes, then lay down. Brad wrapped his arm around her and pulled her in.

"If you're making a case to get naked," he said, "keep talking."

"Maybe you should gather some kindling," Bailey said. "Start a fire."

"There's a monsoon out there," Brad said.

"You're the one who wants the big adventure," Bailey said. Thunder cracked and the room was lit up by the following flash of lightning.

"I don't think even the best Boy Scout could start a fire with wet kindling," he said.

"Where do you think Captain Jack is?"

"I don't know. I doubt he'd head back in this storm anyway."

"But it's weird. He's not answering his phone."

"I think he likes to hit the sauce," Brad said. "He's probably passed out."

"I was thinking that too."

"Great minds think alike."

"I just wish we had warm, dry clothes and a bed." Brad kissed her on the forehead. "It's really cold," Bailey whined.

"I know." The more he tried to comfort her, the more she felt like complaining. Sometimes she felt like a bottomless pit of need. How screwed up was that? Were all relationships this complicated?

"Maybe we should call the Realtor. Or the Coast Guard. Or nine-one-one."

"And say what? That we need to be rescued from our own lighthouse?"

"We could report Captain Not-Jack missing."

"You want to report a man whose name we don't even know missing?"

"We know it's not Jack," Bailey said.

"Actually, it is Not-Jack," Brad clarified. Bailey swatted him. Brad laughed. And not his polite laughter or soft chuckle, both of which were familiar to her as her own heartbeat. Brad gave a full-out belly laugh. It was nice to hear, and it felt good to feel him shake next to her. It was almost worth the bone-chilling cold working its way into her toes.

"We could put his face on a cereal box," Brad said.

"Cap'n Crunch." It was stupid, but it had them both in stitches. A few minutes in wet clothing, and hysteria was already setting in. "Seriously," Bailey said. "I don't want to succumb to hypothermia." Suddenly, Bailey sat up.

"What?" Brad said.

"Where's the kitchen?"

Just as quickly, Brad sat up too. "You're right," he said. "We never saw a kitchen."

"Or a bathroom," Bailey said. "There might be towels, or toilet paper, something."

"Good point."

"And is there only one bathroom? How can we run a B-and-B with one bathroom? I'm not sharing a bathroom with fourteen hundred strangers."

"Calm down. Although I'm glad you're dreaming big. I'm sure there's one down here, and there's probably another one in the locked room."

"We might have to put a third one in," Bailey said. "One on each floor. That would make two for the guests and one for us."

"Let's at least find one for now," Brad said. He got up and began lurching about the room.

"What are you doing?"

"Looking for the light switch." A few seconds later, he found it, and a portion of the room came to life. And there, to the left of the fireplace, was a swinging door. How could they have missed it?

The first glance at their kitchen was a gloomy one. Every appliance looked a hundred years old. It was big enough to fit a table for ten and had a wall of windows looking out, which boded well for a future business, but right now, nobody in their right mind would have wanted to sit in there to gaze at the view, let alone eat. Bailey was relieved there was indeed a bathroom off the kitchen, but it too was in serious need of remodeling. The place was a long way from being a bed-and-breakfast.

Bailey couldn't tell if Brad was mentally calculating what this dump was going to cost them to fix up, and at the moment she wasn't either, because what they needed was some warm clothes or a blanket before hypothermia set in. Brad began rummaging through the drawers. Bailey found one towel in the bathroom, and whether or not it was clean was moot given that it was at least dry.

"I found a towel," Bailey said, holding it up. The kitchen light wasn't bright enough to see whether it was green or dark blue.

"Perfect," Brad said.

"There's only one, and it's small, and it smells."

"See?" Brad said. "Things are looking up already."

"We won't get dry with this," Bailey said, waving the small, smelly towel.

"Once we take these clothes off we can't put them back on, so let's towel ourselves off with our clothes on for now," Brad said. He held something up to the light. "I found a key. Maybe it unlocks the top room." Brad headed for the stairs.

"Now?" she said. "You're going to try it now?"

"Why not?"

"Because it's dark," Bailey said. "And creaky."

"Bails," Brad said. "Don't tell me you're afraid."

"Of course not," she lied. Maybe she should have let him see the obituary. Maybe she should have asked Captain Not-Jack why he wouldn't come in. Or answer his phone. Maybe she should insist that they were not going to spend the night in a creaky, old keeper's house. Half a million dollars. How could it have fetched such a high price? In Bailey's humble opinion, it wasn't worth more than two, maybe two hundred and fifty thousand. She shut down her negative thoughts and followed Brad up the stairs. They were halfway there when someone pounded on the front door. Bailey stopped. Brad kept climbing.

"Did you hear that?"

"What?"

"Someone's at the front door."

"I don't hear anything." The pounding came again, a distinct loud series of knocks.

"There it is again." Brad looked at her as if he truly didn't hear someone pounding on the door. "How can you not hear that?"

"You sound testy."

"Someone is pounding on the door."

"I believe you."

"So let's go answer it."

"I want to try this key."

"You're going to leave me alone with some stranger? Remember the axe murderer?"

"The one you made up? Yes, he rings a bell."

"He's knocking."

"I didn't mean it literally."

"I'm going to answer it," Bailey said. "Maybe it's salvation."

"You think salvation would ring the bell," Brad said. "Now I mean it literally."

"Are you coming?"

"I'll be right down. I have to check this key." Bailey nodded, then hurried to the front door. She was hoping it was salvation, but at this point she would even welcome the company of an axe murderer.

Captain Jack stood in the entryway, holding a bundle of blankets and clothing.

"Oh, thank God," Bailey said. "Come in." Instead he thrust the pile at her and stepped back.

"You should've come back to the boat," he said. "At the appointed time." He sounded angry, and Bailey got the distinct feeling he didn't like being this close to the house.

"What are you talking about?" she said. "What appointed time?"

"Your husband agreed to be back at the boat at five," he said. "Before the storm."

"I'm so sorry. I had no idea. I was wondering." It was ridiculous to stand out here, yelling at each other over the rain. "You're soaked," Bailey said. "Please come in."

"No," he said. "I'll be in the boat. You will be too, first sign of daylight, if you want to get off this island at all."

"I'm sorry," Bailey said. "We'll be there."

"You're welcome to come now," he said. "Sleep on the boat."

"You have room for the both of us?"

"Who said anything about the both of you?" Even in the dark she could feel his eyes on hers. It hung in the air, a flirtation, a come-on. Was he joking? Was she actually thinking about it?

"Why won't you come in?" Bailey said.

"Place is haunted," Captain Not-Jack said. "See you at the boat. First sign of daylight." Bailey stood in the doorway clutching the clothes and watched his tall frame disappear into the darkness. Then she shut the door and hurried back to Brad with the change of clothes.

Appointed time. They were supposed to have been back to the boat at an appointed time. In his excitement did Brad just forget? Or did he miss it on purpose? And what the hell was that about the place being haunted? Captain Whatever-his-real-name-was was a sarcastic man. Obviously, he was joking. Haunted. Oh, well. Every spooky lighthouse needed a good ghost story, right? Maybe it would be good for business. If they ever actually opened. Bailey thought about the obituary she'd ripped off the wall and shuddered. It was normal to shudder when you were wet and freezing, she chided herself. Still, at least she could comfort herself with proof that she wasn't a vampire, for she could not wait for the first sign of daylight.

Chapter 12

"I got it!" Brad yelled. "The door is open. Hurry, hurry!" Bailey had just taken a step up the stairs, clothes still in her arms, when a whir of black whizzed past her, brushing against her legs. She screamed.

"Jesus Christ," she yelled. What was that? And where was it now? It couldn't have been a bat, unless the bat was a cripple and could only crawl instead of fly. What happened to the light? Why was it suddenly dark in here again? Bailey immediately dropped her bravado, along with the blankets and clothes, and began to scream. Joke or not, Captain Jack had really bothered her with that haunted comment. And Brad had missed the boat on purpose, she just knew it, and now they were stuck in here with something rabid and black. "Brad, Brad, Brad!" Soon he pounded down the stairs.

"What happened?"

"Why did you turn the light off?" She was screaming at him, and she knew it wasn't fair, but whatever that thing was, it was still in here.

"I didn't turn it off," Brad said. "You must have." He quickly found his way back to the light switch. Soon the faint light above the fireplace flickered and then remained steady.

"There's something in here," Bailey said. "Some kind of creature." Just saying it made the hair on the back of her neck stand up.

"Where did you get those?" Brad said, pointing to the clothes on the floor. Something whirled past, another flash of black. Bailey shrieked. Instantly, Brad put his arms around her.

"Bails, Bails," he said. "It's a cat." He stood behind her and turned her to face the windows. At first she didn't register anything but the blackness that was the Hudson at night. "Over there." Brad gently turned her face to the corner of the fireplace. There, a black cat stared at her with glowing yellow eyes.

"Jesus," Bailey said. "I almost had a heart attack." She crept toward the cat. "You scared the shit out of me, kitty," she said in a singsong voice, the one she reserved for animals and babies.

"Look at that," Brad said. "Our first guest."

"From the looks of him, he's the original owner."

"Poor guy."

"When's the last time you had anything to eat?"

"Are you talking to me or the cat?"

"I'm talking to the cat. You don't deserve dinner."

"I'm too excited to eat anyway," Brad said. "Come on. I got the door upstairs unlocked."

This time when Brad bounded up the steps, Bailey did her best to keep up with him. She no longer wanted to be anywhere in this house all alone. On their way up the steps she tried to tell Brad about the captain's strange behavior at the door. Then she dropped a subtle hint about missing the designated meeting time. If Brad heard her, he didn't comment. Bailey didn't like this either, but they could have a nice long chat when they were back in their furnished, non-haunted condo in Manhattan.

Bailey stood back as her husband tugged on the door. It didn't budge. "It was open," he said. "It was just open."

"We'll try again in the morning," Bailey said. "We have to change out of these damp clothes." She felt the cat brush up against her legs, weave in between them, and then start again in the other direction. "I wish Jack would've brought us food too," she said. She started back to the stairs. "And I wish we hadn't missed the designated departure time."

At this, Brad finally stopped tugging at the doorknob. "Was that directed at me?"

"Please. Brad. Please. Can we just go change?"

"I didn't know anything about a designated departure time." Brad trailed behind her, his footsteps slow and heavy. Once again, he reminded her of a child. Maybe his brush with death had made him feel young again. Too young for her liking, but what could she do about it? Eventually, he would return to the land of the living.

"Come on," she said. "Let's change out of these wet clothes and go to sleep." *Everything will seem better in the morning,* she added silently. Yet somehow, she just didn't believe it.

"Since when do you have a cat?" Jesse asked. Jesse didn't like cats. Bailey suspected it was because she was a single woman living in a studio apartment. Just a couple of cats away from being dubbed a crazy lady. In the two weeks he'd been living in Manhattan, Blackie had grown fat and spoiled, and Bailey had grown surprisingly attached to him. "He's black," Jesse said, pointing out the obvious. "Isn't that bad luck?"

"He came with the lighthouse," Bailey said. She scratched him behind the ear while Jesse remained in the doorway. "Are you seriously just going to stand there?"

"You know how I feel about cats."

Bailey scooped the cat up and shut him in the bedroom. "Better?" she asked.

"Much." Jesse sat on the couch, as far away from where the cat had perched as she could get. She took a bottle of wine out of her purse.

Bailey waved the bottle away. "I have wine," she said. "And it's chilled. Save that for an emergency."

"This was the emergency," Jesse said. "But I'm all for saving." She tucked the bottle of wine back in her bag. After Bailey served them some chilled Chardonnay, she finally filled Jesse in on their visit to the lighthouse.

"That's it," Jesse said after Bailey confessed to finding the obituary of the past keeper tacked to the wall and the captain's offhanded comment about it being haunted. "I'm never visiting."

"That's too bad," Bailey said. "I was thinking you and Captain Not-Jack might hit it off."

"I'd probably just shorten it to Cap," Jesse said. "Is he really cute?"

"In a Clint Eastwood kind of way," Bailey said. "But I was kidding. He's too old for you."

"You sound keen on him," Jesse observed.

"I am not. He's a total character, that's all."

"If you want me to visit, you need to get an exorcist in there first."

"And a plumber, and a painter, and an electrician, and a carpenter," Bailey said. "It's ridiculous how much work the place needs to become operational. Brad really got taken."

"Can you get out of it?"

"I don't think so—the auction clearly stated the property was 'as is.' I just can't believe people bid so much on it. Don't get me wrong, I don't hate it. There's something hauntingly beautiful about the place."

"Hauntingly. Did you hear yourself? I've changed my mind again. I'm not visiting."

"Seriously," Bailey said. "If we had the money to sink into it, I'm starting to think we could actually make a decent living. People like the allure of staying in a lighthouse. But we don't have that kind of money. I honestly don't know what he was thinking."

"So what are you going to do?"

"Brad's determined he can fix it at cost. He's on Facebook twenty-four/seven trying to round up old pals as volunteers."

"How's that going?"

"If you ever want to lose faith in social media, just trying posting a request for a favor. People are willing to look through your three hundred pictures trekking through a Brazilian rain forest, but they don't want to help refurbish your lighthouse."

"Go figure."

"Anyway, he's been out at the lighthouse for the past week— 'making progress.' " Bailey wasn't normally an air quote type of girl, but this time, she felt it was required.

"You don't seem happy."

"I'm not. It's a total nightmare. We can't even start major renovations until the spring. The river freezes in the winter."

"Sounds like an adventure. It could be fun."

"Whose side are you on?"

"Whoever has the most wine."

"That would be me."

"That inconsiderate bastard!" The women laughed, then fell into an easy silence as they sipped their Chardonnay.

"I hate to ask you this," Bailey said. Jesse sat up straight. Everyone loved to be asked something awkward.

"Shoot," Jesse said.

"You said you've seen this kind of thing before."

"Cats?" Jesse said. She looked around in alarm.

"Would you calm down about the cat? I'm talking about Brad. His little journey."

"You mean his NDE?"

"Yes."

"It's very common."

"He's spending a lot of time chatting with others online. Some NDE group. One of the women—get this—her name is Angelicka Heavens."

Jesse laughed and rolled her eyes. "She's probably three hundred pounds and wears blue eye shadow," she said.

"Here's hoping," Bailey said. "Is there any research—you know—like explaining scientifically what happens in those few seconds of a . . . a slightly inactive brain?"

"You can't say 'clinically dead,' can you?"

Bailey shivered. "I don't like hearing you say it either." Jesse sighed, leaned back in her seat, finished off her wine. Bailey reached over and refilled it.

"There are arguments and 'research' on both sides, Bail. But if you're saying what I think you're saying."

"What do you think I'm saying?"

"Look. The point isn't whether or not life after death exists. The point is, Brad believes it does. And if you swoop in and try to convince him otherwise . . ."

"Yes?"

"I just think it could backfire. Don't you?"

"Yes, which is why I've kept my mouth shut. But, Jesse, I seriously think my husband could have suffered some kind of brain damage."

"Aren't you being a little overdramatic?" Jesse said. This coming from a woman who kept scanning the room for invisible cats. "I'll see what I can come up with," Jesse said as she was leaving. But her tone of voice betrayed her. Once again, she thought Bailey was the one being unreasonable.

The obituary was for a man named Trevor Penwell. Bailey typed the name into the search engine. Certainly an interesting name. It conjured up more of a butler than a lighthouse keeper. She was anxious to see what she would find.

Google was amazing. She found a Trevor Penwell who was a reporter for a small newspaper. A Trevor Penwell who was a racecar driver. A Trevor Penwell who was a boxer. They were all alive. It made her wonder who all the Bailey Jordans were out there, and if they were leading a more exciting life than she. She decided not to Google her name; she really didn't want to know. It wasn't until the third page of the search that she found it.

TREVOR PENWELL
LOCAL LIGHTHOUSE KEEPER DIES

Trevor Penwell illuminated the Hudson River from the Sage Lighthouse for forty-five years. He died at the age of seventy-one of natural causes. Although loved for his sense of humor, endless practical jokes, and trusty black cat,

Web, Trevor Penwell is most famous for his late wife, Edga. Ten years prior to his death, his beautiful Swiss wife hanged herself in the third floor of the keeper's house. She is said to have literally died of insanity, distraught from the loneliness induced by such isolated living. She is rumored to have spent the days before her death pacing the keeper's house and wailing. Visitors to the lighthouse have reported still hearing those mournful footsteps along with echoes of her haunting cries. With the passing of Mr. Penwell, the fate of the lighthouse remains just as much of a mystery. Rumors have it that it will be auctioned to the highest bidder next fall. I wonder if the new owners will get along with the late Mrs. Penwell. Rumor is, she's a scream.

Bailey pulled back from the article and looked around the room. Why did Jesse have to leave before she read this? "Is it true?" Bailey asked the cat, who was studying her from the doorway to the bedroom. "Edga," Bailey said out loud. The cat simply stared. "Web," Bailey said. The cat came forward. So either that part was true, or the cat had simply had enough of Bailey talking to herself and was coming over to investigate. Bailey petted the cat. He looked old, all right, but was he really the keeper's cat? Maybe he was one of his kittens. Everyone had babies but her.

Great, Bailey thought. A wife who went insane and hanged herself. In the very room that was locked. Maybe it had been boarded up from the other side. She wondered what Brad was up to right now. Probably sitting up in the lighthouse tower poring over old weather-keeping records. He'd promised her he wouldn't go up to the third floor until she arrived the next weekend. After all, this was their adventure, not just his. Should she tell him about the obituary and the keeper's wife?

Despite everything, Bailey actually found herself looking forward to going back. This time they would have food, and clothing, and an air mattress. She'd bring some wine; it would be like a little honeymoon. In an isolated, haunted lighthouse. Oh, well, when you were married, you took whatever scraps of romance you could get. Hopefully Edga and Trevor Penwell had their share of romantic moments before she went insane. Bailey was going to do everything in her power to make sure their lives would be different. She would contact a psychiatrist about Brad's behavior. Once he was in his right mind, they would fix the lighthouse up, flip it, and sell it. They'd move back to Manhattan, have babies, and laugh about the day Daddy bought a lighthouse. If only she didn't have the image in her head of lonely Swiss Edga, hanging from the third floor.

Then again, ghosts were very popular these days, weren't they? Maybe it wouldn't hurt if the lighthouse was a little haunted. The sooner the place started making money, the better. Between a little ghost, and Brad's near-death experience, and the Fairytalers "pimping the lighthouse," maybe they could actually turn a profit. They wouldn't have to sell the condo, and when Brad snapped out of it, their true life in Manhattan would be waiting for her. Marriage was all about compromise and patience. In other words, Bailey was just going to have to wait it out until Brad saw things her way. Until then, she was going to find a way to turn the lighthouse into a gold mine.

Chapter 13

Bailey brought Brad a cake. It was made by a local genius on her block, a white sheet cake on which he sculpted a lighthouse with icing. She also brought a nice bottle of wine, and candles. She tucked them away in the kitchen until she was ready to surprise him. She'd also had a wooden sign made. It simply read B&B OPEN on one side and B&B CLOSED on the other. She propped it up on the front stoop, hoping to surprise him with it that evening when they came back from their walk. True to Brad's word, he'd scrubbed the place clean. He was supposed to have stocked the cupboards and fridge with groceries from Island Supplies, but the cleaning took so long that he hadn't gotten around to it. At least they had the basic food groups—sugar and alcohol.

The place still looked like a hovel, but it was a clean one. They stood in the living room. Bailey realized she'd probably spend most of her time here, gazing out onto the water. There was definitely something primal about the sea. "I've been thinking of furnishings," Bailey said. Bailey also wanted a slate tile floor for the kitchen and a nice sage green color on the walls.

So far Brad had remained silent on the subject but Bailey didn't push it, mainly because they'd yet to figure out how to pay for all of it. Bailey had purchased one gallon of sage green paint and it sat unopened in the dining room section of the kitchen. They also couldn't agree on cabinets, countertops, or appliances. Bailey wanted cherrywood, and stainless steel, and slate countertops. Brad wanted to go bargain basement. Where was that mentality when he spent half a million dollars in a matter of seconds? If he was allowed to cause that much damage waving a paddle in the air, she should at least be allowed to spank him with it. Or get her pick of the appliances and furnishings. Brad didn't seem to see it that way.

"Furnishings," Brad said. "We can't afford anything too expensive." His response, said with a smile, irritated her. She swallowed it and smiled back.

"It's an investment. We're committed to this now, we should do it right."

"Bails."

"Can I just tell you what I've been thinking?"

"Sure. As long as you're not too attached."

Too attached? She didn't say it out loud; she wasn't going to let him tease her about her habit of repeating after him, yet she still couldn't stop doing it in her head. She had three catalogues clutched in her hand, with samples of furniture she thought would be perfect for the B&B, a mixture of antique and modern. Leather couch with Victorian coffee table, Persian rug with Pottery Barn chairs—nothing that screamed "theme," no seashells in the bathrooms, no seafaring paraphernalia, just simple, clean, and sleek.

She also pictured black-and-white photographs on the walls, except for the lighthouse loft—which was what she was calling the circular room below the tower. For that she wanted to splurge on original paintings by up-and-coming artists exhibiting in Manhattan. She and Brad could make a night, or several, out of it, visiting art galleries, drinking wine, eating cheese, and dreaming. Just like they'd spent their twenties dreaming. Or rather Brad dreamed and Bailey followed his follies. The fourth catalogue, the one with baby furniture, she kept at the condo. That was for another discussion, when Brad was a little bit more himself.

Brad looked at the catalogues she'd thrust in front of him, but except for once in a while saying, "Mmm," his reaction was halfhearted at best.

"You don't like them?"

"I didn't say that."

"Your body language says that."

Brad uncrossed his arms and sighed. "You have excellent taste," he said, handing the catalogues back to her. "You always have. Of course anything you pick out would be fantastic."

"But?"

"But we have perfectly good furniture." Bailey glanced around the empty space, wondering if Brad was now seeing furniture in addition to bright lights. Brad caught the look of worry on her face and laughed.

"At the condo," Brad said. "Unless we're going to sell it furnished?" The last part was said with a boyish grin and a nervous sweep of his hand through the fuzz on his head. He'd been doing that lately, rubbing his head, like it was a genie capable of granting wishes. It had been months since the accident, but his hair had barely grown back. The doctor said it could be due to stress. Yet another reason Bailey shouldn't be arguing with him. Yet she couldn't believe what she was hearing. He was casually talking about selling their condo. The condo he said she'd never have to give up.

"We talked about this," Bailey said. "You said I could commute. We never talked about selling the condo."

Brad walked to the window. "Captain Jack was right," he said to her back.

"Excuse me?"

"The river that cannot make up its mind."

"That's not fair," Bailey said. "We never talked about selling the condo. Never."

"I know, I know." Brad passed his hand along his fuzzy hair

again and started pacing. "I just thought once you saw this place, felt it, you would know it's home. Where we belong."

Bailey stepped in front of Brad, and took hold of his arms. "I like this place," she said. "I really do."

"But?"

"Home? We've had this place a few weeks. It's nowhere near ready—"

"It needs some work. We need money to do that work."

"We're going to have to find another way. We're not selling the condo."

"There is no other way."

"Get a loan."

Brad walked over and put his hands on Bailey's shoulders. He gently started kneading her. "You just got here," he said. "Relax." She wanted to relax, she really did. Lately, she didn't know how. "As soon as we get a bathtub, I'm going to draw you bubble baths. Lots and lots of bubble baths."

"That sounds nice," Bailey said. "How soon will that be?"

"It costs money to put in new bathrooms, Bailey. Everything costs money."

"I can't believe this place was so expensive," Bailey said. "Half a million and it didn't even come with a tub." Brad stopped massaging her. He crossed his arms and moved away from her. And just when she thought he was going to start another fight, his tone softened.

"We'll figure it out," he said. "I promise. But when we do start decorating the rooms—what do you think of having nautical themes?"

It happened as they were standing there. Bailey was thinking that Brad didn't really deserve the cake or the wine and was contemplating sneaking up the lighthouse tower by herself with a wine opener and a fork when they heard the front door open. They looked at each other. Neither of them moved. They listened to the door shut. Then they heard footsteps, and before they knew it, a short, bald man was standing in front of them.

He looked to be in his fifties. He was wearing a white undershirt, jeans, and a gray jacket.

"You left the door unlocked," Bailey said to Brad.

"You were the last in," Brad said. That was true. But she had cake and wine in her hands.

"Sorry," the man said. "Is this a bad time?" He smiled. His teeth were crooked and yellow.

Bailey shivered. "We're not open for business," she said.

"The sign out front said you're open," the man said.

"Sign?" Brad said.

"Surprise," Bailey said.

The man threw his arms open. "Look at that view."

Brad immediately went into business mode. He stuck his hand out. They shook. "I'm Brad. This is my wife Bailey. Welcome to our bed-and-breakfast."

"So you are open," the man said. "Excellent."

"We're not," Bailey said. "As you can see—"

"Have a seat," Brad said. Bailey was about to point out there was nowhere to sit when the man simply sat on the floor as if it was the most normal thing ever. He tucked his legs up like a yoga master. Then Brad held up his finger and disappeared into the kitchen. Bailey and the man just stared at each other, the man grinning. After a moment Brad emerged with the cake.

"Would you like a piece of cake?" Brad said, displaying it as if he'd made it himself.

"I only eat cake at night," the man said.

"I'd love a piece, Brad," Bailey said. "Why don't we go into the kitchen and cut a piece?" Brad smiled and followed Bailey into the kitchen. He put the cake on the counter, then swooped her into his arms and began to dance with her.

"We've got a guest, we've got a guest, we've got a guest," he sang. Bailey broke out of his arms.

"We can't let him stay."

"Why not?"

"Why not? Because we're a bed-and-breakfast without beds or breakfast."

"I'll take the rowboat and buy eggs." The rowboat. The one that came with the sale of the lighthouse, the one Brad promised to paint yellow, turned out to be a rusting, leaking old thing.

"You cannot be serious. We're not open for business."

"The sign says we are!"

"Seriously. We don't even have pans. Or a new oven."

"The old oven sort of works. And we have a table." Brad gestured to the dining room section where he had set up a card table and folding chairs that Captain Jack had sold him.

"But we don't have pans, or even eggs."

"We don't have to share the eggs. Let him eat cake."

"He only eats cake at night, remember?"

"Well, he can have his breakfast at night."

"Brad. We don't have a license or furniture, or insurance, or even a working shower. We are not open."

"He seems pretty flexible."

"And don't you think that's weird?"

"You really are a jaded New Yorker." He grabbed Bailey's hand and pulled her back into the living room. The man was standing by the windows gazing out onto the river.

"Listen," Brad said. "We aren't really set up to handle guests yet." Bailey squeezed his hand as a thank you. "Unless you pay in cash, and don't mind an air mattress, and are willing to eat cake in the morning," Brad added.

"Our air mattress?" Bailey said. The man grinned again and pulled a wad of cash out of his pocket. "Welcome to our little B-and-B," Bailey said.

Her choices sucked. She either stayed at the house with a strange bald man clutching a wad of cash, or she rowed the leaky boat across the river to buy food, and if she was lucky, a pan. She'd gone from living in a city where she could have anything delivered at all hours of the night to a world where she had to row a boat just to get a pizza. Brad put a tarp on the bottom of the boat and pushed her off. The oars were not easy to pull, or push, or whatever you were supposed to do with them. Brad yelled instructions from the shore. He was lucky she was concentrating too much to let him have it. There was a little seat for her bottom, but the tarp only provided so much protection and water started to leak onto her tennis shoes. Her arms started to ache. She'd only gone a few feet. This was so not supposed to be her job. And what about the romantic weekend with her husband she'd planned? It certainly didn't involve a threesome with a bald stranger with strange cake-eating habits.

Although the cash was enticing. They certainly needed cash. The more money they had coming in, the less Brad would push her to sell the condo. Of course, they were about to spend some of the cash on food. Bailey looked up to see a giant ship coming toward her. It was in the distance, but she still imagined it crushing her like a bug. Could it even see her? Being a smaller vessel, she was pretty sure she had the right of way, but what consolation would that be if she and this wreck of a boat sank?

She started to row faster. There was now an inch of water at her feet and blisters on her hands. This was not a proper boat! And where were they now? All the people who insisted this was all worth it, as long as she had her handsome husband. *A lighthouse! How cool! I'd love to live in a lighthouse!* Bailey was definitely cranky when her feet were wet. At the least, her fear of being crushed by the giant ship was enough of a distraction that before she knew it, she was reaching the shore. The boat slid onto the rocks with a prolonged scraping sound. What did she care? She was done with the little rowboat. She was going to get the captain to bring her back, whatever it took.

Island Supplies was a short walk down the path and through the woods. In the future Bailey planned on having their supplies shipped from somewhere cheaper, but she was stuck tonight. She'd really only brought enough food for herself and Brad, and even though technically they were only supposed to provide breakfast, Bailey figured she might as well have enough for him to join them for dinner. She'd simply pick up more pasta and sauce from Island Supplies, plus maybe some eggs, bacon, and toast for the morning. And pans. *Please, please have pans.* If she forgot anything, they didn't even have neighbors to

run to for a cup of sugar. Wow. Sans neighbors. It was a brand-
new world.

It was kind of exciting to have their first guest. And if he
liked the place this much when it was this Spartan, she could
just imagine how popular they'd be when the place was deco-
rated and ready for business. She was starting to feel affection
for the bald guy. How refreshing to meet someone so happy to
sit on a wood floor and just enjoy the view. Maybe all of their future guests would touch Bailey in some way, teach her something about living an authentic life. And in turn they would
provide much-needed peace and quiet to an otherwise hectic
world. Maybe Brad was right, maybe this was their calling.

Bailey pushed open the door to the small store. A bell jin-
gled. Captain Jack was behind the counter, standing with one
leg propped up on a stool, his elbow leaning on it, looking at
her as if he'd been waiting for her to walk through the door.

"Why, hello," he said. "How's island life treating you?"

"We have our first guest."

Jack frowned. "I didn't realize you were open for business?"
Bailey flinched. Of course he was right, they weren't, but she
didn't like hearing anyone else say it.

"Not officially," Bailey said. "But he kind of just appeared."

"I didn't bring anyone over on the ferry," Jack said.

"Maybe he has a boat," Bailey said.

"I'd be careful," Jack said.

"It's not like we have anything he could steal," Bailey said.

"We may be remote," Jack said, "but we're still expected to
follow the law out here."

"Excuse me?"

"You need permits to run a business. You need to be insured.
Licensed. My guess is furniture wouldn't hurt either."

"I said the same things to Brad."

"Ah. Great minds think alike."

"Well, he's here now, and it's a one-time thing. And he seems
to like the empty space. I think he's some kind of yoga master."

"Well, I won't tell, but again, be careful." Bailey grabbed a
basket and quickly filled it. To her relief, the Jack-of-all-trades

even sold pans. She bought one frying pan and one saucepan. He had everything she could probably want, but his prices were steep. Until a Walmart moved in, he could charge whatever he wanted and get away with it.

Jack watched her as he rang up her purchases. Bailey hated feeling like she was under a microscope and hoped her smile didn't show it. "You weren't at the auction," Jack said.

"No," Bailey said. "I wasn't." She wasn't going to air their personal business, admit that she knew nothing about the lighthouse until it was already signed, sealed, and delivered.

"You were there?" Bailey asked.

"Of course," Jack said. "I was going to bid on her myself, but your little committee beat me to it."

What a strange thing to call Brad, Bailey thought. "Why on earth did you want it?" she asked. "You won't even go inside the house."

"One's personal," Jack said. "The other is business."

"I don't understand."

"Do you think I'm afraid to go into the house?"

"You said it was haunted."

"I'm not afraid of ghosts. Are you?"

"No." Bailey took the newspaper clipping and Internet blog from her purse. She hadn't planned on showing it to him tonight, but it was as good a time as any. She handed it to Jack. "Is this who's haunting the lighthouse?"

He scanned the articles. "Trevor?" Jack laughed. "If he is, you've nothing to worry about. Trevor wouldn't hurt a fly."

"What about Edga?" Bailey said. The minute the name was out of her mouth, she regretted it. The captain's face clouded over.

"We don't like to pick over our tragedies here like vultures," he said.

"Oh," Bailey said. "I'm sorry. It's just—the article says—"

"I know what it says."

"You said you were going to bid on the lighthouse," Bailey said.

"That's right."

"But you didn't?"

Jack laughed. "Didn't get a chance. Your committee—"

"Right," Bailey said. Brad Jordan, committee of one. She picked up the groceries and headed for the door. The conversation had flustered her so much she'd even forgotten to ask him for a ride home.

"The auctioneer opened the bid at a hundred thousand," Jack said. Bailey stopped.

"Wow," she said. "It was really in demand, wasn't it?"

"Brad immediately bid a half a million dollars," Jack said.

Bailey felt her entire body lock up. A cold chill spread down the back of her neck. She tried to keep her voice light. "He what?"

"From one hundred thousand to five hundred thousand." The captain snapped his fingers. "Just like that. Guess nobody ever told them how an auction works."

"He knows how an auction works," Bailey said. She couldn't comprehend what she was hearing, she simply couldn't process it now, yet she still had to stand up for her husband. Captain Jack continued as if she hadn't spoken.

"You should have seen the commotion in the room. A few laughed, thought it was a joke. Others, like me, thought they were completely out of their minds. She's got character all right, but she's not worth anywhere near half a million dollars. I probably don't have to tell you that. Being in the business."

"The property is zoned for business," Bailey said. Her voice sounded like she was flailing. "That increases the worth."

"Sure, sure," Jack said. "Anyway, no use speculating now. The place is all yours." He smiled. When Bailey smiled back, she felt downright ill. *My husband was in an accident,* Bailey thought. *He could have brain damage.* Would this be enough to get him out of the contract?

"Why do you keep saying 'they' and 'them'?" Bailey asked. It was probably just his way of talking, like the annoying way some people referred to themselves in the third person. Or, more likely, Brad had mentioned Olivia while purchasing the lighthouse, pretending as if she were in on the deal. It was all so overwhelming, his insistence that she were somehow still around. Captain Jack stared at her, as if trying to figure her out. His phone rang.

"Sorry," he said. He answered the phone and waved good-bye. She remained standing, so he simply turned his back on her and continued his conversation. Little did she know how much the saucepan was about to come in handy.

Chapter 14

Bailey replayed Captain Jack's words with every saucepan of water that she scooped out of her rowboat and poured back into the Hudson. The auction. The bid opened at one hundred thousand dollars. Brad immediately upped it to half a million dollars. *My God.* Was it true? And if so, why? *Did* Brad know how an auction worked? Or was he brain damaged? Brain damage. Trauma. Aunt Olivia. Now here they were. By the time Bailey made it to shore she was a wreck. Aching arms, and even worse, completely confused.

But no matter what, she wouldn't dream of confronting Brad in front of a guest. Not arguing in front of paying customers was their mantra, and they'd certainly had enough practice. At the surf shop they were too young, naïve, and in love to argue. By the time they even realized they'd driven the business into the ground, it was too late and they were out of there anyway. Mostly they just closed early and took long lunches so they could have sex in the back of the shop on various surfboards. It got to the point that Bailey would start getting turned on any time she saw a new design. At the sweater boutique, they argued a tiny bit. But it didn't matter. All that wool muffled their voices so that they could argue behind a stack of cardigans without being heard. And at the coffee shop they screamed at each other whenever they were grinding beans or frothing milk. Nobody heard them, not even them. Otherwise Brad would just whistle when he was angry with her. He whistled a lot back then. But they were seasoned professionals now. Whatever happened at the auction could wait. They had to entertain a strange bald man. And strange he was indeed.

He had a habit of humming to himself, only it seemed to be one long, guttural tone he was emitting instead of anything remotely resembling a tune. As if he were meditating or chanting. Bailey didn't know if she was supposed to look at him or not look at him during this, so she mostly kept her eyes glued to Brad. Unlike her, Brad seemed completely at ease, even happy to have company. Maybe he just wanted to avoid her. Had he ever planned on telling her what really happened at the auction? What had Jack called Brad? *The committee.*

Once again, their guest was more than thrilled to sit at the little card table in the dining room. His name was Harold and he was taking time to travel the United States since the death of his wife. The pasta with meat sauce Bailey whipped up was her specialty, and Harold the hummer ate with gusto. Maybe she would give all their guests funny nicknames behind their backs. Not to be mean, just to amuse herself, just to cope. Brad looked totally content, and on several occasions shared a private smile with Bailey. Bailey smiled back and tried to push down her urge to confront him. *I love him,* Bailey thought. *Even if he was paddle-happy at the auction.* But then, just as quickly, another thought hit. *He immediately bid a half a million dollars. What if we could have bought this place for a hundred thousand? What was he thinking?! How could he!* When their guest finished his plate, he happily accepted seconds.

"I see you waited until you cleaned your plate before you asked for more," Bailey said. Brad cocked his head and looked at her. Harold just started humming. "Instead of asking for all of it right away, you bided your time—waited to see whether or not you'd be hungry, finished your plate, and then asked for seconds." Harold didn't even look up from his plate, he just kept shoveling it in, humming all the while.

"Bailey?" Brad said.

"That's how these things work," Bailey said. "You don't ask for it all at once, you eat a little at a time."

"Are you all right?" Brad said.

"I'm just happy he understands the concept," Bailey said. "Suppose he asked for it all at once, but halfway through discovered he was full?"

"Okay," Brad said.

"Think of the waste!" Bailey said. "Think of all the money we would have wasted!"

"Island Supplies is pricey, all right," Brad said.

"This is the perfect concept," Harold said when he'd finished his second plate. "A Zen retreat. No phones, no television, no furniture."

"Oh, we're going to have furniture," Bailey said. "And phones. And television. And the Internet. And e-book readers."

"E-book readers?" Brad said.

"All of our guests are going to get a free e-book reader," Bailey said. "Except for you, Harold. We haven't implemented it yet."

"Don't need one," Harold said.

"How about we just keep a shelf of paperbacks on hand," Brad said.

"My point," Bailey said, twirling her spaghetti extra tight on her fork, "is that we are not going to be some low-tech B-and-B out in the boondocks."

"Why?" Harold said. "That's exactly what society needs today."

"Exactly!" Brad said.

"A retreat from technology," Harold said.

"A retreat from technology," Brad said.

"We're going to be an equal-opportunity B-and-B," Bailey

said. "Those who want to retreat can do so. Those who need to Google or Facebook or e-mail or watch *Glee* can do that too." Bailey cleared the plates. "Would you like cake?" she asked their guest. He glanced out the window. Twilight was descending, but there was still light to see by. He shook his head. "Because it's not night?" Bailey asked. Brad gave her a look, but she really wanted to know.

"Where all have your travels taken you?" Brad asked. *So this is how it's going to be,* Bailey thought. *Whenever I ask one of our guests something that embarrasses Brad, he's going to change the subject.* There was an old adage, "Never do anything in your first few months of marriage that you don't want to keep doing for the rest of your life." If she let Brad run over her now, he would continue to do so. Harold was their test subject. She had to show Brad he couldn't run the whole show.

"Is there anything else you don't eat during the day, or is it just cake?" Bailey asked.

"I'm just beginning my travels," Harold said, with a quick glance between Bailey and Brad. "And, uh—it's pretty much just cake."

"Like a vampire with a sweet tooth?" Bailey said.

"Bailey!" Brad said.

"It's okay," Harold said. "You see—I'm starting a new life. And I wanted to shake things up a little bit. I love cake. I really love it. So I decided that whenever I wanted to eat cake, I would do it at night. Under the moon and stars."

"That's beautiful," Brad said. He looked at Bailey for confirmation. She thought it was just weird. The old Brad would have too. He might have said "That's beautiful," but when he looked at her he would have raised his eyebrows, or grimaced, or given her a silly grin, something to let her in on the joke. Now he just looked . . . impressed.

"What about pancakes?" Bailey said. "Or French toast. French toast is basically cake, right? Do you only eat pancakes and French toast at night?"

"I'm not really a breakfast eater," Harold said.

"Me neither," Brad said.

"Most important meal of the day," Bailey said. She gave Brad a look. How could they run a successful B&B if he went around telling people he didn't even like breakfast? "Especially for us, right, Brad?" she said.

"For us?" Brad said.

"What would a B-and-B be without breakfast?" she spelled out.

"Just a 'B,' " Harold answered.

"Exactly," Bailey said. "People would say, 'What do you do?' and we'd say, 'We run a B on the Hudson River.' Now that would just be weird!"

"Bails," Brad said. "Are you okay?"

"God, it's good to be out!" Harold said.

"Bailey and I have done a lot of traveling," Brad said. "One adventure after the other."

"Wonderful," Harold said. "And now you're settling down."

"We're home," Brad said. "Home at last."

"We still have our condo in Manhattan," Bailey said. "But this could be a wonderful place to raise kids."

"Kids?" Harold said. He sounded alarmed and looked around as if they might suddenly materialize. "Well, you'll probably have to get furniture then," he said.

"Don't you like kids, Harold?" Bailey said. She kept her voice light. Harold began to fidget in his chair, like he was a child himself.

"Well, I was one once, so there's that," Harold said. Bailey had forgotten he was a widower. Maybe that's why Brad was giving her a look. Had Harold and his wife wanted children? Had they fought over it? Lost a child? She didn't dare ask and Harold didn't offer. She was going to have to respect the boundaries of their guests. But how could you sit and share a meal and not get to know one another? She already missed the days at the coffee shop where guests would finish their lattes and go home.

Brad said absolutely nothing about them having or not having children. "More wine?" Brad said. Everyone said yes. And now the bottle was empty. She should have bought more. Maybe they could turn a portion of the house into a wine cellar.

"Who would like to go for an after-dinner walk?" Bailey said.

"Perfect," Harold said.

"Let's go," Brad said. For once, they all agreed on something.

It was cool by the river. Bailey loved the fresh evening smell, and the feel of the rocks under her feet. It wasn't the beach, but it wasn't a bad place to stroll. Barges chugged along in the distance, and occasionally sounded their horns. The light from their tower pulsed across the river. Harold carried his little piece of cake in a Tupperware container. At one point they all stopped to look at the lighthouse.

Its beam, spreading across the river, was a sight to behold. A beacon in the night. Bailey felt a surge of pride, as if she'd built the sixty-foot tower herself. Just then she noticed a small speedboat buzzing toward them. Much faster than a rowboat and a saucepan. It reminded her of something.

"How did you get here?" Bailey said. "Captain Jack said you weren't on his ferry."

"I have a kayak," Harold said. "Best investment I ever made."

"I'm going to get a kayak," Brad said.

"*We* have a leaky rowboat," Bailey said. "And a saucepan."

"Who is that?" Harold pointed at the speedboat making its way toward shore. They could make out two men in dark uniforms standing up in the boat.

"Looks like the Coast Guard." Brad had barely finished the sentence when their guest dropped his cake and took off. Bailey stood, stunned, watching his short legs sprint away as if he were on fire. The speedboat flashed a light and sounded an alarm as it pulled up to shore. The two guards jumped out. They introduced themselves and then said they were on the lookout for a man who had escaped from the county prison. Since the prison was less than ten miles away, they thought they'd check in and see if they'd seen or heard anything. Bailey looked down at the piece of cake smashed on the rocks.

"Uh-oh," she said. They glanced around. Harold was nowhere in sight. There were plenty of places to hide. Miles and miles of woods. "He has a kayak," Bailey said. "And he only eats cake at night."

"Do you think they'll catch him?" They were lying on the air mattress that Bailey insisted they move from the loft into the living room. She wanted to be in an open space next to the windows just in case their escaped guest was hiding somewhere. Although Brad insisted he was probably long gone.

"Long gone?" Bailey said. "He's on foot. Or a kayak."

"Still. He was pretty fast. And he had a head start."

"A fugitive," Bailey said.

"A *suspected* fugitive," Brad answered.

"He ran like hell when he saw the Coast Guard."

"I'm so happy I got the cash up front," Brad said.

"We," Bailey said. "We, we, we, we, we."

"What?"

"All night you've said 'I' this and 'I' that. We're a 'we,' remember?" Bailey was ready for a fight. But Brad put his hands on her waist, rolled her to him, and rubbed his nose against hers. Like married Eskimos.

"I remember," he said quietly.

"We'll never forget our first guest," Bailey said.

"I can't believe you thought he was a yoga master."

"Yoga master, escaped convict. They both travel light." Brad laughed, then Bailey joined in, and for a moment they were traveling light. "No wonder he didn't mind sitting on the floor. Any place without bars on the windows was like a five-star hotel."

"And remember when he said, 'I'm so glad I'm out!' My God. I thought he meant, like out in the country. He meant out of prison!" The deep-in-the-gut laughter was a welcome relief. They laughed long and hard, releasing all the energy and stress of the past few months. When they were done they both had to wipe tears from their eyes.

"He didn't even get to eat his cake," Brad said.

"You can't have your cake and eat it too," Bailey said.

"We can. We can eat all of it." For a moment Bailey wondered if he would segue into something sexual, work his lips and tongue down her body. She remembered the thrill of first becoming sexual with him. Raging hormones and stolen moments, and his fingers slipping into her panties, always to find her completely flooded. Now there was usually a tube at the side of the bed. When did everything change? When did they start to need pharmaceuticals to aid in their lovemaking?

Instead of slipping his fingers into her, Brad sat up, eyes bright. He was excited all right, just not the good kind. Ah, the honeymoon stage. The beginning. In love with a lighthouse. How long would it last this time?

When the coffee shop opened, they'd stayed up round the clock. Partly out of excitement, but mostly, Bailey suspected, because of the staggering amount of espresso shots coursing through their young bodies. They'd talked about everything that night. Their customers, the décor, their espresso-making techniques. Brad swore he was going to learn to make a little heart in the foam. He never did. Was this the same thing, was it going to follow the same high, then crash into abject failure? Only here, they were childless and quickly approaching middle age.

"Escaped con or not, Harold still had some valid insights. I'd like to keep this place Zen," Brad said.

"I love you," Bailey said. "But we're still getting furniture, television, and the Internet."

"Furniture, okay," Brad said. "Please. No television, and the Internet only for us. For emergencies."

"But sometimes I just like to zone out and watch TV," Bailey said.

"I know. But you'll get used to it. Wouldn't you rather tune into life? Sunsets, and wildlife, and speedboat chases?"

"What about Matt Lauer? You know I can't start the day without Matt Lauer."

"Let's just go without it for a while," Brad said. "You'll see."

"What happened to 'everything in moderation'?" Bailey said.

"It still applies," Brad said. "But can't we just give it a try?"

"Speaking of moderation," Bailey said. "Tell me about the auction again."

"Why?"

"Because I missed out on it and I want to feel a part of it." She snuggled up to Brad. "What was your opening bid?"

She was testing him, and it probably wasn't a very wifely thing to do, but she had to see whether or not he was going to confess. He didn't. He claimed the bid started at a hundred thousand and he only went up by increments of ten thousand. A heaviness hit Bailey square in the center of her chest. Despite his restlessness and lack of good business sense, her husband, Brad Jordan, had always been honest to a fault. And now, after seeing the light, he was apparently a liar.

"I can't believe the price was so high," Bailey said. "Comparative properties all sold for much, much less. Under three hundred thousand, most of them."

"They probably needed a lot more work," Brad said.

"More work than this?" Bailey said. "Unless we cater exclusively to escaped cons, we can't even have guests here with the current state of things."

"This is why we need to sell the Jag and the condo," Brad said. She wanted to pummel him. She wasn't selling the condo. Especially not when he was lying to her.

"Brad. Captain Jack told me the bid started at one hundred thousand dollars and you—he called you a 'committee,' by the way—immediately upped it to half a million dollars."

"Oh," Brad said.

Bailey sat up. The air mattress tilted and squealed. "Oh? That's all you have to say? Oh?"

"What else is there to say?"

"Oh, gee, I don't know. How about, 'That's ludicrous, Bailey. Why in the world would I do something that stupid'!" She hadn't meant to escalate so quickly, but in addition to a compulsion to throw things, she always did have a lead-foot mouth.

"We had to get it, okay? I couldn't risk losing it."

"But you're supposed to wait. Bid in increments. Maybe it would have sold for a hundred and fifty thousand dollars!"

"No. You should've seen Captain Jack. He wanted it, Bailey."

"He won't even come inside."

"I'm telling you—I may have moved it along quicker, but this lighthouse was going to go for this price anyway."

"You don't know that."

"Bailey, I'm telling you. I know in my gut. If you had just been there. I just had this overwhelming feeling—"

"There was a suicide on the third floor!"

"What?" Brad stood up and looked to the ceiling, where Bailey pointed.

"In the very room we can't get into." They'd tried everything short of breaking down the door. The next plan of action was to call a locksmith. Bailey was surprised Brad hadn't torn into it already, but he'd promised to wait for her.

"Somebody killed themself up there?"

"Edga Penwell. She was the late keeper's wife. She hanged herself."

"And you know this how?"

"Captain Jack—"

Brad threw his arms up. "Captain Jack. I should have known. He could be making it all up. I saw the look in his eye—he was going to buy it. I had to beat him to it."

"Brad!" Bailey put her hands over her face. She was so tired. Brad put his arm around her shoulders.

"I got a good deal. Sorry. *We* got a really good deal."

"In this case, feel free to use the 'I.' Because if I'd been there—" She stopped. They were exhausted and upset. And quickly approaching lines which if crossed could become forever tangled.

"If you'd been there, what?"

"We wouldn't have gone over two hundred and fifty."

"Then we wouldn't be here now."

"You don't know that."

Bailey got up and fetched her purse from the fireplace mantel. She flicked on the light and rummaged in her purse until she found the obituary. She held it out to Brad.

"What is it?"

"Read it."

Brad sighed, but finally complied. He had to hold it farther away from his eyes than she'd ever noticed before. It wouldn't be long before they were both buying reading glasses. How could they be ready for reading glasses but not babies? He put the article down, then looked toward the ceiling again.

"Kind of weird, right? That we can't get into that floor?" Bailey said.

"There must be a lot of energy up there," Brad said. "Energy that needs to be released." Bailey had a lot of energy that needed to be released too, but she kept her mouth shut about that.

"Wonder how much an exorcist goes for these days," she said. Brad stood up, came close to Bailey, and took her hands in his.

"I know it hasn't been easy," Brad said. "But I swear, Bails. This is where we belong. Right here, right now. We're needed here. I feel it." He squeezed her hand.

"Um. What do you mean—we're needed here?"

"It's going to sound crazy."

"Crazy as in—we're supposed to help Edga cross over?" She'd hit the bull's-eye. She could tell by the look on his face. The only reason she didn't lose it was the gentle reminder to herself that a good ghost story might be good for business. But if Brad thought she was using his life mission to make a profit, it would lead to another argument. She was way too tired to argue.

Brad must have been thinking along the same lines, for instead of continuing the conversation, he swept her into his arms and began to dance with her.

"All right, Fred Astaire," Bailey said, slightly pulling away. "It's a little late for dancing."

"It's never too late for dancing," Brad said. "Or cake. Or to try and find your true purpose in life." As if there had been music playing that just stopped, the pair stopped dancing. Brad lifted her chin with his fingers. "It's not too late for you either."

Bailey jerked away. "What do you mean by that?"

"You need to follow your passion."

"Instead of just following you from whim to whim?" She didn't mean to say it. But that was the problem with mouths sometimes. They spat things out that couldn't be taken back. And it wasn't like it was a secret.

"I just want you to be happy."

"I was happy. We were making fantastic money!"

"Fantastic money, yes. Happy? Are you kidding me?"

"I liked my job. I liked Manhattan. I wanted us to live there and have babies."

"Life is fleeting, Bailey. If we had a baby now . . ." He stopped talking. The one thought she wanted him to finish.

"What? Tell me?"

"You'd throw yourself into motherhood like you've thrown yourself into everything else. I'm just afraid—you'd lose yourself."

"So now it's my fault you don't want to have a baby?"

Brad's voice took on a serious, quiet tone. "I just want what's best for you."

"I keep telling you, but you won't listen."

"There's no rush for children, Bails."

"Tell that to my biological clock." Brad got that grin on his face, the one that showed his dimples and made his eyes light up, the one that was impossible to resist. He leaned down to her stomach and poked around.

"Is this where your clock is?"

"Lower," Bailey said.

Brad laughed. He grabbed her around the waist and nuzzled his mouth into her belly button. "We have plenty of time," he yelled into her stomach. "Stop ticking!" Bailey put her hand on top of his head and nudged his head down lower. Finally, her husband got the hint. And this time when they fell back into the saggy air mattress, it wasn't to sleep. When they were finished, Brad rolled over and was asleep and snoring within minutes. Bailey, on the other hand, was wide awake. Mostly because she'd made a decision. She'd list the condo in the morning. Her place was, and always would be, right beside this man.

Chapter 15

Winter on the Hudson River was wild, and beautiful, and completely frozen. Floating snow cones, or ice floes as they were officially called, littered the river bobbing along at a fast clip, as if on a race. Bailey liked to watch them float by, at first down by the water's edge; then when frostbite threatened her fingers and toes, she'd watch them from the windows inside the house.

The icy fingers of winter also played upon the grass and the rocky path along the river, and the pier, making walking treacherous. The sides of the tower were so slick that when the sun shone upon it, it looked as if it were made of glass. Jagged icicles dangled like weapons underneath the tower's iron deck. With the exception of ice-breaking tugs, boats were fewer and farther between, and on stormy days and high tides no one could navigate the stretch of land between their house and the boat dock. When snow fell, it was a devastatingly beautiful but lonely wonderland. Bailey took as many pictures as she could, hoping at least one would capture its pristine grace, its place in history, its power. A few days after the first snowfall, when mud threatened to ruin the wonderland, Bailey and Brad made a snowman in the yard. It was a brief moment of fun, a rest from shoveling and salting and building fires.

It was thanks to Bailey that the fireplace was now working beautifully. The first attempt at using it resulted in a disaster. The main room immediately filled with clouds of black smoke. Luckily, Brad had a fire extinguisher on hand. It would take days to clean the soot off the walls, and floors, and themselves. Brad was so frustrated, he looked as if he were going to cry. So Bailey pretended not to be bothered, and instead talked him into taking a shower together, in their new upstairs bathroom. It helped lighten the mood—that is, until Brad didn't want to make love in the shower because they didn't have a condom. They argued and she finished the shower early, declaring that Brad could be the one to clean the soot from the tub, and the floor, and the towels. Then she turned her attention back to the fireplace.

Bailey was on a mission. She declared the fireplace her project and refused to let Brad in on the repairs. She paid the buyers of their condo an undisclosed price to take back her custom-made mantel, and hired an expert to fix the fireplace before attaching the new mantel.

It turned out to yield quite a surprise. Bailey assumed the black smoke was due to a problem with the flue. She couldn't have been more wrong. The chimney sweep discovered something was blocking the chimney. He crouched in the fireplace, gazing up. With his face obscured, he waved her over with one hand.

"Fifty years," he said. "Never seen anything like this." Bailey hurried over, knelt beside him, and looked up. His flashlight illuminated a large crate blocking the chimney.

"Oh my God," she said.

"It's up there on some kind of hoist," the chimney guy said. "Whatever it is, it must be heavy."

Bailey smiled to herself as she replayed the memory. What an adventure that turned out to be. Lucky for her, Brad was way too busy in the tower, and the yard, and on the dock to notice what was going on inside the house. Had he been there when they lowered it, and she opened it, she never would have been able to hold on to this delicious surprise. And it was great timing; she was able to use the crane Brad had hired to repair some of the stones in the tower wall to lift the surprise up into the Crow's Nest. At first she simply threw a blanket over it, and Brad didn't notice a thing. Then she purchased an industrial cabinet to store and lock it. It even took him a couple of days to notice that. When he did, thanks to his secretive, locked journals, Bailey was able to placate him.

"It's a locked cabinet," she said when he finally asked about it. "For my personal things." He just looked at her.

"It's taking up a lot of space," he said.

"And yet it took you two days to notice it."

Brad ignored the comment. "There's not much space up there to begin with."

"I need it."

"What's in it?"

"Personal and private things," she said. "Just like your diaries."

"Journals." But he let it drop with a shake of his head and a joke about knowing where to look for the bodies if any of their guests disappeared. Since then, Bailey had visited the cabinet every time she needed to remind herself that this was an adventure worth having. It became a hobby that kept her busy, and somewhat sane. The biggest challenge was carving out time when Brad wasn't in the Crow's Nest. She could tell he was a little resentful, as if he assumed he could claim the perch as his own, but he wisely began to let her have her own time up in the nest. It was hard to keep her mouth shut—she normally wasn't very good at keeping secrets, but this one was well worth it.

She was saving it until they'd been in business for a full year. A date that was unknown since they weren't officially open for business yet. Of course, she wondered why the crate had been hoisted into the fireplace, but since Trevor's journals didn't yield anything other than weather patterns and wildlife spottings, she feared they'd never know. For once she was happy that Brad was so out of it, so distracted; otherwise, she might never have been able to pull it off.

And to top it off, once the obstruction was removed, the chimney sweep did a magnificent job restoring the fireplace. Now that the mantel from her childhood home was in place, she felt a little bit more as if she belonged here. But even so, unless you were sitting directly in front of the fire, the keeper's house was steeped in a deep chill. Bailey felt as if she could never get warm, and worried that guests would shun them in the winter. Brad assured her they would work on the heating system, but to Bailey it was just another thing to add to a mounting To Do list. The holidays passed without much recognition. They couldn't host a Thanksgiving dinner without appliances, and although they had several invitations back in the city, Brad didn't want to stop any of his projects. Since even the contractors wouldn't work in this winter wonderland, Brad was trying to start with DIY projects. Bailey was horrified that this included putting down a new kitchen floor. Did he really know how to do that? She certainly didn't. And it took them a while to agree on which tiles they wanted. Bailey still wanted a slate floor, Brad wanted a cheap one. Their weekends were filled with trips to the local hardware store, arguing over floor samples.

Finally, one of the managers offered them a discount on the slate tiles that had caught Bailey's eye. He was probably just trying to get the arguing couple out of his store. Brad used the opportunity to buy appliances at a discount as well. The dishwasher turned out to be black because it was on clearance, and so they had to get a black stove to match. Bailey really wanted a stainless steel refrigerator but Brad pointed out that you couldn't stick magnets on it and he wanted to get plastic letter magnets so guests could leave messages on the fridge. So they ended up with a black refrigerator as well, although Bailey wasn't a complete pushover because she talked him into getting the little white magnets with typed words, insisting it would look classier. Later, even that was a decision she would come to regret.

Because maybe the colorful plastic letter magnets would have been a subliminal reminder to Brad that they needed children to go along with them. Regardless, little by little, they compromised. Bailey and Brad had Thanksgiving dinner in town, at a nice family restaurant. The people they met were polite, but not what Bailey would call friendly. Especially when they heard they were running the lighthouse. They would start out all chatty and smiling, and the minute anyone found out who they were, their demeanor would immediately shift, and they seemed to almost regard Bailey and Brad with suspicion. Was it because of the suicide? Or the auction? Had others wanted the lighthouse for themselves? Bailey spent quite a bit of time pondering the possibilities, but Brad told her she was being paranoid.

Since he thought that was being paranoid, Bailey started keeping other little things to herself. Besides being drafty and constantly damp, Bailey often heard strange noises in the house, especially late at night. She was glad they were sleeping in the tower room, because quite frankly, being in the house after dark spooked her. Maybe it was just the thought of what had happened in the attic. Several nights when she was staying up later than usual and thus still in the house, she thought she heard footsteps from above. It was impossible to mistake the sound; now that they'd ripped the carpets up, the floorboards creaked when walked upon. Brad told her it was the wind. It was true, the sound of the wind certainly did whistle through the house most nights, but Bailey could distinguish between the two.

One night she swore she heard music playing. It was a melodic tinkling sound, like a child's music box. She'd been too afraid to check it out herself, so she fetched Brad from his post at the Crow's Nest. But when they got back to the main house, the music had stopped. They checked out every room, including the attic, which, once they got a locksmith to open the door, turned out to be a large but otherwise unremarkable space. Except for a few boxes with some clothing and books that Bailey assumed had belonged to Trevor and Edga, there was no apparent reason for the room to be locked, certainly nothing of value. Something about the space gave Bailey the creeps, but it was probably just because she couldn't stand up there without imagining Edga hanging from the rafters. Once they cleaned it out, Bailey avoided going up there. And there was certainly plenty of other things to keep her busy.

The kitchen floor was only halfway done, and their new shower was cold and the water pressure was weak, especially with the pipes freezing every other day, and Bailey was dying to get their furniture from the condo in the house, but they had to store it because there was no use putting down furniture when you still had to put in new floors and sand and stain old ones. Brad convinced Bailey that she could put the flooring in the small bathroom herself. Soon there were two of them on their hands and knees grouting tile with the how-to book by their side. She'd been resistant at first, but she had to admit she felt a tremendous sense of pride when it was done. Even if Brad did have to tweak a few tiles after she was done. Next they were on to putting up crown molding and painting. With each project, their bank account took a nosedive. The third bathroom and outdoor repair work would have to wait until the spring when the contractors agreed to start.

Captain Jack recommended several workers, and Brad booked them all on the spot. They agreed to start in March. Bailey continued to wonder what they had gotten themselves into. The only thing that kept her going, besides having so much to do every day that she was literally too tired to think, was watching Brad. Little by little he seemed to be coming back to her, speaking less and less of seeing the light. Although it could have something to do with his online support group. He was still spending a lot of time chatting with them. Maybe Brad was still talking about it the same amount, just not to her. For that, she was grateful. She wondered where they would spend Christmas. Her sister Meg was going through trauma with Thomas, Bailey's nephew. Both Joyce (her niece), and Thomas were teenagers now. Meg complained about them constantly, but always with an undercurrent of fierce love. She was worried Thomas was keeping secrets from her. Meg suspected he had problems with some other boys at school, at least that was the rumor as reported by Joyce, but so far Thomas had refused to talk to her about it. Bailey wondered if he got that from his father. Meg's husband was the type who always seemed to be holding back. It was a constant reminder to Bailey that no matter what crazy things she'd had to endure for Brad, they'd always been 100 percent honest with each other.

Bailey really wanted her family to come visit them, but besides the deep freeze, it just wasn't fair to ask anyone to stay in the middle of a project. Everywhere you turned there were tools, and dust, and something ripped up yet still sitting in the middle of the floor. Lately the electricity had been wonky too. Lights would suddenly flicker or blow out completely. Bailey couldn't believe that she'd gone through an entire package of lightbulbs for the main house in just a month. They would have to hire an electrician to get to the bottom of it. And if that didn't work, then they were going to have to hire a priest.

Keeper's Log
Brad

Bailey is what I call a Full Moon kind of woman. Passionate and unpredictable. I'm trying as hard as I can to make progress on the house, because I can tell that all of these projects are getting to her. She was so proud of that bathroom floor that I just couldn't tell her I had to sneak out in the middle of the night to redo it. Yesterday she cried because she was tired of seeing a screwdriver on the kitchen counter. I wish I could fast-forward to the summer when our new cabinets and countertop are in the kitchen, as well as a dining table filled with witty, conversing guests. I found a gorgeous old Spanish wood dining table at the antique store in town. It seats twelve. The matching chairs all have purple velvet cushions. The color of royalty. What a great metaphor—the way we intend on treating all of our honored guests. I've already bought it and as soon as the kitchen floor is done, I'll arrange for Captain Jack to bring it over on the ferry. I think Bails is going to love it. It was bad timing to move in the winter all right, but there's nothing I can do about that now. If we can just get through this, everything will be so easy in comparison.

Every day I wake up convinced this will be the day I tell Bailey everything. I don't know how habitual liars do it. It's stressful keeping secrets. Of course, I should be used to that by now, shouldn't I? There are other times when I think the kindest thing is to say nothing at all. Why should someone else pay for the mistakes I've made? When will I learn to just tell the truth from the beginning? The more time goes by, the harder it is. Especially now, with all the work we're doing on this place. Don't get me wrong, it's beautiful here. Peaceful. At night the river is deep black, and when the light sweeps over her, it's a sight almost as gorgeous as my wife. I had forgotten how powerful bodies of water can be, how deeply meditative. I love to sit up in the tower with Bailey and watch the light sweep over the depths of the Hudson. I think she's starting to see it too, I think she's starting to come around. We are truly the keepers of the light. Soon, Christmas will be here. Imagine telling her now? I just can't. Besides, that particular truth is nothing more than a technicality. Or am I just justifying? Who knows. I just need to let Bailey fall a little bit more in love with the place, which probably won't happen until we thaw out, and then, I swear, I'll tell her everything. Well, almost everything.

Winter dragged on. Renovations and DIY projects took their toll, but little by little, progress was made. They argued. About Olivia's ashes, where to spend Christmas, the tools that tripped

Bailey up wherever she went, the unbelievable chill of the house, the dust covering everything, and most distressing to Bailey, the fact that they spent days on end without seeing another human being. Bailey wondered if Brad was trying to drive her insane. Just like Edga Penwell, who, if Bailey believed in such things, was still hanging around the house in some shape or form, trying to push Bailey that much closer to the edge. The mysterious noises continued, but whenever Bailey got the courage to try and discover where they were coming from, they would stop. The only thing that carried Bailey through that winter were the walks she took with Brad along the river. No matter what else was going on, there was comfort in pulling on their winter boots and bundling in hats, and scarves, and coats, and walking side by side along the river in the mornings and sometimes again in the evenings. A routine, a chance to bond with nature, a chance to watch their breath in the cold air and remark on the wildlife hardy enough to live out the winter by the river.

Despite her complaints, it wasn't all stress. Besides the daily walks, there were other highlights. The first snowfall. Boats adorned with Christmas lights. The town decorating for the season. And finally one day the kitchen floor was done, and the appliances were in. They still had the old cabinets and countertops, but at least the kitchen was a functioning one. The morning the kitchen was finished, Brad made banana bread. It permeated the air with its sweet scent, and they sat on their new floor, enjoying it with steaming mugs of coffee they bought in town. Then Captain Jack ferried over with much fanfare, tooting his horn and passing by the house several times before docking. Brad ran out to greet him, and a few minutes later, the two of them carried in a dining table the likes of which Bailey had never seen. Gorgeous, thick dark wood and tall, regal chairs with violet velvet cushions. It fit perfectly in the dining space, and Bailey had to admit that they never could have found such a treasure in a catalogue.

They spent their first Christmas alone in the house. Brad bought them each a pair of cross-country skis, and soon their morning walks alternated with cross-country skiing. In the early afternoons they would watch the ice-breaking tugs chopping their way through the river, working hard to keep this portion of the Hudson River viable to boats, especially the barges carrying heating fuel to upstate New York. Wasn't it humbling, Brad said, to live somewhere so vital?

Bailey still missed Manhattan, especially at Christmastime, but it was less and less, and even when homesickness or boredom threatened to choke her, Bailey kept it to herself. Brad was so eager for her to love it here as much as he did. So Bailey and Brad might have survived, even enjoyed the winter, but they couldn't say the same for the dock. Winter ravaged a portion of it, and one day the end caved in under the weight of ice and snow. Brad was told the repair work would take several men and cranes and winches to lift pilings, and it sounded so hideous that Bailey soon tuned it out. Hopefully the contractors that Jack recommended would be as good as he assured them they were. The work, and the costs, were piling up. Day by day, Bailey saw the profit from their condo eaten up by another repair. It was what you got, Bailey said silently, for owning a lighthouse. Spring would bring promise, she thought. She was grateful there was no one around to tell her that she was in for months of misery beyond her wildest dreams.

It started with a tent. Winter was still keeping one icy claw on the land, but spring was just starting to tease. Bailey looked out the window one morning to see a tent set up on the grassy area just beyond the patio. Without stopping to worry that it could be another escaped prisoner, Bailey immediately went out and stood just outside the flap. She was still holding her coffee cup. Brad was up in the tower writing in his diary.

Just as she was pondering how you "knocked" on a tent, a man stepped out. He was in jeans and shirtless. He looked to be in his late twenties, and more than that, he looked as if he'd just stepped out of a page of a magazine. Tall, and tight, and tan, and young. Bailey stopped, took a sip of coffee, and just stared. She was supposed to be watching the sun spill its first rays of light across the horizon, but instead she was staring openly at his arms, and chest, and stomach. She suddenly wanted to spill her coffee on his abs just so she could lick it off. Oh God, where did that thought come from? Was nature turning her into some kind of pervert? Despite her embarrassment, she didn't look away when he caught her staring.

"Hello," he said. Bailey lifted her coffee in response. "Gorgeous morning, isn't it?" His voice was as deep and lazy as the river. He sounded like summer.

"No doubt about that," Bailey said.

"This is some life," he said. "Wouldn't you die to live here year-around?"

"I'm going to," Bailey said.

His beautiful eyebrows furled. "Going to what?"

"Either die or live here year-round," Bailey said. The man perked up. He moved closer to her, so close she once again spilled her coffee. *Note to self: Get a travel mug with an extra-tight lid.* A few splotches ended up on her breasts, and first she noticed it, then she noticed him noticing it. When his eyes finally came back up and locked with hers, she had to take a step back. In a single rush, she realized that he reminded her of Brad when he was that age. When they were that age. Oh God. Were they really not that age anymore? Was their youth really behind them? Was she a dirty old woman? *Cougar. Oh, good Lord, I'm a cougar.* She tried a roar inside her head. It reverberated through the rest of her body.

"This is your lighthouse?" the man said. He sounded so happy, so excited. Just like Brad.

"Yes," Bailey said. *My husband and I bought it,* she knew she should add. But she didn't. *You're gorgeous,* she wanted to say. But she didn't. If it was true that fantasizing and thinking about doing things you shouldn't were just as sinful as doing it, then she was going to have to start asking for truckloads of forgiveness. "Who are you?" she said. He held out his hand.

"Jake." She shook his hand, of course she did, when someone held out their hand you were expected to shake it, it was just common courtesy. Innocent touching. Now, hugging him would be inappropriate. Wondering how his hard stomach would feel against hers was just normal. Although she noticed he didn't really shake her hand, instead he just held it in his. Were her hands really perspiring? Should she apologize? What was going on here? She was a happily married woman, at least she used to be, and she would be again, and she was way too old for him, but definitely not a cougar, and it wasn't like it was a crime, gently holding the hand of a stranger thinking how nice his fingers and palms felt against hers. Appropriately, she pulled her hand away. He tilted his head and smiled. He looked curious, and interested. In her. Had she spiked her coffee too much, or not enough? It wasn't the big questions of life that plagued her, it was the little ones.

"Are you part of the group?" she asked. She wasn't going to call them the "committee" as Brad had called them on a few occasions. He mentioned he'd invited his NDE support group to the lighthouse, but Bailey didn't think they were supposed to be here this soon.

"I've never been a groupie," Jake said with a smile.

Bailey pointed to the tent. "So you're just arbitrarily parked on my lawn?"

"Considering you're paying me, I don't think I should take up one of your rooms as well, do you?"

"Paying you?" she said. "What am I paying you to do?" A hundred dirty answers ran through her mind. Jake laughed as if he knew this.

"I'm your new general contractor," he said.

"You're kidding?" Bailey said. *Thank you, Captain Jack.* Was he old enough to use tools?

"Don't worry," he said with a wink. "You're in good hands." Oh God. She wasn't going to think about that comment.

"Would you like breakfast?" she said.

"I thought you'd never ask." Bailey should invite Brad down for breakfast too, introduce him to the new contractor. Then again, he probably didn't want to be disturbed. Besides, it would give her a chance to explain to Jake exactly how she wanted the repairs done around the place. And it was because she was trying to be polite, getting used to letting others do as they wish in her home, that she didn't even think to ask him to put a shirt on. No shirt, no shoes, but this B&B still had service.

Chapter 16

Holes. There were holes in their yard, holes in the floor of the lighthouse tower, holes punched into the walls of the attic. Bailey thought she was seeing things. Now in addition to tools, and dust, and holes, there were strange men littered about the place. Jake had a small crew, but they were still a crew. Bailey supposed she shouldn't complain. After all, when they were done she'd have new cabinets and two new bathrooms, and beautifully stained floors, and a dock you could walk on without plunging into the Hudson River, and a new outdoor patio where guests could barbecue and sip wine at night while watching the ships go by, and lights that actually followed the law of the switch.

But in addition to their home and yard, it was official, their pocketbook also had holes. The last of the money drained out of their account so fast, it made Bailey's head spin. And Brad was becoming more distant than ever. His NDE group had to postpone their first visit. It was like watching a child disappointed by a father who'd promised to take him to a baseball game but left him waiting all alone on the curb instead. Bailey and Brad were either fighting or suffering alone in silence. By the time months had passed and the house had actually taken shape, Bailey's marriage was falling apart. It was time to use the contact Jesse had given her and call in help. Since there were no psychiatrists on the island, it was time to ship one in. His name was Martin Gregors. He used to be the head psychiatrist at Bellevue; now he was in private practice to an exclusive clientele in Manhattan. Normally they could never have afforded him. But despite how she felt about living in one, Bailey was beginning to discover the power of a lighthouse. Instead of his astronomical fee, Martin agreed to a free weekend at the lighthouse, in exchange for casually checking out Brad. Bailey just wanted to know how much she should worry about her reclusive husband and his attachment to "his committee."

But that wasn't the worst of it. There was still the matter of Olivia. Brad had out-and-out refused to find a final resting place for the ashes. The urn was up in the lighthouse, in the eye, where the light pulsed nightly, a permanent fixture in their lives. At odd times, she would catch Brad talking to the urn as if Olivia were right there beside him. Bailey wanted her gone. She'd tried everything she possibly could with Brad, and he'd stubbornly refused to get rid of her. He was convinced their guests would love her. Bailey was convinced that anybody in their right mind would peg him as a lunatic. Hopefully Martin was that right-minded man who could point Brad in a healthier direction.

Bailey was proud to give the good doctor the tour. Most of the furnishings that used to be in their condo fit surprisingly well in the keeper's house. The leather couch, the Persian rug, the dark wood coffee table. Maybe Bailey had been furnishing a Victorian lighthouse all those years without realizing it. Some kind of strange fated destiny of which she was blissfully unaware.

Bailey took pleasure in gauging Martin's reaction to the place. Brad should be alongside her, showing off his land. Instead, he was in the Crow's Nest doing God knows what. Gregors was a short, slim man in his forties with thinning blond hair and black-rimmed glasses. Although he was wearing jeans and a dark blue T-shirt, she somehow imagined him always wearing suits. He had an ease about him that made Bailey feel comfortable right away. He'd probably cultivated that over the years he'd spent listening to other people's neuroses.

"You've done a remarkable job," Martin commented as they took the tour of the upstairs.

"Thank you. We've tried to keep the furnishings to the original time period. This keeper's house was built in 1892. The lighthouse is built onto the back of the house and can be accessed from a little bridge on this floor. There are only twenty-nine iron steps up to the top."

"I can't wait to see it," Martin said.

"It is something. I mean, the light itself isn't much to see, except at night. It's really something to stand up there watching the room blink light and dark."

"Amazing."

"It's also where my husband Brad spends most of his time. With Olivia."

"I see."

"I hope you can help my husband. He hasn't been the same since the accident."

"Where he had a near-death experience?"

"Yes. Last summer."

"Fascinating." They stopped in the largest of the three guest rooms, apart from the attic, which they'd decided not to rent out unless they absolutely had to. Strange noises could still be heard up there late at night. Several of the workers had soon refused to go up after dark. Even Brad reluctantly admitted to hearing the footsteps. So that guests wouldn't try and claim the attic for their own, they'd left it unfurnished. Martin insisted on seeing the space. Instead of recognizing that it was just an empty old attic, he loved it. He paced over the thick wood floors, once in a while touching the high beams and gazing out the small window. Bailey tried not to gaze at the ceiling and wonder from which spot Edga had hanged herself. She assumed it was by the window. It was human nature. We all liked a good view, even if we were on the way out. "Why, this is like a studio apartment up here," Martin said. "Or will be when you furnish it."

"Little by little," Bailey said. She glanced around, wondering if the ghost would make an appearance. Flicker the lights, squeak the floorboards. Bailey could hardly stand to be in the space at all. She decided not to mention any of this to Brad's new therapist; he might see to it that she was the one on the couch.

"Shall we go to the lighthouse now?"

"Lead the way," Martin said. He was equally impressed with the lighthouse loft. It was by far Bailey's favorite place. She'd always wanted a loft apartment. They'd painted the concrete floor maroon. The kitchen was in the middle of the space with a granite island directly in the center. On one side of the open kitchen was a couch facing the window, with the view of the Hudson River. On the other side, their king-sized bed was situated next to the fireplace. They'd turned a closet into a small bathroom. It was modern and old-fashioned at the same time. The spiral staircase up to the tower was on the far wall.

"This is just fantastic," Martin said. Bailey could tell he was hating his guest room more and more.

"Yes," Bailey said. "Although it gets a little drafty." Martin murmured something politely. She wanted to point out that he was getting to stay for free—in exchange for shrinking her husband's head, that is. Something she wasn't convinced he was even going to be able to do.

"It was something cleaning these stairs," Bailey said as they headed up to the tower.

"Cast iron," Martin commented. "Remarkable." Bailey felt a flush of pride, even though Brad was the one who had spent his entire fortune on the house. It truly was a remarkable renovation. Bailey could see the value of the place increasing as the years went by. And she was excited about having guests. It shouldn't be a problem getting people to come and stay.

"In the old days they had to carry whale oil up here to light the tower. Of course, this isn't bad—just twenty-nine steps if you count both staircases. Some lighthouses have hundreds of steps they used to navigate."

"That would be something," Martin said. She hoped she wasn't boring him with too many facts. Just like her father. Maybe in the end, no matter what you did, everyone turned out like their parents. She wondered what Martin thought of that—after all, he was the expert—but now was probably not the time to talk shop.

"Knock, knock," Bailey said as they entered the small, round tower.

"Who's there?" Brad cheerfully called back. Bailey and Martin climbed into the tower. It was a tight fit with all three of them. If Brad was surprised to see her with a guest, he didn't show it. Officially they were still waiting for their license to come in.

"This is Martin Gregors," Bailey said. "Martin, this is my husband, Brad." Martin grinned and stuck his hand out. He purposefully avoided looking at the urn, which was sitting just to the right of the desk where Brad was shuffling through a pile of papers.

"Would you like to go out on deck?" Brad said. "It's a bit narrow out there, but the three of us would fit. That is, if you're not afraid of heights?"

"I'd love to go out," Martin said. Brad opened the small hatch and climbed out first. As Brad predicted, the three of them fit on the narrow deck, but barely. They held on to the railing and Bailey was still awestruck standing out, gazing at the river. It wasn't too terribly high, but it would still kill you if you jumped.

"You're incredibly lucky," Martin said. "This is a special, special place." Brad beamed and shot Bailey a satisfied look. They

climbed back into the tower. Martin finally turned his attention
to the urn.

"And who is this fine woman?" he asked in a theatrical voice.

Brad treated them to another wide grin. "Martin," he said.
"I'd like you to meet my aunt Olivia."

Martin bowed. "The pleasure is all mine," he said. Bailey
stared, open-mouthed. He'd better be working up to a plan
with this bullshit, or it looked like she was going to have to
throw him off the tower along with Olivia's ashes.

But instead of shrinking Brad, Martin Gregors spent the rest
of his weekend just being a guest. He read more than one paperback thriller. He constantly quizzed Bailey on all the options for
breakfast, and even roped her into making him eggs Benedict,
which required a special trip to Island Supplies, and since he
had no interest in rowing over there, she had to do it herself.
She was astonished how lazy he was. Somehow he paid Captain
Jack enough to deliver him dinner from the Italian restaurant in
town. He didn't even ask if they'd like to order as well. She had
to sit near him and smell meatballs and garlic bread and pretend she was perfectly happy with the stew she'd made a few
days ago. He didn't even eat it all. She watched in horror as he
threw out half a piece of garlic bread and a full meatball.

He played chess with Brad and spent the entire game pretending to talk to Aunt Olivia himself—especially whenever
Brad made a move the good doctor considered risky. "Ah, doll,
look where your nephew just moved his bishop!" Bailey couldn't
believe it. She was dying to kick him out. He didn't even take
walks. How could you live by the river and not take one freaking walk? Now, that was unhealthy.

Instead, he put on a blue shag robe and never ventured farther than the patio. On his second morning with them, he
stood on the patio, and Bailey saw him bend down and put
something in the pocket of his robe. She was dying to know
what it was. There couldn't have been anything that interesting
on the ground, could there? Was it a pebble? A bit of sea glass?

Around three o'clock he started in on the red wine he'd bought in town, and at ten P.M. he stumbled up to the attic, where he slept on a Japanese-style mat he brought himself. There, he found Bailey with her hand shoved into the pocket of his robe.

"What are you doing?" It was an excellent question. So insightful.

"Going through your pockets before I wash this robe," Bailey said. God, she was good.

"You're going to launder my robe?"

"Of course," Bailey said. "We are a full-service B-and-B."

"Excellent." Martin Gregors heaved his huge duffel bag onto the bed, zipped it open, pulled out an enormous pile of clothes, and thrust them on Bailey.

"You brought all this for one weekend?"

"I was going to ask if I could use your washer and dryer. You know how hard it is to do your laundry in Manhattan."

Yes. You just drop it off and they do it for you. Cheapskate. Bailey almost tripped going down the attic steps with a pile of his dirty clothes in her arms. All that for what? It was a penny he had in the pocket of his robe. A freaking penny. Apparently, it did bring good luck, for she was the one now doing all of his laundry. She missed the ex-con.

And to top it all off, Martin Gregors thought Brad was completely normal. Although "normal" wasn't the word he used.

"I think he's delightful," Martin Gregors said on his last day with them. "And not at all brain damaged." Bailey couldn't believe it. "He's simply grieving in his way," Martin continued. "He knows Olivia is gone. Some people visit a grave, others keep the ashes. I can't see the harm in it."

"He talks to her," Bailey said. "I hear him up there."

"Again, nothing to worry over. Now, if she starts talking back, that's when you should give me a jingle." Martin laughed heartily at his own joke. Bailey wanted to punch him.

"And what about his obsession that Olivia didn't make it into the light, that she's 'earthbound and trapped'?" She felt guilty for quoting Brad, but Martin wasn't taking this seriously. And it was serious. Something had been off with the light lately. Bailey suspected Brad was somehow altering the pulse so he could signal Olivia. She didn't know how he was doing it, but he was doing it.

"I thought the light was automated," Martin said.

"It is. But—"

"Run by the Coast Guard."

"Yes."

"Yet somehow your husband has found a way to alter it?"

"Just slightly."

"I see."

"You think I'm seeing things? I know the light better than you do." They were in the dining room, where Martin seemed to spend most of his time, as if waiting for the second Bailey was going to feed him again. He pulled out a chair for her.

"Where did you grow up?" he asked casually.

"Fall River, Massachusetts," Bailey said.

"Ah. And now you live by a river. Interesting." She didn't know how it happened. Suddenly he seemed so interested in her, and the next thing she knew, she was running off at the mouth like a leaky faucet. Spilling the beans about her obsession with Brad, her professor father, her flighty mother, the sibling rivalry she had with her sister Meg, her obsession with Brad, all of their failed businesses, her aching desire to have a baby, and to her horror, she even blurted out her fears of a ghost in the attic and her sexual attraction to Jake.

"My goodness," he said when she was finished. She hated him again. "If you would like to make an appointment—"

"Me?"

"I'd be more than happy to have you as a client. I know you can't afford me. We could work out some kind of exchange. Maybe a weekend free here every month."

"God, no!"

"Excuse me?"

"I mean. That's very—generous. It's just. This isn't about me. Brad's the crazy one."

"I don't use the term 'crazy.' Unless of course, they really are." He threw his head back and laughed. Bailey had to get him to see that Brad was the one who needed help.

"Brad is obsessed with death. He spent a half million dollars on this lighthouse!"

"A half a million. My goodness. I had no idea. I thought two, maybe two-fifty." She hated that his assessment was right on. Bailey grabbed Martin's arm.

"He thinks he's seen the afterlife. And apparently, it's so wonderful, and beautiful, and brilliant that he no longer wants to be here on earth!"

"Again, Mrs. Jordan, this is all so new. He's still grieving. He faced mortality. That can do strange things to a man. I think you're just going to have to be patient. Have you told him how worried you are?"

"I try," Bailey said. "He assures me he's better than he's ever been."

"Well, hang in there. And if you change your mind about therapy—for you—if you ever want to talk about how conflicted you feel in this marriage—"

"I do not feel conflicted."

He abruptly left the table. "You have my number," he said. She turned to watch him walk out of the room. Brad was leaning against the kitchen counter, arms folded across his chest, watching her. Oh, great. How much did he hear? Oh God, not the part about Jake, right? Brad returned to the Crow's Nest, buried himself on the computer, went to bed early, and pretended to be asleep when she slipped into bed next to him.

The next morning she made sure Martin's eggs were runny and his coffee tepid. As soon as breakfast was over, she showed him the door. She watched him walk down the pathway, duffel bag full of clothes she'd laundered herself, in hand. In the distance, Captain Jack, who was waiting to take him back to the mainland, waved. Bailey halfheartedly waved back. It was too far to know it for a fact, but she was pretty sure that Captain Jack winked at her. No doubt Martin would spend the ferry ride talking about how crazy *she* was. After all, she wasn't really his patient, so he wouldn't be bound by confidentiality. Their guests weren't supposed to talk about them behind their backs. They were supposed to talk about their guests behind their backs. It wasn't fair. And the worst bit about it was the little voice that now whispered to her every night before she fell asleep. Maybe the doctor was right. Maybe she was the one who needed therapy.

Chapter 17

Everything was as ready as it was going to be to take advantage of summer, which they predicted would be the busiest season of all. The last thing to click into place was the business license. When it finally arrived, they framed it and hung it above the fireplace next to the large mirror with ornate gold frame, one of their many purchases from the antique store in town. The owners, a nice middle-aged couple, gave them a great deal on everything. In return Brad and Bailey promised to plug the store. On their way out, Bailey invited them to come to the lighthouse sometime, maybe for dinner or a movie on the patio. To her surprise, the couple quickly dismissed the invitation. What was with everyone in town? It had to be the suicide. She prayed they wouldn't say anything to their future guests. If they didn't want to be friends with them, fine, but poisoning their guests would be crossing a line. Brad told her she was being paranoid and insisted they hadn't brushed off the invitation—which he pointed out wasn't for a specific date, it was just a general comment, one that didn't require an affirmative response. He was probably right. Now she had "paranoid" to add to her growing list of neuroses.

Bailey soon got over it. The morning Brad turned over the VACANCY sign and Bailey placed the guest book on the small table in the entryway was a landmark moment. They had worked hard, and the place looked magnificent. Bailey was surprised how proud she felt. She and Brad were beaming like new parents. They spread the word about town and among their friends, and placed ads in the local newspapers. They had a modest website created, with pictures of the renovations, and Brad started writing a keeper's log that he posted on the site. And then, they waited.

Brad often waited in the kitchen with his KISS THE COOK apron and new set of bright red nonstick pans. Bailey sat through numerous practice omelets. One day, Brad told her he had a surprise for her. It arrived by mail, which meant rowing to shore and checking their post office box. This time, however, it was an easier ride. Brad had bought a new rowboat, which he also painted yellow. It was so much easier to row. A few hours later, Bailey stood in the kitchen next to the large box she'd picked up at the post office in town. The row back hadn't been as smooth; the box nearly sank the boat.

"What say ye?" Brad bellowed like a medieval guard addressing a commoner. He gestured for her to open the box. She tore into it and pulled out a shiny, deluxe espresso machine.

"It's a little small," Brad said. "I thought it would be bigger."

"I love it," Bailey said. She threw her arms around Brad and held him. "Thank you." She knew it wasn't polite to ask, but she couldn't help it. They really had to start tightening their purse strings. "How much did it cost?"

"Half a million," Brad said.

They had dinner in town. A great little Italian restaurant with a back deck bordering the water. Bailey loved the little lights strung around the deck, and the red and white checkered tablecloths and the giant breadbasket with oversized bottles of oil and vinegar. She even liked the bug candles. They had a routine. Every morning Brad cooked breakfast and Bailey made cappuccinos. They fed the cat and walked along the river, trying to get to know the local boats, fishermen, and wildlife. Then together, they would do the dishes. After that Brad would go off to the tower and do whatever it was he was doing up there. Writing in the keeper's log, taking photographs from the deck, and, Bailey suspected, keeping up with his NDE group online.

Bailey spent part of the morning sitting on their back deck, jotting down marketing and customer service ideas. Then she'd do a quick cleaning, so that when their guests did finally start arriving, they would be dust free. Sometimes she would read a book, or take a second walk, or join Brad in the tower. Tuesdays they would go into town. They'd hit the antique store, the bookstore, the ice cream shop, and the Italian restaurant. Thursdays Bailey did the shopping at Island Supplies. There was a larger grocery store farther out, but when she bought a substantial amount, Jack would always give her a free ferry ride home. At night, after dinner, they would take another walk and relish the lights on the boats, and from town across the river, and of course, their own tower, spreading its beam as far as the eye could see.

It was exactly nine-thirty on a Tuesday morning when Angelicka Heavens walked into the keeper's house. The name sent Bailey's alarm bells ringing. The woman Brad had been speaking with online. Petite, silky blond hair, twenties, roaring blue eyes, tan, straight white teeth, big lips, big breasts. So much for three hundred pounds and blue eye shadow. Wait until she told Jesse.

"Call me Angel," she said. Her voice was loud, and too high-pitched for Bailey's liking.

Really? Not Licka? Bailey wanted to say. "Welcome," Bailey forced herself to say. "Are you traveling alone?" *Please be with a husband. Or a boyfriend. Or a pimp.*

"I'm with the group," Angel said. Bailey's ears perked up. Group was good. It meant money. But she didn't have a group reserved. Bailey glanced at her laptop on the little antique desk

where she'd set up shop in the living room. There were no
reservations on the calendar hanging on the wall behind her
either, although in protest to Aunt Olivia, Bailey had covered
each and every square of days gone by with little notes. *Walked
by the water. Fed the ducks. Vacuumed and mopped main room. Chatted with Captain Jack. Sat with Brad in the tower and tried to throw a
sheet over Olivia's urn—*

That didn't go over well. Brad told her she wasn't a bird cage
or a piece of abandoned furniture. Bailey told him she wasn't
anything—she was ashes, she needed to be tossed in the sea.
Brad retreated and didn't speak to her the rest of the day. That
was yesterday. This morning they'd exchanged pleasantries,
painful given the fact that she could see Brad was forcing himself to speak to her. She was going to have to be careful when it
came to Olivia.

"I don't see a group reserved," Bailey said.

"I'm the first one here, aren't I?" Angel said. She smiled and
rolled her eyes. "I'm never fashionably late. I hate that about
myself. I even wait on purpose. I get all ready, then force myself
to leave at least ten minutes after I actually want to leave. And
I'm still the first one." She smiled. She didn't look as upset as
she was claiming to be.

"How many are in your group?" Bailey asked. So this was it,
the NDE "committee" was actually coming. Since the cancellation a while back, Bailey assumed they hadn't yet been able to
coordinate another date. Apparently, they had. So much for
Brad keeping her in the loop.

Angel began to count on her fingers. Her nails were long
and painted bright pink. "How many are on the board? I think
seven?" Brad called it the committee, this woman was calling it
the board. And nobody even bothered to tell her they were
coming. Maybe Bailey should charge a little bit more for such
late notice. And they were going to have to share rooms.
Should she include the attic? Just last night, she'd once again
heard noises coming from up there. This time, it sounded like
someone pacing the floor. Brad, Mr. Near Death Experience,
actually told Bailey she was paranoid. He even admitted to jok-

ing about it in his keeper's log. Bailey didn't mind. If any "ghost lovers" came in, she'd have stories to tell them. Then she'd refuse to let them sleep in the attic. If the ghost-hunting guests insisted, she'd make them sign a fake waiver and charge them fifty bucks a night extra. She didn't feel bad about the plan—if her guests wanted a haunted experience, she would help create one. Nothing would get them going more than sleeping in a space so haunted that they had to sign a waiver and pay extra for it.

"You're in luck," Bailey said. "As long as you're willing to share rooms?"

"Of course," Angel said.

"But in the future you'd be safer making a reservation."

Angel tilted her head and lifted her thinly sliced eyebrows. "We have a standing reservation," she said. "We're the board."

"Right. The board."

"It's so amazing, isn't it? Owning a lighthouse?!"

From the way she talked you'd think Angel owned part of the lighthouse. "Brad and I consider ourselves very lucky," Bailey said. *At least we used to.*

"Brad," Angel said. Her smile was huge. So were her blue eyes. And her breasts. It was at that moment that Bailey started to hate Angel just a little. First Allissa, now Angel. Was she doomed to be jealous of women from A to Z, and she was only on the As?

"That's my husband," Bailey said, mostly because "Angel" looked as if she came to wed him.

"Oh, hello!" Angel said. "I didn't know our Brad was married." She laughed, a musical sound that also made her cleavage jiggle. Bailey's hatred deepened. Regardless, she managed a pained smile.

"Childhood sweethearts and still going strong." If she could call wanting to strangle him at that very moment with her bare hands "going strong."

"How are you handling this?" Angel said. Her head was cocked and she was looking at her with a mix of pity and admiration.

"This?" Bailey said. "You mean running a B-and-B?" She pulled her hand away.

"I meant Brad's transformation," Angel said. "His journey into the light."

"Transformation." The word hovered around Bailey until she envisioned her husband wrapped in a giant cocoon, struggling to become a butterfly. She imagined ripping his wings off before breaking from the fantasy.

"What group did you say you're with again?" Bailey asked although they both knew perfectly well she'd never said. "Are you all . . . transformers?"

Angel held up a finger and the grin was back. "We call ourselves Journeymen, but maybe I'll suggest a change. Transformers. Although isn't that the name of those robotic toys that morph from like a car into a raging cyborg or something like that?"

"So you met my husband online?" Bailey said. So that's what he'd been doing with himself all day. So much for watching birds and ships, and writing down weather patterns.

"Intothelight-dot-com," Angel said. "It's such a miracle to have found each other. You don't know how isolating it is to have this miraculous, life-altering experience and no one to share it with. We're so lucky to live in the age of the Internet!"

"Yes," Bailey said. "So lucky." *Get back to basics,* Brad said. *Commune with nature,* Brad said. *What is the city doing to you?* Brad said. This was his solution? Picking up young busty girls just back from the dead and inviting them to spend the night? Had she been totally duped? Was he going to run some kind of midlife crisis right under her nose?

Now she was the one hearing ghosts, and he was picking up blondes on the Internet. She'd made a huge mistake, selling the condo. For the first time in a while she let in the prickles of regret she'd been keeping at bay. She shuttered the thought and forced herself to be businesslike.

"I'll show you the choice of rooms. You'll get first crack although we'll still have to double up. How many men, how many women? Are there any couples?"

"Oh no, we're here just for us. No spouses allowed. I guess we'll let you stay!" Angel laughed and began counting on her fingers again. "Three men, four gals."

"Well, we'll figure out the room arrangements when you're all here. How would you like to pay?"

"Oh, but you see, Brad invited us," Angel said.

"Yes, he invited you to take your vacation here—"

Angel placed her annoying hand on top of Bailey's. "Why don't you speak with him. Of course we'll be happy to make a small donation, and one woman is bringing coffee and cookies." She clapped her hands and laughed.

"I will definitely have a word with my husband," Bailey said. She wasn't going to let Tinker Bell see how upset she was. Brad couldn't have invited seven people to stay for free, could he? At this rate, they'd be broke within the year, and back in Manhattan, but this time living in boxes under a bridge.

Bailey mechanically gave Angel a tour. She watered it down, given the fact the girl was trying to sneak in for free. Why should she get the full treatment? Angel wanted to stay in the attic. Should Bailey tell her about the noises? The footsteps? The squeaks and groans? The keeper and his wife? Maybe "journeymen" liked ghosts. Or maybe they'd have a séance and get the poor lost souls back into the light.

Instead, Bailey tried to make a practical appeal. "It gets hot up here," she said.

"I'll open the window."

"It's haunted."

"Excuse me?"

"There's a ghost who lives up here. I think it's the ex-keeper's wife. She went insane."

"I don't believe in ghosts," Angel said. "They're just journeymen who can't find the light."

"Be that as it may—"

"I don't mind sharing the attic with spirits. I don't mind sparseness. I don't mind the heat."

"All righty then," Bailey said. *Just don't come running into our room in the middle of the night in your little nightie.*

"Is Brad here?"

"He's in the tower."

Angel jumped up and down and clapped her hands. "Take me to your leader," she said.

"He's my husband. Not my leader."

"Well, he has been to the other side and back."

The other side, maybe, Bailey thought. But she didn't know if he was back. And she was beginning to wonder if he ever would be.

The old Brad had been a man of the world. In Europe, he was like a wind-up toy that kept going, and going and going. Country after country. He didn't mind wrinkled clothes, or new people, or foreign languages, or foreign smells, and he absolutely thrived on not knowing where they were going to be tomorrow, or even where they were going to sleep that evening. They went to Spain, Italy, France, England, Ireland, and Scotland. They said *hola,* and *buongiorno,* and *allô,* and cheerio mate, and top of the mornin' to ye. Then Brad was sick of Europe. He wanted them to go to Hong Kong, and Saigon, and Bangkok, and Vietnam, and Taiwan to "see where everything is made."

Bailey saw her life flash before her. A life filled with suitcases stuffed with smelly wrinkled clothing, and un-mailed postcards, and cheap souvenirs. She was homesick for the United States. She wanted to settle down. Even then, she wanted to have a baby. "Wouldn't it be wonderful," she said, "to go back to the States and hang out on a beach in California?" And right then and there, Brad Jordan forgot all about Asia. Their life of starting up start-ups was born. Would it have been better if they had just kept traveling? After all, here they were in one place, and Bailey was starting to feel a tiny bit trapped. Bailey dropped Angel off in the tower and pretended to busy herself in the loft below. It had been two hours and they were still up there.

And whatever they were talking about, it must have been hilarious, for Angel was doing an awful lot of giggling. From now on, Bailey realized, she was never going to be alone in her own home. She was never going to be able to walk into the kitchen in her underwear. She would always have to check herself in the mirror when leaving their room. "We're going to need to declare days off," she'd said to Brad.

"We'll have them," he answered. "It's called winter."

She heard female laughter again and looked up. Sure enough, Angel and Brad stood on the tower deck. Angel's long blond hair blew gently in the wind. Bring on winter, Bailey thought, pouring herself a glass of wine even though it was only two in the afternoon. Bring it on.

PLEASE SIGN OUR GUEST BOOK!

Brad Jordan is the greatest keeper alive! LOVING my stay.
Angelicka Heavens

Chapter 18

The rest of Brad's "committee" arrived together. They'd met at the ferry, which deepened Bailey's suspicion that Angel had arrived early just to get time alone with Brad. They gathered in the main room for bedroom assignments and introductions. There was Vera, a thirtyish woman who was indeed over three hundred pounds and wore blue eye shadow. Her smile was just as large, and Bailey felt guilty even though it had been Jesse's joke and not hers. Then there was Daniel. He was a skinny man in his fifties. He wore what looked like a long white dress—although to be fair, it was probably more of a smock. Worn brown sandals adorned his rather large feet. Bailey always hated looking at men's feet. His were especially horrifying. Granted, it was a bit hypocritical for a nail biter, but seriously, she was going to have to get him to cover those things. At his side was an enormous German shepherd. Daniel introduced the dog as "Tree."

Bailey and Brad hadn't even discussed pets. They were both animal lovers, but this was a business. Was a large, somewhat sullen-looking German shepherd a good or bad thing?

"Is he house trained?" Bailey asked.

"He's way better than me," Daniel said with a wink. And so much for there not being couples. There were two young couples in the group. Sheila and Chris, and Kimmy and Ray. Sheila and Chris held hands. Chris wore a T-shirt that read: MY WIFE WENT TO HEAVEN AND ALL I GOT WAS THIS LOUSY T-SHIRT. He grinned when he saw Bailey reading it. Kimmy and Ray didn't look so loving, or happy. Kimmy looked shell-shocked and Ray looked like the one who had just tossed the grenade.

"We told him not to bring the dog," Kimmy said. She pointed at Tree in case there was any confusion. Her voice was timid and shaking. Yet she held her chin up and clearly enunciated every word.

"And I told you," Daniel said, "not to bring the husband." He threw his head back and laughed.

"Ray doesn't like dogs," Kimmy said. Ray lifted his shirt. A large scar cut across his stomach.

"Doberman pinscher," he said.

Vera held up her index finger. "Pencil sharpener," she said. "Third grade. Stuck my finger in there on a dare. Hurt like a motherfeather."

"Is this show-and-tell?" Chris said. "Because I don't think you want to see mine." He winked and pointed to his groin.

Bailey wished Brad would come down from the tower.

"Tree doesn't bite," Daniel said.

"Tree barks," Chris said. "Get it? Like tree bark?"

"They get it, honey," Sheila said.

"Wow, tough crowd. You'd think people just back from the dead would appreciate a little humor."

"Chris," Sheila said.

"You with me, buddy?" Chris said to Ray.

"I'm not your buddy, dude," Ray said. He leaned over and whispered something to Kimmy.

"Can we go to our room now?" Kimmy said.

Daniel shook his head. "We're sleeping outside," he said. "And next year no spouses means no spouses."

"And no dogs means no dogs," Kimmy whispered.

"Did you say you're sleeping outside?" Bailey said. Daniel turned around. Strapped to his back, folded like a large hot dog, was what Bailey assumed was a tent. "Under the stars," he added. "Close to the essence." Vera heaved a bag of her own on top of the little antique table Bailey used as a desk. It barely fit. She opened it up and began pulling out locks and chains. The rest of the group moved in slightly to have a look.

"This is for the fridge," she said, holding up the largest lock. "And there are several more for the cupboards." Bailey didn't mean to laugh, but she truly thought it was some kind of a joke.

"I'm a sleep-eater," Vera said. "You must lock up all food products."

"Of course," Bailey said. "We strive to accommodate everyone."

"What if somebody else wants a little snack?" Chris said. "Are you going to make copies of the keys?"

"Absolutely not," Vera said. "Our keeper here will have the only keys."

"I'd rather you not call me your keeper," Bailey said. It made her sound as if she worked at a zoo. On the other hand, maybe that's what they should call her.

"You can get a snack before I lock everything up," Bailey told Chris. What was she saying? This was a bed-and-breakfast. Not a bed, breakfast, and snacks. "Or you can buy your own snacks in town," she added. "Island Supplies."

"You must keep them locked between midnight and six A.M. every single night," Vera said.

"Of course," Bailey said. "We once had a guest who only ate cake at night," she added. None of them seemed impressed. Bailey let each couple have their own room, Daniel headed outside to pitch his tent, and that left Angel and Vera to share a room. They were booked solid. Bailey turned the sign to No Va-cancy. *We're full up,* she thought. *And totally broke.* What with feeding them, and cleaning up after them, and locking up after them, and apparently giving them snacks, their guests were actually going to cost them money. Oh, well. Maybe it would be good publicity. Besides, they needed the practice. And really, how much could guests complain if everything was free?

PLEASE SIGN OUR GUEST BOOK!

The water pressure in the shower is low.

I can't believe we have to share a bathroom. Someone left wet towels on the floor.

The hostess didn't seem happy to see us.

I heard the fridge is going to be locked at night. Isn't that a bit extreme?

There is a draft in the attic. And where is the music coming from? Sounds like a child's music box. I hope it doesn't play all night long.

Bailey didn't even get a minute to talk to Brad alone. He spent the afternoon with the group, then they had dinner on the patio. Their first barbecue. In the few weeks that Bailey was in Manhattan, Brad purchased a deluxe grill set that was at least four feet long. Bailey wondered what it cost him. They were both keeping things from each other. Secretly purchasing items, inviting guests behind each other's backs, even changing around décor. A picture Bailey bought in the antique store, a black-and-white photograph of the main street in the 1800s, had been moved. Bailey hung it on one side of the fireplace, and behind her back Brad moved it to the other. She didn't bother mentioning it, although it struck her as a petty thing for him to do. In the past he might have done it as a joke, but Bailey had waited and waited for him to mention it, but he never did. Although given that he'd let go of the nautical theme (bar little blue glass bowls of seashells in the bathroom), she didn't even mention the switch.

And she would've been fine with him purchasing the grill too. Of course they needed a grill for their back deck. And didn't men who liked to barbecue also like children running around in the backyard and coaching Little League games? Maybe Brad just needed to ease into being a father. First came the house, then came the barbecues, and maybe the babies would follow. Luckily, the deck already came with two picnic tables that were rusty, but otherwise in decent shape. Bailey painted them evergreen. Then she bought two potted rosebushes, several tomato plants, and little pots of herbs that she positioned around the deck. They also purchased little white lights at the hardware store in town and Brad strung them along the side of the house and across the deck, attached to a tree on the other side. It was pretty. The mosquitoes, however, were not. There was always something. Everything good in life came with a little sting, or several little bites. It was just the yin and yang of the world, Bailey supposed. Fortunately, several well-placed citronella candles seemed to be doing the trick. If not, Bailey was sure she'd read about it in the guest book.

Dinner was simple. Hot dogs, hamburgers, and veggie burgers for Daniel. Bailey bought thick homemade buns in town, made potato salad, and bought coleslaw. They had bags of chips, and sodas and wines. Just adding up the cost of dinner irritated Bailey. How could he have invited them for free? Vera was eyeing the large cooler.

"You'll have to put a lock on that as well," she said.

"It's just raw meat," Bailey said.

"I once ate twelve sticks of butter," Vera said.

"I'll lock it," Bailey said. After dinner they held a group meeting on the deck. Before it began, Brad took Bailey aside.

"Ray is going to be a problem," he said. Bailey glanced over. He was wearing the same scowl from this morning. He and Kimmy sat as far from the group as possible. "Maybe you could take him for a walk," he said.

"Along with Tree?" Bailey said.

"Fantastic," Brad said. She was being sarcastic. He used to know her sarcasm as well as he knew his own.

"Ray hates dogs," she said.

"Then leave the dog," Brad said. Bailey shook her head. She was going to leave the dog but walk one of their guests. At least Tree looked content, sprawled out underneath one of the pic-

nic tables, waiting eagerly for scraps to drop. Bailey walked over
to Ray and Kimmy.

"I'm skipping the group meeting," she said. "Going for a
walk." The couple just looked at her. "Ray," she said. "Would
you like to join me?" To Bailey's surprise, he jumped up and a
look of pure relief crossed over Kimmy's face.

"Sold," he said.

They skipped rocks. They walked along the shore. Bailey didn't
try and make conversation, and Ray seemed to appreciate it. She
wondered what the group was talking about. Sharing their experiences, most likely. But hadn't they already done that online? As the sun slipped lower into the sky, ships began to
disappear and a sprinkle of stars began to show their first light.

"I hate this," Ray said. "I hate all of it."

"You mean the group thing?"

"The group thing. The nosy neighbors. The look that comes
over her face when she talks about it."

"What happened to her?" Bailey couldn't help it. Guess she
was one of the nosy ones. Ray didn't seem to mind.

"Car accident."

"Brad too," Bailey said.

"Were you driving?"

"No," Bailey said. "God, no. Thank God."

"I was driving," Ray said.

"Oh," Bailey said. "I'm so sorry. I didn't mean—"

Ray held up his hand. "It's all right. I wasn't at fault. Some
asshole out of nowhere. Turned headfirst into us."

"Oh my God."

"It was a couple of years ago. Physically, we're healed. But
she's never been the same."

Never? Bailey thought. *Years?*

"It's like she's half in this world, half in the next. It makes me
so damn angry."

"I'm surprised you wanted to come," Bailey said quietly.

"She tricked me," Ray said. "Didn't know it was a group thing
until we arrived at the ferry."

"Oh, boy," Bailey said. "I'm sorry."

"I'm getting used to it," Ray said. "She's sneaky now. Never used to be. But she sure is now." *At least she didn't buy a lighthouse behind your back.* Bailey bit back the words. She wasn't going to start complaining about her husband to total strangers. Ray took a silver flask out of his pocket and drank. He offered it to Bailey. She shook her head. He took a rolled cigarette out of his pocket. "Do you mind?"

"Is it . . . ?"

"It's the good stuff," he said. He held out his arms. "Perfect environment for it." When he offered her a drag, she didn't refuse. She hadn't been high since she and Brad were in Amsterdam. All those years ago.

They sat near the river, on a patch of grass by the rocks. It was so peaceful out here. Still, she wondered what was going on at the "meeting." When the light from the tower swept through, they could see a man walking toward them. It wasn't until he was right on them that Bailey recognized him.

"Chris," she said. "Please, join us."

"Is that what I think it is?" He pointed to the joint. Ray held it out. "Thanks." He took a seat next to them.

"What are they doing?" Bailey asked.

"Comparing stories," Chris said. "It's a little much." Bailey and Ray laughed.

"We were just talking about that," Bailey said.

"I've never doubted her story," Chris said. "I believe every word of it. But . . ." He stopped, passed the joint back to Ray. Ray handed it to Bailey.

"Feel free," Bailey said. "We've been there."

"It's all she ever talks about anymore. And it's been three years. You'd think she would have—I don't know. Moved on by now. But it's like she's gone off to war, and now she's home—but she wants to go back. I mean—I'm not even looking forward to heaven. What do I know about fluffy clouds, and harps, and floating around all day. I'd go fucking crazy."

"Is that what she saw? Harps and fluffy clouds?" Bailey was glad Ray asked it so she didn't have to.

"Not exactly. She did go through a tunnel. Then she saw her grandmother. She told her to go back. It wasn't her time. She had things to do."

"And?" Bailey said, sensing there was more to the story.

"She's going nuts trying to figure out what her purpose is. It's absolutely tormenting her. Like she's been given super powers, only she doesn't know what to do with them or who she's supposed to save."

"Survivor's guilt," Bailey said.

"Huh?" Ray said.

"They have survivor's guilt. They've been 'saved.' Given a second chance. Come back to life. Now they think they owe somebody something for that. But they don't know who to make the check out to or how much it's supposed to cost them." Intellectually, Bailey understood Brad felt guilty, but she thought it was all about Aunt Olivia. But how would she feel if she'd died and come back? She already felt guilty for living such a nice life when others were born into lives, and countries, and cultures where they had nothing. Where the goal of day-to-day life was to get through it alive.

Was it just dumb luck that some people had it easy and others had to struggle? And wouldn't that feeling of guilt be even stronger if she actually did almost die and then was given another chance? She would probably feel exactly like Brad did. She would be struggling, trying to prove her worth in the world. Maybe it was just the pot, maybe it was having others around who were going through the same thing, but in that moment, she felt she understood what Brad was really going through. It made her love him all the more, made her want to do everything she could to assure him he deserved to live.

"I'm just so grateful that she's alive," Chris said. "I don't have a right to complain about anything."

"And that's our burden to bear," Bailey said. The three fell quiet again and simply passed the joint around. *This night was meant to be,* Bailey thought. *It's going to bring me and Brad closer than ever. I'm going to be the most understanding, supportive, loving wife ever.*

"You must be especially bummed," Chris said to Bailey.

"Why's that?" Bailey said. *Because my husband bought a lighthouse behind my back?*

"You know," Chris said. "Because when the voice told him he had a choice—"

"Wait," Ray interrupted. "What voice?"

"God? I don't know. It sure wasn't his grandmother. He said he saw this incredible light—"

The most incredible love he's ever felt. . . .

Chris turned to Bailey. "Sorry, you've probably heard this a million times."

"Go on," Bailey said.

Chris directed the rest of the story to Ray. "While he was in the light, he heard this male voice. It told him he could either stay or go back—it was his choice. Only he didn't want to go back. In fact, there was only one thing he was tempted to go back for. And it wasn't even his wife. It was his shoes."

Bailey, who had just taken a big draw on the joint, began to choke. The men stared at her, waiting for her to finish, waiting for a reaction. She hoped she wasn't showing one. Finally, Chris patted her on the back, and she was able to get it somewhat under control. As under control as someone who felt absolutely sick could be. Worse, she was high, and she desperately wanted to be sober. How could she handle this news high? His shoes? He didn't want to come back for her, he came back for his shoes? Was it true? Was that what he was telling people? People as in everyone but her? *I came back for you,* he told her. *I came back for you.* Bailey let out a nervous little laugh.

"Seriously?" Ray said, still staring at Bailey. "Are you serious?"

"I feel for you," Chris said to Bailey. "It would have killed me if my wife had said something like that."

"That's beyond painful, man," Ray agreed. "His fucking shoes?" He looked at Bailey again. "Is he Arab?" He was waiting for Bailey to say something. She couldn't. She'd lost the ability to speak. He turned to Chris. "Don't Arabs worship shoes or something?"

"It's the opposite," Chris said. "Shoes are an insult. If you throw them at somebody."

Bailey looked at the ground. If she threw something now it would have to be a lot heavier than a shoe. Maybe if she looked at the ground hard enough, they would just go away. Maybe she would go away. She would float off to another world and feel love like she'd never felt before, and not care about anyone or anything on earth. And if she did care about anything, if she did want to come back, she only knew one thing for sure. It wouldn't be for a pair of shoes.

A sharp pain in her heart. The telltale sign of unstoppable tears. She held herself in. She would not cry in front of her guests. In the future—note to self—she wouldn't take them for walks, and she probably shouldn't smoke pot with them either. But it was too late. What was done was done. She couldn't change anything. Nothing she did to Chris could take back the story that came out of his mouth. She could rip his stupid T-shirt off and shove it down his throat and it still wouldn't change things.

She jabbed at the ground. The joint was already out, crushed. She reached for it and tried to unfold it into something she could light. Her hands shook. She dropped it the first three times she tried to pick it up. She felt as if her insides were going to fall out. She asked Ray for a lighter. But he was too entranced in the story.

"His shoes?" Ray said again. Were they really still talking about this? Wasn't it time to stop? Bailey really wanted them to stop. If only she could get her tongue to work. It was the pot, it was turning their conversation into the movie *Groundhog Day*.

"Yeah," Chris said. "I guess he had just bought new shoes, and it was the only thing he was tempted to go back for. But nothing else mattered anymore."

"Ouch," Ray said.

"But that's what the group is for, right? To say those horrific things they've been keeping bottled up inside them. I mean, obviously, the two of you have worked through that, right?" Chris said. He glanced at Bailey.

"Ray?" she said. "Lighter?"

"I don't think there's anything left," he said.

"I was a Girl Scout," Bailey said. "I'm going to try." Ray handed her the lighter. She burned her fingertips and her lungs when she tried to dredge something out of the joint. It wasn't the story he'd told her. Sitting in their condo, he'd held her hands, he'd looked into her eyes, and he'd told her, "I remembered you. I came back for you."

And now, here he was, in his lighthouse, sitting less than twenty feet away telling strangers a totally different story. And she didn't have to ask which story was the truth. It explained a lot. Brad making huge decisions behind her back. Moving away, telling her she could commute, avoiding the topic of having kids. Oh my God. That was the reason he'd asked Bailey to take Ray for a walk. It wasn't to get him away from the group, it was to get *her* away from the group. Her husband's guilt. His moodiness. His preoccupation with death. It wasn't about Olivia. It was about her. All they'd been through, all she'd done for him, or tried to do for him—meant nothing in the end. Brad died, went to another world, and felt love like he had never felt before. In the end, she hadn't even meant as much to him as a new pair of shoes.

Chapter 19

There was somebody to blame, there had to be. His mother. Hadn't Martin Gregors hinted as much? Given what horrible maternal instincts the woman had, it was no wonder Brad couldn't form intimate attachments with anything but shoes. If she could get Elizabeth to the lighthouse and entice Martin to come back, maybe he could do a little instant family therapy. Best-case scenario, Elizabeth was sober and ready to fall on the sword for what a horrible mother she'd been. Mother and son would make up, Elizabeth would spend the rest of her life making her son feel like he finally had a mother, and presto chango, Brad would be ready to become a father.

Worst-case scenario, maybe Martin could help Brad let go of his mother once and for all, and in doing so, he'd be able to fully commit to Bailey and their future bambinos. Time was running out. As soon as the morning was over, Bailey would sit down and write a letter to Elizabeth Jordan. She would get her to come to the lighthouse, whatever it took. But first she had breakfast to contend with.

Never again would Bailey believe in the phrase "The more

the merrier." Everyone was up early, but nobody was getting along. Kimmy and Ray wanted to leave and demanded that Bailey get in touch with Captain Jack. Bailey tried to explain that breakfast was included with their stay, but upon remembering nobody here was paying for their stay anyway, it didn't much matter. Except for the fact that it was just barely seven A.M. and Captain Jack had made it clear on numerous occasions that unless it was an emergency (meaning willing to fork over big money), he wasn't going to make any runs before ten A.M. When Kimmy and Ray heard that, breakfast was suddenly an enticing option.

Bailey went looking for Brad, but he was already out of bed and hiding God knows where. She hadn't been able to sleep a wink last night. Brad was right beside her, snoring softly in their bed, while a thousand accusations swam around in her head. But she couldn't bring herself to confront Brad about the story he'd told the group. Not yet. She was way too hurt—an ache in her heart rose every time she replayed the conversation in her head, and she was liable to say things she could never take back, or worse, threaten a breakup. And in his current state of mind and support from his fellow zombies, there was more than a chance Brad would be happy to see her go.

Zombies. Did she really just call them that? Since when had she become so spiteful? She hated it, she hated all this "near death" stuff. She wanted to be as far away from it as possible. Yet since their arrival, her husband had definitely perked up. There was a bounce in his step, a permanent smile on his face. Would the horrors never end?

Bailey headed for the kitchen. It's where her husband should have been standing in his KISS THE COOK apron, getting ready to make breakfast for their guests. The old Bailey would have fantasized about what he was wearing under the apron and dared to get a quickie in before anyone caught them. Maybe the new Bailey would feel the same way. Maybe she would open the door and he'd be waiting for her, naked except for the apron. Instead, Bailey opened the door to a disaster.

Cupboards were flung wide open. The refrigerator door was open-mouthed and near empty, for almost every single item from within it was out on the counters, and on the table, and on top of the door to the unhinged stove. An empty bag that used to house white fluffy bread was discarded on the floor, along with a carton of eggs stacked with cracked and empty shells with the exception of a single egg, broken and dripping a gooey yellow tear, and next to them an open jar of mayonnaise and a decimated jar of pickles.

If only it stopped there. A bag of flour had been ripped open and white powder coated the kitchen as if it had snowed indoors. Bailey just stood, stunned. *Raccoons,* she thought. *We have raccoons.* But she didn't see any paw prints in the flour. She glanced at the tide clock that hung above the door. The hand was hovering over High Tide, and slightly shaking, as if traumatized by the kitchen intruder.

And that's when she noticed the sink. Something metal and coiled was resting in its bottom. The locks and chains. She'd forgotten all about them. But there they were, all tossed in the sink in one big rusty heap. Panic took hold of Bailey. She had locked everything up last night, just as she promised. The key was actually on a side table by their bed. She'd forgotten the key this morning, but she'd definitely locked them last night. "Brad?" Bailey yelled at the top of her lungs. "Brad!!"

Bailey stomped over to the fridge and shut the door. She peered into the oven and pulled out a tray of cookies. They weren't even baked. Raw cookie dough sitting on the pan, half of them gone. Bailey shut the oven door and turned it on. Might as well bake the rest. What in the world had this woman done? Dry flour, raw cookie dough—what else? A saucepan on the stove with one or two kernels of corn left in it. The empty can of corn lay on its side on the counter. She'd eaten half a loaf of bread, gnawed on a huge chunk of a frozen pizza, and alas, it appeared she had indeed eaten a stick of butter. *"Brad,"* Bailey yelled again. She didn't know where Vera was, but she couldn't be feeling well. The kitchen door flew open, but it wasn't Brad, it was Angel. She was wearing the tiniest jogging shorts and bra Bailey had ever seen and she didn't have a single imperfection on her body.

"Oh my God," she said, taking in the room. "Are you having a hard time of it?"

"What?" Bailey said.

"Not that I'm much of a cook either," Angel said. "I mostly eat raw."

"I'm sure you do."

"What," Angel's eyes darted around the destroyed kitchen, "are you trying to make?"

"This isn't my mess," Bailey said. "I believe Vera was sleep-eating."

"Oh my God," Angel said again. "I thought you were supposed to lock everything up." Bailey went to the sink and hoisted up one of the lock and chains. "She either has another key or she picked the locks," Bailey said.

"I'm going for a jog," Angel said. "Then I'm doing calisthenics. Then I'm going to meditate and watch the sunrise. But after that, and my shower, I'm totally available to help you clean up."

"Oh, I'm not cleaning up," Bailey said. *"Brad!"* Bailey turned to Angel and gave a fake smile. "Have a good run," she said.

"I'm not married yet," Angel said. "But can I make an observation?"

"No," Bailey said before she could censor herself.

Angel threw her head back and laughed. "I love your sarcasm," she said, placing her hand on her heart. "But do men really like to be screamed at?"

"Oh, I have a whole repertoire of things that Brad would like even less," Bailey said. Then, just to spite Angel, Bailey took a deep breath and yelled for Brad again, the loudest one of them all. Would she have done it if she thought guests were still sleeping? Who knows. But she'd already run into Kimmy and Ray begging to go home, Daniel was out in his tent, and Sheila and Chris were standing just outside the window by the river holding hands. Bailey didn't know where Vera was, but from the looks of the kitchen, she was either in some kind of food coma or in such pain, a little yelling certainly wasn't going to do much more damage. Angel didn't leave. Bailey turned her back to her and started making coffee. She would make herself a cup of coffee (maybe with a little shot of the strongest something she could find), she would go for a walk herself, and only then would she come back and tackle the kitchen. Hopefully, by then she would be able to locate her MIA husband.

"I would offer you a cup of coffee," Bailey said. "But I don't want to." Angel laughed again, but this time it was muted and off-key. "Run," Bailey said. "Run, run, run." This time, Angel left.

Coffee with shot of Baileys in hand, Bailey stepped outside, took a deep breath, and tried to calm her mind. It was nice and cool. The sun was slow to sizzle around here, and Bailey liked it that way. The birds were out full force, chirping and flitting about. She didn't know one bird from another, but Brad did. She'd read a few of his keeper's blog entries. He was very specific. *Saw an osprey this morning singing her heart out.* Since when did he know species of birds? Three sailboats dotted the river, making their lazy way down the Hudson. As Bailey neared Sheila and Chris, she could see Daniel and Tree approaching from the other direction.

Sheila held out her hand. She was holding a rock. It didn't look like much to Bailey, just a black rock, but Sheila looked rather excited about it.

"Isn't it a miracle?" she said. Bailey looked in Sheila's eyes. Large, hazel, and unblinking. Behind her, Chris gave Bailey a knowing look. But when Sheila whipped around to see his reaction, he too was looking at the black stone like it was a miracle. "It's so smooth," Sheila said. "So wet and perfect. I feel connected to it. I truly feel at one with it." Just then, Daniel passed. He swiped the rock out of her hand and without a second glance pitched it far into the river without breaking stride.

"Let go!" he shouted. "It's gone now!" Tree ran past, drool dripping from his mouth. He let out a loud, excited bark that made Bailey jump and jostle her coffee. The hot liquid spilled onto her wrist. Bailey took another sip of the spiked stuff anyway, stopping short of licking her wrist, and kept walking. Jake soon passed her from the other direction. Even though his work as a contractor had finished, he had asked Bailey if he could stay the summer. Brad wasn't thrilled with the idea, but after all, he was staying in his tent, not taking up one of their rooms. Bailey hated to admit it, but she liked having him around. He was a very pleasant distraction. Besides, with the exception of the fact that the man seemed to like to dig holes, he and his crew had done a good job. Sure, they took longer than she would have liked and they cost an arm and a leg, but what contractors didn't?

They stopped to chat, and soon Bailey felt someone else watching them. She turned around to find Daniel staring at them openly. Did she laugh a little too loud at Jake's jokes maybe? Or did her flushed cheeks give her away? After a few minutes, Jake left to go kayaking, but Daniel lingered, watching Bailey.

"He's a little young for you, isn't he?" Daniel said.

"Yes," Bailey said, looking him up and down. He was wearing the same white dress and sandals from yesterday. "And that outfit is a little too Jesus for you."

Brad was in the kitchen, fully dressed and no apron in sight, when Bailey walked in a half an hour later. He was standing, dumbfounded, staring at the mess as she had done an hour earlier. When he turned to her, she answered before he even asked any questions.

"I did lock everything up." She went to the sink and held up the locks and chains. "She either stole the key from the table next to our bed or she picked the locks."

"Unbelievable," Brad said. "Now we don't have any eggs."

"We should ask Vera to replace them."

"It's not her fault," Brad said. "She has a disorder."

"And I feel bad for her. But it's not our fault either, and we're trying to run a business."

"It's just a dozen eggs."

"And bacon, and half a bag of flour—"

Brad put one hand to his head and held the other up to stop her. "I can't," he said. "I'll get sick." Bailey stepped closer and looked at Brad. His eyes were slightly red; his hair was sticking straight up.

"You smoked last night too, didn't you?"

"It was just a little—what do you mean, 'too'?"

"I smoked with Ray and Chris."

"You did?"

"Yep. Who did you smoke with?"

"Vera passed a joint around to the group."

"I'm no prude—but shouldn't a known sleep-eater not get herself all toked up and hungry before bed?"

"I can't control our guests," Brad said. "And neither can you." He grabbed a broom out of the closet and began sweeping the flour from the floor.

"Did I say I could?" Bailey said. Brad looked at her as if he didn't know what she was talking about. "Control our guests?" Bailey added.

"I just meant it might not be smart to smoke pot with our guests," Brad said.

"Like you did?"

"That was different," Brad said.

"Why? Because you've all been to heaven and back and that gives you some kind of ganja pass?" She had better be careful. She was never very good at hiding her sarcasm. One slip and she'd be calling them zombies.

"No, because I was a guy with a room full of women. You were a woman alone with two strange guys."

"Are you holding me to a different standard with our guests than yourself?"

"Hey, guys." Bailey turned, startled. Angel stood in the doorway, glowing and sweaty. She was all smiles.

"When's breakfast?"

"There's been a delay," Brad said, gesturing around him.

"Great," Angel said. "Then I have time for a long shower." She paused and held eyes with Brad, as if hoping he was imagining her in the shower. Which he probably was.

"Don't use too much water," Bailey said. "We do have other guests." Bailey walked over to the doorway until Angel stepped back. Then she shut the door to the kitchen so that once again she and Brad were alone.

"Yoo hoo!" Vera barged through the door. She paraded through the mess as if she didn't even see it and sat at the kitchen table. "Cream, two sugars," she said. Bailey opened her mouth, but a few seconds later she felt Brad's hand around her waist, gently pulling her behind him.

"No problem," Brad said. "I'm making a fresh pot as we speak."

"Great!" Vera said.

"How do you feel?" Brad said.

"What?"

"I mean—how did you sleep?"

"Deeply," Vera said. Bailey tried to move past Brad. He pulled her in and whispered in her ear.

"Don't."

"But she—"

"Doesn't remember," Brad finished for her. "She's a guest. Remember?"

"Fine," Bailey said. "Captain Jack should be pulling in any minute. I'll see if he can take me to Island Supplies for bacon and eggs, and bread, and flour." Brad leaned in and kissed her mid-list.

"Thank you," he said. "I don't know what I'd do without you." Bailey grabbed her purse and headed for the door.

"Hey," she said. "When we get a minute alone, I want to hear all about your group meeting." *Word for word,* she added silently. *Word for freaking word.*

It was their first full house for breakfast. In addition to the group, they were joined by Jake. Bailey slightly hated to admit it, but she loved taking in Brad noting how good-looking Jake was, even with his shirt on. "Mr. *GQ*," Brad whispered to Bailey under his breath. It almost made up for Angel, who was wearing a low-cut top that was also tied in a knot just above her belly

button, and cut-off jean shorts. Bailey had never been able to
pull off shorts that tiny, not even when she was young. Brad had
not only done a great job cleaning up the kitchen, but his
scrambled eggs with peppers and onions and crispy bacon was
fabulous. Bailey made chocolate-chip pancakes that were also a
big hit. It was so easy to make people happy. Just make sure
they're well fed. Delicious, comforting foods and good company. It would have been perfect, except for one thing. Bailey
couldn't wait for them to be gone. Would she feel differently if
they were paying? She didn't think so. She wanted time alone
with Brad. She had to confront him about his changing near-
death story. Who had he lied to? Her or the group? Maybe he
just didn't want the group to know that he loved his wife so
much that he was willing to give up heaven for her.

The biggest problem with that theory was that she just didn't
believe it. She was the one he had lied to, she could feel it. So
what did that mean? Could she really blame him for something
he felt or didn't feel when he was dead? Wasn't it a little like
being angry with someone for having a sexy dream about someone else?

Speaking of sexy dreams, if Jake stayed any longer she was
going to end up having a few hundred of her own. Bailey
looked around the table with a fake smile on her face. Nobody
was talking. Which was totally fine. Wasn't it? Certainly it meant
they were comfortable and relaxed. Just quietly stuffing their
faces. God, it was strange to watch strangers chew. Bailey wasn't
sure she liked it. She should stop watching them. Were they
watching her chew? She didn't like that thought either. Now
she was happy everyone was quiet. Imagine, everyone talking
and chewing at the same time like a bunch of animals. Maybe
she should institute some kind of mandatory no-talking rule.
Besides, when they did start talking, she was probably going to
get the same questions over and over again. *What's it like to live
in a lighthouse? How does a lighthouse work? How much did you say
you paid for this candle in the wind?*

She wondered if it was fine with Brad that nobody was conversing. Did he have some fantasy of stimulating breakfast con-

versation every morning? Intelligent and inquisitive guests debating art and politics over pancakes?

"I can't believe you're able to eat," Angel said. She was looking at Vera. Vera's fork froze by her mouth.

"What do you mean?" Vera asked.

"Angel," Sheila said like a mother warning a child.

"What?" Angel said. "I don't mean because of her weight"—Vera audibly gasped. Angel continued as if she didn't hear her—"but because she totally ate her way through the entire kitchen in her sleep!"

Stricken, Vera's head swiveled around the table. One by one, heads ducked into their plates. Angel was the only one who continued to stare, unabashed, at Vera. "I did not," Vera said slowly. "Everything was locked. All the food was locked," she repeated when nobody said anything.

"Yeah," Angel said. "Even that didn't stop you." Angel laughed and looked around the table for support. "Did I say something wrong?" Angel said. "I didn't mean to—I just think if you're going to get up in the middle of the night, pick seven locks, and eat half a bag of flour, raw bacon, eggs, and raw soup from the can, then at least you'd better have a sense of humor about it, you know?"

Vera's fork dropped to her plate with a clatter.

"There's no such thing as raw soup," Ray said. "It's just soup. Either hot soup or cold soup. Still soup."

"Okay, whatever," Angel said. "Half a bag of flour, raw eggs—I can say raw eggs, right? And cold soup from the can. Happy now?" Ray glared at Angel and then looked at Kimmy as if he wanted her to do something about it. Kimmy's eyes filled with tears and she stuck her face as close to her plate as she could.

"I ate all that?" Vera whispered. She stood and grabbed her stomach.

"We don't know for sure," Bailey said. "Maybe you just—opened things up."

"And ate them," Angel said. "Opened things up and ate them."

"Maybe it was someone else," Sheila said. She gave her husband a look. He didn't notice it, just happily continued to shovel food into his mouth. He was humming too, something Bailey found disconcerting. It was hard to concentrate on what everyone was saying and try and figure out what tune was playing on his jukebox-for-one. She was pretty sure it was "You Can Leave Your Hat On."

"Someone else?" Vera shrieked. "Like who?" She continued to swivel her head. "Who?"

"You sound like an owl," Daniel said. "Hoo, hoo. Hoo, hoo!"

Vera pointed her fork at Daniel's face. "Could have been that dog of yours."

"Could've been," Daniel said happily. "He'll eat anything."

"Can he pick locks too?" Angel said. Daniel stopped and dramatically looked to the ceiling with his fork hovering in the air while he thought about it.

"No," Daniel said in a thunderous voice. He waved his fork like an orchestra conductor. "He cannot pick locks. No thumbs." He looked at Vera as if to say, "Back to you."

"I can't pick locks either," Vera said. "At least I don't think I can."

"I've heard about sleepwalkers having all sorts of secret talents," Sheila said. From the tone of her voice, she was very excited to share this news. She was practically bouncing in her seat. "Things they can do when they're doing their zombie thing that they can't do when they're awake."

"Zombie?" Vera said. "Did you just call me a zombie?" Bailey couldn't believe it either. Thank God she wasn't the one who said it.

"Maybe," Sheila continued, "we should put a paint set and paper by your bed tonight. You could be like one of those monkeys who can paint. You never know."

"She'd probably eat them," Ray said.

"Ray," Kimmy whispered. "Don't."

"Are you calling me a monkey now?" Vera shouted. "Which is it, Sheila? Am I a monkey or a zombie?"

"A *talented* zombie," Sheila said. "My God. Why does everyone blow past my compliments and go straight for the negative?"

Bailey glanced at Kimmy. She was practically vibrating in her seat. She was pushing food around but she hadn't taken a bite. "Is everything okay?" Bailey asked her. Kimmy looked up, eyes brimming with tears.

"I don't eat eggs. Or bacon. Or sugar. Or flour."

"Bet Vera wishes she could say the same thing," Chris said. Sheila elbowed him. He went back to eating and humming.

"Oh," Bailey said. "Would you like oatmeal and fruit?"

"We don't have oatmeal and fruit," Brad said.

"I'm just trying to establish a baseline," Bailey said.

"I'd love oatmeal and fruit," Kimmy said.

"Great," Bailey said. "Next time I'll make sure to have it."

Vera pushed away from the table, still clutching her stomach. "I feel sick," she said. When nobody responded, Vera said it again at ten times the volume. "I feel sick!"

"You were fine a minute ago," Sheila said. "Sit down. It's psychosomatic."

"Or just psycho," Angel said.

Vera cried out, "I have a disease. How dare you make fun of me!"

Angel flinched. All of her, that is, except her boobs, which remained in exactly the same perky spot. "It's a joke! My God, can't you people take a joke? In Egyptian times they would have hidden all the food in a tomb." She leaned forward and whispered, "You'd probably get lost and die looking for it. Even if you could pick locks."

"I don't pick locks," Vera cried. "I've never picked a lock in my life. Who did it? Who opened the locks?" Heads began swiveling around the table, taking each other in. Vera pointed to Chris. "Did you come in for a midnight snack?"

"How would we get the key?" Chris said. "We don't pick locks either."

"Personally, I suspect Tree," Daniel said cheerfully. He snuck the dog a scrap and patted his head. "He's my furry, lock-picking spy."

Vera looked at Bailey. "I trusted you," she said. "I trusted you with the key."

"My wife is innocent," Brad said. He put his arm around Bailey and gave her a nervous pat. Bailey looked at him. He gave her one of his fake smiles.

"Oh my God," Bailey said. "You think I just left the key lying around, don't you?"

"It's no big deal," Brad said. "Sometimes you're a little . . . you know."

"No, I don't know. Why don't you tell me?"

"Bailey, relax. Creative. You're a creative soul and sometimes, you know, you're a little forgetful."

"Oh, really? Well, at least I don't forget the important things."

"Right," Brad said. He gave Bailey a quick peck on the cheek. "You are wonderful," he added nervously.

"Like, say—if I died and went into the light." The table immediately fell silent. Even Chris stopped humming. Stricken, Brad looked at Bailey. "I certainly wouldn't forget who I was. Whom I loved. I certainly wouldn't forget *you*."

"He didn't forget you," Ray said. "He just cared about his shoes more."

"You told her?" Brad said. He pushed himself away from the table and stood as if he were in a bar about to start a brawl.

"That's what you're going to take from this," Bailey said. "I find out I'm worthless and you want to fight him for telling me?"

Brad turned to Bailey. He reached out as if to touch her, but then thought better of it. "Worthless?" he whispered. "How could you think that?"

"You said," Bailey said. Her voice was starting to waver. She was going to cry. "You came back for me."

"Bailey," Brad said. "Bailey, Bailey, Bailey."

"Which was it?" Bailey demanded. "Me or the shoes?" Brad didn't answer, but he did sit back down beside her.

"This is like a fucked-up version of Cinderella," Ray said.

"I think I need to see a doctor," Vera said. "What if I swallowed something poisonous?"

"You'd be dead by now," Daniel said.

"If I were you, I would sue," Chris said.

"Excuse me?" Bailey said.

"She warned you about her condition. She trusted you with the key," Chris said matter-of-factly.

"Exactly," Vera said. She pointed at Chris. "What he said."

"I did exactly what you asked," Bailey said. "I locked everything. The key is probably still right by my bed where I left it." She felt Brad's hand land on top of hers under the table. He gave it a little squeeze. He was trying to tell her to calm down. He was worried she was going to start throwing things. What if she just threw the salt and pepper shakers? That wouldn't be so bad, would it?

"I think I'm sweating," Vera said. "I'm sweating but also slightly chilled. Is it just me?"

"Oh, just go outside and walk it off," Daniel said.

"If you do die," Sheila said, "we'll totally try to contact you."

"A walk is an excellent idea," Brad said. "Bailey, would you like to take a walk with me?"

"No," Bailey said. "But make sure you take your shoes." Brad hung his head. Bailey felt a rush of guilt and a desire to comfort him. She reminded herself that it was his blatant lies that got them here. "Maybe Vera would like to go for a walk," Bailey said. "Maybe all of you would like to go for a walk." *Before I tip this entire table upside down or launch every object on it at your heads.* Vera looked ready to veer into another monologue about her impending death.

"Some joint we own here," Angel said.

Brad abruptly stood. "Everyone," Brad said. "Please join me in a walk. Please."

"We?" Bailey said. "Some joint *we* own here?"

"Angel's right," Sheila said. "All this negativity won't be good for business."

"Thanks for the tip," Bailey said.

"I have to agree too," Kimmy whispered. "We don't want to make our guests feel uncomfortable."

"We?" Bailey said. "Why are all of you saying 'we'?"

"Seriously, people," Brad said. "I need everyone on the committee outside right now."

"She has a point," Daniel said. "We're in this for the long haul. We need to put the lighthouse ahead of our differences."

Bailey felt a ripple of dread wash over her. Brad looked as if he had just been shot.

"Bailey," Brad said. "There's uh—something—"

Bailey screeched back from the table and stood. "We?" Bailey said again.

"Oh my God," Kimmy said. "She doesn't know."

"Brad?" Bailey said. She was afraid to say more.

"Oh, honey," Vera said. "It's okay. We're your family now. One big happy family." She reached over as if to grab Bailey and crush her in a bear hug. After seeing the look on Bailey's face, she shrank back. Bailey opened and closed, and opened and closed her mouth like a baby bird. There were just no words. She was even too numb to throw anything.

"Bailey," Brad said. "I'd like you to meet the board."

"The board," Bailey repeated. It came out as an eerie whisper.

"Olivia's Lighthouse Conservation Society," Kimmy said in the loudest voice she'd used so far.

"We all own equal shares in the lighthouse," Daniel said. "Except for Tree. He's like you. The keeper's companion."

"No," Bailey said. "Uh-uh. No."

"Daniel was joking," Brad said.

"Oh, thank God," Bailey said. They got her good. She thought she was going to faint there for a minute.

"You're not just a companion. You're a partner too," Brad explained.

"Yes," Angel said. "And we're your partners in crime!"

"Um. It's not uh, legal, for individuals to run a lighthouse," Brad said. He laughed nervously. "It has to be owned and run by a nonprofit conservancy group."

"Otherwise the light has to be decommissioned," Daniel said.

"And I couldn't let that happen," Brad said. "I had to save her—I mean him—you know?"

"No," Bailey said. "I see your mouth moving. But I have no idea what you're saying." Maybe she had died too. Maybe they were all dead. Maybe it was like that Nicole Kidman movie where they were all dead only they didn't know it. It was comforting. If she was already dead, she wouldn't have to feel guilty about killing them all with her bare hands.

"Captain Jack was going to buy this place and shut down the light!" Brad was out of his seat again and talking fast, as if his mouth could outrun the trouble he was in.

"Are you saying what I think you're saying?" Bailey said.

"Don't worry," Brad said. "You and I are officially the keepers. We can never be fired."

"Fired," Bailey said. She was afraid if she stopped repeating everything he said, she would self-destruct.

"We are the keepers of this lighthouse," Brad said. "You and I."

"And we're the board," Angel said. "Who owns it." Everyone glared at Angel. She shrugged. "Like a Band-Aid," she said. "Gotta rip it off."

"It's a technicality," Brad said.

"A technicality," Bailey said.

"Exactly," Brad said.

"Exactly what?" Bailey said.

"We don't technically own the lighthouse," Brad said. "I mean, we own part of it. We share in the guardianship with the board. The board owns it. We, the board, are a nonprofit corporation whose mission is to preserve and run this lighthouse." Bailey nodded. Bailey sat back down. Bailey resumed eating. Bailey did not dare look at anyone. "Bailey?" Brad said.

"Let's go for a walk, Brad," someone said.

"Don't forget your shoes," Bailey said once again. Brad stood a few minutes longer, staring at her. Then someone, Bailey didn't know or care who, gently took Brad's arm and led him out. One by one everyone left the table until Bailey was sitting alone with Jake. Not that she cared. She was too stunned to even fantasize. For a few minutes they ate in silence. Then Jake pushed his plate away and patted his stomach with a big smile.

"So," he said. "What's it like living in a lighthouse? Is it as much fun as you thought it would be?"

Chapter 20

Keeper's Log
Brad Jordan
July

We have a dive-bombing bird patrolling the patio.
She's an aggressive blackbird, protecting her nest,
which I'm assuming is in the large oak near the patio,
but it's so tall and thick with leaves that I've yet to be
able to spot it. Guests are getting pretty freaked out.
She will actually brush your shoulder or the back of
your head with her body. She will only make contact
when your back is turned, so in that way she's a bit of
a coward. Experts call it "mobbing." Still, it's unnerv-
ing. Once she headed straight for my eyes, and I stood
stock-still. I couldn't believe she was getting more aggressive, attacking face-to-face. I still didn't move. At
the last minute, she swerved, while sending out a
warning cry. My heart was pounding in my chest—it
was a bit like being in a 3-D movie, seeing her come at

me like that. She's incredibly fast. That's the maternal instinct for you. It's made it near impossible to have dinner or movie nights on the patio. We will just have to wait until the babies are born and have flown far, far away.

I'm worried sick about Bailey. Since learning the truth about the lighthouse, she's taken to standing by the kitchen window, waiting for the bird to strike an unsuspecting guest, and recording it all on her iPhone. Then she posts it to the B&B's Facebook page (Did I mention we have a Facebook page?!) with comments like, "Hilarious!" and "Check this out!"

Angel got the worst of it. The bird smacked into her head three times in a row. I suspect it has something to do with the shampoo she uses. When she stands close to me I always get a hint of strawberries. Angel said Bailey asked her to go out and wipe down the picnic tables. We had a good rain last night, and nobody had been near them since, so they certainly didn't need wiping down. Angel screamed every time the bird slammed into her head, and Bailey uploaded the video to YouTube. I haven't said anything to her. Lately it seems the only thing that makes her smile is recording the bird mobbing people. I'd sacrifice myself, stand there all day letting the thing tear me apart for her, but any time she sees me she puts the iPhone down and turns away. I've been sleeping on the couch in the main room. It's not too bad except one of our guests likes to play a music box all night long. My guess is it's Kimmy. I haven't brought it up because I guess it soothes her to sleep.

I wish Bailey knew how sorry I was. I don't know how to explain the feeling that came over me during the auction. I know it sounds ridiculous, to speak of a

higher power. But at the time, I had to do it. I had to
save this lighthouse. I felt as if someone's life de-
pended on it, maybe not my own, but—I don't know. I
felt as if the lighthouse deserved a voice. And I was
that voice. That's no excuse. I should have told Bailey
the truth from the beginning. I'm no stranger to that
concept, though, am I? Now would be the time to tell
her every secret I've ever kept, and yet here I sit,
silent, again. She's still here. By some miracle, she's
still here. I'd give my life for her. I just wish she knew
that whether I deserve it or not, I thank every star in
the sky for her existence. I'd give anything to take
away her pain, and I've never loved her more than I
do right now.

In addition to recording unsuspecting members of the
board getting whacked by their dive-bombing blackbird, Bailey
was also doing a lot of reading. Fantasy books mostly, and the
occasional biography of violent savages. Captain John Smith
was a whaling pirate. He fell in love with Pocahontas. He be-
headed three men. Now, there's a man who would have ravaged Bailey on the deck and willingly planted his seed in her.
Not that she wanted Brad's seed at the moment. She didn't
know what she wanted. Aunt Faye advised Bailey to get a lawyer.
For once, Brad's charm had failed him. To Faye, lying about
real estate was a crime for which there was no parole. Faye
urged her to come back to New York, offered Bailey her old job
back. Bailey hadn't said yes, but she hadn't said no. She just
didn't know. Jesse had been a bit more diplomatic. She suggested that maybe Bailey had been correct after all, maybe
Brad had suffered some kind of head trauma. She urged Bailey
to consider taking him in for tests before she made any "dras-
tic" decisions.

Bailey didn't tell her mother or her sister. Meg was still having some kind of problem with Thomas, but whenever Bailey
pressed her for details she changed the subject. If her sister
wasn't going to open up to her, then Bailey wasn't going to

open up either. And telling her mother would mean that Brad would be in for a lifetime of resentment from Ellen Danvers. Nobody lied to her little girl. Her father would've probably been a bit more neutral, argued both sides like a litigator, then pronounced a verdict in favor of Bailey. The thought made her feel good, but she still didn't tell them. She didn't need more people in her head adding to the confusion. She even called Martin Gregors. He was surprisingly sympathetic toward her.

"It sounds as if he's really betrayed you," he said. At first, Bailey was thrilled to hear he was on her side.

"Exactly," Bailey said. "I'm totally shocked."

"Do you have a lawyer?"

"What?"

"It just doesn't sound legal. He would have needed your approval to buy the lighthouse, no?"

"Not initially. He had cash from Olivia. But when I sold the condo, we sank the profits back into this place." Bailey suddenly felt guilty for building this "case" against Brad.

"Definitely grounds for a lawsuit," Gregors said.

"I don't want to sue my husband, Dr. Gregors." What she didn't tell him was that there was no need to sue. Brad had already fallen on the sword, offered Bailey anything she wanted. He offered to try and convince the board to dissolve the conservancy. He said they could decommission the light and just run it as a private B&B. He offered to try and sell it and give her the money. He even offered to have himself declared temporarily insane to see if they could somehow get out of the contract. He was scrambling, not knowing if he could actually make good on any of his promises, but he was sincere in at least making the attempts. "I just want . . ." Bailey stopped talking. What did she want?

"What do you want?" he echoed.

"I don't know."

"Would you like to come to my office in Manhattan and talk about it?"

"I don't know."

"Look. You've had a shock. It's normal to be indecisive."

"I guess."

"If you decide you'd like to start seeing me, my door is always open." Bailey nodded even though he couldn't see her and hung up without saying good-bye, hoping it would make her seem a little bit more decisive.

They were having another board meeting on the patio. It was a tricky place to eavesdrop without being seen. Of course she was "invited" to the meeting, she was after all on the board. But she didn't want to attend any of their meetings. Besides, Bailey had received an e-mail for a paying reservation for the upcoming weekend. Paying reservations took precedence over freeloaders even if they were members of the board. If preserving the lighthouse was truly their aim, then nobody could argue that a paying guest took precedence over them. Bailey had at least made one decision. It was time for the board to hit the road. They could hold their meetings online.

"Penny for your thoughts?" Startled, Bailey turned from the window. Jake was standing just a few feet away from her.

"Hello," Bailey said.

"Am I interrupting something?"

"Just peeking in on the group," Bailey said. "See if they need anything."

"I'm going to town," Jake said. "I wondered if you'd like to join me?" Town. She needed things in town, didn't she? They had plenty of groceries, so that was out. And they didn't need furniture, or books, or—what else was in town?

It didn't matter. It was what wasn't in town that mattered. The people taking over her patio, sucking up all her energy, they weren't in town.

"I'd love to go to town," Bailey said. "I must go to town." Jake's smile seemed genuine.

"Hope you don't mind sharing my Jet Ski," he said. Was there a twinkle in his eye? Was she allowed to do this? Was she allowed to share a Jet Ski with another man?

"I could call Captain Jack," Bailey said. After all, she had to at least appear to not want to get on his Jet Ski, didn't she? Even though she could already feel herself pressed up against him.

"Great. You call the mighty captain and I'm going to hop in the shower. I'd really like to take you to dinner and I don't want to be tossed out for smelling like the great outdoors."

Dinner? Bailey thought. She didn't know about dinner. But she didn't say that, she just nodded again. Jake went off and Bailey glanced out the window. Brad was holding court, waving his hands as he spoke. When he finished everyone laughed. Bailey marched out to the patio, silently practicing her spiel on the way.

I'm going to town.

I'm going to town with Jake.

I'm going to town and Jake happens to be going to town.

Jake asked if I wanted to go town with him. On his Jet Ski. We're going in the ferry instead. He wants to take me to dinner.

Jake asked if I wanted to go into town with him and since we'll probably be there at dinnertime, he asked if I wanted to have a bite. He's in the shower now so he doesn't smell like the great outdoors.

As Bailey approached the patio she could hear Brad talking.

"Olivia was like a mother to me. I really hope she made it to the other side."

"Maybe we can try contacting her." It was Angel. Of course.

"Contacting her how?" Bailey said. The group stopped talking and stared at Bailey. "Like a séance?" Bailey said.

"Bails," Brad said. He stood. "Are you going to join us?"

"No," Bailey said. "I'm going to town with Jake. On his Jet Ski."

"What?" Angel said. Bailey flicked her eyes over to Angel. She didn't look happy. What? The woman wanted her husband and the handyman?

"I'd like to go to town with you," Brad said.

"Jake asked first," Bailey said. "I'm going into town with Jake," she said. "On his Jet Ski."

"Fine," Brad said.

"Fine," Bailey said.

"I hope his little Jet Ski is safe."

"Oh no," Bailey said. "There is nothing little about his Jet Ski."

Brad clenched his fist, but put on a smile. "I want you to have a good time," he said. "You've been working too hard." Darn right she had. Dishes, floor, linens, uploading videos to Facebook.

"We're probably going to grab dinner in town too," Bailey said.

"Dinner?" Angel said. She sounded furious. What was her problem? Did she expect Bailey to hang around to make sure Angel got *her* dinner? This was a B&B, not a B&D.

"Enjoy," Brad said through clenched teeth.

"Oh, I will," Bailey said. They locked eyes, but it might as well have been horns. *Barcelona,* Bailey thought. She hadn't seen his nostrils flare like that since Barcelona.

They were twenty-two and Spain was their playground. At the dance club hugging the ocean, Bailey wore the tiniest blue dress that showed off her cleavage and three-inch pumps that elongated her legs. She'd spent hours getting ready while Brad went to the Miró museum, and even though he said she shouldn't have missed it, it was well worth it because she looked hot. Every Spanish man on the dance floor thought so too. She lost count of how many men she danced with, how many she kissed; even a boy in a wheelchair. Earlier in the day, Brad had kissed both cheeks of a beautiful girl who had done nothing more than give him the time and tell him his Spanish was good for an American.

"It's Europe!" he said when she complained. "Kissing is like shaking hands." If that were the case, Bailey was going to shake, lip-to-lip, every boy's hand she could. And she did. By the end of the night, Brad was positively shaking with jealousy. He stormed up to her in the middle of one of these "shakes," gently took her arm (although she suspected he wanted to pull it out of the socket), and pulled her to the side. Several men threw their voices up in protest. Bailey winked at them and was

all smiles until she saw the look in Brad's eyes. He was truly furious. Was he actually jealous? The realization sent a thrill
through her body. Brad Jordan jealous of her! For the first time
in their love-stalking relationship the power dynamic had see-
sawed in Bailey's direction. She was going to enjoy every single
second of it. There were a hundred beautiful, exotic, foreign
girls around them, but Brad was only focused on her.

"Something wrong?" Bailey said.

"You!" Brad said. "And all the kissing."

"It's Europe," Bailey said. "It's like shaking hands."

"I get it, okay," Brad said. "You're mad about the girl. But all
I did was kiss her on the cheeks, Bailey. The cheeks. You're
locking lips with every Spaniard in sight!"

Bailey stood up straight, put her hands on her hips. "Admit
that you liked that girl," she said.

"No," Brad said. "I won't."

"You're telling me—if it had been some old lady and not
some hot little thing, that you would have acted the exact same
way."

"Yes," Brad said. "Now let's go." He started out the door, as if
she would just agree, as if she would just follow. Instead, she
didn't move. How long until he turned around? He went all the
way out the door. Not a glance back. He was so sure she would
follow him. Knowing he would eventually come looking for her,
she made her way back to the dance floor and tried to lose herself among the sweaty, swaying bodies. She didn't look to the
exit once. She danced alone, moving away when men tried to
press their bodies against hers, because now that she'd made
her point with Brad, she had no need for strange boys. He was
the only boy she wanted. Instead, she found joy all alone, in the
middle of the massive crowd, sweat pooling into the nape of
her neck, music thundering through her body. It may have only
been minutes, but it felt like she danced like that for hours.
When she was ready to go home, she happened to glance up to
the second-floor mezzanine overlooking the dance floor. And
the first person she locked eyes with was Brad. He'd been sitting front and center, watching her. He looked at her with such

devotion and desire that had she been struck by lightning at that very moment, she would have died the happiest girl in the world. She knew then and there that they would marry someday. And now? How would she feel if she got struck by lightning now? She'd be slinking into heaven with her tail between her legs. For no matter how you looked at it, she was using a young, gorgeous contractor and his big Jet Ski to get back at her husband for lying about a lighthouse.

Despite everything, it was nice to be in town. They strolled through the antique store, and the bookstore, and even the florist before ending up in the café where they ordered lattes and chatted on overstuffed couches in the back room. Jake talked about his travels: his trips to Beijing, and Thailand, and Hong Kong, and Bailey pretended to listen.

"You are a thousand miles away," Jake said. Startled, Bailey looked up. He was staring at her again, with an intensity that was hard to miss. It was a look that conveyed she was the center of his attention. A flutter gathered in her stomach. She was glad Captain Jack had agreed to ferry them both ways, for despite what she'd allowed Brad to think, it wouldn't be right to be pressed so close against him.

"Sorry," Bailey said. "I'm a little distracted." Jake leaned forward.

"Distracted," he said. "Just like your light." Her light? Oh no, was he going to turn into one of them too?

"My light?" she repeated out loud.

"The tower beam," Jake said. "It's been quite erratic the past two days."

"It has?" Had Bailey even looked at the light the past two days?

"Last night it flashed three times in a row. Like an SOS signal." Bailey snuck a guilty look at her cell phone. The Coast Guard had called several times that morning. She'd been too upset to call them back. It had to be about the light. This was so typical. They were spending all their money to save a lighthouse that didn't even work.

"Olivia," Bailey said.

"Who?" She hadn't meant to say it aloud. But there it was. Maybe Brad was messing with the light, trying to "contact" her. The group was a bad influence. They were probably all in it.

Bailey held up her cell phone. "I have to make a call," she said. "Thank you for telling me."

"Oh," Jake said. "So it's not a ghost?"

"A ghost?"

"Some say the place is haunted."

"I've heard," Bailey said. "No. It's not a ghost. Just a middle-aged man and a crisis."

"Don't tell me you're calling yourself middle-aged."

"I meant Brad. But I'm also—"

"Beautiful." The word hung in the air, suspended. It sent an electric thrill down her spine.

"Thank you," she said. She held up her phone again. "I'm also married."

"Happily?" Jake asked.

"Not always," Bailey said. "But for the purpose of this discussion it's definitely 'ever after.' "

Later, back on the island, Bailey would replay her silly words. "For the purpose of this discussion." Was she leaving open the possibility that she and Brad wouldn't make it "ever after"? Was she making a subconscious decision, already backing away from him, disengaging, qualifying their marriage? Could she say for sure they were going to make it through this? Could anyone?

Chapter 21

"I swear to you," Brad said. "I am not messing with the light." They were standing in the tower, whispering despite the impossibility of anyone hearing them.

"He said it was blinking three times fast, like an SOS signal," Bailey said.

"If that were the case, wouldn't we have heard from the Coast Guard?"

"They called," Bailey said. "I didn't answer."

"Bailey. If they thought we were messing with the signal, they would have been knocking at our door in seconds flat."

"You think he's lying?"

"I don't know." She waited to see if he would lecture her about going into town with Jake. He didn't mention it, although she knew he saw Captain Jack ferry them back and forth. Why didn't she go on the Jet Ski? Why did Brad get to be the only one on bad behavior? Not that he'd done any of it to hurt her. Bailey knew Brad would never purposefully cause her pain. It made it all that more difficult to be so angry with him.

"We have a paid reservation request for this weekend," Bailey said.

"But the group is staying through next week."

"Then they are going to have to pay," Bailey said.

"I promised them—"

"We're still the keepers, right?"

"It's in the contract. No one can ever take this place away from us, Bails. I swear. We can stay here until the day we die."

"We just can't pass it on to our children." *We don't have children* was the elephant in the lighthouse.

"We can appoint the new keepers," Brad said. He avoided all mention of children.

"Okay then. The board. They either start paying or start packing."

"Does that include your little tent friend?" And there it was at last, a hint of jealousy. It didn't feel as good as Bailey thought it would.

"Yes, it includes him," she said. "Everyone who wants to stay has to pay."

"We have so many things left to do," Brad said.

"You mean contact Olivia?"

"Do you have to sound so sarcastic?"

"You won't even believe me when I tell you the keeper's house is haunted!"

"Because it's not. It's an old house."

"But you believe in Olivia's ghost?"

"No. Not exactly. Olivia is not a ghost."

"And yet you want to hold a séance."

"It's not a séance. It's—an energy circle. Today is Wednesday. When are the guests arriving?"

"Friday," Bailey said reluctantly.

"Then let's let the board stay until Friday morning," Brad said.

"Fine," Bailey said. "But they have to be out by nine A.M."

"Nine A.M.?"

"I'll have three rooms to clean."

"I'll help."

"We'll still need the time."

"Okay. Nine or ten A.M.—"

"Nine A.M."

"Deal."

"So what is—an energy circle?" Bailey was trying. She was really, really trying. But she couldn't get rid of all her sarcasm, she just couldn't. Even so, Brad looked grateful. His face softened and he looked so hopeful it almost broke her heart.

"We'll just . . . sit around in a circle holding hands and concentrating our energy on sending Olivia to the light."

"That's a freaking séance."

"Call it what you like."

"It's a séance."

"Stop saying that."

"Fine. But I'm sitting in on it and you can't stop me this time." To her surprise, Brad took her hand.

"I was hoping you'd say that," he said.

"You were?"

"Yes. If Olivia does come through—you two have a bit of healing to do, don't you think?"

"Oh. Yes. Of course." *If by healing you mean I want to kick her big ashes out of my house.* "Will you blog about this séance—energy circle—in your diary? Sorry. Keeper's log?"

"Nah."

"I think you should."

"Why?"

"Business," Bailey said. "Everyone loves a good ghost story."

"Bailey," Brad said. "That's not the right frame of mind."

"You're the one who wanted a lighthouse bed-and-breakfast," Bailey said. "I'm doing everything I can to build clientele."

"And you think they want to hear about ghosts?"

"I don't think," Bailey said. "I know." It was true. Ghosts were very "in" right now.

"Fine. I'll mention it in my log." Bailey went to hug him, kiss him. Then she remembered she was angry with him. Brad looked elated, then pained.

"I'm so so sorry," he said. "I love you. You know that, right?"

"I know," she said. "But you shouldn't have kept such a huge secret from me."

"You're right. I don't like to do it. I don't know what's wrong with me. I'm a coward—"

"Leave the criticizing to me, okay? I don't like to hear you putting yourself down."

"I have to tell you something else," Brad said. "Something I should have told you eons ago." Just then, the beam across the river flickered. Instead of four light and one dark, it flashed three times quickly. Brad and Bailey stepped toward the window, staring at the light. Soon after, both of their cell phones started to ring. "Coast Guard," they both said at once. Slowly, they looked up at the automated light. Neither of them had touched it. Neither of them had been anywhere near it.

"I guess the light doesn't like you keeping secrets either," Bailey said.

"Or it doesn't want me talking," Brad said.

"Well, you were saved by the light, then," Bailey said. "I'd rather not deal with your next deep, dark secret until we finish apologizing to the Coast Guard."

"Bailey," Brad said. Bailey stepped forward and kissed him on the cheek.

"Seriously," she said. "I can only deal with one crisis at a time, okay? Unless you're having an affair—"

"God, no. Never. Never, Bailey—"

"I was kidding. Relax. Is it life-threatening? Are you sick?"

"No."

"Does it require our immediate attention?"

"I guess not."

"Later, then. Okay?"

"Okay."

Bailey smiled. At the moment, she really, truly didn't care what it was. She had more than she could handle. But it was weird, the light freaking out just as Brad was about to bare his soul yet again. He was probably giving off so much energy it was interfering with the electricity. A far-out concept, yes. But Bailey was starting to get used to the "far-out." Unfortunately, she doubted the Coast Guard would be so open to her explanation. Bailey took Brad's hand and they went downstairs to face the firing squad.

Bailey was up early the next morning. She didn't sleep well after the lecture from the Coast Guard. It was their light, they had the access to it, they were the ones who automated it, yet because they couldn't figure out what was wrong, Brad and Bailey were the ones getting blamed for it. Bailey probably shouldn't have insisted it was their problem, but really, was she wrong?

And although she couldn't get rid of the Coast Guard, the board was going to get the axe. She was going to make breakfast extra special just in case their guests took her "pay if you want to stay" speech the wrong way. On her way through the living room she noticed that the guest book was open. A new entry had been scribbled in last night.

WHAT A TREAT. WHAT HOSPITALITY. THANKS A LOT.

It wasn't signed. It was also in red pen instead of the black that Bailey kept next to the book. But the most striking thing was that it was written in all caps. Didn't they know all caps was offensive? *WHAT A TREAT. WHAT HOSPITALITY. THANKS A LOT.*

Oh my God, Bailey thought. *Who wrote this?* It was meant to be sarcastic, snide. Here they are, staying for free, getting waited on hand and foot—okay maybe breakfast was a little tense the other day, but come on. This kind of rudeness could not be tolerated. She picked up the phone and called Captain Jack.

They were all seated, waiting for their food. The smell of eggs and bacon and pancakes permeated the room. Bailey even had fresh fruit and oatmeal for Kimmy. Even Vera seemed relaxed. Ever since the sleep-eating incident she'd been sharing a tent with Daniel. New love must have done the trick, for Vera hadn't broken into the kitchen since. Bailey would have never put those two together. She had a lot to learn about reading her guests. Which meant the culprit could be anyone. Bailey stood at the head of the table with her hands full. But instead of plates to pass out, she was holding blank paper and red pens. Captain Jack had come through with the red pens, although it had cost her.

"Before you eat, you'll need to make a comment on this sheet with this red pen," Bailey said.

"Bailey?" Brad said. He was leaning on the kitchen counter behind her. Bailey ignored him. She already knew what Brad's handwriting looked like; he didn't need to participate.

"You can write whatever you want, as long as it's in capital letters."

"Bailey?" Brad said again. "A word?" He was using a tone of voice she knew well. If she didn't give in and talk to him, he would escalate. It was just as she feared—they would never be alone to fight. Sheila was holding the entire stack of paper and pens, looking confused.

"Please take one and pass it down," Bailey said. "I'll be right back." She joined Brad by the counter and tried to keep her voice low.

"What?"

"What are you doing?" Bailey took Brad's arm and led him to the guest book. She opened it to the correct page and pointed to the comment. Brad read aloud.

" 'What a treat. What hospitality. Thanks a lot!' " He smiled, looked at Bailey. "That's awesome," he said when she didn't respond. Bailey wanted to hit him over the head with the book. She was starting to think that married couples should be allowed a couple of free wallops a day.

"It's sarcastic, look. Red letters and all caps."

"Maybe they're just passionate. Red is the color of passion." Brad always looked for the best in people. It wouldn't have been the first thought that crossed her mind. Red was also the color of rage, and hot tamales.

"Trust me," Bailey said. "It's not a nice message."

Brad glanced toward the kitchen. "So what's the plan, Nancy Drew? Are you collecting handwriting samples?"

"Damn right I am," Bailey said.

Brad threw his head back and laughed. "You can't do that," he said. "It's freedom of speech."

"Freeloaders don't have a right to freedom of speech," Bailey said. She turned on him and marched back into the kitchen. She stood at the head of the table. "Did everyone write down something in capital letters?"

"I don't get it," Sheila said. "What are we supposed to write?"

"How about a good-bye letter?" Bailey said. She smiled ear to ear to help ease the blow. "I'm sure you—as the board—will all be thrilled to know that this coming weekend we are going to have our first paying guests. Therefore, this will be your last night staying here for free. If you would like to continue staying, you will have to pay for your rooms. And tents," she added with a glance to the campers.

"What about our energy circle?" Sheila said.

"The séance will be tonight," Bailey said. "Seven P.M. sharp."

"It's an energy circle," Angel said.

"Can you please pass your papers up and I'll get breakfast served," Bailey said. She was losing her patience. Why did they have to keep talking back? Bailey glanced at the papers as they came in. "Did everyone put their names on it?"

"What subject are you teaching?" Angel said with a snort. "I forgot to check the syllabus." Brad took the sheets out of Bailey's hand and set them on the counter.

"Who wants what for breakfast?" he said, slightly pushing Bailey out of the way. Bailey subtly went over to the pieces of paper. Nobody put their names on it.

WHAT AM I SUPPOSED TO SAY

I LOVE LIGHTHOUSES!!!

I'M HUNGRY

YOU ARE BEAUTIFUL

THIS IS STUPID

And the rest were blank. Bailey turned to see if she had any champagne left in the fridge, for she needed just a little something to take the edge off, when she noticed someone had written something on there as well, using the magnetic letters.

GET OUT

Was this a joke? Had Vera written a message to herself while sleep-eating? To top it off there wasn't any orange juice left, let alone champagne. Brad served their guests, but he didn't even ask Bailey if she wanted a cup of coffee. By the time she got to the pot it was empty. She set about making a new one. She opened the drawer to get a measuring spoon. Brad brushed by her, and in doing so his hip slammed the drawer on her thumb.

Oh God, the pain. The red-hot pain roaring through her thumb. Instant, irrational rage. Bailey doubled over and screamed. This was the worst morning ever. She was tired, she was pissed, she was caffeine- and food-deprived, her husband loved his freaking shoes more than her, she just found out they didn't even really own this blinking albatross, one of their free-loading guests was an ungrateful son of a—

And now she slammed her thumb in the drawer. Her arm lashed out, and she picked up the first object she touched. A stick of butter in a ceramic tub. She hurled it across the room. It smashed against their mahogany cabinets and then dropped to the sink with a deafening clank.

"Bailey, Bailey, Bailey." Brad tried to take hold of her hands. He was probably just trying to stop her from throwing anything else. But she wanted to. Hearing that butter tub clank and smash felt so good! Dare she say it even calmed her down a little. What could she throw next? Maybe something softer so it wouldn't alarm their guests. Although it wasn't like she was aiming at them or anything. Brad was still trying to reach for her.

"Don't touch me," she said. "It hurts." All the guests were openly staring at her. "It hurts," she said again. "It really, really hurts."

"Do you want some ice?" It was Jake. He was out of his seat and hovering over her. Bailey looked at Brad as if to say, "See? He's being attentive." To her horror, Bailey felt tears coming to her eyes. Her entire life, she'd always cried at all the wrong things, at all the wrong times. Usually in public, in front of strangers. Set her on a couch with a box of Kleenex and a Hallmark movie and NADA.

"I'm okay," Bailey said. Jake nodded, moved past her, then at the last minute shuffled through the papers on the counter, placed one of them on top, and gently slid it toward her.

YOU ARE BEAUTIFUL

Startled, Bailey looked away. He thought she was beautiful like this? Roaring and shouting and hurling sticks of I Can't Believe It's Not Butter across the room? Ah, the young, always attracted to drama. He probably thought she was a wildcat. Men loved crazy women in bed. Was she wild and crazy in bed? The last time she and Brad made love she didn't even take off her nightgown, and in the middle of it she glanced at her crossword on the end table by her bed and figured out that six down was "astray."

But that didn't mean she didn't still have it in her. She used to be wild in bed. Oh, the nights she and Brad took chances, made up positions, talked dirty, screamed, even bit each other. She used to have to force him to use condoms. Now she couldn't get him to go bareback for anything. He was probably wearing one right now just to be extra safe. Bailey took a deep breath. She'd better get a hold of herself. Her guests were still staring.

"It's okay," she said. "Everything's okay. As long as nobody needs any butter."

Later, after insisting she clean up alone after breakfast, Bailey noticed the guest book was once again open. There was another message. In red pen. And all caps.

**BREAKFAST WAS TRULY TERRIFYING!!!
NEXT TIME PASS OUT HELMETS.**

Bailey turned to scream for Brad, only to find him standing directly behind her. She pointed at the latest comment. "I didn't throw it anywhere near them," she wailed.

"I know," Brad said. He pulled Bailey into him and kissed the top of her head. "Still," he said. "We might want to just consider the helmets."

Chapter 22

Everyone sat in a circle in the main room. There were a few candles lit, but nothing over-the-top. To anyone walking in it could have been a book group or a support group with soft lighting. Bailey wanted to set up chairs, but Daniel insisted they sit on the floor. Bailey thought he would have gotten along great with the ex-con. What was his name again? Harold. How could she forget? Didn't you always remember the name of your first prisoner? Bailey wondered if he'd ever been caught and where he was now. It would be that way for as long as they ran the B&B. People would come in and out of their lives, full of stories and life and drama, and then just disappear. Or go back to jail. Maybe some would return year after year, but otherwise it would be like watching a revolving soap opera where the main characters were constantly replaced by new actors.

Vera was the only one who came dressed for a séance. She wore heavy eye shadow, fake eyelashes, and a long purple dress, complete with a headband wrapped around her head like an amnesia victim. Bailey looked around at the eclectic little group and thought, *If my parents could see me now.* At that moment, they were probably sitting at the dining room table discussing the latest articles in the *New York Times*. If they knew what Bailey and Brad were up to, her father would shake his head and say, "What kind of California hippie-dippy thing are you into?"

"It's not my fault," Bailey would say. "Brad has brain damage, and I'm just trying to drum up business. Ghosts are really hot right now thanks to cable television." The fascination probably had something to do with the fear of death. Ghosts were proof that an afterlife existed. Everyone was searching for the answers. Except the group surrounding Bailey. They all thought they had the answers.

They started by finishing up minutes from their last meeting. "So," Vera said. "What question did we leave the group with last time?" Sheila raised her hand. Vera nodded.

"You asked who's thinking of writing a book about their experience," Sheila said.

"Right," Vera said. "And show of hands, who's writing a book?" Everyone but Bailey thrust up their hand.

"You're going to write a book?" Bailey asked Brad. Was that the other "secret" he'd been referring to the other day?

"I've already started," Brad said. Would it be rude, Bailey wondered, if she pinched the bridge of her nose really hard and closed her eyes?

"You were only dead for thirteen minutes," Bailey said. "It will have to be a very short book." Although the others didn't seem to appreciate her humor, Brad threw his head back and laughed. After all these years, one thing was for sure. He got her. Maybe love did conquer all, even the supernatural.

"Bailey has a great sense of humor," he explained to the group. "It was her sharp tongue I fell in love with."

"And the things I could do with it," Bailey said.

"See?" Brad said. He beamed and scanned the group for approval.

"Moving on," Angel said.

"My book is going to combine my near-death experience with sleep-eating," Vera said. "I'm going to call it *Does My Corpse Look Fat?*" Bailey slapped her hand out of her mouth to keep from laughing. "It's okay," Vera said. "You can laugh. Humor is part of it."

"Mine is going to be like *The Wizard of Oz*," Daniel said. "Only no Dorothy or yellow brick road shit. Just me and Tree meeting Our Maker as we navigate a long and bumpy tail."

"Did you mean 'trail'?" Kimmy whispered. She spoke so softly everyone leaned forward to listen.

"No," Daniel boomed. "I mean tail. Turns out Daniel and Tree are climbing up a huge dragon's tail, but you won't know it until the end. And if any of you steal it, if I see any mention of dragons in your books, I will hunt your asses down. You'll see what "Fire Breather" means then!"

"What about you, Kimmy?" Vera said.

"Mine isn't really a book," Kimmy said. "Just some poems about my experience."

"Read us one," Sheila said.

"Oh God," Ray said.

"You should be more supportive," Chris said. He put his arms around Sheila.

"Yes, Kimmy, read us one," Ray said, staring at Chris.

"Are you sure?" Kimmy said.

"A short one," Vera said. Kimmy cleared her throat. Then she stood. Bailey doubted anyone really heard the poem; the shocker was Kimmy's theatrical voice when she recited it—or one might say, "belted" it.

"I was dead. But now I'm not. What should I do? In life's web I'm caught." When she finished yelling her poem, she bowed.

"Happy now?" Ray said to Chris. Since Chris and Ray looked as if they were contemplating punching each other out, Bailey began applauding, and as the rest joined in and Kimmy took her seat, the tension momentarily eased.

"Sheila?" Vera prompted.

"I'm going to write about how this experience changed my marriage." Was it Bailey's imagination, or did Sheila glance at her after saying that? "It's made it so much stronger, happier. We truly appreciate each other now." She did! She'd just glanced at Bailey again.

"What about you, Brad?" Vera said. "What's your book about?"

"It's just a continuation of my journals," Brad said. Bailey didn't pipe in and tease him about him keeping a diary or pout that he'd never let her read them because for some reason her husband had just turned a thousand shades of red. What was making him blush? What was in those journals?

"We should talk about Olivia now," Vera said. "So we can send her our energy."

"Certainly," Brad said. "Olivia Jordan was—"

Vera leaned over and touched Brad's arm. "Not you, sweetie," she said. "You're too close. I think we should let Bailey talk about Olivia."

"Oh," Brad said. "Sure." All eyes turned to Bailey.

"I'm really just here to watch," Bailey said. The last thing she wanted to do was talk about Olivia.

"I'm sorry," Vera said. "In order for this to work, everyone must participate in full."

"It's okay," Brad said. "Just say a few words about her."

"Okay," Bailey said. "Well. She was Brad's aunt. She absolutely doted on Brad. She was in her seventies. She lived in a very clean and simple one-bedroom in the Riverdale section of the Bronx. It was a rental. Which is totally wild when you think about it."

"What's wild about it?" Vera asked.

"Because she was rich," Bailey said. "She could have bought a place. She even had a niece-in-law who was a pretty good Realtor, if I do say so myself."

"Go on," Vera said.

"Well, I got my license about a year ago, and even though I mostly dealt with high-end condos and penthouses—"

"Not about you, dear. Go back to talking about Olivia."

"Oh," Bailey said. "Right. Well. She liked to play poker, but of course we only found that out after she died."

"It was quite a surprise," Brad said. He held up a deck of cards. "I brought this to honor her." Bailey hoped she was sitting in a spot dim enough that nobody could see her expressions.

"It was a surprise," Bailey said. "She didn't even hang out her

real calendar when we visited. And she kept a Jag in the garage
we didn't even know about. We had to sell that when we moved
here."

"Why don't you talk to Olivia," Vera said. "Tell her what's on
your mind." Everyone looked at Bailey. She looked at Brad.
Why was this being geared toward her? Brad was the one with
Olivia issues. But Brad didn't look as if he were about to speak.

"Well," Bailey said. "I think we'd all like to know where she—"

"Speak directly to her," Vera said. "As if she were right in
front of you." Bailey nodded and tried not to roll her eyes.

"Olivia. We'd all like to know where you would like us to
spread your ashes. Is the Hudson River okay?"

"Bailey!" Brad was out of his seat. Olivia's urn was sitting on
the fireplace mantel. He looked as if he were about to throw his
body in front of it. Bailey threw her arms open.

"Am I wrong? Aren't we here to say good-bye? Release her?
Go to the light, Olivia! Go to the light!"

"I miss the light," Sheila said.

"Me too," Kimmy said. Bailey was outnumbered. Chris and
Ray were too busy eyeing each other to come to her defense.

"We all miss the light," Vera said.

"I don't," Brad said a little too loudly. "I really don't. Not anymore."

"That's because you live in the light, brother," Daniel said.

Angel turned to Bailey. "You've no idea how good it feels,"
she said. "I wish you could experience it."

"Oh, I've heard," Bailey said. If Bailey wasn't mistaken, Angel
had just found a polite way to tell her she wished she would
drop dead.

"If you don't mind me saying," Vera said. "You sound a bit . . .
unhinged." Bailey looked around to see who she was talking
about. They were all staring at her. Wait—they were all staring
at her. They thought *she* was unhinged? The back-from-the-
dead board thought she was unhinged? She was going to have
to watch her temper or they'd see unhinged.

"I think we've gotten off track here," Bailey said. "This isn't about me. I'm just going to sit back and let you guys do your thing."

"But it is about you," Vera said. "Can't you see that?"

"I have no idea what you're talking about." Bailey turned to her husband. "Brad? Tell them this isn't about me."

"It's not," Brad said. "Entirely about you."

"It's about your hostility," Angel said with a huge smile, as if she were a television host picking the winner of a lottery. Bailey laughed. This had to be some kind of joke.

"Let's all join hands and guide Olivia into the light," Bailey said. She grabbed Sheila and Kimmy's hands. Brad was sitting across from her in between Angel and Vera.

"You're the one we're trying to guide into the light," Angel said.

"Excuse me?" This was getting ridiculous. Brad and his posse of back-to-lifers.

"The group helped me come to a few revelations," Brad said. "My worries aren't about Olivia. They're about you." Bailey nodded as if this made perfect sense, as if she were astutely listening. All the while a hum filled her ears. Her leg took on a life of its own, shaking with nervous energy. She was absolutely going to kill him.

"Do tell," Bailey said.

"Don't be angry," Brad said. "I'm trying to help. I'm trying to make things right." Brad took a deep breath. Angel squeezed his hand. "I've been carrying a huge burden," Brad said.

Bailey shot out of her chair. "Don't you think this is best handled privately?" she said.

"We're like family," Angel said. She put her hand on Brad's shoulder. "We're just here for support."

"You are not like family. You're not even a friend."

"Bailey."

She held her hand up to stop Brad. "It was nice meeting all of you. Good luck. I probably won't see you again before you leave. Bright and early tomorrow morning."

"Brad tells us you gave up the guitar?" It was Sheila. She was looking at Bailey with definite sympathy.

"Are you kidding me?" Bailey said.

"Is it true?" Sheila said. "Did you give up your dream?"

It was a million years ago. For his twenty-first birthday, Bailey secretly bought Brad tickets to see Bruce Springsteen. It was a sold-out concert. In order to pay the high price set by a scalper, she'd sold the acoustic guitar her parents had just bought for her twenty-first birthday. For the short time she had it, she dreamed of becoming a famous songwriter. She imagined playing with Brad, taking their show on the road. But she had to have those tickets for his birthday. Brad loved the Boss. The stinky scalper kept her waiting two hours in the rain, in the dark, under a scary overpass. A drunk who was living there in a cardboard box kept growling at her. She gave Brad the tickets, brimming with pride that she'd just given him the best birthday present ever. She never mentioned the hell she'd gone through to get the tickets, and she'd even kept her mouth shut every time Brad chided her for giving up the guitar so soon. Apparently, he'd always known what really happened to it. Her mother must have told him. She was going to have to have a word with her too.

"I'm sorry, Bailey," Brad said. "But ever since I've had this . . . experience . . . I keep thinking about you. Everything you've given up for me. And it kills me."

"Really? Does it?"

"It does, really."

"Then why are we here, Brad? Why did you lie to get me here? Why did I give up my job? Sell our condo? If you care so much about what I want, why are we still using condoms?" She didn't care anymore that she was airing her business in front of strangers. They would all be gone tomorrow. It was Brad she cared about, Brad she had to get through to. He had it all wrong. He was the one who needed help.

"He's very upset," Angel said.

"Do you mind," Bailey said, "not telling me how my own husband is feeling?"

"I asked them to be involved," Brad said.

"That's crazy," Bailey said. "This should be private."

"We've gone through something powerful—"

"I don't want to hear it, okay? I already know how great the light is. In fact, I also know that you didn't come back for me. That the only thing you were even remotely sorry about losing was your freaking shoes!"

"That's a gross misrepresentation—"

"None of us cared about anything when we were in the presence of the light," Vera said. "It's very powerful."

"Blah, blah, blah," Bailey said. The more enlightened they proclaimed to be, the more juvenile Bailey felt.

"Wow," Angel said. "I can see why he doesn't want to have kids." Bailey didn't think. She heard Angel's words and just reacted. She felt herself moving. She felt the object in her hand, heavy, cold, and smooth. She didn't put a name to it, or to what she was doing. She heard her husband yell, but it didn't faze her. She felt her arm pull back. She threw as hard as she could. Olivia's urn soared across the room and smashed against the wall between the windows. Bailey braced herself for a storm of ash, a small cloud of dust, pieces of Olivia hovering above their heads before snowing to the ground and covering everything and everyone within reach. Instead, smashed shards of the urn and a deck of playing cards flew up in the air in a giant arc, like an invisible card shark playing a game of fifty-two-card pickup. When the cards finally fell to the ground, they seemed to cover every surface. The queen of hearts landed at Bailey's feet. The queen's eyes bored into hers with a vacant stare, much like the expression Olivia wore when she was alive. Goose bumps prickled up Bailey's arms. Stunned, she looked to Brad for an explanation. He looked just as shocked as she did. It took Bailey a few seconds to remember why she threw the urn in the first place.

"Tell me," Bailey said. "Tell me you did not tell this group that you don't want to have kids." Brad didn't answer. He simply hung his head.

"Right now," Kimmy said. "He doesn't want to have kids right now." Bailey looked at the cards scattered across the living room floor.

"Where's Olivia?" Brad said.

"I don't know," Bailey said. "And I really don't care."

Chapter 23

PLEASE SIGN OUR GUEST BOOK!

I like to listen to the music box, but I can't see it. My Scout leader says you shouldn't play it all night long. I am missing a box of Thin Mints. Did you take it? You will pay for that.

Keeper's Log
Brad

I don't know how things have gone so wrong. Bailey is still here, at least physically. Mentally, she still hates me. I guess I don't blame her. But I'm trying to do the right thing. I just don't always know what that is. Maybe I shouldn't have let Angel stay. Despite what Bailey thinks, it's not because of me. She has a little crush on Jake. And she's paying her way now, so how could I say no?

I don't know where Olivia's ashes are, and I have to be careful questioning Bailey about it. Do I think those playing cards magically appeared in the urn? No, of course not, I'm not that far gone. But maybe Olivia's spirit influenced whoever did it. It was her way of telling us she's found her own resting place. Okay, it sounds crazy. But no crazier than looking all over the place for her missing ashes. Every time I see a bit of dust on the furniture I think, Is that you, Aunt Liv?

On another note, I will never play Pictionary with Bailey again. She gets way too angry if I don't understand her absurd pictures and she never gets mine, although she's right, I don't take it seriously.

Tree wasn't a happy dog. And who could blame him? Daniel had abandoned him without a second thought. He likes it here, he told them as he departed. Even though she hadn't exactly bonded with him, Bailey felt for the dog. It was traumatic being abandoned. Web, on the other hand, seemed to like having another animal around. Normally curled up in the Crow's Nest, the cat had taken to following the dog at a safe distance. Bailey found it hilarious and thought about filming it for YouTube. Sadly, Tree had no interest in Web. Instead, he was taking his anger out on a specific patch of dirt by the patio, digging as if trying to create an escape tunnel of his own. On several occasions, Bailey had come into the kitchen to find garbage scattered about. At first she thought Vera was back, but she quickly spotted Tree's paw prints in the ground coffee littering the floor. He had also taken to barking and whining whenever they left him outside alone. He was now sleeping at the foot of Brad and Bailey's bed every night, snoring to high heaven.

Their first series of paying guests came with their share of baggage, and not just the Louis Vuitton kind. There were the newlyweds, who, in their eighties, kept joking they were really the "nearly deads" (oh, if only they knew Brad's story!). They stayed in their room the entire weekend. If it weren't for the bed creaking and the headboard continuously knocking against the wall, Bailey would have worried they had actually died up there. They insisted on breakfast in bed, and when Bailey took them their tray, she was horrified to see they were watching hardcore porn on their laptop.

Bailey was shaken, but soon comforted by Brad, who thought it was the funniest thing he'd ever heard, and finally, in shared laughter, the patch of ice between them slowly began to thaw. Besides game night on the patio, when the Girl Scouts came for a stay, Bailey finally started movie night as well. The projector jumped in a few spots, but otherwise Bailey was sure the girls enjoyed watching *E.T.* and eating popcorn and Reese's Pieces. She certainly did.

That is, until one of the girls accused Bailey of stealing several boxes of Thin Mints. As if she would do that! Oh, how they turned the place upside down. Bailey was convinced it had to be one of the other girls; after all, Angel didn't eat, Jake was always outside, and the elderly couple never left the bedroom. That left her and Brad. Brad finally paid for the missing boxes of Thin Mints, something that absolutely infuriated Bailey. She didn't mind donating to the troop, but she thought Brad's action was an admission of guilt. Besides, if she were to steal cookies, she would have taken the Peanut Butter Patties.

And when the Girl Scouts complained of hearing scary creaking and moaning during the night, Bailey was forced to stick to her ghost stories. And yes, it might have caused at least one Girl Scout to start wetting the bed, but Bailey had no choice. The truth—that the moans and creaks were coming from horny senior citizens—could have scarred them for life. In the end, Bailey was just as happy to see the paying customers leave as she was the freeloaders.

For the most part she had avoided seeing Jake. He was still outside in the tent, paying a nominal fee of $25 a night. In the summer, it would be a nice little extra income having people pitch tents on their property. He kept to himself, although every day Bailey would catch glimpses of him. He usually ran along the river in the morning, came in for a shower, dressed, showed up for breakfast, then disappeared all afternoon. Sometimes he took the ferry into town, sometimes he disappeared into the woods. In the late afternoon he would usually float down the river in his kayak. She would often see him chatting with other boaters or sitting on the patio reading a book. It was a whole week before he approached her again. It was a Thursday and the Girl Scouts and elderly couple had just left. Bailey had already stripped the beds and washed the sheets.

It was a gorgeous summer day, perfect for hanging things out to dry. Bailey brought her large basket and clothespins, carefully lifting one corner out at a time. If the wet sheets hit the ground, it would be game over. This was a far cry from Manhattan, where she would drop off piles of clothes at a laundry service before work, then pick them up hot, fresh, and folded in the evening. But this was nice too, out in the fresh air, hanging sheets.

"Need a hand with that?" She knew it was Jake before she even turned around. She might go as far as to say she'd been expecting him.

"Sure," she said. She handed him a corner and a clothespin. They worked in tandem, and the sheets were hung in no time. There was something so nice about seeing the sheets sway on the line, the smell of fresh detergent wafting through the air.

"Go for a walk?" Jake suggested.

"Why not," Bailey said. "A short one."

"Short it is," Jake said. He picked the upriver direction, where as you walked along there were fewer and fewer people as opposed to downriver, where Captain Jack's ferry could often be spotted moored on this side of the river. Jake walked at a bright clip, his strong calves and back muscles slightly flexing as he strolled.

"You remind me of Brad when he was younger," Bailey blurted out. Jake stopped abruptly and Bailey ran into him. It was a chest-to-chest bump. Jake put his hand out to steady her, first on her waist, then resting for a few seconds on her hip.

"Is that a good thing or a bad thing?" He was speaking in a low, quiet voice, almost a whisper.

"Youth is always a good thing," Bailey said, pulling away. "But mostly I'm referring to your sense of adventure, tackling the world on your own."

"I hope I won't always be on my own."

"I'm sure there are several girls waiting in the wings as we speak." Bailey suspected it was one of the reasons Angel was hanging around. A small smile confirmed her suspicion. "Do you want to get married someday? Have kids?" How easy the question tripped off the tongue, as if the two breezily went hand in hand.

"Of course. I can't wait to have kids." His exuberance caused Bailey a sensation of physical pain. She smiled through it.

"You'd have to give up some of your freewheeling lifestyle," Bailey teased.

"That's exactly why I'm doing this now," Jake said. "Traveling, living out of a tent. Getting it out of my system. I figure my twenties are for exploring. Thirty to thirty-five is for love. Thirty-five is when we start trying to have kids. Loads of them. Nothing less than a truckload." When he grinned, a dimple popped up on the left side of his face, just like Brad. God, he was cute. "I figure if I get this out of my system now—no regrets—I'll be able to concentrate on being the best husband and father I can be. I want exactly what you two have," he added.

"Except with kids," Bailey said. They were nearing the end of the gravel. From here out they would be walking on grassy banks. Bailey stopped to wipe a trail of sweat from the nape of her neck. In the distance a Coast Guard on patrol waved at them, and they waved back.

"You'd be a fantastic mother." Jake sounded so earnest that Bailey had to laugh.

"I don't think so," she said. "I still have temper tantrums."

"You're passionate. I like that about you."

"Brad doesn't want to have kids." She didn't know why she

blurted it out. Normally, she used the "We're waiting for the right time" line, or the "We're saving up for it," or "As soon as . . ." with anything plausible to fill in the blanks. But it felt good to tell the truth.

And the truth, the painful truth she hadn't wanted to face, the one he'd confided to his NDE group, was that Brad Jordan simply didn't want to have children. Ever.

"Not carry on your genes? It's almost criminal." Bailey laughed again. Jake held out his hand to help her up the embankment. She couldn't help but feel a little thrill when their hands touched. "Although," Jake said when they reached the top of the embankment and sank into the soft grass, "if it's because he just wants you all to himself, I can totally see that too."

Bailey laughed again, as if he were joking, and forged ahead. He was shamelessly flirting, but really, as long as she didn't lead him on, what was the harm? Angel hung over Brad so much it was as if she'd mistaken him for a coatrack. Could there be some truth in what Jake said? Was Brad afraid to have kids because he didn't think he'd be number one anymore? It was common for new mothers to dote so much on their children that they ignored their husband.

And if that was it, if that's what he was afraid of, maybe all she had to do was find a way to assure Brad he would always be number one. Or at least on an even playing field with their kids. Wouldn't they both want to make their children the number one priority? Not that they would give up on their romance. They could have date nights. Wasn't that what mature adults did? She would have to find a way to work this into a conversation with Brad. After all, if they could juggle a bed-and-breakfast, surely they could find time for a child. What was one more mouth to feed as long as they were making breakfast anyway?

"Thank you," Bailey said.

"For what?"

"You've given me a new perspective," Bailey said. Jake raised his eyebrows. Bailey leaned over and kissed him on the cheek. "I have to turn back now," she said.

"I'll come with," Jake said. "Although I was hoping to walk all day."

"You need to find a girl your own age," Bailey joked.

"Age is irrelevant," Jake said. "Marriage, however, is a different story."

"Tell me about it."

"Are you happy?" There he was again, on about happiness. Ah, youth. Another nervous laugh escaped from her. How many did that make today? Was it some kind of female/hysteria/hormone thing? She was no better than a giggling schoolgirl. And she was fighting fantasies of Jake throwing her down on the soft grass, covering her body with his young, strong one, and taking her right there and then. Hello, Coast Guard! It's high tide all right! Menopause. How many years did she have? Twelve? Fourteen? She wanted to be a mother by then. Why else put up with her period, month after month, year after year, since she was twelve years old? She would make a fantastic mother. And Brad, despite his fears, would make a fantastic father. He would not be abandoned by Bailey, not even after the birth of their child. She had been right about one thing. This all stemmed from his mother. And his father too, walking away from Brad before he was born. No wonder he was afraid to have kids. Now, why hadn't the psychiatrist pointed this out? Bailey was so wrapped up in her thoughts that she barely noticed the silent walk back. Before she knew it, they were back where they began, with the sheets still swaying in the sun.

"I can't thank you enough," Bailey said. What happened next would have been slow motion if it were a movie. She started to walk away. He grabbed her wrist and swung her back. Like a perfectly practiced dance, they bumped into each other again, only this time in addition to their chests, their lips came together. And although she did nothing more than freeze in place, and Jake was the one who did the kissing, it still lasted seconds too long. Seconds that made all the difference between innocent peck and "something going on."

Bailey pulled back as soon as her brain started functioning. "Jake," she said. Jake grinned and held up his hands.

"No lecture necessary. It will never happen again. But I had to do it. Just once." He winked at her and took off again, in the same direction from where they'd just returned. Bailey was shaking her head and gently touching her lips, and smiling to herself, when she felt someone staring at her. Startled, she looked up. There, in the lighthouse tower, hanging over the outside rail, focusing rays of jealousy just as strong as the beam from the light, was Angel. Angel had seen the kiss, and Bailey had been judged, juried, and sentenced.

Chapter 24

PLEASE SIGN OUR GUEST BOOK!

Thank you for my stay. I heard noises in the night. It sounded very creaky. I heard footsteps and a loud screaming. Nobody believed me. Then they heard it too. Then they believed me. I should have earneded my ghost badge. But they don't have a ghost badge. They should have a ghost badge. Because I would have earneded it.

Megan Girl Scout Troup #14

P.S. Did you take Dahlia's cookies? She is really really mad.

Keeper's Log
Brad

Thank you, dear readers, for following this amateur keeper's humble blog. I will attempt to answer some of your insightful questions below.

Full moons. Half moons. Crescent moons. Crickets. The sounds of life on the river. A gentle rhythmic sloshing. Fish plopping. Birds chirping and singing. Ducks clucking. Frogs croaking. I've even grown to like the gentle buzz of mosquitoes. Tugboat horns.

Canadian ducks. Wood geese. Osprey. Beavers. Frogs. Bald eagles!!!!!!

I am thinking of turning the two front rooms into a miniature museum. The antique store has some nice memorabilia that I'm pretty sure I could mark up by fifty percent (am I starting to sound like my wife?), and I can get photocopies of original lighthouse plans and pictures from the library and county clerk's office. I'm also very excited about the postcards. They should be back from the printers any day now. It's a gorgeous shot of the keeper's house and lighthouse taken by yours truly at sunrise. Do you know how many times I saw the sunrise in Manhattan? Zero. Here? Every single day. Bailey seemed to like the museum idea (as long as she's not running it) but she also wants to play up the ghost angle. The other day she suggested turning the third floor into Edga Penwell's original room. She even suggested adding a hanging noose! I'm very worried about her and I think I convinced her that her idea was not only morbid, but slightly deranged. I probably shouldn't have used those words. Bailey never forgets anything.

I'm just starting to understand tide charts. Sometimes the tide clock in the kitchen works perfectly, other times it's way off. Unlike my dear wife, I do not think anything supernatural is controlling the clock. Also, I think I've figured out what is wrong with the light. I'm convinced it's a simple wiring problem. So much for Bailey's ghost. The Coast Guard should have it fixed soon.

Last night two Coast Guarders, Joe and Mike, stopped by for peach pie and coffee. Although we bought this one in town, it would be nice if we started baking our own pies. Next time I'm in town, I'll pop into the bakery and see if I can charm the recipe out of Madge.

The section of dock leading up to the keeper's house is sagging under from loose and rotted boards. Bailey's right, I need to fix them before someone gets hurt.

Okay, yes, once in a while people complain they hear music at night. They say it sounds like a music box, only ten times louder. Footsteps, creaking, and moaning have also been reported. Guests who stay on the third floor often report small items missing. If it continues, I'm going to install cameras and recording devices to get to the bottom of it.

We're booked solid for the next two months!!!!!

What do I think about the kiss? Who sent me this question? What kiss?

Bailey had never been a morning person. It took her several minutes of rubbing her eyes and staring for the large black object at the foot of the bed to really come into focus. A guitar case. Brad was already out of bed. She pulled the case close to her and ran her hands along the top of the case. She couldn't believe it. How sweet. She opened it. It was an oldie but goodie as far as she could tell. Brad probably bought it at the secondhand shop in town. She gently lifted it out and strummed. She could really learn to play it this time. She and Brad could play duets at night on the patio. Make beautiful music together. This could only mean one thing. He didn't know about the kiss.

Bailey tried forgetting about it. She cleared out the front two rooms that Brad wanted to turn into a museum gift shop. She roped off the broken section of the dock and put an orange cone in the middle of it. She made a peach pie. Brad had gone on and on about the one from Madge's. Was she actually jealous of an aging, overweight baker? And just when she finally thought she could breathe again, when it had all blown over, she saw Angel hanging around Jake. They had taken to kayaking together in the mornings. Angel was going to tell Brad about the kiss, Bailey just knew it. She took her cell phone up to the lighthouse tower and called Jesse. As soon as Jesse answered, Bailey launched in with all the drama.

"Girl Scouts are mean. A horny elderly couple almost broke the bed, I kissed another man, and Brad bought me a guitar." There was a few seconds of silence before Jesse replied.

"Despite my striking array of options, darling, you do know which subject I'm going to insist you expand upon." Bailey smiled. She loved when Jesse morphed into her thirties moviestar voice. "And before you start in on the jokes," Jesse continued, "I was a tomboy. So I don't give a shit about the Girl Scouts, and nobody wants to hear about blue-hairs doing the nasty."

"All right," Bailey said. "The guitar it is!"

"Bailey."

"All right, all right. Remember Jake?"

"Oh no."

"He kissed me. I just kind of stood there and let him."

"Oh my God."

"Seconds, Jesse. It was over in seconds."

"You're talking to a nurse in the emergency ward. Seconds can mean the difference between life and death."

"Should I tell Brad?"

"Is Jake still camped out on your lawn?"

"Yes."

"Oh, boy."

"But Angel's still perched in our attic."

Jesse laughed. "First Allissa and now Angel," she said. "You've had a rough year."

"Yes," Bailey said. "Sending hot blondes to earth to tempt my husband and torment me. The big guy does have a sense of humor. But speaking of the Fairytalers, we haven't heard from them since we moved in."

"Is that a good thing or a bad thing?"

"I almost want to use Allissa to drive Angel out. Kind of like getting a cat to get rid of a rat." The two laughed, enjoying the same sense of humor. "So," Bailey said. "When are you coming out?"

"Thought you'd never ask. Guess who has next weekend off."

"Thank you, thank you, thank you."

"You're welcome. Don't kiss anybody else until I get there."

Bailey made up her mind. She was going to tell Brad about the kiss. What choice did she have? Angel was going to tell him, or had already told him, although if that was the case, Brad was doing a pretty good job of hiding it. Their new guests were a young French couple with an adorable baby, and a middle-aged man who was way into bird-watching. All of them had risen early; the couple was off to the city for the day (although Bailey tried to warn them it was too long a trip for one day), and the man was apparently out bird-watching. Bailey had hoped the couple would stay around so that Brad could see how adorable their baby was, but she was learning there was no controlling their guests. Just over two hours to Manhattan and two hours back. Ridiculous. They should have just stayed closer to the city. But they insisted on doing it anyway. Maybe they didn't understand English as well as she thought they did. The third booking canceled at the last minute, which meant they were charged anyway. The woman wasn't happy, but Bailey gently reminded her that there was a twenty-four-hour cancellation policy.

Even Angel and Jake had gone on some all-day hike. If you didn't count Tree, who was busy digging holes in their yard, Bailey was all by her lonesome. And although she had always been an animal person, Bailey hadn't really bonded with the dog, but Brad sure had. Usually once a day Bailey would come across Brad hugging the beast to his chest, rubbing his head and cooing, "Who's my boy?" Bailey and Brad were alone for the first time since the summer began. This was her chance to come clean. Besides, if anyone had a couple of free passes coming, it was Bailey. After all Brad had put her through this past year, he certainly couldn't justify getting upset over a harmless kiss.

It was the perfect moment. Brad was happy because the Coast Guard had fixed the light. Bailey was too—after all, what was a lighthouse without the light? She hadn't realized how much she missed the gentle pulse at night. She was even getting used to being on the deck of the tower, especially during the day. Plunging to your death seemed less likely when the sun was shining across bright blue skies. Bailey met Brad outside and suggested a walk along the river.

"We're booked solid," Brad said as they started off.

"I know," Bailey said. "And Jesse is coming next weekend." Brad put his arm around Bailey's shoulders and pulled her in.

"Thank you for the guitar," Bailey said. "That was so sweet."

"What?" Brad said.

"Funny," Bailey said.

"I don't get it," Brad said.

"Are you going to teach me, or should I try and take lessons in town?"

"Is this about the other day?"

Bailey breathed in the warm summer air. She was just trying to thank him for a present and let him know she was going to actually use it. Was it just her or was every conversation they had lately more complicated than it had to be? "I'm not sure what you're referring to—I'm just thanking you for the guitar."

"The séance. Or whatever it was. I didn't mean you had to run out and buy a guitar. Unless you wanted to, of course. But, Bailey, I haven't heard you mention the guitar in years."

"Then why did you buy me one?"

"I didn't."

"You didn't buy me a guitar."

"No. But if I was supposed to, I'm sorry. I'm really sorry."

"Brad. When I woke up this morning there was a guitar at the foot of our bed. I assumed it was from you." Bailey could tell by the frustrated look on his face that he had no idea what she was talking about.

"You have an admirer, huh?"

"Doubt it," Bailey said. "Or maybe it's for you. It's not like there was a name on it."

"Show me." They climbed back into the tower and descended the spiral stairs to their loft. Bailey was relieved to see the guitar still sitting at the foot of the bed. For a split second she'd feared it would be gone, like a suspense movie in which dead bodies kept disappearing. Brad examined the guitar.

"It's a decent one," he said.

"I thought so," she said.

"It was just sitting here? Like this?"

"Pretty much," Bailey said. "Except the case was closed." She turned the lid down. There was nothing on the outside of the case to give them any clues.

"It's either Angel, Jake, the French couple, or the bird-watcher," Brad said, listing them on his fingers.

"You forgot the baby and the dog," Bailey joked.

"Angel is the only one who was in the group meeting the other night," Brad said. "When you talked about playing the guitar."

"I might have mentioned it to Jake the other day," Bailey said.

"Oh?"

"We went for a walk."

"Okay." Brad appeared to be watching her very closely, as if bracing himself for something. Was Bailey right? Did he suspect something?

"He's a young flirt, just like you," Bailey said. "You know how Aunt Faye is always kissing you on the lips?"

"Uh-huh," Brad said.

"Well, at the end of the walk, before I even knew what was happening, he kissed me on the lips."

"He what?" And there it was, a twinge of jealousy. Maybe this was good. Maybe this was what they needed.

"I was as surprised as you were—"

"I'm not surprised. I'm livid."

"Livid? Come off it. I just told you it was nothing."

"Right. Like kissing your aunt Faye."

"Exactly. And besides, I reminded him that I was a married woman, and still very much in love."

"Did you?"

"Of course."

"Then you must have known the kiss wasn't nothing. If the kiss was nothing, you wouldn't have had to say something, now would you?"

"Brad. You know me. I get so paranoid."

"Well, that makes two of us. Because when I hear that some guy is going around kissing my wife and giving her guitars, I get a little paranoid too."

"We don't know it's from him," Bailey said.

"No? Who then? Angel? You two aren't exactly BFFs."

"That's because she only has eyes for my husband."

"And Jake. Don't forget Jake. All the women want Jake." Brad turned and headed for the down staircase.

"Where are you going?"

"Never mind." She knew that tone of voice. It was his jealous voice. She had to run down the stairs to keep up with him. In her haste, Bailey tripped on the last step. She threw her hands out to protect herself, but it was too late. She smashed her lip on the concrete floor. When she lifted her head she could see blood dripping from her mouth. *Please, don't let me lose a tooth—*

it was her worst nightmare. She didn't even know how Brad heard her cry, he was so far ahead, but suddenly he was kneeling beside her.

"Honey, honey, honey. Are you okay?" He helped her sit up and insisted on examining her. Thankfully no teeth broken, just a split upper lip. She started to cry. They sat on the bottom step and he pulled her in.

"Don'tstartafight," Bailey said.

"I can't understand you with that fat lip, baby," Brad said. He kissed her nose. "I'm sorry. If you tell me it was nothing, I believe you. I'm just glad you finally told me." Bailey stopped sniffling and pulled back.

"Whaddayamean?"

"Seriously," Brad said. "We'd have better luck playing Pictionary." Bailey punched him on the shoulder.

"I knew about the kiss," he said. "I couldn't understand why you were keeping it a secret." Despite Brad's objection, Bailey struggled to get up.

"Whotoldyou?"

"Let's not start."

"Angel!" she said.

"She just happened to—"

"Ohshejusthappenedto." *That's it.* "We'rekickingherout."

"Then we're kicking Jake out too."

"Finetheycanbothgo."

"We need to get you some ice. And pen and paper. Really, I've no idea what you said. I think you called her a hobo."

Bailey tried not to laugh because it really hurt. But something about it, along with lack of sleep and too much cooking, cleaning, and kissing, had already put her close to the edge. Soon, she was in hysterics. Brad joined in, and as they crossed the yard to the house, they were laughing so hard they had to lean on each other just to keep upright. Tree, who had been in the middle of digging, heard the commotion. He came barreling across the yard and jumped on the center of Bailey's chest, which started them laughing all over again. Everything was going to be all right. This felt good. Maybe everything was going to be all right. Maybe they could get back on the right track. She should've known Brad was going to ruin it.

"There's my boy," Brad said, rubbing the dog's head as he stood, paws on his chest. "See?" he said to Bailey. "We don't need a baby, we've got a four-legged one right here."

Chapter 25

The French couple, Rachel and Dean, were back from the city. They couldn't have seen much of it, but they looked happy and relaxed anyway. They sat on the back patio drinking wine. Their adorable baby was sleeping next to them in a stroller. Bailey's brilliant plan was already in motion. They were going to take a nice romantic stroll upriver while Bailey and Brad watched the baby, a gorgeous eight-month-old named Simone. Bailey couldn't help but feast her eyes on her tiny blond curls and chubby cheeks, and fat baby legs, tiny drool running down her chin. Brad was more interested in cleaning the grill. If Bailey had anything to say about it, that was going to change.

She watched the young couple take off hand in hand for their walk. "I'm going to take these wineglasses in before we attract bugs," Bailey said. "Will you watch Simone?"

"Who?" Brad said.

"Seriously?" Bailey said. She pointed at the baby.

"Oh. You're just going to be a few seconds, right?" Was he afraid to be around babies? Was that what this was all about?

"Just going into the kitchen," Bailey said. "Scream if she tries anything." Bailey took the wineglasses in and stood at the kitchen sink, watching him while she washed them. He stood with his hands on his hips, staring down at Simone. Bailey hoped the poor child didn't wake up and see the stressed look on Brad's face. She'd probably burst into tears.

Bailey finished washing the wineglasses, and just as she was heading back outside, the phone rang. It was a woman wanting to make a reservation, and she had a million ridiculous questions from the thread count on their sheets to whether or not there was any possibility they would be awakened by a rooster. Bailey couldn't even tell from the woman's voice whether or not they wanted to be awoken by a rooster. Anything was possible.

"We're not a farm," Bailey said. "There are no roosters. Just the occasional tugboat or foghorn."

"Oh," the woman said. She sounded disappointed.

"But some say the lighthouse is haunted," Bailey said. "So you never know what you'll hear."

"Really?" the woman said. Now she sounded excited. "Does the ghost ever sound like a rooster?" Bailey was pretty sure she could get a recording of a rooster.

"Absolutely," she said. When she was done answering the rest of the woman's questions, she headed back to the patio. Brad had his back to the stroller and had gone back to cleaning the grill. Bailey stepped around to the front of the stroller. It was empty.

"Brad!" She startled him. He turned around ready to scold her, and then saw what she saw.

"It's gone?"

"It?" Bailey said. "You're calling her an it?"

"It's a girl?"

"She's a girl. Where is she?"

"I don't know. She was right there!"

"Oh my God. Oh my God."

"Don't panic."

"Oh my God."

"We'll call the Coast Guard!"

"Why? Do you think she went for a swim?" Just then Jake and Angel came around the corner. Jake had Simone in his arms, and he was bouncing her up and down. She was screeching with laughter.

"Oh my God," Bailey said. She lunged forward and took Simone out of his arms. Bailey wanted to cry.

"You can't just take a baby from her stroller," she said.

"We were just over there," Angel said.

"I don't care where you were. It's kidnapping."

"Calm down, Bailey," Brad said.

"I'm sorry," Jake said. "You're right. But she was just sitting here all alone—"

"Brad was watching her," Bailey insisted. Wasn't he? Angel and Jake glanced at Brad.

"We're really sorry," Angel said.

"Did you leave the patio?" Bailey asked Brad. He held a scrub brush out.

"Just to grab this," he said. "I was only gone a few seconds."

"It only takes a few seconds!"

"Bailey, nothing happened, okay? Sit. Breathe. And please— let someone else hold the baby."

Angel lifted the screaming child out of Bailey's arms. She immediately settled down and began to play with Angel's long blond curls, identical to her own. "She probably senses your fear," Angel said.

Brad came over and put his arms around Bailey. "I'm really sorry," he said. "I've learned my lesson. It really scared me too. Okay?"

"Okay," Bailey said. All he had to do was stay on the patio for five freaking minutes and watch a baby sleep in a stroller. Rachel and Dean would have been mortified. But when they came back an hour later, they looked as carefree as ever. Angel even told them about the mishap, and instead of looking horrified, they laughed.

Rachel put her hand on Bailey's shoulder and patted it. "It's okay. You lose the baby. You find the baby. It's life!"

"Believe us, getting an hour alone was much appreciated.

Once you have a baby—your life is—how do you say? Gone!"
Dean said.

"Gone," Brad repeated.

"They're joking," Bailey said.

"No, we are not," Rachel said.

"About this, we never joke," Dean said. "My wife and I. We no
longer even make love. Our noises wake up the baby."

"Oh, the noises we used to make," Rachel said.

"I'm sure you must get some time alone," Bailey said.

"You are right," Rachel said. "But we are so tired. When our
time is free all we want to do is sleep."

"We love to sleep," Dean said. "And we don't mean the sex."

"No more sex," Rachel said. "Sleep."

"It's just a phase," Bailey said. "Happens to all new parents."

"You have children?" Rachel said. Bailey tried to smile. Didn't
she read somewhere that smiling could make you feel better even
if you didn't mean it? Fake it until you make it? Why did people
with children always feel compelled to ask people so obviously
without children that question? Didn't they know it was like a
knife to the heart?

"No," Brad said. He sounded chipper. In his case, it wasn't
even a butter knife.

"Not yet," Bailey said.

"Don't do it," Dean said. "I mean this. If you still like the sex,
don't do it."

"We like it," Brad said. "We like the sex."

And to prove it, that night Brad tried to seduce Bailey. He
began kissing her neck, caressing her stomach.

"Forget it," Bailey said. She pushed his hand away.

"What's wrong?"

"Having a baby isn't the only way for a woman to lose interest
in sex. In fact, not having a baby can make a woman completely
dry up!"

Brad sighed, threw off the covers, readjusted his pillow. "I
thought we agreed," he said. "It's just not the right time."

"Be honest with me, Brad," Bailey said. "I mean really, really honest."

"What?"

"You're just making up excuses. You say it's not the right time. It's never going to be the right time. If people waited for the right time, this would be one very lonely planet!"

"I don't mean perfect, just—"

"What? We don't have enough room for a baby? We have a whole house! And the longer we wait to have a baby, the more expensive it will become—"

"I just lost someone else's baby today. Is that the kind of man that should be having his own?"

"You were careless. But as you said, lesson learned and tragedy averted."

"I really thought you were going to let this go for a while. Just let us be, you know? Let us grow and make something of this business, and find yourself—"

Bailey sat up. That was it. That was the end of sleep for her. "I'm really starting to resent all this 'find yourself' crap," she said. "What if I'm supposed to be a mother? What if that's what I need to 'find myself'?" Brad didn't answer. Bailey snatched her pillow and a blanket from the bed. She stood in the middle of the room, not sure where to go. Then she headed up to the tower. Since she knew she was going to be up for most of the night, she might as well keep watch.

The Hudson River was deadly calm. The light was a comforting pulse. Bailey sat in Brad's "captain chair" and stared out at the blackness below. She could almost hear the water gently lapping the shore. She replayed the recent argument with Brad. Then she replayed every argument and "discussion" they had ever had about having children. And every time Bailey tried to do what Brad asked, put it out of her mind, she just couldn't. Everywhere she turned there were babies. There was even a new sitcom on television. It featured a cute couple, about their age, who had just had their first baby. The comedy played up the many difficulties of having a newborn.

Sleep deprivation. Guilt. Diaper changing. Spats with your spouse. Date nights gone awry. Bailey watched it without laughing. She watched it with the jealousy of a woman watching her lover with another. She imposed their faces on the sitcom characters, imagined it was her with baby poo in her hair while her laughing husband tried to warn her about it. Her showing up for her lawyer job on two hours of sleep and taking a pacifier out of her pocket instead of a pen. It was Brad standing on the other side of the crib saying, "She has your eyes, but my charm."

If she got pregnant right now, she would be thirty-seven when she gave birth. Fifty-eight when the child turned twenty-one. That she could handle. And what if they had trouble conceiving? After all, what about all the times in their younger years when they'd carelessly made love without condoms? Tons of times and no accidents. The irony. It was only now that they were older and therefore less likely to conceive right away that Brad started using protection. He could have avoided a ton of fights if he'd just gone ahead and tried to conceive. In all likelihood she wouldn't have gotten pregnant anyway. IVF could take years to work, couldn't it? All the more reason to start now.

The light started to flicker. Bailey sat up. Sure enough, when it was supposed to go to "one dark," it didn't. It bounced up and down like a jerky image from a faulty movie projection. Shit. Shit, shit, shit. Brad wasn't going to be happy about this. She glanced toward the spiral steps, unsure if she should call Brad up or not. Was he lying awake, like she was, wondering how to fix this between the two of them?

Now the light was only flashing three times and staying dark for two. This was bad. The phone immediately rang.

"I'm sorry," she said as she picked it up. "I don't know why this keeps happening."

"Well, shut her down for the night," the guard said.

"Yes sir. Very sorry." Bailey waited and watched. Instead of shutting off right away, the beam flared. It spread across the river brighter than she'd ever seen it, almost blinding, and stayed on for five whole seconds before it shut down. Her heart thudded in her chest. If it had been that bright from up here, what it must have looked like from out there. It would have totally blinded any ships in its path. Bailey waited for her eyes to accustom to the dark before glancing out at the river. She stepped onto the deck and welcomed the cool night air against her flushed skin. That was truly weird. It was so bright! Had Brad's light been like that?

"Olivia?" Bailey whispered into the night air. "Are you the resident ghost?" If so, she was a long way from the Bronx. There was no answer. Not that she expected one. That was the problem with ghosts. If you believed in them, you could find them anywhere. From the pulse of a light, to the creak of a floorboard, to the cry of a baby. Speaking of crying babies, Bailey wondered how the bird-watcher was coping. It really wasn't fair that he had to listen to a baby cry all night. Bailey would check in with him at breakfast. But he was only getting a discount if he insisted on one. After all, she and Brad had a lot to save up for.

Chapter 26

Bailey and Brad sat in the main room while two members of the Coast Guard they'd never met before paced in front of them. Just when Bailey had started to like Joe and Mike. Was this on purpose? Were they bringing in the big guns? Or one big gun and one little one, an observation Bailey kept to herself. The larger one did all the speaking, while the shorter one did all the glaring.

"The purpose of a lighthouse is to provide safe passage. You do understand this concept, do you not?"

"We do." Bailey was going to let Brad do all the talking too.

"We are responsible for the care and maintenance of the light." *So why are you yelling at us, then?* Bailey wondered.

"Yes sir."

"The light is automated. It's been working perfectly for decades. The batteries and the wiring have been replaced. The only conclusion we can come to is that you are deliberately messing with it."

"No sir."

"So why in the world are we seeing SOS signals coming out of here if it's not some kind of a gimmick?"

"I promise you. It is not."

"Because word on deck is you're spreading rumors about ghosts and holding séances in here. Would that be correct?"

"It was just a support group meeting," Bailey chimed in. "And Captain Jack was the one who started the ghost rumors."

The guard tipped his hat and tucked his thumbs into his pants. "Captain Jack," he said. "Why, you're not listening to that old man, are you?"

"He was just saying that Trevor Penwell's—"

"Trevor Penwell operated this lighthouse for twenty-five years. And not once . . . not once did we see the kind of 'malfunctions' we're seeing now. No SOS signals, no séances, no ghosts."

"Right," Brad said.

"If you think you're going to turn our little community into some kind of Amityville Horror just to attract guests—"

Brad stood. "I promise you, we don't even believe in ghosts, do we, Bailey?"

"This is a lighthouse, sir," Bailey said. "I've done my research. All lighthouses have resident ghosts. It's harmless."

"Bailey," Brad said under his breath.

"But I assure you, we're not the ones promoting this. It's an old, creepy house."

"It's not creepy," Brad said.

"But it is creaky. Guests come in and they hear what they want to hear. And you have to admit—with the suicide on the third floor—"

Both guards immediately looked up. "What suicide?" the taller one said.

"Edga Penwell," Bailey said. "Ten years ago, was it?"

"Lady, I have no idea what you're talking about."

"We weren't around ten years ago," the shorter one said.

"Doesn't mean we don't know every bit of gossip in this town."

"I get the feeling it's something none of them talk about very much," Bailey said.

"That would be a first."

"We're so sorry about the light. I've had electricians look at our wiring and everything. I don't know what to do."

"We're going to shut it down," the guard said. "From now on, no more light."

"But we're a lighthouse," Brad said.

"Well, you're going to be a darkhouse now."

"For how long?" Bailey said. The only reason Brad had bought this place—handed their property over to a board—was to keep the light going. Without it, they had nothing.

"A lighthouse without a light," Brad said.

The guard wasn't moved by their plight. "If you want, you can stand out on the deck with a flashlight," he said. "Otherwise, she goes dark until we get to the bottom of this." They were put in their place. Bailey didn't even bother to correct the pronoun. So much for men and their phallic symbols. They all wanted the lighthouse to be a "she." After they left, Brad disappeared into the tower to sulk, and Bailey was left to clean.

Just when Bailey thought she had become quite accustomed to the oddities of her guests, she was surprised yet again. She came into the kitchen one morning to find the bird-watcher sitting naked at the dining room table. She let out a little screech.

"Sorry, sorry," he said, standing.

"Don't get up!" Bailey yelled. She whirled around so that her back was to him.

"I'm sorry," he said. "Usually you're all asleep at this hour."

"You do this every morning?"

"Yes ma'am." He was way older than her, with a huge stomach and gray hairs and sagging skin, and he was calling her ma'am.

"Mr.—" She suddenly couldn't remember his name. She'd been calling him bird-watcher so long she'd forgotten everything else.

"You can call me Tom."

"Why are you naked?"

"I'm sorry, ma'am. It's for my wife."

"Call me Bailey."

"I'll just go to my room."

"Just get some clothes on and I can make you breakfast."

"I know you don't serve breakfast this early and I've got a long day of bird-watching ahead, so I'd best get a move on."

"I'm up now. Definitely won't be getting back to sleep now." *Not after the image of your naked aging body burned on my brain.*

"Appreciate it." He scooted out of the kitchen, and she forgot to keep her eyes averted, so she caught an unfortunate sight of white buttock as he exited. Was this the dream Brad had in mind? He was upstairs snoring peacefully with the damn dog. Bailey started with the pot of coffee. The French couple, baby and all, were late sleepers. When Tom came back down, he was in his khaki bird-watching outfit: pants, vest, hat, binoculars, boots.

"Coffee?"

"Black, please." Bailey served him a cup, then tried to find out if he wanted eggs or pancakes, but he insisted on nothing more than a bowl of cereal. She served him, then began making the batter for the pancakes anyway. She would eat them herself.

"So," she said when he was nearly done, "you just come in here every morning and sit naked at my kitchen table?" Oh, God. The seats. Did he always sit in the same chair? She was going to have to boil the cushions. Was there a way of telling him it was unsanitary without hurting his feelings? "I'm afraid we can't allow—"

Tom held up his hand. "I'm sorry, ma'am, it won't happen again."

"You said something about your wife?" Tom looked up at her. He had a sweet round face and big blue eyes. He nodded, and they filled with tears. "Tom?"

"She passed away last spring."

"I'm so sorry."

"I never went swimming with her."

"Pardon?"

"She loved going to the beach. She loved summer. Even at her age. Wearing shorts and swimsuits. She loved it. Somewhere along the way, I became self-conscious about this." Tom patted his protruding stomach. "I refused to go with her." His voice started to crack. "All I cared about was what other people would see. What they would think of me. I let years go to waste. I made her go alone every single time. One of the last things she said to me was, 'Tom. People don't care half as much as you think.'" He glanced at Bailey and chuckled. "Although you should have seen the look on your face. I guess I should have left my shorts on." Bailey laughed, and then he laughed and soon they were in hysterics. Bailey started unbuttoning her shirt.

"What are you doing?"

"We'll leave our undergarments on," Bailey said. "But what do you say we give the Coast Guard something to honk at."

Rachel and Dean, contrary to their usual noon wake-up call, were up soon after Bailey had taken off everything but her bra and underwear. And at the least the stereotype about the French being more comfortable about sex and their bodies proved true in this case, for they too undressed after hearing about Tom's wish to get over his insecurities. The Frenchman was very skinny and hairy. The baby was chubby and adorable. The woman was very petite, and she even decided to go topless. After a while it all felt very normal. That is, until Jake and Angel walked in. Bailey was immediately jealous, not wanting to look at either of them stripped down. She didn't have to worry because Jake just leaned against the counter and stared at Bailey, which was what he was doing when Brad walked in.

Brad let out a few expletives of his own. "Bailey?" he said, trying to make his voice sound under control. "A word?" When Bailey followed Brad into the living room, she imagined that Jake was watching her walk away. She didn't dare turn and look to see that was the case, but she could feel it happening anyway. "What the hell is going on?"

"We're helping Tom feel comfortable with his body," Bailey said.

"Say more." Bailey tried to fill him in. Brad just kept shaking his head. "Please," he said. "Put your clothes back on."

"Fine. But if I died and you wanted to get naked, I would only hope there would be people willing to support you." Bailey started back to the kitchen. Brad reached out and stopped her.

"Where are you going?"

"My clothes are under the dining room table," Bailey said.

"I'll get them," Brad said.

"Would you be acting this way if Angel had her clothes off?"

"Excuse me?"

"Bet you wouldn't ask her to put her clothes back on." Bailey could feel the bitterness coming out of her mouth, and she knew it wasn't fair to blame all her jealousy on Brad, but she couldn't help it. That's what years of marriage did. Like little particles, little layers of dust accumulating year after year, and even though you tried to clean it out, the little misunderstandings, the tiny resentments, the disappointments, the words you couldn't take back, the times you'd been taken for granted, the broken promises, they remained, no matter how much you cleaned.

"I would certainly ask her to put her clothes back on," Brad said. "Just like I'm going to ask them all to put their clothes back on. Do you really want us to get some kind of bizarre reputation? Did you learn nothing from the séance? The whole town thinks we're nuts!"

"I'm sorry, I'm sorry. I just felt so proud of Tom for breaking out of his shell. I think this was very therapeutic for him."

"I'm sure it was. But we're not running a nudist colony."

"Aye aye, Captain."

"I can't believe you all did this."

"Birds of a feather," Bailey said. "Birds of a feather." Brad stared her down. Then he shook his head. Next, he took off his T-shirt.

"What are you doing?" Bailey said.

"I can't have you looking like the cool keeper, now can I?"

"Our poor children," Bailey joked. "They'll have two cool parents and no discipline." She just said it to be funny. Or so she told herself. But she was saying things about kids all the time now. It was probably manipulative. Show her one marriage that wasn't. Brad pulled Bailey into him and kissed her neck.

"You look mighty fine in your underwear, Ms. Jordan," he said. "But if you ever take your clothes off around that horny man-boy in there who is so obviously hot to trot for you, we're going to be wanted for the suspicious disappearance of a missing person. You got me, babe?"

"Got ya. He wasn't here when the whole thing started."

"You got your mulligan. We'll start fresh."

"Really?" Bailey called after him. "Hot to trot?"

"Drinks on deck," Brad was calling it. Since the aging projector Brad bought in town couldn't show a flick without skipping some parts, and game nights had caused more fights than they'd had in their entire marriage, he decided from now on they would just drink. He invited Captain Jack, Jake, and Angel, and of course Dean and Rachel. To Bailey's disappointment, little Simone was sleeping. The only reminder of her existence was a baby monitor propped on one of the picnic tables.

Bailey thought they should offer cocktails, but all they had was wine and beer. Nobody seemed to mind, but Bailey used the opportunity to bring up the margarita machine she'd wanted to buy. Why was it that Brad got every toy he asked for yet she couldn't have hers? Then again, if she had a margarita machine close at hand, she might really start using it, running to it every time a guest stressed her out or Brad found some way to dash her hopes of becoming a mother. She'd start drinking in the morning while doing the dishes and having a little pick-me-up during the day. No. No matter what, they weren't buying that machine.

And like she said, Rachel and Dean seemed happy with wine,

the other men stuck with beer, and Angel insisted on drinking only fizzy water because she was going to go for a run in the morning. In theory, Bailey was totally supportive of exercise. But she noticed a tendency among those who did it religiously to always find a way to drop their healthy habits into conversations. "Sorry I couldn't call you back—I was at the gym." Or, "I can't drink, I have to run in the morning." Or, "I would love to catch a movie with you, right after my spin class." Really, Bailey never walked around telling people she was making beds and mopping floors and making breakfasts and taking morning walks.

Well, maybe she did, but once in a while a girl had to vent. Bailey sipped her wine and just listened to the conversations around her. They talked and laughed, and drank, and came and went from the table, but Bailey just sat there looking at the baby monitor. She wished the sweet little girl would wake up so she could hold her and play with her and smell her hair. Would this be her life? Living vicariously through the children of their guests?

From the monitor came a slight crackle. Bailey leaned forward to listen closer. Suddenly, there was a faint tinkle, like a bell ringing, and the sound of laughter. Everyone who was still at the table froze. Rachel stood up first, grabbed the monitor, and looked up toward the room.

"Someone's in there with her." The laugh had definitely not been a baby's laugh. Captain Jack's face had gone as white as a sheet, so white Bailey couldn't look at him. Everyone began the race to the stairwell together. When they reached the room, they were all breathless. The baby was standing up in the crib, looking at the corner of the room. There was no one there. Rachel grabbed her and held her.

"She's fine," Dean said.

"Who was laughing?" Bailey looked around for Brad. Since he wasn't in the room, she turned and screamed his name. She felt a little guilty when the French couple slapped their hands over their ears, but it did the trick. Brad came running up the stairs.

"Where were you?"

"Sorry," Brad said. "I was getting Angel a drink. What's wrong?" Bailey filled him in, and was happy when Rachel and Dean added to the story. At least it wasn't just her this time crying ghost. Brad and Jake began a room-by-room search. Bailey pulled Captain Jack out of the room.

"What aren't you saying?" she whispered. Captain Jack shook his head and looked away. "Tell me."

"It sounded just like her," Captain Jack said.

"Who? It sounded just like who?"

"Edga." Jake and Brad came stomping down from the third floor. Brad was carrying a picture frame. It had obviously been smashed; tiny shards of glass at the edges were all that remained intact. He turned the picture to Bailey. It was a black-and-white of a young couple. They were both very attractive, and smiling. Everyone looked at Captain Jack.

"That's Edga and Trevor," he said. "It was taken on their first day here."

"Who is that?" Rachel said. "Is it the ghost who was laughing?"

"An American ghost!" Dean said. "We love it."

"Not when she's laughing at our baby, we don't," Rachel said.

"Where did that picture come from?" Bailey asked. "I've never seen it there before."

"Neither had I," Brad said. "It was in the middle of the floor."

"Middle of the floor," Jack repeated softly. "Underneath the highest rafter."

"How did you—"

"Right where they found her hanging," Jack finished. He shook his head and started for the stairs. Bailey hurried after him. He kept a fast clip and was soon out the door, almost running back to the ferry. Bailey went after him.

"Someone is playing a trick on us," she said.

"I warned you," Jack said. "Edga is still around."

"She is not. I'm telling you—"

Jack whirled around. "Who?"

"I don't know."

"I'm sorry, Bailey. But it's no trick. Strange things have been happening in the house and with the light since she died. I'm sure the Coast Guard has paid you a few visits about the light?"

"Of course. We think it's just a malfunction—"

"It's her. I'm telling you, it's her. She wasn't happy here. And if the look in your eyes is any kind of a clue, I don't think you are either. It's starting to scare me."

"Scare you?"

"You remind me of her. In so many ways. She was so in love too. But it drove her crazy. She started to get paranoid."

"Are you saying I'm paranoid?"

"If you're not, you should be. You have a ghost! If I were you, I'd pack my bags and move out."

"I don't see that happening."

"Good night, Bailey. Think about what I said."

"What would we do? Have another auction?"

"No. I'd buy her off you."

"Is that what this is all about? You want the lighthouse for yourself?"

"No," Jack said. "I want to burn it." With that and a tip of an invisible hat, he was once again off and running.

Chapter 27

On their second to last morning at the lighthouse, Bailey made Rachel and Dean French toast. Maybe that was a mistake. They were still talking about the sound of a woman's laugh coming through the baby monitor.

"Angel left the table right before it happened," Bailey said. "She said she was going to the bathroom."

"You think it was her?" Dean said.

"It had to be," Bailey said.

"Why didn't she tell us?" Rachel said.

"Because she knew you wouldn't like her sneaking into your baby's room."

"We have to ask her. Is she coming to breakfast?" Bailey looked out the window to see if she could spot her jogging down the path, but there was a thick layer of fog that morning, obscuring everything.

"She won't tell us the truth," Bailey said. "We'll have to get her to laugh instead and then see if we recognize it."

"What's going on in here?" Brad entered the room freshly showered. Bailey loved how he smelled.

"We're going to make the blonde with the big boobs laugh," Dean said. Brad looked around to see what he was talking about.

"Your wife thinks she is the ghost," Rachel said.

"I'm making French toast," Bailey said. "Do you want some?"

"Do you make English muffins when the British come?" Dean said.

"No," Brad said. "But we hang out two lanterns." The couple just cocked their heads and looked at him. Bailey laughed. Dean thrust a syrupy knife in their direction.

"Ah, joke!" he said. "Very good. You can make the blonde laugh with that one, no?"

"Bailey?" Brad said. "A moment."

"We don't need a moment," Bailey said. "They were just talking about hearing someone laugh on the baby monitor, and I just happened to remember that minutes before, Angel had excused herself to go to the restroom."

"So?" Brad said.

"So obviously, she popped her head into the baby's room, the baby did something funny, she laughed, then she lied about it." Bailey kissed Brad on the cheek and handed him a cup of coffee.

"That's not possible," Brad said. Jake stepped into the room.

"What's not possible?" Jake said.

"Nothing," Brad and Bailey said at the same time.

"The blonde with the big boobs is our ghost," Dean said. "At least we think so. But first we have to say the English muffin joke and make her laugh."

"I don't get it," Jake said.

"To be honest, we don't either," Dean said. "They are serving us French toast, because we are French, no? So I ask if they serve English muffins to the British. He says, 'No, but we hang out the lantern.' "

"Two lanterns," Brad said. "Two if by sea."

"The British are coming," Bailey said.

"Oh, so you are buying English muffins, no?"

"Would you like some French toast, Jake?"

"What were you saying about Angel?" As if on cue, Angel appeared in the doorway. She was in her usual running gear, tiny shorts and a tight sports bra. Bailey couldn't stand the way the woman had to pop into the dining room in her sweaty little outfit every single morning before showering.

"Hi, y'all!" she called. "God, it's so gorgeous out there. Oh my God, is that French toast? That smells delish!"

"If you go by sea, you can have two English muffins," Dean said. He threw his head back and laughed, then stared at Angel, who just smiled back. He looked at Bailey and shrugged, like, *I tried.*

"I'm just going to have grapefruit," Angel said, patting her flat, tanned stomach.

"Did you go into the baby's room last night?" Jake said. "Were you the woman we heard laughing on the monitor?"

Interesting investigative style, Bailey thought. *Confront the suspect directly. One problem. Suspects will lie.*

"You got me!" Angel said.

"What?" Brad said.

"I should have 'fessed up. I love babies. I just couldn't help a peek. She was awake when I went in and gave me the cutest little look. She just tucked her chin into her shoulder and smiled at me. I had to laugh."

"Angel," Brad said.

"I know, I should have told you," Angel said. "I'm so sorry."

"It's okay," Rachel said. "We always have to peek at her too."

"I can't wait to have kids," Angel said. She snuck a glance at Jake, who was smiling at her without any hesitation at all.

"Beautiful women make beautiful children," Jake said. There was a beat, then he glanced quickly at Bailey. Their eyes connected for several seconds.

"I'm going to shower," Angel said. She headed out of the room.

"Wait," Brad said. Angel turned back around. "Why are you lying?"

"Brad?" Bailey said. "What are you talking about?"

"Angel wasn't using the upstairs bathroom," Brad said. "She

used the one down here. I was in the kitchen when she came out. We were having a chat when all of you started running upstairs."

Angel threw her arms open. "Got me again," she said.

"So you weren't peeking in the baby's room?" Rachel said.

"I was down here," Angel said. "With Brad."

"Well, not with me. I was just in the kitchen getting more wine when she came out of the bathroom." Bailey felt a stillness settle in her chest as she looked from her husband to Angel. They were both speaking in measured voices, as if reciting lines from a play. Why in the world would Angel lie about chatting with Brad in the kitchen? Unless they were doing more than chatting.

"I just thought you guys would feel better if there wasn't some ghost hanging about the place," Angel said. "I mean, we all get to leave. But you two have to live here. And frankly, I would be totally freaked out if I were you."

"Why don't we let Angel take her shower," Bailey said. "Running might make you look good, darling, but it doesn't do much for your smell." There was just a slight hesitation before Angel laughed. And if anyone was unconvinced seconds ago, it was now quite clear. Angel's laugh was nothing like the woman on the baby monitor.

"Bailey?" Brad said. "A word?"

"No," Bailey said. "Whatever you have to say in front of me, you can say in front of our 'guests.' " Granted, it probably wasn't nice to put air quotes around the word "guests," but Bailey was sick of Brad pulling her aside to scold her in private. She'd warned him about this: Who wanted to live twenty-four/seven with strangers? Did he think they were never going to fight in front of anyone else? It was exhausting always being "on," having to watch every single thing that came out of her mouth.

"Wow," Jake said. "The tide clock is going nuts." Everyone looked at the clock. Sure enough, the hands were swinging like a pendulum from High Tide to Low Tide.

"Can't blame that one on me either," Angel said.

"You're the one who confessed to something you didn't do,"

Bailey said. "And my guess is it's because you feel guilty. About something."

"Bailey," Brad said.

"So what exactly were you two chatting about anyway?"

"Thank you for breakfast," Jake said. "Can I help with the dishes?"

"We've had enough of your help around here," Brad said.

"What is that supposed to mean?" Rachel lifted Simone out of her high chair, even though the baby looked as though she could keep eating until sundown.

"Thank you for the nice place to stay," Rachel said. She grabbed Dean by the shoulder and yanked him up mid-bite. "Let's go," she said in a loud stage whisper.

"I'm sorry if it's a little tense in here," Brad said.

"We had a lovely time," Rachel said.

"You're here one more night, aren't you?" Bailey said. The couple looked at each other.

"We want to see more of Manhattan," Rachel said. "We're leaving early."

"Thank you for coming," Bailey said.

"We're so sorry," Brad said.

"Stop apologizing," Bailey said.

"Good luck," Rachel said. They scooted out of the room like racewalkers. Bailey hadn't noticed before that their suitcases were propped by the door.

"I don't think Captain Jack will be here for another hour," Bailey said.

"We'll wait outside," Rachel said.

"Don't forget to sign the guest book!" Brad called after them.

Chapter 28

PLEASE SIGN OUR GUEST BOOK!

Although we very much appreciate your French toast, we do not like to hear couples fighting so early in the morning. It is a shame the Oprah show is over, you could have some national American-style therapy. May we suggest that your ghost is not happy with your fighting? Your light is not working, your tide clock is going berserk, and ghosts are laughing at you. Although you mentioned wanting to have children, I would suggest healing the rift between the two of you first. Regardless, we appreciate your attempt at jokes, and if we were ever to come again (which we will not) we would like to try those English muffins. We still do not understand how they are like lanterns, but we laughed anyway.

Keeper's Log

Bailey is furious with me, and I don't blame her. How can I tell her what I told Angel? How could I have told

Angel what I told Angel? Everything is going south.
Like our French visitors stated, even the clocks in this
house are going crazy. Here's something else I can
never tell Bailey. I'm going crazy. I'm bored with tide
charts and weather reports, and now that the tower is
dark, I don't know—it just feels like something is
missing. I never really thought about the fact that we
would be surrounded by people all the time. I have to
keep in mind that summer is almost over, there will
be less visitors in the fall, and even less in the winter.
Maybe we're just having growing pains. I can think of
a thousand places I'd rather be. Maybe I'll throw myself into setting up the museum. We only have a few
bits in there. I'm going to start giving official tours to
the community too. We can't have them thinking
we're trying to turn the place into a haunted house. I
think tours and a museum is a good place to earn
back some respect.

Bailey was nervous. Her entire family—parents, sister, niece
and nephew, and Aunt Faye—were all coming to visit. Jesse was
supposed to join them as well, but she'd canceled at the last
minute. Apparently, another nurse had taken ill and Jesse had
to cover her shift. Bailey was disappointed, but Jesse promised
to come the following weekend instead, and at least by then
there wouldn't be too many people around to take away from
their time together. This way, Bailey could just focus on her
family, then next weekend get some much-needed alone time
with her best friend.

It should have been a time of celebration, a time to relax and
just enjoy themselves. If only Bailey could figure out a way to
get rid of Jake and Angel. It was annoying, thinking of the two
of them all snuggled in the tent night after night. And then
there was the little Angel. Brad was still insisting that nothing
had happened between them. Bailey wanted to believe it, but it
just didn't make sense. Unless she felt guilty about something,

why in the world would Angel claim to be the woman laughing on the baby monitor?

And if it wasn't her, who had it been? The only other women present, Bailey and Rachel, had been on the patio. Despite their protests to the Coast Guard, Bailey had been trying to play up the ghost business to garner interest and business. But she didn't believe in ghosts herself, so who was sneaking around their house?

Bailey waited with Captain Jack for her family to arrive. It was chilly enough to see their breath in the morning air. The river smelled a little bit like oil. She hoped her parents didn't notice it. Even if they did, they would have to be impressed by the parade of river traffic and wildlife, and the rich variety of plants growing wild throughout their property. Oh, please let them be impressed, because she was showing off a lighthouse that wasn't lit.

Brad borrowed Captain Jack's shuttle van, picked them up at the train station, and drove them to the ferry. In tow were her parents, Jim and Ellen, her sister Meg, and Joyce and Thomas, her niece and nephew, ages thirteen and sixteen. Meg's husband was always traveling on business, so it was no surprise that he couldn't join them. Aunt Faye was supposed to arrive later in the evening with Jason. Bailey was a bit surprised to hear that Jason was tagging along, but she wasn't going to tell him it was close friends and family only—after all, it wasn't his fault he got the Fairytalers' sale over her. Business must be good if they were both taking off at the same time, although they were only staying for one night.

Bailey's parents had never pressured her to have children. They didn't have to. The fact that they'd raised Bailey in a somewhat normal, happy childhood was pressure enough. Why wouldn't she want to pass on the happiness she'd been handed as a child? Parents who might not be overly effusive—okay, maybe to some her father was downright boring—but he was educated, and stable, and always there. Yes, he liked quiet nights with books, and long walks, and even when he argued he sounded more like a polite guest having a debate, and he was a definite homebody, but he was her father, and he was as solid as a rock.

Her mother had been flirtatious, bordering at times on flighty. Ellen had been the fun parent, Jim the disciplinarian. Bailey was a little jealous that when it came to her relationship with Brad, she was definitely more in the role of her father than mother. Ellen always went on about how easy it had been to raise three children, and Bailey knew most of the credit had to go to her father, who took over when her mother was done playing or having fun, and she was free to go off and have "me time" in an era before "me time" was even a thought in housewives' heads. Ellen just couldn't fathom why Bailey and Brad hadn't given them grandchildren yet. Bailey's biggest problem was that she agreed with her mother 100 percent. Every time she tried to explain Brad's hesitations, her mother looked at her as if she was just making excuses. "I'm going to have a talk with him," she'd warned Bailey several times on the phone before their visit. At first, the very thought sent Bailey into a tailspin of panic, and then she thought, what could it hurt?

Maybe a little prodding or induced guilt from her mother would do the trick. Her father would stay out of it and focus more on the lighthouse. A researcher at heart, he would arrive with more knowledge of the workings and history of lighthouses than Bailey would learn in the next ten years. She smiled to herself as she thought of her parents, looking forward to seeing their sweet faces.

Her sister Meg was another story. Meg's workaholic husband had basically left her a single mother. She was five years older than Bailey, terrified of not being young anymore, furious she'd "wasted her youth," and adamant that Bailey and Brad were the smart ones for not having kids. Add to the mixture the fact that Joyce and Thomas were teenagers. Bailey thought they were terrific kids, but of course they were still kids, and Meg had had her share of squabbles and rebellion with Thomas lately. Bailey just prayed Meg would keep her opinions to herself and not start touting the joys of childless living.

* * *

"The first lighthouse was the Pharos of Alexandria," her father announced on the ferry. "280 BC in Egypt."

Bailey leaned up and whispered in Brad's ear. "Alexandria or Alex," she said. "I like those names." *They'd make cool kids' names.*

"Wonder if they made it into a bed-and-breakfast," Brad said to her father. "I wonder how Cleopatra or King Tut liked their eggs."

"Well-preserved, I imagine," Jim joked back.

"Did they like use candles or what?" Joyce said.

"Pretty wimpy lighthouse if they used candles," Thomas said. "One little puff and ships crash."

"They used fires and reflexive mirrors," Jim said. He turned to Brad. "Yours has an occulting white light instead of twin arrow beacons, right?"

"Right, Dad," Bailey said. She could tell he was trying to turn this into a lesson for the kids, both of whom looked ready to throw themselves off the boat and swim for it.

"You see, a flashing light is when the light has longer periods of darkness and less light. What they have is longer periods of light than dark, right, Brad?"

"Four seconds light, one second dark," Brad said. His voice was strained. Neither of them had broken it to her father that they were having light malfunctions. Her father was an absolute non-believer in anything supernatural and would spend his entire trip trying to find a logical explanation for the odd mishaps.

"You see, instead of rotating, an occulting light has a screen that is periodically raised and lowered around the light source," her dad continued.

"Can I work the light?" Joyce asked.

"It's fully automated," Jim said. "That's the beauty of it, they don't even have to touch it."

"It used to be lit with whale oil," Bailey said. Now she too was "teaching," but what kids weren't interested in whales?

"That's totally cruel," Joyce said.

"Awesome," Thomas said. "Moby freaking Dick!"

Captain Jack, who hadn't been able to get a word in since her father stepped into the ferry, chimed in. "They didn't tell you about the light freaking out all the time? The Coast Guard keeps shutting it down."

Both Bailey and Brad gave Captain Jack a dirty look, but it didn't seem to bother him.

"Your lighthouse is freaking out?" Jim said. "Is that why they auctioned it off? Did you buy a clunker, dear?"

"No, we didn't buy a clunker, Dad. Just some wiring problems they haven't worked out."

"Ah, so you're no longer blaming the ghost?" Jack said. Joyce and Thomas, who had been hunched over since they arrived, suddenly sat up like someone had zapped them in the base of their spines.

"Ghost?" Joyce said. "You have a ghost?"

"Is it an evil spirit?" Thomas said. He looked at Joyce and waited for a reaction.

"It's a wiring problem," Bailey said. "We're going to fix it and then reapply for permission to use the light again."

"You didn't say anything about ghosts," Meg said. "You know Mom and I don't like anything creepy."

Jim leaned over to Brad and said in a loud whisper, "That's why Ellen picked me over John Boyd."

Ellen's laugh rang out. "Johnny Boyd was pretty creepy," she said.

"Ghosts," Joyce said, getting in Bailey's face. The young might be beautiful, but they certainly didn't have better breath. It was all Bailey could do not to side-step her niece. "Spill, details," Joyce continued. "You know I watch *Ghost Whisperer* religiously."

"It's just a rumor," Bailey said. "It's an old house. A beautiful, old house. You're going to love it."

"How can you even call it a lighthouse if there's no light?" Jim asked.

"I'm sorry, Dad. It just happened."

"I'll take a look at it," her father said. Bailey smiled and concentrated on not rolling her eyes. Joyce and Thomas started whispering about ghosts, Meg and her mother began worrying about whether or not they were going to be able to get a wink of sleep, and Captain Jack, who seemed thrilled he'd been able to break the news that Bailey and Brad hadn't, began to whistle. It was the longest little ferry ride of Bailey's life.

PLEASE SIGN OUR GUEST BOOK!

Are there any other kids on this island besides my stupid brother?

PLEASE SIGN OUR GUEST BOOK!

Lovely. Some of the furniture is in need of dusting. Although maybe it's on purpose, to give the lighthouse a more authentic look. Either way it's just lovely! I would be happy to dust for you, darling.

PLEASE SIGN OUR GUEST BOOK!

I wish Grandpa would stop talking.

PLEASE SIGN OUR GUEST BOOK!

You'll miss me talking when I'm dead.

PLEASE SIGN OUR GUEST BOOK!

Mom and Dad seem really proud of you. Can we lock the kids in the tower until they appreciate the goddess that is their mother?

Aunt Faye and Jason arrived fashionably late, loaded down with their own sheets and pillows. Faye grilled Bailey about the comforter on her bed, which was only a few months old. Bailey had to stand by while Faye inspected the room. Ellen, Meg, and Joyce watched joyfully from the doorway, Meg and Ellen with glasses of wine. Faye did this to all of them when she visited, and it was always fun to watch as long as it was someone else's turn. Just like the saying, "Doctors make the worst patients," real estate agents made the worst guests. Bailey wasn't looking forward to Faye pointing out the many flaws in the rest of the old building. There was only so much you could do when you lived so close to water. Bailey was now used to what she jokingly called the "great sea smell," but she could tell by Faye's up-turned nose that she was going to hear about it later.

"I can't wait to see the lighthouse tower," Faye said. "That was our favorite Nancy Drew, remember, Ellie? Nancy and the light-house tower."

"The light isn't working," Joyce said.

"What on earth?" Faye said.

"First it was the batteries, now they think it's a wiring prob-lem," Bailey said. "The Coast Guard is working on it."

"It's because of the ghost," Joyce said.

"Would you stop?" Meg said. "Faye, why don't you take these two back to the Rotten Apple with you."

"I'd put them to work," Faye said. Bailey couldn't help but feel a twinge of jealousy. She missed her work as an agent. It was one thing to put up with whiny clients when you stood to get a pile of money at the end of it; it was quite another when you were barely making ends meet and still had to clean their dirty sheets and dishes. Let's face it, she was a cook and a maid.

"So," Faye said when she was done inspecting her room. "Have you guzzled all the wine, or is there anything left for me?"

It was so nice to have her family around. Bailey noticed with affection that Thomas and her dad hung around Brad for the most part while the "girls" caught up. Jason tried joining the men at first, then gradually drifted over to the women and stayed. Despite her tendency to criticize, Faye was impressed with the lighthouse, and they all felt a little bit of awe as they stood on deck watching the ships pass below.

"They're going to get this light fixed while you're here," Bai-ley said. "I can feel it." She gave them the tour, pointing out all the technical terms she'd learned in the few short months she'd been here, something that seemed to impress all of them. They were set to have a barbecue that evening. Captain Jack even promised them some fresh fish caught by one of the lo-cals. Bailey was taking anyone who wanted into town where they could have a few hours hitting the antique shop, bookstore, and ice cream parlor. She was happy to see that Brad was throwing a football by the water with Thomas and her dad, and several times when she looked over they were all laughing. Her family wasn't perfect by any means, but surely Brad could see that for the most part, they brought joy. Once again she was reminded that he didn't grow up with this—his frame of reference was much, much bleaker, and it had to be the reason he was afraid to have children of his own. Maybe a long weekend with her family was just what the doctor ordered.

By the time they had spent a few hours hitting the little shops in town, Bailey was starting to feel a sense of pride and excitement. The gang thought everything was so quaint, and even Jason was starting to ask how much property cost in the area.

"I couldn't live here full-time, mind you," he said. "But it is a charming spot to get away from it all."

Faye pulled her aside after they hit the ice cream parlor, cornering her when she had her mouth full of Rocky Road. "You and your charming husband seem very happy." Bailey glanced over at Brad, who was leaning against the counter listening to her father. Who knows what he was going on about, but Brad was in for a long one. Brad felt her watching him and met her eyes. He gave her a little eyebrow movement, then smiled.

"We have our moments," Bailey said.

"And are any of these moments leading up to a little something in the oven?"

Bailey laughed. "I can't believe you still use that expression."

"I'm old," Faye said. "If I can get over it, you can too."

"We've got enough on our plates right now raising a lighthouse," Bailey said.

"Your eggs don't last forever, darling," Faye said. "Take it from me."

"You wanted to have children?"

"I still do," Faye said.

"Right," Jason said. "You changing diapers."

"Oh, it's not a reality anymore," Faye said. "Doesn't mean I don't want them. In theory."

"In theory, they are perfect," Jason whispered loudly to Bailey.

"If I were you, I'd carry on that man's adorable genes right this instant," Faye said.

"It's not that easy," Bailey said. She maneuvered away from Faye and managed to herd the group back outside. They only had an hour before they had to catch the ferry back to the house. Everyone was tired, and Brad suggested they head back to the ferry anyway and get Jack to take them home early. He wanted to go out on the rowboat with Thomas before it got dark, and her dad was eager to start the barbecue. As they approached the ferry, they noticed Jack speaking with a woman. Her back was to them, but from behind she was tall with a nice figure and long, dark hair. The rest of the group continued toward the pair, but Brad stopped in his tracks. His arm shot out and grabbed Bailey as she went by.

"What?" she said.

"You tell me," Brad said. "What did you do?" She looked at Brad's face. He was ten years old again. Just then, the woman with Captain Jack turned around. It was amazing how good she looked for a woman who had done years of hard drugs and alcohol. Elizabeth Jordan. What had she done indeed.

Chapter 29

He'd been so relaxed with her family, so happy. Every time she looked over at Brad, he was telling a joke, or patting Thomas on the back, or listening to her father with genuine interest. Every time she'd looked over at him, a strong feeling of love washed over her, and a physical sensation that was even stronger than touching him. When someone is yours, they are yours. Their smell, their smile, the way they glance at you over the heads of others, seeking out your head. You know you'll be in bed with that man and get to snuggle up to him and talk about everything happening in your day. Now with the B&B they got to gossip about their guests, saving up little tidbits from the day to share with each other at night.

With one glance at his mother, it was all undone. His smile, his good posture, his dimple. How long had it been since he'd seen her? Definitely over five years. The enormity of what she'd done was just starting to hit Bailey. But she hadn't meant for Elizabeth to just show up unannounced. She'd expected a phone call, a letter, a text, something. Any kind of warning at all. She wished she could turn back time, watch all of them walk backward so that she could do something to make Elizabeth Jordan disappear. Should she confess or pretend she had nothing to do with Brad's mother showing up out of the blue?

"Bailey invited me," Elizabeth called out. Everyone was just standing in a half circle several feet away from her, enrapt but keeping their distance like it was feeding time at the zoo. Bailey didn't dare look at Brad, but she could feel his eyes on her.

"I sent your mom one of those postcards," Bailey said. "I casually said I hoped she'd visit sometime. I actually didn't know you were coming, Elizabeth."

"You sent letters, you texted, you called," Elizabeth repeated. "You practically stalked me."

"It's been a long time, Mom," Brad said. Bailey let out her breath. At least he was talking. She'd seen Brad descend into periods of silence. He'd gone days in the past without speaking. Those had been some of the worst days of her life. He hadn't done it since their worst day at the coffee shop when the beans were bitter, and the milk wouldn't froth, and the inspector found a family of ants underneath a shelf of coffee mugs and fined them a thousand bucks. Bailey was the one who'd eaten the scone and forgotten to clean up the crumbs that attracted the ants.

And it had come at the worst time—a long line of customers that Brad was trying to impress and an espresso machine on the fritz, and even though she had sworn up and down that she had carefully checked the date on the milk, it was obvious that she had not. He didn't stop speaking to her to be deliberately cruel, it was just a genuine depression that settled over him, leaving him mute, a man without words. As long as he was talking, even if it was angry talk, it was better than the wall of silence.

"Everybody on the ferry," Bailey said. She was determined to muscle through this. Maybe it was a good thing her family was there; they could help distract Brad from the thing that was his mother. She was dressed as if going to a cocktail party: a tight green dress with sequins. Her hair was shiny and black as if just dipped in a well of ink. Her face was heavily made up, fake eyelashes, dark eyeliner, strong pink lipstick. She looked great for her age, but she looked a bit trashy too. But as far as Bailey could tell, she was sober, and that was saying something.

"You all go on ahead," Brad said. "Bailey and I are going to row over."

"What?"

"We have to get the boat back anyway," Brad said. "You left it moored behind Island Supplies last time, remember?" Moored was a nice word for it. She'd actually kicked it a few times before hitching a ride with Captain Jack.

"Maybe Thomas would like to go with you," Bailey said. Brad put his arm around Bailey and pulled her close. Then he whispered in her ear.

"Don't even try," he said.

"Brad and I will see you all over there." Faye and Jason swept Elizabeth up in the boat. Surely they didn't think she could afford one of their penthouses? And was it her imagination or was her father staring at Elizabeth? Her mom had a jealous streak, just like Bailey, so for her father's sake she hoped he would stop soon. Maybe it was a good thing she was going in the rowboat after all. Maybe she and Brad could row off into the sunset and leave all of them behind. She still couldn't tell how much trouble she was in; Brad was playing it close to his chest. They didn't speak as they trudged from the ferry to the rowboat about thirty feet away.

Brad's back muscles flexed as he pulled the boat from the grass embankment to the water. Bailey waited until they were both ass-in-rowboat to speak. "I didn't think she was going to just show up like that, I swear," she said. Brad pushed off, and the little boat glided out with a whoosh. Bailey had to grip the side to keep her balance. The new rowboat was better than the old one, but it too had sprung a leak. Even though Brad had patched it, water was still trickling in, getting Bailey's shoes wet. She hated having wet feet, but she found she could only complain about so many things at one time. "Please don't be mad. Not with my family here. I don't think I'll be able to get through the next few days if you're mad at me." It was true too.

Bailey soaked up Brad's moods like they were her own. It didn't seem to work so much the other way around—many were the times that he'd been clueless that Bailey was upset. Especially when he was in workaholic mode. This would often make Bailey even more upset than the original event. How in the world could he miss the fact that she was upset? Many were the nights when the fight would end with Brad throwing up his arms and yelling, "You don't even remember what you're so upset about!"

"That's not the point."

"How can that not be the point? Why am I being punished for not noticing that you're upset when you don't even remember what you're so upset about?" Often Bailey had no reply but to stomp away. Brad didn't have that option. In this rowboat it was sink or swim.

As Brad pushed off in the rowboat, Bailey watched the ferry make its way across the Hudson River. He followed her gaze. "It's just you and me," he said. His words washed over her like the remnants of a familiar but long-forgotten song. He used to say that to her all the time. In front of their fireplace in their little café in Colorado, the one time they got it to work, just one glorious almost-hour before they were overtaken with smoke and found out it would cost three thousand dollars to clean the chimney and repair broken bricks and the flue, and Brad swore they would fix it as soon as they started to turn a profit and Bailey insisted they would start turning more of a profit if they had a roaring fire for people to sip their coffee by, and they never did fix it because they didn't stay long enough to turn a profit because the fireplace may have been the first, but wasn't the last item that needed fixing, so yes, they only got one fire, one hour, but oh, what a fire it was, what a magical hour.

Crackling orange heat sparking out at them like the tips of fat burning fingers, and Brad's smiling mouth and dimples, and his beautiful eyes staring into hers. Then he took her hand and kissed the tips of her fingers one by one, slowly working up to using his tongue on her palm, such a simple gesture but the sensation so erotic it led to her reaching for his belt buckle. They made love so much when they were in their twenties.

When they hit thirty they vowed they would do it five times a week no matter what. In reality they averaged once or twice a week, and lately, not even that much.

"You're not rowing," Bailey said. They'd barely made any progress. The ferry had long reached the other side. They would be wanting dinner soon. "They're going to kill each other," Bailey said.

"You and me," Brad said.

"And baby makes three." Bailey said it before she could censor herself. It just flew out of her mouth. That was something else they used to say. Oh yes, there was a time when they did talk about it, actually when Brad talked about it. What were they, sixteen? He would say, "You and me," she would repeat, "You and me," and he would smile at her with that look of being up to no good and add, "And baby makes three." It used to send a chill down her spine. He wanted to have babies with her back then. He teased her about it. What happened? Had she missed some tiny, precious window of time? Her biological clock was fine, but had her husband's run out?

"Have I told you lately how much I love you?" Brad said.

"Are you going to push me overboard and pretend it was an accident?" Bailey said.

"No," Brad said. "But I do have something to tell you." They were thirty feet from where they pushed off, and a long, long way from the lighthouse.

"Push me off instead," Bailey said. "Say it was an accident." Nobody ever wanted to hear "I have something to tell you." Did anything good ever follow those words? The last time Brad said that to her, he'd bought the lighthouse.

"Bailey, please."

"Look. My mom and dad are here. And my sister. And my niece and nephew. Your mom is here."

"Thank you for reciting the guest list, gorgeous, but I still got something I have to tell you." He'd called her gorgeous. This couldn't be too bad.

Or was it worse?

"Haven't you ever heard of a time and a place?"

"Did you tell my mother that Aunt Olivia left us money? Is that why she's here?" Bailey looked at the sky. Lazy strips of blue intersected fluffy white clouds. A tugboat honked downriver. She couldn't lie to Brad. Lying in a marriage was a no-no. Especially if she could easily get caught. And of course Elizabeth would bring it up, why wouldn't she? But if she admitted that the only reason Elizabeth was here was because she happened to mention that Olivia left them a fortune, then the chances of Brad reconciling with either of them could be slim.

"That's one question answered," Brad said. "You should have asked Olivia for a few poker-face tips."

"Are you mad at me?" Bailey said. "I just wanted—"

"Me to get over my mommy issues so we could have a baby?"

"Wow," Bailey said. She couldn't believe how well he knew her. "That's outrageous!" Bailey said. "I cannot believe you just said that to me."

"I don't care," Brad said. "It's okay."

"So why did you row me mid-river?"

"I never get to talk to you alone anymore."

"Whose fault is that?"

"Why do you sound argumentative? I'm just trying to talk to you here."

"Okay. I'm sorry. I did want you to make up with your mother. Or kick her out of your life for good."

"Because you think that's why we don't have a baby?" Bailey grabbed the oars and pulled, pulled, pulled. "You're going the wrong way." She glared at Brad, then, forgetting which direction they were going, she laid on the oars once again and pushed, pushed, pushed.

"I. Don't. Know," Bailey said as she exerted herself and the rowboat inched toward the lighthouse. "I've turned over every scenario."

"Oh, you have, have you?"

"Yes," Bailey said. "I have." She should really let him do the rowing. It was killing her. And they were barely getting anywhere. And his arms were folded across his chest and he was leaning back in the little boat and he looked so freaking smug. He unfolded his arms, held them aloft.

"Let's hear the scenarios."

Bailey paused from her rowing and looked up at him. Her hair was starting to frizz to the sides. Sweat was pooling under her armpits. She wanted to dump him off the boat. She also needed him to start the grill. Life was a constant series of conflicting wants and needs.

"You don't want me to list them right now."

"Oh, but I do."

"You're impotent, you're selfish, you're scared, you think I'll love our baby more than I love you, you're lazy, you're spoiled, you have mommy issues, you want to sleep with other women, you think I'll get fat, you think we'll stop having sex, you never grew up with a loving family so you don't believe they exist, you think I'd be a terrible mother—"

"Bailey Rene Jordan!"

You asked.

"Scream it again. I don't think the tugboat driver heard you over his whistle." The boat bobbed in the water as they fell silent. Bailey trailed her hand in the cold river.

"You brought me out here so I couldn't throw anything, didn't you?" Bailey said. Brad smiled.

"It's a bonus," he admitted.

"So what did you want to tell me?"

"My mother is not a well woman."

"That, my darling, is no secret."

"If she thinks she can get a piece of what we have, she'll say anything to get it."

"Okay."

"I mean anything."

"I believe you."

"So if she starts talking crazy this weekend, you have to promise me—promise me you won't believe a word she says."

"I promise."

"I mean it, Bailey."

"You're starting to scare me."

"Sorry. I just can't stand the thought of her getting between us."

"She won't. And I'm sorry for contacting her. But you never know. Maybe she's changed."

"I love you."

"I love you too."

"I'm sorry I haven't given you everything you wanted."

"Life's a journey, babe. Not a destination."

"Am I glad to hear you say that. Because I think we're way off course."

Chapter 30

Elizabeth Jordan had a lot to say, and apparently most of it came from AA. Several times, while they were preparing the barbecue, Bailey heard her interject "one day a time" into the conversation, even when it didn't quite seem to fit. Brad and Bailey's father were manning the grill, Thomas and Joyce were halfheartedly throwing a Frisbee, which more often than not Tree caught in his mouth, Faye and Jason were drinking gin and tonics, and Meg and her mother were telling Bailey about their latest mother-daughter quilting project, something they'd taken up together years ago.

"We're getting good at it," Ellen said. She glanced at Brad, then lowered her voice. "Should we start making a baby quilt?"

"Definitely not," Elizabeth said with a derisive laugh. She looked at Bailey for support. "Am I right, or am I right?"

"Mom," Brad said. "Would you go inside and get more lemonade?" Brad had fabulous hearing. Even when immersed in another task several feet away, he was still listening, watching. It used to flatter Bailey; now it just comforted her, knowing he always had his ear out for her.

"Why would you say that?" Bailey asked. *Because he didn't have such a great childhood himself?*

"Brad's too much of a child himself," Elizabeth said. "And of course—"

"The lemonade, Mom?"

Elizabeth stopped talking and stood up. "One day a time," she said, heading into the kitchen.

"Do we even have lemonade?" Bailey asked Brad.

"No," Brad said.

Things were so much easier for Bailey with her mother around. She helped strip and wash sheets and towels, cook meals, and it seemed every time Bailey turned around her mother was cleaning either the kitchen or one of the bathrooms, singing to herself as she went. Her mother always seemed to truly enjoy domestic life. Did Bailey? She didn't think so. She certainly wasn't singing, or even whistling. There hadn't even been any ghostly activity since her family arrived. But the best news of all was delivered by the Coast Guard. They dropped by with what they said was their last attempt to replace batteries and wiring, and before they knew it, the light was back on and shining. It was cause for celebration. Everyone stood by the river, gazing at the light, toasting with a bottle of champagne that Brad bought in town.

"You're so lucky, Aunt Bailey," Joyce said. Even Thomas seemed impressed. Elizabeth was standing near Brad, her arm hooked in his. He'd been hanging awfully close to her lately, as if trying to monitor her every word. Bailey had thought about the conversation out in the rowboat several times since. She knew Brad was embarrassed by Elizabeth, but Bailey of all people knew what the woman was like. What was he so afraid of?

"This is a good sign," Meg said. "The light coming back on."

"This is actually decent champagne," Jason said. He held the glass out and eyed it. "How many bottles did you buy?"

"One," Brad said.

Jason's satisfied look turned to one of pure horror. "What time does the liquor store close?" he said.

Brad looked at his watch. "About an hour ago," Brad said. Jason and Faye exchanged a look.

"We're not in Kansas anymore, Dorothy," Jason said to Faye.

"Wrong, Toto," Faye said. "We are in Kansas, and—"

"*That's* the problem," they said in unison.

"We have wine in the house somewhere," Bailey said.

"Who's the good-looking young couple in the tent?" Jim asked. Bailey had forgotten all about Jake and Angel. In fact, she hadn't seen them around at all lately. Bailey filled them in, leaving out the bit about Jake having a crush on her and Angel on Brad.

"They met here and fell in love," Bailey said.

"You should put that in the brochure," Faye said. "Now. The light is on, the champagne is gone. I think I'm going to head to the house and read. Did you just hear me? Read? My God, what is the country doing to me?" She and Jason belted out a laugh, then the two of them turned and headed for the house.

"We'll find the wine, don't worry about us," Jason said over his shoulder.

Meg, Ellen, and Bailey stayed up long after everyone else went to bed. Bailey brought out a bottle of wine that she'd kept secret, and the three of them sat talking and enjoying it. The stars were out, and even the chill in the air was comforting as long as you had a shawl or a sweater, which, thanks to Ellen, they all did.

"I'm kind of looking forward to winter," Bailey said. "I don't think we'll have many guests, and I'll finally get to be alone with my husband."

"He seems to be doing better," Meg said. "I mean, I haven't heard him talk about any of that near-death stuff."

"Ever since I smashed Aunt Olivia's urn and a deck of cards flew out instead of her ashes, he's stopped obsessing," Bailey said.

"What?" Ellen said. Bailey filled them in, leaving out the bit about the séance and purposefully throwing the urn. Luckily, they were too curious about Olivia's whereabouts to question her story. "Where are the ashes?" Ellen asked.

"We have no idea," Bailey said. "But Brad thinks it's some kind of message from Olivia."

"Seriously?" Meg said. "Like what? She scattered herself?"

"I didn't say he was cured," Bailey said. "Just slightly improved."

"What did Elizabeth mean about Brad not wanting children?" Ellen asked. "Is it true?" Bailey should have never given her mother more wine. Half a glass and she would say anything.

"Of course not," Bailey said. "You can't believe a word that woman says." Was that what Brad was so worried about? That his mother would start saying things like that? Or was it something more specific?

"I think she has a crush on your ferry captain," Meg said. "What's his name?"

"Jack," Bailey said. "Except that it's not." Ellen and Meg cocked their heads and Bailey explained the joke.

"Kind of weird, isn't it?" Meg said. "That you don't even know his name?"

"I guess," Bailey said. "If we lived anywhere else. But around here, it's a little more laid back. People are free to be who they want—or not to be."

"So what does Brad say about having children?" Ellen said. "Does he want them?"

"We know Mom certainly wants more grandbabies," Meg said. "Mine are teenagers now, so they don't count anymore."

"Hush, you," Ellen said. "You know how much I love Joyce and Thomas."

"Then what's with the pressure? I'm sure if Bailey wanted children, she would have had them by now."

Bailey felt a familiar angst rise in her, but then she realized she was the one who had given Meg that impression all these years. Any time anyone in their immediate family mentioned children, Bailey acted like it was her that was waiting. Had she been trying to protect Brad all these years, or herself?

"I hope mine turn out like Joyce and Thomas," Bailey said.

"They're so perfect." Meg and Ellen exchanged a look. Bailey realized what she'd done. She'd completely forgotten about their trouble with Thomas lately. He'd been so well-behaved here she was starting to wonder if they had been exaggerating his problems. The look between her sister and her mother told her otherwise.

"What?" Bailey said. "What was that?"

"Nothing," Meg said quickly.

"Meg." Apparently Bailey wasn't the only one shielding her family from truths.

"Nothing, really," Meg said. "It's just Thomas. He's been—I don't know. Such a boy lately, I guess."

"Meg," Ellen said. "It's more than that. Just because he's a boy. That's making excuses."

"Would somebody please fill me in on the details?"

"He's been violent lately, okay?" Meg said. "Are you happy now?"

"Of course not," Bailey said. "Why would you even say that?" Meg looked on the verge of starting a fight herself, but Bailey saw tears lurking. Maybe the bottle of wine hadn't been such a good idea. The more they drank and relaxed, the more they were starting to unravel. Bailey leaned forward and studied her sister's face. There was no humor there.

"What do you mean violent?"

"He's been in several fistfights after school," Ellen chimed in. "Hanging around the wrong boys. Smoking pot and getting tattoos." Bailey almost choked on her wine. Coming out of anybody else's mouth it wouldn't have been that shocking. Listening to her mother say it with a straight face was another story. "He stays out late too," Ellen continued. "Meg can't get him to come in."

"All right, Mother," Meg said.

"What does Andy say?" Bailey asked.

"He's tried talking to him, we've both tried."

"You've tried, darling," Ellen said. "But that husband of yours has been MIA."

"Andy's been traveling a lot this year," Meg explained.

"And that's part of the problem," Ellen said. "Boys especially need their fathers."

"Well, what would you have Andy do, Mom? We're lucky he even has a job in today's market."

"Why didn't you tell me all this before?" Bailey said.

"You've had your hands full," Meg said. "And I don't want anyone thinking bad of him. He's a good kid, you know? He's still a good kid."

"Of course he is," Bailey said. "I had no idea. He seemed a little quiet, but he's been great here."

"So far," Ellen said.

"Really, Mom," Meg said. "It's not like he's going to start a fight with anyone here. It's just that school."

"He's not in school during the summer, and he's been in a fight almost every week," Ellen said.

"Every week?" Bailey said.

"Last week he sent some boy to the hospital and now he's going to have to go to court," her mom said.

"Oh my God. Meg. I can't believe you didn't tell me."

"Thanks, Mom."

"Don't blame Mom. This is serious. I can't even imagine Thomas beating someone else up, let alone putting them in the hospital."

"I know, I know, okay?" Meg said. "Maybe going to juvie is what he needs."

"Maybe he should stay here for the rest of the summer," Ellen said.

"I thought you said he had court," Bailey said.

"It's in two weeks," Meg said. "He does seem happier here."

"Yes, that's it. He should stay here!" Bailey said. And that's when she realized, microseconds too late, that she was the one who shouldn't have been drinking the wine.

Chapter 31

In a marriage, you learned to predict how your spouse was going to react to any given situation. It was probably an ancient survival instinct, like animals in the wild growing thick pelts to keep their bodies warm. After so many years of being together, Bailey was confident in her "Brad-reading" skills. From the little things, like the fact that he would order bruschetta in every restaurant, stop to talk to each and every elderly person they passed, and floss his teeth after dinner, to the big things, like whenever anyone brought up a political issue without actually having facts to back up their positions, they were in for a barrage of cold, hard facts from Brad, delivered with a passion five times bigger than theirs, to the knowledge that whenever she brought up the subject of having a baby, she knew he was going to find an ingenious way of changing the subject. Bailey thought she had a pretty good handle on Brad Jordan's moods, his moves, his basic patterns of interacting. But this, she never expected. Turning down one of her close family members? When she put up with an entire near-death, co-lighthouse-owning, sleep-eating, spandex-wearing, dog-abandoning committee? And it was only for the last two weeks of summer. From the way Brad was acting, you would have thought she'd asked him to adopt Thomas as their own.

Bailey sat on their bed while he paced, and defended his argument against having Thomas stay. Bailey was trying to give him her full attention, but she was distracted by Tree, who was sitting at the base of the stairs leading up to the tower. He was gazing up the spiral staircase and whining. He'd been doing this a lot lately and they had no idea why. There was no way they could carry the big shepherd up the stairs, and he cried as if he were dying to go up, but he'd yet to put even a single paw on a single step. Brad whistled and pointed to the bed. Tree stopped whining, and gracefully leapt onto Bailey's side of the bed, where he stretched out as if he owned it. Seconds later, he was snoring. Males, Bailey thought. She'd never been able to fall asleep that fast. Brad continued talking.

"Don't you think we have enough on our plates? Should we just keep piling on more?"

"It's not like he's moving in with us forever. It's only a couple of weeks."

"It's too much responsibility."

"It's not like we'd have to babysit him every second, Brad. He's sixteen."

"Sixteen," Brad said. "Sixteen." He stopped pacing for a second and looked out the window as if the number sixteen were hovering above the Hudson River. "Sixteen," he said again softly. Brad actually looked as if he were about to cry. Just when Bailey thought they were getting past things, settling in. If he started up about the light again, Bailey was going to hurl herself off the tower. "Sixteen," Brad said again. Somehow, his button was stuck.

"I think we've established that," Bailey said. What was the matter with him? Just a few hours ago he was throwing around a football with Thomas.

Brad turned from the window and fixed his intense gaze on Bailey. "Do you think everything happens for a reason?" Brad said. "Or is everything just one big cosmic joke?" This one lifted Bailey off the bed.

"Since when did my nephew become a cosmic joke?"

"That's not what I meant."

"What did you mean, then?"

"Never mind." Brad headed for the down staircase, then stopped at the edge. Slowly, he turned back to face her. "There's nowhere to go."

"What?"

"This is our house, and I just want to go to the kitchen, or the living room, or the museum, and yet I can't, because there are people everywhere. There are always people everywhere." Brad went to the dresser, and for a split second she thought he was going to sweep everything off it, including a mirror propped against the wall, but instead he just put his head down on its hard surface and groaned.

"Yes," Bailey said. "Sometimes it sucks."

Brad lifted his head, then walked over to where Bailey was standing and took her in his arms. "You tried to warn me," he said. "You told me this was a mistake." Bailey pulled away. Now he sat on the bed while she started to pace. She couldn't let Brad panic. Panic was bad. Panic was dropping everything and running again. And this time, panic would leave them homeless and broke. Was this all because she'd invited Elizabeth? From the minute he'd rowed her out in the middle of the Hudson River to warn Bailey not to listen to anything his mother had to say, he'd been acting funny.

"You've had a long day," Bailey said. "Why don't you rest? I'll go downstairs and keep the crew entertained. You can write in your journals, or go through weather maps, or just take a little nap."

"I hate the weather maps, Bailey. I've just been pretending to like them."

"Okay."

"Did you hear me say you were right? This was a mistake. This was one big, colossal mistake." It was happening, Brad was entering panic mode. She would have to go easy on him. She wasn't even going to point out that it was ludicrous to use "big" and "colossal" in the same sentence. Go with colossal, she would have said. It's a stronger word and renders "big" obsolete. Instead, Bailey sat down beside him and put her arm around him.

"You need to stop thinking this instant. You're tired."

"I'm not just tired," Brad said. "I'm bored. I'm bored to death out here. You were right. Manhattan is where it's at. I miss Manhattan, don't you?"

"So we'll go for a visit. Stay with Aunt Faye, or Jesse, or at a hotel."

"You could get your job back, right? Faye would take you back."

Bailey concentrated on her breath. In, out. In, out. She thought about suing the psychiatrist who came for the weekend and failed to see that her husband needed help. Bipolar. Manic-depressive. Was that him? The words were thrown around too much these days. Besides, she didn't want a medicated husband. He had his quirks, but she'd always just chalked it up to Brad being Brad. But this, she hated to see. He was truly in a state of turmoil. It made it impossible to be angry with him.

"Stop worrying. Stop thinking. This is our home now." At first Bailey was just saying it to calm Brad down. But as soon as the words came out of her mouth, she knew it was true. She liked living here. She liked new people coming in and out, bringing their stories, and their weird questions, and their quirks, and having a few laughs or even arguments at the breakfast table. She was starting to notice little things too, like, so much for dogs—people actually looked like their luggage. Angel had pink bags, and Vera had oversized bags, and the horny old couple had green bags. It was fascinating. Maybe she could get Brad to blog about that. She for one certainly wasn't ready to give it all up.

She didn't even mind the strange noises at night anymore—

an intriguing mystery never hurt anyone. She liked looking out at the light spreading its beam across the river at night, and imagining all the other nights in history that it lit the way for ships going by. She liked their morning walks with Tree running up ahead or lingering behind; she liked noticing the birds, and plopping fish, and blooming plants. She liked knowing answers to questions guests asked and researching the ones she didn't, then eagerly anticipating a future guest asking the question again so she could get it right this time.

She was looking forward to fall. Then winter. Then spring. She felt as if she were a part of something. She didn't even have the urge to go into town much anymore. She was just . . . content. For the first time in a long life of moving around, she felt as if she truly belonged somewhere. And here, not even a year into it, Brad was starting to freak out again. Maybe life *was* just one big cosmic joke.

"I might have had my doubts at first, but this life isn't so bad. We're here. We're doing it. We've put so much into this. We're going to be just fine."

"We could let someone else on the committee run it," Brad said. "Kim would be my first choice. She was the most stable of them all, don't you think?"

Bailey took a deep breath so that she wouldn't let him have it. "I don't care what it says on paper. This is our home now." *You wanted a lighthouse, you got a lighthouse, and now you're going to live in your lighthouse!* Thomas was also staying for the rest of the summer, and that was that. There was no need to get into that now either.

"Are you happy here?" Brad said. "Are you happy with me?"

"Yes," Bailey said. "A thousand times yes. We have everything we need. You and me. A really cool place to live. Family and friends, and a somewhat weird, but sweet dog. Everything else is just icing. It's time to stop searching for something we've had all along, Jordan. I can't keep uprooting our lives whenever you get scared." Brad rubbed his eyes. Bailey put her hand on his head. His curls had grown back, as lush and thick as ever. She loved the feel of it beneath her fingers. "Go to sleep. I mean it. The doctor talked about this. He said you might need to rest a lot more than you used to."

"You're right," Brad said. "I'm so tired."

"And when you're feeling better, I'll help you with the museum. You just need a project. Then you won't be so bored."

"I guess," Brad said. It wasn't exactly a ringing endorsement, but Bailey would take it.

"It's settled, then." Bailey gently pushed Brad down on the bed. She covered him with the small blanket at the foot of the bed and gently kissed him on the lips. By the time she was down the first few stairs, he had already begun to snore alongside Tree. Bailey was jealous. She had the strangest feeling that as far as she was concerned, it was going to be a long time before she had another good night's sleep.

Bailey spent the last few hours with her family while Brad slept. They walked along the river, waved at ships, picked up little pieces of sea glass—or river glass, as Meg corrected them—and tried to guess names of birds, and insects, and plants that littered the way. When they headed back to pack, Meg took Bailey aside.

"So what did Brad say about Thomas?" In the distance, Thomas was throwing rocks into the river. From the frequency with which he was glancing over, Bailey realized that he too was waiting to hear the answer.

"He said absolutely," Bailey said. She plastered a huge grin on her face. "What did you think he was going to say?" The two women laughed and even Thomas sported a hint of a smile. Bailey glanced up at the tower, wondering if the light was going to strike her down for her lie. It was the first time she could ever remember going against Brad's wishes. She was allowed at least one veto, wasn't she? Of course she was. She just prayed Brad would see it that way.

It was torture trying to entertain Elizabeth without Bailey's family to keep her sane. Elizabeth didn't like getting up early.

By the time she shuffled into the kitchen in her robe and slippers, Bailey had already cleaned up from breakfast. Elizabeth expected to be served no matter what time she rolled in. Elizabeth also didn't like going for walks (the rocks hurt her feet), or sitting on the patio (too many mosquitoes), or being in the keeper's house alone (too creepy). When Bailey pointed out that Thomas was in the attic, Elizabeth continued to complain as if she didn't hear her. *One day at a time,* Bailey found herself repeating in her head, *one day at a time.* Elizabeth, Bailey realized, hating herself for the thought, had been easier to tolerate as a drunk. She may have put down the drugs and booze, but her personality had never recovered. Bailey had fully expected Elizabeth would take off the minute she learned that the lighthouse was officially owned by the Olivia Foundation and she would never have any legal claim over it. The reason Elizabeth was continuing to hang around soon became apparent.

Whenever Captain Jack's ferry chugged by their side of the island, Elizabeth would just happen to appear on the shore, always dressed in something short and tight, and suddenly the rocks didn't bother her feet so much. Bailey could smell her perfume from miles away. Brad was flummoxed. He pointed out that Captain Jack wasn't rich. Bailey countered that in this case, she thought it was just pure lust. Brad slapped his hands over his ears and refused to listen to any more. Bailey would have actually supported the match if she thought Jack had any interest in Elizabeth. But if he noticed he had an admirer, he sure didn't act like it.

"If you ever do make headway," Bailey told Elizabeth one day, "be sure and find out his real name for me." Bailey should have never said this. Elizabeth seemed to take it as her personal mission. Although it did seem to perk her up quite a bit. She began complaining less and chattering about Captain Jack more.

Thank God for Thomas. Bailey was actually enjoying having him around. If only she could say the same thing for Brad.

Despite the fact that Thomas was behaving exceptionally well, and making a point to express how much he appreciated their offer to stay, and trying to engage Brad in various activities, Brad began retreating. More and more he was taking the rowboat into town without inviting anyone else along. What he even found to do in town, Bailey couldn't imagine, but she didn't press him. At first she was just grateful that he was still speaking to her. But now it was getting ridiculous. Thomas was a great kid who needed a little help and attention from an adult male. And her adult male was sulking. She was going to have to figure out what was wrong with him. It wasn't until Bailey vaguely mentioned something around Elizabeth that she realized Elizabeth Jordan knew something Bailey didn't. They were sitting alone at the breakfast table. Brad had finally yet reluctantly agreed to let Thomas go rowing with him. Bailey eagerly watched them from the window. From what she could see, Thomas was the one doing all the talking, and it broke her heart, and quite frankly made her angry, that Brad still seemed so sullen.

"I don't get it," Bailey said, mostly to herself. "Thomas wants Brad to like him so much." Bailey could feel Elizabeth staring at her. She turned. Elizabeth held her gaze even as she stirred her tea.

"It has to be difficult for Bradley," Elizabeth said. Bailey winced inwardly. She hated when Elizabeth called him Bradley.

"It's difficult for all of us," Bailey replied, even though she wasn't quite sure what Elizabeth was referring to.

"Still, having a boy that age around all the time?" Bailey slightly nodded, although again, she was confused. Okay, so teenage boys could be tough. But there weren't other boys his age around to get into fights with, and he was genuinely a nice kid.

"I'm not sure what you mean," Bailey said. It was the look that Elizabeth gave her that set the alarm bells ringing in Bailey's head. It was a clearly a look of triumph.

"Well," Elizabeth said. "I guess you'll just have to ask your husband, then."

Chapter 32

Elizabeth began to give Bailey daily reports on her attempts to ferret out Captain Jack's real name. She flirted with Louis, the sixty-something-year-old owner of Louis ZA!, the best pizza shop in town, but if he knew Captain Jack's real name, he wasn't about to tell her. He simply joked about it. "He won't tell you, eh? That's our Jack! I never knew he had such a closed mouth! Especially the way he chows down on our extra-large, extra-cheese, extra-thick-crust, meat lover's special! Don't worry about him, pretty lady. What can I get you? A personal-sized margherita pizza, maybe?" And she got pretty much the same reaction everywhere. From the bank, to the flower shop, to the antique store, to the bookstore, to the ice cream parlor.

"I even bought a triple scoop with sprinkles," Elizabeth said. "And they still wouldn't break." Even though it was nice to see Elizabeth with a raison d'être, she was worried it was all going to get back to Jack. She didn't want him thinking they were nothing but a bunch of snoops. And Elizabeth had been hogging a lot of Brad's time lately too. It seemed every time Bailey turned a corner, Elizabeth was off with Brad for a private walk or having an animated chat by the windows in the kitchen, and every time Bailey walked into the room, they would immediately stop talking and just stare at her. Bailey was starting to feel like the odd man out. At least next weekend would be good. Jesse was coming, and they were also having a going-away party for Jake and Angel, who had just announced that they were going to go off and see the world. Bailey was relieved. Things had been so stressful with Brad that she was ashamed to admit she'd entertained a few fantasies about Jake lately. It was just so flattering, the way he still looked at her once in a while, as if he would drop Angel in a heartbeat if only Bailey said the word. It was normal to fantasize, Bailey told herself, men probably did it every second of the day. But she did feel guilty. Her best friend would straighten her out. Yes, a dose of Jesse was exactly what she needed.

She also talked Brad into having another movie night on the patio. She picked *Planet of the Apes* since it was Brad's favorite and Thomas had never seen it. It didn't go as well as Bailey had planned. Thomas actually made fun of the movie all the way through, and even though he didn't say a word, Bailey could tell that Brad was furious. Thomas was probably just acting out. How could the kid not pick up on how cool Brad had been toward him?

Later, when they were alone, in the kitchen, Bailey finally confronted Brad. But he wasn't about to concede any guilt. He just threw his arms up. "I didn't want him here in the first place!" he said. They heard a floorboard squeak. Their heads swiveled to the door separating the kitchen from the living room. It was still slightly swinging as if someone had just gone through it, and the tide clock was swinging to High Tide.

"Oh God," she said. "What if that was Thomas?"

"He shouldn't be sneaking around," Brad said.

"It's the kitchen. He could have been coming in for a snack."

"Maybe it was my mother."

"Your mother would have just stayed," Bailey said. "You have to go talk to Thomas."

"And say what?"

"Tell him you want him here."

"Bailey."

"I don't get you. You're not like this." Brad didn't answer. But he did look as if he was at least taking in what she was saying, so she kept going. "You are someone who cares about people. You're hurting his feelings, honey."

"I know," Brad said. "I'm sorry. I'm really really sorry."

"I think you need to tell him that," Bailey said. "Please." Brad nodded and picked up an apple from the bowl on the counter.

"I'll go see if he wants this," he said.

"Thank you," Bailey said. He got as far as the door when Bailey called out to him. "Wait." Brad stopped. Bailey opened the cupboard and reached around to her secret place in the back. She threw him the bag of the really good chocolates. Brad laughed, tossed the apple back at her, and went to find Thomas.

It seemed to work. Thomas went back to following Brad around, and although Brad wasn't exactly his normal exuberant self, Bailey could see that he was at least making an effort. The week flew by and before she knew it, she was in Island Supplies buying items for the going-away party. She kept her eye on Jack as she shopped, and as usual he watched her openly, sipping now and again from what appeared to be a glass of Scotch.

"My mother-in-law is subtly asking around town about you," Bailey said. Jack let out a loud laugh.

"Subtle my ass," he said. "She came in the other day and practically tried to fingerprint me." Bailey laughed too.

"You know she's not a bad-looking woman," Bailey said.

"Never said she was," Jack said.

"She's been asking everyone in town your real name."

"And?"

"Sealed like a drum," Bailey said.

"I'll drink to that," Jack said. And he did. On second thought, getting involved with a booze hound probably wasn't the smartest move Elizabeth could make.

"Do you have any steaks?" Bailey asked. Jack often got great shipments of meat and fish. The only problem was you never knew when he was getting what. Although it fit Bailey's new, "go with the flow" lifestyle. She never knew if they'd be having pork chops, or tilapia, or rib eye. Jack took whatever sales were being offered.

"Expecting some nice juicy ones tomorrow. You having a party?"

"Yes," Bailey said. "And you're invited."

"It's not a surprise wedding, is it?" Jack asked. "With me as the groom?"

"Come now," Bailey said. "I don't hate my mother-in-law that much." Jack laughed again. Mystery name, drinking, and womanizing aside, Bailey did really like Jack.

"So what's the occasion?" Jack asked.

"Jake and Angel," Bailey said.

Jack dropped his glass on the counter. He grabbed the bottle, poured another drink. "Oh yeah?" he said. It wasn't his usual voice. It was as if he was trying to sound curious, but underneath he was really furious. Bailey wondered if he had a secret crush on Angel. "What about them?" He was definitely having some kind of reaction.

"It's a going-away party," Bailey said. "They're leaving."

"What do you mean, 'they're leaving'?" This time, Jack didn't even try and hide his reaction. Was it because of the drinking? Bailey made a show of cocking her head.

"You sound upset," she said. Actually, he sounded downright pissed off, but Bailey didn't want to start a fight.

"No, I just . . . You know. It figures, doesn't it? Get a good contractor in town and he takes off at the drop of a hat." Was that it? Had Jack been getting a take for recommending Jake?

"Of course we could still use him," Bailey said. "But the kids are in love. Gotta let 'em go and see the world, right?" *So that married women like me don't end up accidentally getting kissed again.* She wasn't about to say that to Jack either. He switched back to his happy-go-lucky self.

"I'll bring the steaks," he said. "And wine. What does Brad's lovely mother like to drink?"

"She's a recovering alcoholic," Bailey said. "She no longer drinks." Jack suddenly looked like he wanted to uninvite him-

self. He fell into a brooding silence as he rang up her purchases. Maybe all men were somewhat like Brad. Flirting and
joking one minute, scowling the next. It was impossible to figure them out. They weren't too good at picking up on women's
subtleties either. Bailey had to stand there for quite a while,
looking forlorn, before he finally caught on that she wanted a
ferry ride home.

Jesse arrived late Thursday afternoon, and Bailey was thrilled
the weather couldn't have been nicer. Summer was still hanging on to its warmth during the day, yet giving the air a touch of
a breeze in the evening, hinting that fall was on its way. Sunsets
lately had been lazy and breathtaking. Red and purple stripes
raced across the sky, then melted in a soup of dark orange before falling to navy and then black. And then the stars would
come out, popping across the sky and shining like crystal
droplets. Bailey couldn't wait to just gaze at the stars with her
friend and catch up on their lives. Sure enough, Jesse fell in
love with the place on sight. It made Bailey feel good to hear
her go on about how beautiful, how remarkable it all was. Brad
seemed proud too, and Bailey hoped it would help him get
over his recent doubts.

Bailey wished Elizabeth weren't in the master bedroom so
that Jesse could stay there, but Jesse insisted she liked the smallest room anyway. It had a nicer view onto the river and she
loved the wood-burning stove. Although it was nice to have dinner and a walk along the river as a group, Bailey was looking
forward to some much-needed alone time with her friend.
Luckily, Jake and Angel voluntarily retreated to their tent, and
Brad invited Thomas and Elizabeth up to their loft to watch a
DVD. Bailey and Jesse took a bottle of wine into the main room,
joined only by Tree, who curled up at Bailey's feet.

"You seem really happy," Jesse said.

"I am," Bailey said. "Mostly."

"Mostly?"

Bailey filled Jesse in on Brad's recent sulking. She admitted
it was probably all her fault for inviting Elizabeth Jordan. Jesse

pointed out that the fact that Bailey had stayed with Brad despite learning that their home was owned by a committee earned her a lot of leeway. Bailey agreed, although she wasn't sure Brad did.

"What about the ghost?" Jesse said. "Any recent sightings?" Bailey decided not to tell Jesse the truth. What good would it do to tell her about the woman talking to the baby, or Olivia's ashes disappearing, or the music box playing late at night? Filling Jesse's head with a bunch of stories before sending her upstairs to bed right underneath the attic would be a form of abuse.

"All quiet lately," Bailey said. "Personally, I blame the Girl Scouts. Just making up stories to get badges." It prompted Bailey to fetch the guest book, and the two of them spent considerable time laughing over some of the entries. The rest of the evening Jesse regaled Bailey with stories of the ER and dating in New York City, which was scarier than some of her most traumatic patients. Several hours and a few bottles of wine later, they were ready for bed. Bailey decided to just curl up and go to sleep on the couch. She didn't feel like walking over to the lighthouse; besides, Tree was probably already snoring in her spot.

Bailey lay on the couch, eyes open. Except for the hum of the fridge and the occasional chirp of a cricket, it was all quiet. She debated going back to the tower. Maybe Brad was awake, waiting for her. But she was tired and had drunk too much wine. The last thing she needed was to trip on the spiral staircase and break an ankle.

She wasn't aware of falling asleep, but the next thing she knew she was standing in the lighthouse loft, wearing her wedding dress. In real life, her dress had been beautiful but simple. A classic style, no frills. In the dream, it was all lace and bounce and layers with a plunging neckline. Tree was beside her with a dozen yellow roses in his mouth, whining up at the tower. Suddenly, Bailey heard Brad shout from above.

"Help!" She started up the iron staircase leading to the

Crow's Nest. Tree barked out a series of warnings, but refused to follow. It was difficult to climb the steps—her crinoline kept catching on the treads—and then Tree grabbed her train and tried to pull her back down. She knew if she wanted to save Brad, she'd have to let the dress rip. As soon as she had the thought, she heard the deep tearing sound of the material being yanked away. She hauled herself up through the small door; her arms felt weak, her body heavy.

The first person she laid eyes on was the naked bird-watcher. He was sitting in the Crow's Nest with the psychiatrist Martin Gregors. Bailey realized, before they even opened their mouths, that they were up there discussing *her*.

"She never finishes anything," Martin said.

"Me?" Bailey said. They ignored her.

"She blames Brad," the bird-watcher said.

"Ironic, isn't it?"

"I don't blame Brad," Bailey said. "I just . . . tolerate him sometimes."

Bird-watcher started counting off Bailey's offenses on his fingers. "They had that surf shop and she never even learned to surf."

Martin pecked out a note with his index finger on his iPad. Therapy had gone digital. Where had she been? She leaned over to see what he was writing. *Never learned to surf.*

"It takes years to learn," Bailey said. "I concentrated on setting up shop instead."

"How could Brad keep it going when she hated the sport?" Bird-watcher said. In real life Bailey would have been mortified for forgetting a guest's name—Business 101: use their names!—but in the dream she just wanted to pluck him like a turkey and stuff him.

"I let you sit naked at my dining room table!" she yelled.

"What about the sweater shop?" Martin asked.

"She was allergic to the wool, remember?" Bird-watcher said.

Martin started to chuckle. "Would you buy a sweater with snot—"

"Hey," Bailey yelled. "There was never any snot—"

"And the coffee shop," Martin said. He swiped his finger across the keyboard. Bailey heard the sound of an espresso machine start up, and suddenly the two men were drinking lattes.

"I loved the coffee shop," Bailey said. "I almost learned to make little hearts in the foam."

"Almost doesn't count," Martin said.

"I thought you couldn't hear me."

"She blew their entire nest egg on a fireplace," Bird-watcher said. "Tanked the whole business." Tom, Bailey thought. His name is Tom. But he was being so mean. She wasn't going to use his name.

"It was cozy, Birdman," Bailey said. "People love to read by fires. Hello! Colorado! Skiing. Snow. Cozy fireplaces? It was a good idea."

"She's so oblivious to her role in all the failures," Martin said. He wrote *OBLIVIOUS* in huge letters on his iPad. They floated into the room and danced about. Bailey didn't know the technology had progressed that quickly. This was just a dream. They were lies, all lies! Weren't they?

"Help!" Brad yelled. She'd forgotten all about him.

"She does look pretty good naked," the Bird-watcher said. "Except for her thighs."

"Assholes!" Bailey said.

"Help," Brad yelled.

Behind her came a hideous clanking sound. Without turning around, Bailey knew it was Vera, scrounging for food in her sleep. Next came Faye and Jason, talking about her, their voices trying to compete over the clanking.

"They don't even own the lighthouse," Faye said.

"Real Estate 101," Jason said.

"Own your property," they finished together.

"Help!" Brad shouted. Bailey started for the deck. Captain Jack appeared and blocked the way through the little gate to the outside.

"Leave the light on for me," he said with a wink. She tried to kick him but he vanished into thin air. She hauled herself onto the deck. It was cold. The night sky was pitch black. Yet a small portion of the deck was lit up. The iron glowed a ghostly green. There, dangling something over the rail, was Olivia. Bailey stepped closer. Olivia was holding one of Brad's new shoes. The ones he had on when he died. Attached to the shoe, hanging upside down over the sixty-foot drop, was Brad.

"Help," Brad said.

"Stop," Bailey cried out to Olivia. "Whatever he did, we can work it out."

"Why do you always blame me?" Brad said. "Surf! Snot! Fireplace!"

"Drop him," Bailey said. While still dangling Brad with one hand, Olivia pulled out a deck of cards with the other. She tossed them in the air and they made a perfect arch before falling back into her hand in a neat little pile. Then they spread out toward Bailey like a fan.

"Pick a card," Olivia said. "Any card. Red, he lives. Black, he dies." A music box began to play. Brad moaned. And moaned, and moaned. It took Bailey a while to realize it wasn't him moaning. But it wasn't until she heard a bloodcurdling scream that she woke up.

Chapter 33

It was jarring, the abrupt switch from such vivid dreaming to sitting up on the couch, heart hammering with fear. Who was screaming? She should move, do something, but she was frozen. Footsteps thundered down the stairs. Elizabeth appeared at the landing, wide-eyed, hair sticking out all over the place, robe pulled tightly around her.

"What?" It was all Bailey could croak out. Another set of footsteps came beating down, and soon Jesse joined Elizabeth. Bailey was finally able to move. She went over to Jesse, who looked as pale as she'd ever seen her.

"A man," Jesse said. "In my room."

"Oh my God," Bailey said.

"And music, and moaning," Elizabeth said. She slapped her hands over her ears as if she could still hear it. Bailey looked at Jesse. She nodded in agreement.

"Thomas," Bailey said. She started for the stairs. Just as she said his name, he appeared at the top. Any suspicion Bailey had that it was him evaporated. He was so terrified he almost plunged into the group trying to get down. His hair was also sticking every which way and his face was slick with sweat. He tried to talk, but he was breathing too hard. With a shaking finger, he pointed up the steps.

"Man?" Bailey whispered. Thomas shook his head. His finger remained pointing up.

"Woman," Thomas said. "Hanging. Swinging. Screaming." He looked from one face to another, as if searching to see some signs that at least one of them believed him. "I swear!"

"Edga," Bailey whispered.

"Who the fuck is Edga?" Jesse said. Some color was back in her face.

"Out," Elizabeth said. "Now." She stumbled toward the patio as if she'd been drinking. Jesse and Thomas quickly followed. Bailey glanced at the stairs, but there was no way she was going up there. So much for the movies, where everyone was brave or stupid enough to chase after every little noise. Bailey too ran for the patio. Then, without discussing it, they all made a run for the lighthouse tower. Over the bricks, then through the grass, passing Jake and Angel's tent. Bailey, in bare feet, prayed she wouldn't step on anything sharp or gooey.

Halfway there, a wave of anger hit Bailey. Someone was messing with them. She did not believe in ghosts. Was it Jake and Angel? She considered going back to their tent, but there was enough doubt to keep her away. What she should have done was grab a large kitchen knife and storm up to the attic. Just as they reached the entrance to the lighthouse, the door flew open and Brad and Tree came barreling out. Tree took the lead, and barking furiously, blew past the little group toward the house.

"What happened?" Brad shouted. "He was going berserk!" Bailey flung herself into Brad's arms. It was such a welcome feeling. His strong chest, his faint cologne, his arms around her. Her Brad, her husband, her life.

"Did I really get snot on the sweaters?" Bailey said.

"What?" Brad looked down at her with a mixture of amusement and concern.

"I want to go home," Elizabeth yelled, ruining Bailey's touching moment. "Now!" Brad glanced at Thomas.

"Dude," Thomas said. "We saw a ghost."

"I didn't say ghost," Jesse said. "There was a man. In my room."

"Jake and Angel?" Brad said. Bailey pointed at their tent. "Let's go," he said. Bailey was glad she hadn't rushed the tent alone. Jake and Angel were both inside, tucked into their sleeping bags, startled awake by Brad and his flashlight. "Sorry, sorry," Brad said, turning off the light and backing out of the tent. After some maneuvering and swearing, Jake appeared, shirtless with tiny shorts, and Bailey was happy for the cover of darkness, didn't want to be accused of checking him out, which she soon realized was exactly what she was doing.

"What's wrong?" Jake said. "What's going on?"

"Someone broke into the house," Bailey said quickly, before anyone could utter the word "ghost."

"Where's that ferry captain?" Elizabeth said. "I want to go home."

"Are they still there?" Jake said. He looked at Brad. "Let's go." The men headed for the house.

"Wait," Bailey said. "What if he's armed?" The men ignored her and soon Thomas was at their side. "Thomas," Bailey said. "No." Now there were three men ignoring her. Bailey ran to catch up. "Wait for me," she said.

"And me," Jesse said. Elizabeth crawled into the tent with Angel. Now, this was more like the movies.

The main room was silent. Brad turned on all the lights. Then he headed for the stairs.

"Wait," Bailey whispered as loud as she could. "Kitchen knife." Brad hesitated.

"She's right," Jake said. "Wait here." He disappeared into the kitchen and soon came back holding a large knife. They took the stairs as a group, at first trying not to make a sound.

"If he's still there," Jesse said, "he can't get past us." It made sense, so they dropped the stealth act and ran up the rest of the stairs. Brad flipped on each and every light switch they passed.

"If we kept the carpeting, it would have been quieter," Brad said. Bailey let it go, deciding now was not the time to "agree to disagree." One by one they took the rooms on the second floor, flooding it with light. As Brad opened closets and looked under beds and behind curtains, Jake followed with the knife. The first two rooms were empty, there was no doubt about it. When they got to Jesse's room, she plowed in first. Now that she'd recovered from her shock, she appeared to be furious and ready for a fight. But her room too was empty. Brad knelt on the floor, trying to find footprints or any evidence of a man being in the room.

"Nothing," he said. They all looked to the attic. Bailey caught the look on Thomas's face.

"You should stay down here," she said. "In case someone tries to get past you."

"Sure," Thomas said. "Good idea."

"Jesse?" Bailey said. She could tell her friend was dying to come up to the attic with them, but like Bailey recognized the terror on Thomas's face.

"I'll stay here too," she said. "Thomas will protect me." Thomas straightened up a bit and nodded. Jake, knife held high, led the way. Brad flipped on the light at the foot of the stairs.

The attic was one large space. No closets to hide in. The mattress was on the floor, no space to hide under it. There was no one hanging from the rafters. The window was closed. Bailey prayed they would at least find a music box, or a footprint, or a piece of frayed rope. Anything to prove it wasn't all in their heads. But there was nothing.

"They had plenty of time to flee," Bailey said. "We should have come directly up here."

"No," Brad said. "Not by yourselves."

"He's right," Jake said. "We've no idea who we're dealing with."

"Should we call the police?" Bailey said.

"And what?" Brad said. "Start more rumors of ghosts?"

"I heard moaning," Bailey said. "And music."

"But nothing for the police to go on," Brad said.

"Let's check out the downstairs," Jake said. "Just to be sure." In silence, the group headed down. Brad, in the lead, was the first to stop short when they reached the main room. There, in the middle of the floor, sat Olivia's urn. Brad hurried over to it, opened the urn, and looked inside.

"She's here," Brad said.

You mean, *she's back*, Bailey thought.

Brad insisted he was going to change all of the locks, just to be safe. There was a small possibility, Bailey said, that she'd forgotten to lock the patio door. She'd been distracted by Jesse's visit, and she just couldn't swear to locking it. It was one of the hazards of having so many people in and out all of the time. Bailey couldn't tell whether Brad was freaked out or relieved to have Olivia's urn back. He returned it to the tower. Bailey told Brad that she couldn't remember where she put the broken pieces of the urn she'd hurled across the room, but she was deeply relieved she hadn't destroyed the real thing. They'd find the urn and trace where it was purchased. What Bailey didn't tell Brad was that she knew full well she'd wrapped the broken pieces of the urn in tissue paper and placed them in their bottom dresser drawer. She was afraid to tell him that it was missing. She didn't want to get him any more wound up than he already was, and she needed him in bed beside her.

The fake urn was their only clue as to who might have made the switch, and it was gone. She was exhausted; she just wanted to crawl into bed with Brad and get at least a few hours of sleep. They had to at least get through the good-bye party.

It took everything to convince Elizabeth that Captain Jack wasn't about to ferry across in the middle of the night to take her back to town. Besides, she wouldn't even be able to get a bus out of town until the next day. So instead, she insisted on sleeping in the lighthouse loft with Brad. Bailey thought Elizabeth would change her mind when she told her she'd have to sleep on a cot, but she accepted it without hesitation. Bailey would have been fine with Elizabeth leaving in the morning, but she seemed to perk up when she heard Captain Jack was going to be at the party. Thomas and Jesse decided to spend the rest of their evening camped out in the main room. Bailey worried about them being alone in the house, so Jake and Angel agreed to camp out there as well, along with Tree. Bailey still wasn't convinced that Angel had nothing to do with the mysterious goings-on, but at least they would soon be out of their lives for good. What Bailey and Brad needed was a fresh start. New guests, new locks. No talk of ghosts. If they had to, they would install a security system with cameras in every room. If there was anything good about starting and failing at so many businesses, it was that they certainly weren't the types who were going to let anybody else scare them off. They were too good at doing it to themselves.

Chapter 34

The evening of the party started out pleasant. Everyone was still slightly on edge from the previous night, but equally determined to enjoy themselves. The air was sweet with lilac and honeysuckle. Horns from tugboats tooted gently, crickets started their nightly hum even though dusk had yet to fall, and birds called long and high to each other. Steak and shrimp sizzled on the grill. Jesse had spent the day making strawberry shortcake, and it looked divine. Elizabeth decked herself out in a red sundress with matching pumps. Jake and Angel seemed more in love than Bailey had ever seen them. Jake didn't even glance at her once. Not that she wanted him to. It was natural to notice when someone who normally paid you a lot of attention was ignoring you, but it certainly didn't mean Bailey wanted the attention. In fact, she felt closer to Brad than ever. Last night, after all the trauma, it was nice to lie in bed next to him. If Elizabeth hadn't been camped out in their room, Bailey would have initiated a little lovemaking. She was dying to be alone with him tonight, dying to get absolutely everyone out of the house. It would be their first time alone in a long time.

Jesse popped up beside Bailey. "Bailey," she said. "Do you need some help in the kitchen?"

"I'm not even in the kitchen," Bailey said.

"Right," Jesse said, giving her a look. Then she slightly raised her voice. "Earlier you said you needed some help in the kitchen?"

"I did?"

Jesse grabbed Bailey's arm. "You, me, kitchen," she said. Jesse hooked arms and began dragging her inside. "You've lost touch with deception. You're definitely not a city girl anymore." They entered the kitchen. Jesse hopped up onto the counter and began swinging her feet, bouncing them off the cabinets.

"Spill," she said.

"What?"

"You've been staring at him all night."

"Who?"

"Jake!"

Bailey felt her face flush. She hoped it was just Jesse who'd noticed her indiscretion. "It's nothing," she said.

"I get it," Jesse said. "It's flattering when someone has a crush on you."

"Exactly."

"As long as that's all it is."

"Absolutely," Bailey said. "I'm sure Brad has had the odd fantasy about Angel too."

"Speaking of Angel," Jesse said. "Did you see her ring finger?"

"No," Bailey said. "Did he give her a big rock?"

"He didn't give her any rock," Jesse said. "But she does have a tan line."

"What?"

"Where it looks like a wedding ring used to be."

"I never noticed," Bailey said. "Wait. What are you saying?"

"That she could already be married," Jesse said.

"She's awfully young."

"You've been with Brad since you were ten," Jesse said.

"Yes, but we delayed the wedding considerably." From the kitchen window Bailey could see Angel chatting with Elizabeth and Captain Jack.

"You want to rip her eyes out, don't you?" Jesse said.

"I just hope she's not lying to Jake," Bailey said. "He doesn't deserve that."

"She seems awfully sneaky to me," Jesse said.

"They're both so young and impulsive," Bailey said. "Although at least Angel's never tried to kiss Brad. At least I don't think so. She better not have."

Jesse hopped off the counter and plucked a strawberry from a bowl. "Are you still thinking about that kiss?"

"No. It was nothing. I already confessed to Brad and everything."

"How'd he take it?"

"Jealous, but didn't overreact."

"So why are you still obsessing over it?"

"I'm not."

"I know you." Bailey sighed and threw a strawberry at Jesse. "Can't fool me," Jesse said as she ducked.

"It's no big deal. He's leaving. Thank God. They just—remind me of us at that age. Sometimes I wish we had it all to do over again, you know?"

"What would you do differently?"

"I don't know. Learn to surf. Get allergy medication. Forget the fireplace. Stop insisting Brad use condoms."

"I have no idea what you're talking about. Except for the condom bit. Which I know you don't mean. Trapping a man into having kids has never worked."

"I know." Bailey stood at the sink and glanced out the window. "Jake told me he'd have kids with me. Can you believe it?"

"Sounds like more than a kiss to me."

"He didn't mean it. He was just being young and outrageous."

"He's sexy."

"I guess I just feel guilty," Bailey said.

"For being attracted to him? That's just human nature, my friend."

"No," Bailey said. "For considering it for half a second."

"An affair?"

"Running away with him. Having a baby. I mean, I never would have done it. But just the fact that I allowed myself to fantasize about it, even for a second, made me feel like I'd done something terrible. Like I'd cheated on Brad."

"Stop torturing yourself. You didn't do anything."

"I liked the kiss."

Jesse shrugged. "Not a crime either. He kissed you, right?"

"Yes. But, Jesse? I thank God he's not staying." From behind them, someone cleared their throat. The sound hit Bailey like a gunshot. She and Jesse whipped around. Jake was standing in the doorway.

"I uh—was sent in on a beer run," he said. From the grin on his face, there was no doubt. He'd heard every single word.

"Oh my God, oh my God, oh my God." Bailey couldn't stop saying it. Jake had already exited with the beer, grin still plastered on his face. "Oh my God," Bailey said again. "This is bad." Confessing your guilt to your best friend was one thing. Having the object of the guilt overhear then being forced to sit through dinner with him, and his fiancée, and his grin, and your husband, was unbearable. If only Bailey had never learned to talk. Somehow, Jesse helped Bailey go through the motions. Bailey sat at the picnic table opposite Jake and Angel while Elizabeth held court.

"I'm so envious of you," Elizabeth said to Jake and Angel. "Traveling is what life is all about. I can't imagine being stuck in one place for too long." Was it Bailey's imagination, or did she just cast a knowing look Brad's way? Angel followed Elizabeth's glance and also smiled at Brad.

"Brad inspired us," Angel said.

"You both did," Jake added, looking at Bailey. "We want to be just like you two."

"Only happier," Angel said. Bailey glanced at Angel. She had such a pretty, innocent face. Then her eyes fell to her hands. Sure enough, there was a tan line around what looked to be a ring on her wedding finger. Should she say something to Jake? Then again, wouldn't he have already noticed? Then again, he was a guy. They weren't always the most observant. Then again, he'd noticed plenty of little things about Bailey, so he was observant. Unless he was only observant with Bailey because he liked Bailey better than Angel. In which case, didn't he kind of deserve what he got? Running off with a woman he didn't like well enough to notice she used to have a wedding ring on her finger? Or maybe it was an ex-husband and he knew all about it, and seriously, it was nobody else's business. Bailey wished Jesse hadn't pointed it out.

"Bailey and I were happy," Brad said. "Even if we weren't always the best travelers." Bailey glanced at Brad. "I might have told her a few stories," he said. Bailey scanned her memory, wondering which "few." Did he tell her about the time she threw all the cups and saucers within reach at the Parisian café? Or the hotel in Rome where he stood on the sidewalk below their room and she shouted at him from their window for a full thirty minutes? Or the sunburn in Barcelona where she cried anytime anything touched her and had to stand like a statue for the entire day? Brad missed exploring Gaudí park, something he really wanted to do, but never got the chance because they left early the next morning for Portugal.

"I can't wait," Angel said. "Everybody thinks I'm so high maintenance, but I'm not. Have I or have I not been sleeping in a tent for like a whole month?"

Had it been a month? Bailey didn't think so. Although in some ways it felt like years.

"And you look so gorgeous," Elizabeth said. "How do you do it?" Bailey got the feeling Elizabeth was just being nice to Angel to upset her. Jesse came to the rescue.

"I think Brad and Bailey are amazing," Jesse said. "Besides the traveling they've done, now they live in a lighthouse. How cool is that?"

"Makes me want to go through our old pictures and post-cards," Brad said.

"They're in the desk in the Crow's Nest," Bailey said. As soon as she said it, another thought hit. *I know that because I saw them when I put the broken urn in there.* It was really because she'd tried to snoop and peek at his journals, but that drawer had been locked. She put the pieces in the opposite drawer, vowing to ask Brad why he needed to lock drawers.

"I'll get them," she said. She stood.

"Wait," Brad said. "I didn't really mean we'd bore our guests with them."

"I'd love to see them," Jesse said.

"Wait," Jake echoed. He turned to Angel. Bailey recognized the look. It was the one men gave women when they were afraid what they were about to say was going to make them mad, so they made themselves look as vulnerable as possible so they wouldn't get their face eaten. "I think we should postpone our trip," Jake said in a rush. "Stay here for a while."

"No!" Bailey said. All heads turned to her. Perhaps she'd been a tad too emphatic. "Seize the day," Bailey said with a fist shake. "Carpe diem!"

"How could we leave now?" Jake said. "In the middle of a good ghost story?"

"Ghost story?" Captain Jack said. Elizabeth pushed her chair back from the table. Her glass tipped over and she knocked into Captain Jack.

"So sorry," she muttered. She didn't even reach to pick up the glass, she just pushed away from the table. "I have to powder my nose," she said. *Oh my God,* Bailey thought as she watched her stumble away. *She's drunk.*

Bailey and Brad simultaneously reached to clean up the mess. When Brad's hand brushed hers, Bailey took it and gave it a reassuring squeeze. He looked at her and they locked eyes. She smiled. She knew he'd noticed his mother's drunken state as well. She wanted him to know she was there for him. He smiled at her and gave a nod that would have been imperceptible to anyone else.

"Let's have the ghost story," Captain Jack said loudly. Since Elizabeth had left the table and Thomas had his mouth full, everyone turned to Jesse.

"I had just fallen asleep," she said, "when I heard a noise." Bailey was happy the sun was still up and they were in a large group outside of the house. She'd yet to admit it, but the thought of the place being haunted was starting to get to her. A few years ago she wouldn't have believed in a near-death experience, or Olivia being a card shark, so who's to say there was no such thing as ghosts? "I opened my eyes and I saw a man in my room—he was standing just a few feet away—near the dresser." Dresser, Bailey thought. An image flashed through her mind. Olivia's broken urn, wrapped in tissue paper. Bailey hadn't put it in Brad's desk—she'd thought about it and then didn't want him to come across it and be upset—so instead she'd put it in the master guest room dresser.

"We should get one of those ghost hunting shows out here, Aunt Bailey," Thomas said.

That's not a bad idea, Bailey thought. She caught Brad looking at her.

"Publicity is part of the fabric of our society," she said. "Deal with it." She expected a lecture; instead, Brad just laughed.

"I love you," he said. He said it loud. He said it in front of everyone. He said it like they were the only two people in the world. Bailey felt a rush of warmth all over her body.

"I won't let you turn this place into some kind of spectacle," Captain Jack said.

"Won't let us?" Brad said.

"This ghost nonsense," Captain Jack said. "You're turning us into a laughingstock."

"At least our ghost is friendly," Bailey said.

"And tall," Jesse said. Bailey shivered. She couldn't imagine waking up to see a tall, strange man standing near the dresser. *Wait,* Bailey thought. *The little guest room dresser.* She hadn't put the broken urn in the master dresser. Since they saved that room for higher-paying guests, she'd put it in the bottom drawer of the little guest room dresser. Bailey stood from the table.

"Nature calls," she said. *Tall,* she thought as she headed upstairs to the guest bedroom. *Our ghost is tall.*

Bailey bounded up the steps to the second floor. She rounded the corner, headed for the last guest room on the right. She stopped short when she saw Elizabeth standing over the bed in the master guest room. She was slightly bent over. Bailey was worried she was going to get sick. She hated to admit it, but her first clenching fear was for the beautiful down comforter on the bed. As Bailey got closer, she noticed Elizabeth was holding a wallet and dumping its contents out on the bed.

"Elizabeth?" She whirled around. Bailey stepped into the room. Elizabeth was holding a man's wallet. A driver's license was dumped on the bed. It was a picture of Captain Jack. Elizabeth brushed past Bailey and quickly closed the door. "What are you doing?" Bailey asked even though it was pretty obvious.

"Look," Elizabeth said. She pointed at the license. "Edgar. No wonder he wouldn't tell anyone his name."

"Edgar?" Bailey said. She picked up the license. Sure enough, there was Captain Jack's face. Edgar Penwell, the name read. "Oh my God," Bailey said. She looked at the rest of the items strewn on the bed. Photos. Of Angel and Jake, and Angel and "Edgar," and Jake and Edgar. But it was one particular photo that drew Bailey's attention. Angel in a wedding dress. Standing next to Jake in a tux. *So that explains the impression of a ring on her finger,* Bailey thought. *Good catch, Jesse.* Bailey picked up the wedding photo and turned it over. Mr. and Mrs. Jake Penwell. Bailey looked at Elizabeth. Her eyes were clear, her posture steady.

"You pretended to be drunk," Bailey said. Elizabeth shrugged.

"I've certainly had enough practice."

"And when you spilled the drink?"

Elizabeth wiggled her fingers. "He didn't even feel it slipping out of his pocket."

"You shouldn't have done this—"

"I did it for you."

"Me?"

"You said you were dying to know his name."

"Since when have you ever done anything for me? Or Brad, for that matter?" Bailey knew it wasn't the time to start a family fight. They had to get this wallet back to Captain Jack— Edgar—and she had to sit somewhere and think about what this all meant. Tall, the ghost was tall. Bailey hurriedly put everything back into the wallet.

"Go back downstairs," she said. "And act as normal as possible."

"I can put it back—"

"No," Bailey said. "Not yet. Please, Elizabeth. Not a word."

"Fine."

"And you're still going to have to act a little drunk." Bailey felt guilty—it would continue to hurt Brad—but she couldn't take the chance that the captain would get suspicious.

"What's with you?" Elizabeth said. "Do you recognize the name?" Elizabeth hadn't been around enough to put any of it together. Jake and Angel Penwell. Nor, of course, did she know about Trevor Penwell or his supposed wife Edga.

"I can't explain anything now," Bailey said. Even if she wanted to. "Trust me. I need you to go back downstairs and keep him occupied."

"Not a problem," Elizabeth said. Before Bailey's eyes, she suddenly became inebriated again. She stumbled to the door. For a split second she straightened up and grinned. "How's that?" she said. Bailey felt a little sick to her stomach.

"Perfect," she admitted. "Don't let any of them leave. Including Jake and Angel."

"I doubt I'll have to try very hard. Jake's been looking at you like he's a lion and you're a tasty little gazelle."

Bailey laughed. *I never thought I'd say this,* she thought, *but I kind of like this Elizabeth Jordan.* It didn't last long.

"You have no clue, do you?" Elizabeth said softly. For a split second Bailey thought she was talking about Edgar, and Jake, and Angel. Then she realized she couldn't have been.

"I have lots of clues," Bailey said. "I just can't put them all together."

Elizabeth laughed and Bailey almost liked her again. "There's a reason," she said, "he won't have a baby with you."

And just like that, Bailey hated Elizabeth Jordan again. But Bailey didn't have time to obsess on Elizabeth's parting comment, or the pitying look on her face, or the ice-cold spear that stabbed Bailey when Elizabeth whispered the words. She wanted to convince herself that Elizabeth was just trying to upset her, but she could tell that Elizabeth was being truthful. She knew something about Brad. Brad who just squeezed her hand across the table and loved her out loud. Brad out in the rowboat, looking terrified. *Please, don't believe a word she says.* But Elizabeth hadn't looked vindictive, just sad. Bailey didn't have time to ponder it anymore. She ran to the guest room where Jesse had spent the night.

Edga Penwell, Bailey thought bitterly as she knelt down beside the dresser drawer. She'd fallen for it. *The lighthouse keeper's wife. Went insane. You have the same look in your eye.* She was going to get the captain for this. She opened the drawer. There it was, wrapped in tissue paper. Bailey knew what she was going to find, even before she unwrapped the pieces. Most of all she was angry at herself for being so naïve. After all, the only "proof" she'd had that Edga existed was the obituary, a "report" from a blogger, and an old photo of a man and a woman. The obituary was the only thing that would have taken some time to fake, but it certainly wouldn't have been impossible. Bailey suddenly remembered all the funny looks and silence from townspeople whenever she gently tried to bring up the subject of the late keeper's wife. At the time she thought they just didn't want to discuss the "tragedy."

So Edga was really Edgar. And it didn't seem likely that he'd ever tried to hang himself in the attic. And if he was a ghost, he was such a good one that Bailey was definitely going to cash in on him. So were he and Trevor lovers?

Bailey opened the tissue paper, and carefully inspected the

broken pieces. Finally, she found it. A small sticker on the back of one piece. *Island Supplies.* He'd been behind it all. With a little help from Jake and Angel. Bailey had played right into his hands from the moment she stepped into the house and saw the obituary, then accepting the "contractor" he'd recommended while Brad started corresponding with a woman who had also had a near-death experience. Actually, Angel had joined the lighthouse committee right after the auction. The plan was in motion right after Captain Jack lost the bid. Now she knew the "who." But why? What did they have to gain? Wishing you owned a certain piece of property was one thing. But who would go to these lengths to get it? And had they now given up? Was that why Jake and Angel were leaving? No wonder the ghost was so active last night. Captain Jack was getting desperate. Bailey had to talk to Brad and figure out why they were doing this. And then, of course, they would be left with the biggest question of all: What did they plan to do about it?

Chapter 35

Bailey put Edgar's wallet and the piece of urn with the Island Supplies tag into a bag and headed downstairs. Elizabeth had kept her word, and everyone was still on the patio, eating strawberry shortcake, drinking, and chatting. Now what? Should she call the Coast Guard? Turn the three of them in for breaking and entering and impersonating a ghost? Did she have enough proof? She could just see herself trying to talk to the Coast Guard. *He's tall. He owns this broken urn. His name is really Edgar, and he's a liar.*

Not exactly fingerprints and DNA, now was it? She could at least kick them off the property and warn them never to come back. But not until she figured out why they were doing all of this, and she didn't think coming out and asking them was going to be very productive.

She snuck past them and ran to the lighthouse tower. For now, she would tuck the wallet and urn away. Maybe she'd start with Jake. What a jerk. Coming onto her when he was married. Of course she was married too, but he was the one who was pushing it. Had that all been part of the act? They must think she was quite the fool. Bailey wanted to catch Brad's eye as she snuck past but he was too busy hovering over Elizabeth, who was enjoying her drunken act a little too much. Bailey could hear her laughing across the lawn. Tree was the only one who noticed Bailey, and the partiers must have been refusing to give him scraps, for he abandoned his spot underneath the picnic table to follow Bailey.

Once up in the loft, Bailey tucked her "evidence" bag into the top of her dresser drawer. Wait. Anyone could get into it. She glanced at the top of the dresser where Brad had left the key to his upstairs desk. Where he kept his journals. She would not read them, she would not do that to him, she would simply lock the evidence away. Bailey took the key and climbed up to the Crow's Nest. Once again, Tree whined from the steps.

She unlocked Brad's bottom drawer. For a moment she just stared at the journals. She really wanted to look at them. Just one journal, just one page. If it had been anybody but Brad, she knew she would have. She wasn't a perfect person, and she would have had a glance. But this was Brad. Her Brad. For him, she would lock all her temptation in a little box. She quickly threw the bag into the drawer and was about to shut it when she saw the envelope. It was wedged between journals. Something made her pull it out. Her name was on it. *Bailey.* It was Brad's handwriting. Now what? Was she allowed to snoop into something that was addressed to her? Survey said: yes. She quickly put the envelope in her pocket, then shut and locked the drawer as fast as she could.

There. She didn't read the journals. But she did have an envelope with her name on it in her pocket. Her heart was hammering as if she'd just done something she shouldn't have.

"Good doggie," she heard someone say from below. Bailey froze. It was Angel. Bailey crawled over to the opening and peered below. Angel held something out to Tree, and he immediately snatched it up and took it to the farthest corner of the room. A bone, no doubt. Angel looked around. Bailey had left the top drawer of the dresser slightly opened and Angel noticed it immediately. Bailey watched, shocked, as Angel walked right over to the drawer, opened it, and started pawing through it. Bailey wished she had a camera or her phone to snap a picture of the live evidence. What in the world was she looking for? Had Captain Jack—would she ever get used to calling him Edgar?—noticed his wallet missing and dispersed a team to find it?

Bailey was about to go downstairs and confront Angel when she spotted something shining. It was coming from underneath her locked armoire. She walked over and bent down. It was another one of the playing cards. The sun coming in through the porthole shined on the white edges, making it almost glow. When she stood back up, she was directly in front of the cabinet. A crawling sensation rippled up her spine. My God. This was it. Why hadn't she realized it before? Bailey quickly turned the combination lock and opened the cabinet. The fourth-order Fresnel lens was still there lovingly restored and shined to a high polish by yours truly. The original. With its brass frame and beehive glass prisms, it was not only a piece of history, it was a work of art. Imagine, someone stuffing this up a chimney!

"Oh my God." Bailey whipped around. Angel stood behind her, mouth open, arms reaching out as if the beehive lens before her was a long-lost child. "It's really here," Angel whispered.

"So this is what you're after," Bailey said. Angel looked completely awestruck. Whatever else she was, she wasn't a poker player. It gave Bailey a new admiration for Olivia's vacuous expression.

"I didn't know it would be so beautiful," Angel said. She was right. The green glass was exquisite.

"They actually used to pour whale oil in here," Bailey said. But Angel didn't seem interested in its historical properties.

"It's been right here? All along?"

"No," Bailey said. "It was hidden in the chimney."

"Shit," Angel said. "Jake was sure it was in the yard." That explained the large holes everywhere.

"Why?" Bailey said. "Why do you want it so badly?"

"What?" Angel was distracted, still staring at the lens.

"Brad doesn't even know I found it," Bailey said. "It's a surprise. For our one-year anniversary."

"I thought you guys had been married since you were in diapers?"

"We met when we were ten—married less than nine—I meant the one-year mark since we opened this B-and-B—"

"Wait," Angel said. "Brad doesn't know?"

"Thus the meaning of surprise," Bailey said.

"We'll split it," Angel said. "Just you and me." A horrible image of the gorgeous lens, shattered, rose to Bailey's mind.

"Split what?"

"You have no idea, do you?"

"I have a lot of ideas." *Pushing you off the tower and treating you to a real near-death experience is one.* "Just not sure which one you happen to be referring to right now."

"An original Fresnel lens. It's worth at least a quarter of a million," Angel said. "Maybe more."

Bailey turned and stared at it again. "Oh my God."

"It's our chance to get away!" Angel said. "Nobody has to know."

"Not so happily married to Jake, I take it," Bailey said.

"Marriage sucks," Angel said. "You know yourself."

"Actually," Bailey said. "I wouldn't trade mine for anything in the world. Not even this." Bailey gestured to the lens.

"Fine," Angel said. "Then you keep Brad and give the lens to me."

"You're insane," Bailey said. "It belongs to the lighthouse."

"Now you sound like Trevor," Angel said.

"He refused to sell the lens too," Bailey surmised.

"If he would have just gone with the plan. But no. *It belongs to the lighthouse.* What is with you people?"

"Were he and Edgar lovers?" Bailey asked.

"What?" Angel sounded appalled.

"Obviously there was no Edga Penwell, so he and Trevor—"

Angel slapped her hands over her mouth. "Ewww," she said.

"That's very homophobic of you," Bailey said.

"Not ewww because you suggested they were gay. Ewww because they were brothers. He made the Edga stuff up just to scare you."

"When did Trevor find the light?"

"A few months before the auction," Angel said. "It was just lying in the first floor of the tower. Discarded along with seagull carcasses. Trevor did a lot of work restoring it. Labor of love, he called it."

"I can see why," Bailey said. "So Trevor knew it belonged to the lighthouse. But Jack—Edgar—just wanted to sell it."

Angel rolled her eyes. "Who cares about a stupid old lighthouse anyway? They're history. Useless. Uh, hello, GPS!"

"I wouldn't expect you to understand," Bailey said. "But some things are worth preserving."

"And sometimes you have to know when to let go," Angel said. "I'm surprised you haven't figured that out by now." Angel took a step closer to Bailey. Tree began barking wildly at the base of the stairs.

"It weighs six hundred pounds," Bailey said. "You can't just take it."

"Maybe not now," Angel said. "But you're the only one who knows it's here."

"How did Trevor die?" Bailey asked. She was trying to stall, and trying to figure out what to do, and trying to figure out exactly how frightened she should be. Were they all just thieves, or murderers too?

"You've seen too many movies," Angel said. "Heart attack. Dropped dead right in here, as a matter of fact," she said.

"Back up," Bailey said.

"Or what?" Angel smiled and stood straighter. She didn't look so angelic now. Footsteps sounded from below. *Please let it be Brad,* Bailey thought. *Please let it be Brad.*

"Angel?"

"Up here, Jake," Angel said. She stared at Bailey. "You had your chance," she said.

"I was going to say the same thing to you," Bailey said.

Jake's head appeared in the opening. "Hey," he said.

"You two should leave," Bailey said. "Now."

"What's going on?" Jake said. He pulled himself up with ease. Angel pointed to the cabinet.

"Look," she said.

"Holy shit," Jake said. He reached out as if to touch it. Bailey threw her arm up and blocked him. Probably not very smart, initiating physical contact so soon, but she hated the thought of him touching it.

"I'd like you two to leave now," Bailey said. To her surprise, Jake nodded. He reached for Angel's hand. She didn't take it.

"That's it?" Angel said. "A year of our lives hanging around this concrete sponge-pad-lightbulb and you're just going to give up?"

Now I can tell they're married, Bailey thought as she listened to Angel screech at Jake. "Concrete sponge-pad-lightbulb?" Bailey said.

Jake gave a soft smile. "That's her nickname for the lighthouse," he explained. "It's very damp here."

"I see," Bailey said.

"What exactly do you want me to do?" Jake said. "She has the lens, it's over."

"But Brad doesn't know about the lens yet," Angel said. "She was saving it for a surprise." From below, Tree let out a series of little barks. Bailey wished he would just get over his fear and climb up the ladder already. She'd seen a television show once, *Dogs with Jobs.* They could climb ladders.

"I still don't know what you want me to do," Jake said.

"Make her give it to us," Angel said. "It's family property. Your family, not hers."

"This lighthouse isn't owned by individuals," Bailey interjected. "You should know—you're on the 'committee.' " Bailey had to admit, it felt good to use air quotes and let just a little of her sarcasm fly.

"And didn't that piss you off?" Angel said. "Your husband took your money—"

"I thought it was his money," Jake said.

"They're married," Angel said. "It's their money. How many

freaking times do I have to explain that to you?" Jake shrugged. "As I was saying," Angel said loudly, "he took your communal money, blew it on this concrete sponge-pad-lightbulb, and then turned it over to some stupid committee! What a winner you have in that one!"

Bailey was no longer afraid of Angel, no matter what she intended on doing. She walked right up to her and put her index finger in the middle of her chest, where she had to admit, she poked her just a little bit, and it felt good.

"Don't you ever, ever talk about my husband like that again. Do you hear me?" Bailey turned away so she wouldn't wrap her hands around Angel's little neck. She pointed to the windows looking out over the river. "This is living history!" Bailey said. "It's the dawning of America. It's Indians naming the river. It's Henry Hudson exploring. It's George Washington, and the Civil War, and the Declaration of Independence, and the Erie Canal, and steamboats, and railroads, and Morse code—"

Bailey could feel herself getting worked up, almost feverish. But it was true. She understood what Brad had been trying to explain to her for the past year. This was a magical place. They were lucky to be its keepers. Jake at least seemed to be listening, so Bailey kept talking. "Lighthouses saved lives. Now I know your near-death experience was all a big hoax, but you know what? I feel sorry for you. Because 'seeing the light' is what allowed my husband to grasp what you seem to be incapable of grasping. There are some things in this life, this short, amazing little life, that matter. Who we are and where we come from is one of them. And this lighthouse is a symbol of that. And that lens isn't your lottery ticket, it's a treasure that belongs right here where people can appreciate it as long as humanly possible."

Bailey heard clapping. Startled, she looked up. Brad was standing there, grinning. Thomas stood beside him, following Brad's every move. She'd been so wrapped up in what she was saying, she didn't even hear them coming up the steps. Wow. She was a tad disappointed. For a second she'd thought this was going to end a little more dramatically, i.e., Jake and Angel wrestling her out on the deck, trying to push her off the tower. Bailey ran to the cabinet and opened the doors so that he could see the lens. "Surprise," she said. Brad stepped forward. Bailey beamed as if she'd given birth to the light herself. The look on his face was all the thanks she needed.

"Holy mama," Brad said.

Bailey laughed. "Holy concrete-sponge-pad-lightbulb," she said.

"Hey," Angel said. "That's my line."

"Finders, keepers," Bailey said. She moved out of the way to let Brad have a closer look at the glowing prisms of green light, the piece of history that was sure to draw visitors from all over the world. As she stepped out of the way, she came in contact with Angel's foot. She couldn't be sure that Angel tripped her on purpose, but the next thing Bailey knew, she was flying forward. She fell right in front of the gate to the deck. Her chin bumped Brad's little desk as she went down.

What happened next was nothing anyone could have predicted. Jake stepped forward, and Bailey would always presume it was to help her up. But Thomas didn't see it that way. Afraid that his aunt was in trouble, he grabbed the nearest object he could get his hands on, which just so happened to be Aunt Olivia's urn. Bailey looked up, saw Jake bending over her, saw Thomas behind him, urn coiled back, ready to strike.

"No!" Bailey shouted. She lunged up, and Thomas, unsure and off balance, froze with the urn held just below his chin. The top of Bailey's head smacked the bottom of the urn. She immediately felt dizzy, and everything around her blurred into little dots. She cried out and fell back to the ground.

"What are you doing?" Brad shouted. "You could have killed her."

Bailey wanted to admonish Brad, tell him not to be so hard on Thomas, but she couldn't talk quite yet. She could hear Thomas put down the urn and begin to speak rapidly, apologizing, explaining, and Bailey wanted to tell him it would be all right. She tried to put her thumb up for "thumbs up!" but wasn't sure she pulled it off.

"What have I done?" she heard Thomas yell. He was in a panic, and the next thing she knew, he ran past the little group huddled around Bailey and climbed out to the deck. Bailey's vision returned in time for her to see Thomas climb onto the railing, below which was a sixty-foot drop.

"Thomas," Bailey said. She tried to move but it hurt. "Help," she said to Brad. Brad ran out to the deck, and Bailey could only watch and listen.

"I'm sorry," Thomas shouted.

"It's okay," Brad said. "Really. Buddy. She's okay." Bailey could hear the fear in Brad's voice.

"I'm not your buddy," Thomas said. "You hate me."

Bailey felt sick. She lifted her head. "Thomas," she called out. "Come down. I love you."

"I don't hate you, Thomas. Far from it," Brad said.

"I heard what you said. You told Aunt Bailey you didn't want me here."

"Oh God," Bailey said. She grabbed onto the desk and hauled herself up. Jake and Angel were gone.

"Thomas," Bailey said, managing to stand at the entrance to the deck. "He said that because . . ." She looked at Brad for help.

"Because you remind me of my son," Brad said.

Chapter 36

"What?" Bailey thought she said. But no words came out. Besides, Brad wasn't even looking at her, he was still trying to talk to Thomas. "I had him when I was seventeen," Brad said. "Close to the age you are now." Bailey slid back down the wall. She wanted to continue helping Thomas, but her legs would no longer support her. "Having you around—it's been hard," Brad said. "Because I've been carrying this secret so long. And you make me wonder what my son is like."

"You hope he's nothing like me, right?" Thomas said.

"The opposite," Brad said. "I'd be proud if he was like you."

"So would I," Bailey said. "Please, Thomas. You're scaring me. Come down." She found her legs again. She would be fine as long as she didn't look at Brad. Not for a single second. Brad held out his hand to help Thomas down. Finally, with a brief nod, he took it. Only when they were safely inside the Crow's Nest did Bailey let out her breath. She wrapped her arms around Thomas. "I love you," she said. "Please. Don't ever do anything like that again."

"I'm sorry," he said. "I won't." Bailey was going to have to call

Meg, and they were going to have to get Thomas help. But for now, he was safe. Bailey took a step toward the stairs and another wave of dizziness came over her. Brad's arms were around her in an instant, and she needed him too much to protest.

"Let's get you to the bed," Brad said. "Then I'm calling for an ambulance." Funny, Bailey always got a kick out of seeing the ambulance boat race by.

"I'm fine," she said. "I don't need it." As they came down one set of spiral stairs, Elizabeth came barreling up the other.

"What is going on?" she said. "Jake, Angel, and Captain Jack took off like there was a fire! They left without me!"

"Want me to go after them?" Thomas said.

"*No!*" Bailey and Brad yelled together.

"They're running from justice," Bailey said.

"What?" Brad said. As he laid her down on the bed, Bailey filled him in as best she could. She wondered if he was relieved his mother hadn't really been drunk, but she couldn't focus on his face. She got so wrapped up in the story, for a few seconds she forgot all about his devastating declaration just moments earlier. But she wasn't going to say anything in front of Elizabeth and Thomas. Nor was it wise to get into it with what was turning out to be a splitting headache.

"Are you sure I shouldn't call the doctor?" Brad said.

"Just give me aspirin and let me sleep," Bailey said.

"That's not a good idea," Thomas said. "She could have a concussion."

"You're right," Brad said. "See? I'm glad you're here. Stay with her and keep her awake while I call the Coast Guard," Brad said. Brad patted Thomas on the back, and taking his mother with him, he ran out of the room. Thomas sat on the edge of the bed and took Bailey's hand. Bailey let him do all the talking, which wasn't easy, for what she suddenly wanted more than anything was just a little bit of sleep.

They didn't talk about it for three days. First, even though she didn't have a concussion, Bailey was on pretty strong painkillers and she needed her rest. Second, they had to wait for the report to be filed against Edgar, Jake, and Angel, who seemed to be long gone. The ferry was abandoned on the other side of the river, and Island Supplies was closed and locked. Then they had to wait for Meg to arrive to pick up Thomas and for Elizabeth to say her good-byes. Bailey wished she and Brad were on better terms because it tugged at her heart strings to see him hug his mother good-bye. Elizabeth had really come through for them, and it did seem as if she had changed. Life really did seem to offer second chances. Bailey listened as Brad and Elizabeth bantered back and forth about future visits. Is that the way life would unfold? Brad would finally have his mother back in his life but would lose his wife? Soon, the house had emptied out, and although it was a relief not to have to take care of anyone else, Bailey didn't look forward to being alone with Brad now that this thing hung between them.

Bailey finally opened the letter that she'd stolen from Brad's desk, praying it would be a heartfelt apology, something she could hold on to, something that would help her forgive him. She opened it, and prayed.

> Dear Bailey,
> I'm a coward.
> I love you,
> Brad

That was it? That was his big apology? She felt guilty for stealing that? It was a good thing he never gave it to her. Instead of helping her process her anger, it just made her more depressed. She tore the letter into tiny pieces and threw them away. She never wanted to get out of bed.

On the third day of Brad bringing her ice packs, and meals in bed, and cups of coffee or tea, and flowers, and paperback books, Bailey finally let it out in the open. Brad had just come to take away her breakfast tray. She stopped him. He sat on the bed and just looked at her.

"You have a son," she said. It was difficult to say the words; they felt thick in her mouth.

"Yes," Brad said. She winced. She couldn't believe how much it hurt, how terribly shocking it all was. She had been holding out hope that somehow it wasn't true, just a fabrication designed to talk Thomas down from the ledge.

"Do you remember the summer you graduated from high school?" Brad said.

"Cynthia Hargrave," Bailey said. Brad wasn't expecting the name to come out of her mouth. It took him several seconds to recover.

"You knew?"

Bailey laughed, even though it wasn't funny. How could he not remember the yard sale? Bailey was the one who'd pushed them to go, mainly because she was dying to see Cynthia's house. Her father was a surgeon. They had a mansion, and horses, and an in-ground pool. Bailey didn't know people like that had yard sales. Bailey was busy checking out the clothes Cynthia had for sale, which were way nicer than anything Bailey owned new. Brad was looking through a stack of college textbooks that belonged to Cynthia's older brother. Brad bought one of the books—*Sexual Deviancy*. Cynthia followed Brad around the yard that day in her little white shorts and sparkling gold bikini top. She laughed loudly at everything he said and flipped her hair so many times it was a wonder she wasn't bald by the time they left. She wouldn't even take money from Brad for the book. And just as they were leaving, she grabbed it away from him, took a red marker out of her white shorts, stuck it in her mouth, pulled it out (still chewing seductively on the cap), and wrote something in the book.

Bailey had kept her jealousy in check because Cynthia Hargrave, who had been the most popular girl in school, liked her boyfriend. Bailey reached for the book, but Cynthia snatched it away and made Brad take it.

"For your eyes only," she said with a wink. Bailey silently wished she would choke on the cap to the marker. But she held it together. She simply linked arms with Brad and pretended it didn't bother her. That is, until they were safely down the enormous driveway and way out of earshot. Then Bailey let Brad have it. At first, Brad seemed amused and doubly flattered. First by the attention from Cynthia, then by Bailey's jealousy. But when she wouldn't give up her sour mood, and he wouldn't admit to flirting back, it disintegrated into a fight that led to their first breakup. Later, when they were at Brad's house and he was in the shower, Bailey snuck a peek at the book.

> *Brad,*
> *Come to my bed and be a sexual deviant with me.*
> *Love,*
> *Cindy*

Bailey wanted to rip it out. She wondered now if events would have changed if she had. Instead, she confronted Brad with it, as if he were responsible for writing it himself, as if he had already slipped into the sheets with Cynthia. She even blamed him for buying the book in the first place, although it was exactly the type of book Brad would have picked up and read. The second half of the fight was a doozy. They broke up for the rest of the summer.

"But how did you know I slept with her?" Brad said after Bailey recounted the story.

"I didn't for sure," Bailey said. "But come on. Do you really think I expected you to never sleep with anybody but me?"

"We were so young," Brad said. "Not that that's an excuse."

"It's no excuse for doing it with her," Bailey said. "But I never wanted the burden of being the only one for your entire adult male life. Believe me."

"Thus your first year of college," Brad said.

"Thus my first year of college," Bailey agreed. That was their second breakup. When Bailey was seized with panic that she would never sleep with another man besides Brad. She told him they both needed their freedom. It lasted six months. Long enough for Bailey to experience that she wasn't really missing anything.

"So tell me everything," Bailey said. It wasn't a new story, or even a particularly surprising one. A pregnant teenage daughter didn't sit well with the Hargraves. Her father was so enraged he threatened to press statutory rape charges against Brad. Cynthia had been a month from turning eighteen. Later, Brad would realize Dr. Hargrave's threats wouldn't have landed him in jail at all. The age of consent in Massachusetts is sixteen. At the time, however, Brad had no clue what they could or couldn't do to him, but he believed Dr. Hargrave was capable of getting his way. He believed he'd do serious jail time. So Dr. Hargrave offered Brad an alternative. He could avoid jail if he gave up all parental rights. Soon after, the Hargraves moved out of the state. Bailey couldn't believe she hadn't put it together sooner, but she spent the rest of that summer in New York City with Aunt Faye. When she did come back, all she knew was that Cynthia and her family had moved.

"When did you find out she had a boy?" Bailey asked.

"Remember the older brother?" Brad asked.

"Of course," Bailey said. She held him responsible too. He was the one selling the textbook.

"I contacted him," Brad said.

"When?"

"When we got back from Europe," Brad said. Bailey cringed. While his son was being born, Brad was traveling through Europe with her.

"He told me it was a boy. Warned me to stay away. Said everyone was fine."

"So that was it?" Bailey said.

"No," Brad said. "Five years later I contacted him again." This time, Cynthia was married to a doctor. The man had legally adopted Brad's son. "That was the last time I ever made contact," Brad said. "My son was healthy. He had a father. What was I supposed to do?"

"Tell me," Bailey said. "That's what you were supposed to do."

Bailey spent several days just trying to breathe. She felt an enormous sadness. A son had missed out on his father. A father had missed out on his son. She had been living with a man she thought she knew inside and out, and yet he had this larger-than-life secret. She wanted all those years back so they could do it right. She was furious with the Hargraves for threatening a seventeen-year-old kid with jail. Especially one without a family support system. Even if she could go back, there was probably little that could have been done to change that aspect of it. She wondered what Cynthia was like now, wondered if Cynthia ever felt bad that her son had missed out on his real father.

Did the boy look like Brad? Have his dimples? Was he impulsive and energetic? Handsome? Every new round of thoughts brought fresh tears. In the days following the revelation, Bailey's tears could have filled the Hudson. Because even if she could see the impossible situation Brad had been in at the time, what about now? Bailey had stuck by his side through thick and thin for the past twenty-six years. All that time and she had no idea that his unpredictable moods, inability to stay in one place, and fear of having children had a source. And even if Bailey couldn't blame everything on this secret, it had undoubtedly played a huge role in every aspect of their lives. And maybe Brad got some kind of relief out of punishing himself by not having any more children, but what about Bailey? What had she done to deserve it? After several days of barely speaking to Brad, she confronted him. He was working on the pier, trying to patch up a few broken boards before winter hit. Bailey stood over him, watching until he looked up. He saw her red eyes, evidence of more tears, and even though she hated to see how pained he was to see her cry, she remained steely.

"Are you going to try and find him?" Bailey said.

"No," Brad said.

"Why not?" Brad turned away, began to hammer. "Why not?"

"It's too late," he said without looking at her.

"He's twenty-one," Bailey said. "Why don't you let him decide for himself?" Brad didn't answer. Bailey watched him take his anger out on the boardwalk for a few minutes longer, then she turned to go on one of many solitary walks along the river.

PLEASE SIGN OUR GUEST BOOK!

What a glorious fall day. We so enjoyed the rowboat, the walks
along the river, and the roaring fires in the evening. We never expected
asparagus in our omelets and cranberries in our pancakes, and now
we don't know how we shall live without it. And the quiet! It's nice to
see a couple enjoy each other without having to talk. We have four
children, and in our house this kind of silence would mean that
something had gone horribly wrong. It was nice to be reminded how
precious silence can be. It was the best gift you could have ever given
us. We hear there is a ferryboat and grocery store for sale. If we didn't
have those darn kids, we might buy them ourselves! We will definitely
be back!

In between ignoring the occasional guest, Bailey and Brad
threw themselves into setting up the museum. Bailey gathered
articles about lighthouses, which she framed and mounted on
the wall. She even became somewhat crafty, using shells, and
bits of worn glass, and driftwood she'd plucked from the river
to decorate the frames. Brad built a display case for the original
Fresnel lens, and even set up a kerosene lamp with a silver
bucket next to it that they labeled WHALE OIL. During this time
he held several board meetings through Skype, all of which Bailey refused to attend, although she did read the minutes afterward. The board was excited about the lens, of course, and was
taking precautions to get it insured.

They stocked the little gift shop as well. They would sell
miniature lighthouses, postcards, and candles for a start. Bailey
wasn't thinking about her future; rather she threw herself into
the projects so she wouldn't have to think. Winter would soon
be upon them, and lately by early afternoon, the horizon would
turn into an endless gray, an on-the-verge-of-a-storm gloom,
and in the mornings the ground would be covered with frost,
and besides Captain Jack taking off, all anyone in town could
talk about was the winter, wondering how bad the river would
freeze this year.

Bailey wished she could enjoy it more. They had holidays
looming, Thanksgiving and Christmas. She wanted to be happy.

She wanted a big turkey and a table full of guests, and a Christmas tree, and Christmas carols, and roaring fires. She even wanted Captain Jack back. She wanted to see his ferry decked in lights, she wanted to buy overpriced eggnog from Island Supplies. She probably would have forgiven the old captain if he stayed. Sure, he would have been brought up on trespassing charges—other than that, what else could they have charged him with? Impersonating a ghost? Jake had certainly destroyed quite a bit of their property while searching for the lens, and of course had charged them for his contracting work in the meantime, but Bailey still thought she and Brad would have gone pretty easy on them. Unfortunately, sometimes people just didn't give you a chance to be the bigger person. The biggest wedge between Bailey and Brad was no longer the past, but the present. Bailey wanted Brad to find his son. He adamantly refused. So the two of them mirrored what the river was soon to become. Bailey was frozen, and Brad was immovable. Bailey even missed the days of Olivia. After Thomas almost destroyed the urn a second time, it had quietly disappeared from the Crow's Nest. Brad didn't tell her what he did with it, and Bailey didn't ask.

Chapter 37

Keeper's Log
Brad Jordan

You're not supposed to meet the love of your life at ten years old. But if you do, like I did, you're not supposed to sleep with other women. But if you do, like I did, you're supposed to be a stand-up guy. I wasn't. I gave up all parental rights to my son. Signed a document and everything. Then I kept it from the woman I love more than life itself. Sure, I was young, and stupid, and scared. And I was probably a little bit relieved at the time too. Relieved that someone else was taking the decision out of my hands, relieved that I could convince myself there was nothing else I could have done, relieved that I was just able to walk away, bury that one night of my life that would come to follow me the rest of my days.

If I had it to do over, I pray I would be a stand-up guy. Although Hargrave certainly had the money to hire the best attorneys. And if I had to do it all over, I still would've believed his lies that I was going to do serious jail time. I should've said, 'Bring it on,' but of course I didn't. But I do know that if I could take it all back, I would have told Bailey. Right? I probably would have lost her. She would've walked away. Who would she be now? Would she be happier? Would she have children? Would she have lived all her life in one place that she could call home instead of being dragged all over the place?

I really did buy this lighthouse so that I could give her a home. I wanted her to have a safe port in the storm. Bailey is still in shock, I can tell by the way she moves, how she holds her body, how difficult it is for her to look me in the eye. But she's still here, isn't she? We're working on the museum, and the gift shop, and she's even trying out new recipes on the few guests we've had since the incident.

Bailey wants me to contact him. She says my son is a grown man and he has a right to decide whether or not he wants to meet me. And I could tell him how I thought about him every single day. On his birthday, holidays, every time I passed a kid that would be around his age. I know Bailey is right, but something holds me back. Is it fear? Or am I still the same old selfish son of a—

Oh God. Bailey's right. This *is* a fucking diary.

Bailey woke up one morning to find a bedraggled, bloated blond woman in the kitchen. Bailey didn't even have time to speak before the woman launched herself from her seat at the head of the dining table and reached out to her.

"Money means shit," she said. "Fame means shit." Bailey nodded slowly, backing up while trying to remember which drawer held the sharp knives. She should never have started watching that zombie series with Brad. "We bought the penthouse despite that dorky chocolate-chip-scented candle and slide show of the Frick museum!"

"Allissa?" Bailey said. It was her voice, but it definitely wasn't her body. Wow, people really did let themselves go when they found true love.

"Like I don't already have a million pictures of where I got married!"

"But didn't the scent of chocolate chips make you feel warm and cozy?"

"No. I don't eat chocolate chips." *You didn't then,* Bailey thought. *But it certainly looks like you do now.* She was mature enough not to say it. Besides, Allissa didn't look fat by any means, she just wasn't her previous skeletal state. She looked better, but between the weight gain and black mascara running down her face, Bailey wouldn't have recognized her in a million years. It was then that Bailey noticed Allissa came with baggage. Four large Louis Vuittons, to be exact.

"How did you get here?" Bailey said. "The ferry is no longer in service."

Allissa gestured out the window. "I came in one of our smaller yachts," she said.

"Of course you did." Bailey gestured for Allissa to sit while she shuffled over to the coffeemaker.

"All he does is work, work, work!" Allissa whined.

"Greg?"

"Of course, Greg. Who else? Our yacht captain?" And if she hadn't already, Bailey would have recognized Allissa's sarcasm anywhere.

"Bear with me," Bailey said. "Just starting the coffee."

"We have some made on the yacht if you'd like me to have someone bring it. Speaking of which, where should Manuel put my luggage?" Upon mention of the name, a short middle-aged man wearing a tux and white gloves entered the kitchen and stood at attention. Apparently, he'd been listening and waiting on the other side of the door. For some reason, he looked familiar.

"Allissa," Bailey said. "You didn't make a reservation." Not that they had any other guests, but Bailey wasn't really in the mood for any, especially someone as high maintenance as Allissa. Allissa gestured at Manuel, who immediately pulled a checkbook out of his breast pocket.

"I'm staying at least a month," Allissa said. "Will fifty thousand do? Consider the extra a donation to your sad little gift shop museum thingy you have going on in there. You don't even have blankets or chocolates, for God's sakes." Blankets and chocolates. They actually weren't a bad idea.

"Upstairs, first room on the left, Manuel." He smiled at her, and recognition dawned.

"Carlos?" Bailey said. "Is that you?"

"His name is Manuel now," Allissa said.

"But you're Carlos, right? With the shopping cart and the megaphone, and the end of the world?"

"Allissa offered me employment," Carlos said.

"Don't say I never give to the homeless!" Allissa said.

"What about the end of the world?" Bailey said.

"It's easier to accept when you have a hot meal and a place to sleep," Carlos said.

"Do you live in the penthouse?"

"My God," Allissa said. "I'm not Mother Teresa."

"Studio in Harlem," Carlos said. "And I still have my shopping cart."

"Can you please stop chatting up the help?" Allissa said.

"Would you like help with the suitcases?" Bailey asked. Carlos-Manuel looked stricken at the idea. He shook his head, hurried over to the four large suitcases, and lifted them with ease, proportioning two on each side.

"Inappropriate!" he whispered at her as he scurried by. Bailey was relieved to see some of the old Carlos was still in Manuel.

"Since you've already had coffee, would you like something else to drink?" Bailey asked.

"Fresh-squeezed orange juice, please," Allissa said.

"We just have store-bought," Bailey said. Allissa nodded, but it appeared to make her sad. Bailey bit back asking if Allissa wanted her to drop everything and grow the tree. "I could put some champagne in it and make it a mimosa," Bailey said.

"I'm pregnant," Allissa said.

"I'll drink the champagne," Bailey said.

Allissa lit up the minute she saw Brad. Color came flooding back to her pale cheeks, and when she smiled her eyes seemed to sparkle. This time, Bailey wasn't jealous. It was good to see Allissa come back to life, and Bailey felt a familiar surge of pride that her husband had that effect on people, even if by "people" she meant women. The three of them had dinner together and allowed Allissa to hold court. Bailey was surprised to hear Allissa say that she didn't want her child to be raised by a nanny. She must have read Bailey's mind.

"I know I seem spoiled," she said. "And I am. But I wasn't always. I grew up with two parents, and no nanny, and so will my child. I'm not saying I'll never have help. Or 'me time' or 'spa time,' but being a mom is a full-time job, and I intend to do that job."

"I'm proud of you," Bailey said. "That's great."

"But Greg is never home. I'm all alone in that humungous place all the time. I mean, so far I keep myself busy with television shoots and the like, but it's all going to change when we have this baby."

"A baby does change everything," Bailey said. She didn't dare glance at Brad.

"I'm so jealous of you two," Allissa said. "You'd be the perfect parents. And look at this quaint, cozy little place. What kid wouldn't want to grow up in a lighthouse!"

"Have you talked to Greg about this?" Bailey said. "He's crazy about you. I'm sure he'd be willing to cut his hours when the baby comes along."

"Being crazy about someone doesn't necessarily mean you're always going to do the right thing, you know?" Brad said.

"We're talking about Greg here," Bailey said.

"Right, right, but just so you know, you can be totally, madly, in love, crazy about someone and still not do the right thing," Brad said. "Whatever that is."

Allissa looked from Brad to Bailey and back.

"Whatever that is?" Bailey said. "Do you honestly think, where a child is concerned, that there's any room for murk?"

"Murk?" Allissa said.

"You know—murky," Bailey said.

"Oh. Murky," Allissa said.

"Murky waters," Brad said.

"Exactly," Bailey said. "Where a child is concerned, there are no murky waters. Just murky, knuckleheaded men."

"Tell me one seventeen-year-old who knows how to handle something like that? You have no idea of the kind of pressure that can be put on someone."

"Greg's a lot older than seventeen," Allissa said. "But he'll be flattered."

"Being young is one thing," Bailey said. "Pressure is another. But lying to the person you love—the person who's done nothing but love you through coffees, and sweaters, and freaking surfboards—being by that person's side for give or take twenty-six years, obviously give away the night you spent with that little tramp from next door—that's a horse of a different color, buddy. That's—that's just unforgivable." Bailey stood up from the table. She knew she was being unfair to Allissa, but it had all just bubbled out of her. She had honestly and quite naïvely thought she was over the shock of Brad having a son. She had rationalized it away—he was so young, it was so long ago. Intellectually, Bailey had maturely processed it, but inside, she was still raw, and terribly sad, and angry.

Allissa's mouth was hanging open. Brad put his head down on the table. "Do you see me, Brad? I'm not even throwing things. But I can't sit here and listen to poor little Allissa whine because she's pregnant."

"Hey!"

"Your husband will do the right thing. I hope. I don't know how you make men appreciate babies. If I knew that I'd have one of my own by now. But at least you know you'll be able to raise this child no matter what."

"Am I missing something here?" Allissa said.

"I'm sorry," Brad said. "I'm so, so sorry."

"I'm sure you are. But I'm not even the one who matters now," Bailey said.

"Thank you," Allissa said.

"I don't want to discuss this," Brad said. "Not here and now."

"Here and now is all we have, Brad. You should know that better than anyone. You have to find him. You have to find him and tell him everything and get this terrible, terrible weight off your chest."

"I hear you," Brad said. "And I've thought about it—I seriously have. But I can't, I just can't."

"I am so sick of listening to your excuses," Bailey said. "All these years, the millions of excuses you had not to have a baby. And now this. This is not like my husband. My husband is not a coward!"

"Greg?" Allissa said. "Are we still talking about Greg?"

"No," Bailey said. "But if you want to talk to Greg, then call him."

"I'd rather he suffer for a while," Allissa said.

"That's very mature," Bailey said. "Both of you. Very mature." She turned and walked in the direction of the tower.

"She's become more aggressive since living on the water," Allissa whispered to Brad.

Bailey stood in the tower, gazing out at the water. Something in her had cracked and split wide open. She wanted to cry, she wanted to rage, she wanted to leap off the tower. Yet she had no right, because there was a young man out there who was the innocent player in the drama. Brad had a son, and he wasn't even going to make an attempt to see him? Just like him. Just like writing in those notebooks all those years, never sharing a word. Slamming doors. Starting over. Again and again. Keeping this secret from her. Denying her a child of their own. And not even coming out and denying it, but stringing her along, putting it off as if it were a project he didn't want to face, as if it were August and he didn't understand why she was bitching at him to take the Christmas lights down from the rim of the roof.

Was the universe testing their love? She felt as if she'd invested so much, given so much, opened herself up time and again. Was it too late to leave? Wouldn't the time have been when she was in her twenties with all the optimism and angst those years bring? Bailey noticed a kayaker coming toward shore. She grabbed the binoculars and peered out. She could have sworn it was Jake. She wondered what the little ghost maker was up to now. She hurried out to catch him.

Down at the water's edge, there was no sign of the kayaker Bailey had spotted from the tower. Nor was there a kayak pulled up on shore. It was as if he'd disappeared into thin air. Or maybe he'd been a mirage. Bailey's fantasies were now imagining Jake where Jake wasn't. She would have to ask Brad if he'd seen him.

Bailey was cleaning up the kitchen when she smelled paint. She entered the main room. It was coming from upstairs. She hurried up and found Allissa standing in the middle of the second bedroom, paintbrush in hand. Pink paint splattered onto the newspaper below. One whole wall had been slathered with pink. Before Bailey could lose it, Allissa turned and treated Bailey to a horrific sight. Allissa's face was bloated. Black tears ran down her face. Her lip was quivering.

"I'm gggoing to pppaint the other wall blueeeeeeeeeeeeee."

"Jesus." Bailey hurried toward her and took the paintbrush out of her hand. "You shouldn't be around paint fumes."

"I have to finish it."

"Come downstairs. I'll make you some juice. We'll figure this out." Allissa reluctantly let Bailey take the paintbrush out of her hands. Bailey turned to see Brad in the doorway.

"I have to finish it," Allissa said, reaching for the paintbrush again.

"I'll do it," Brad said. Bailey walked Allissa downstairs, made her some juice, and then tucked her into the couch for a rest. She took her cell phone out front and put in a call to Greg. Then she went back upstairs and watched Brad paint a baby's room. When he finally turned around, it was Bailey who had fat black tears running down her face.

Chapter 38

Can a marriage just end like that? From a million little paper
cuts? From a paintbrush filled with pink paint? Tiny threads
of resentment had weaved into one giant tapestry in Bailey's
mind, but the image that threatened to unravel it all was her
husband painting a baby's room in their house, which wasn't
really their house, for a baby that wasn't their baby. Without
speaking, because she couldn't, there were no words, just a lump
in her throat that threatened to choke her, Bailey turned from
the scene in front of her and crossed over the bridge to their
watch room. Normally she preferred to walk outside and enter
the tower from below. It was nice to have a separation of home
and work. But at the moment all she wanted to do was pack a
bag and get out of Dodge. Brad followed her, dripping pink
paint as he did, calling her name, softly at first and then almost
shouting it. He knew. He could feel her leaving. Marriage was
that too, tiny clicks and blinks, and sighs, and energy that you
could feel, predict. One of their biggest fights was caused when
Bailey rolled her eyes at something he said. It was also the
greatest make-up sex she'd ever had. That was marriage too, a

sudden wave of passion that would carry you over to the next moment, and then the next, and then the next. But she didn't have anything left to carry her to the next moment. The rowboat of their marriage was sinking fast.

Brad watched her pack a bag, pacing behind her in the circular room. He asked questions she couldn't answer. "Where are you going?" "How long will you be gone?" "What can I do?" "Why won't you talk to me?" *Please, baby, please.* Bailey turned and looked at Brad. She wished she had the answers. She wished she could comfort him, make all of this go away. But she couldn't, she simply didn't know how. *Yellow,* she wanted to say. *We'll always have the color yellow.* But when she said it in her head it sounded melodramatic and silly, so instead she said nothing at all.

Jake was waiting outside, standing on the patio. He saw her suitcase, then locked eyes with her.

"I don't want to be with Angel," he said. "I want to be with you." Bailey smiled, a tired, flattered little smile. "I didn't want to do those stupid ghost things. But it was harmless, right? A few recordings—music boxes and a woman laughing—a duplicate urn, a few wires cut to make the tower light freak out, the wrong battery in the tide clock. I swear I wouldn't have done anything to really hurt anyone. And my feelings for you . . . They were totally real. I mean it, Bailey. I think I'm in love with you." It was absurd, listening to his speech while her husband stood behind them, dumbfounded, still dripping little splotches of pink paint wherever he went. Bailey brushed past Jake and entered the main room. Jake and then Brad followed. Allissa was still curled up on the couch, her cell phone clutched in hand.

"Listen," she said. She pressed Speaker and played a message. Greg's voice filled the little room.

"Honey," he said. "Honey, honey, honey. I love you. I love our baby. I'm coming. Don't go anywhere, I'm coming. I'm taking a vacation. We'll stay out there together, then come home together. Having a family with you is all I've ever wanted. Nothing else matters. Do you hear me? You and this baby are all I've ever wanted."

Bailey looked at Brad. He stared back, and between them, it was clear. She was listening to the very words she wished he would have said to her.

"That's how I feel," Jake said. "About you."

Allissa sat up and straightened her long, blond hair, now sticking up like a science experiment. "Do I know you?" she said.

"He was talking to me," Bailey said. "Not everything is about you."

"You're not getting my wife," Brad said.

Allissa looked confused. "I don't want her," she said. There was a loud pounding on the door. Brad answered it and came back with the Coast Guard.

"Is it the light again?" Bailey asked. For a split second, she wanted the light to be malfunctioning. She wanted the place to be filled with ghosts, she wanted Olivia around to save their marriage. Or she wanted the storm to be the biggest one ever, she wanted the Coast Guard to forbid her to leave her home, her husband.

"We just thought you guys should know there's a storm coming in, and it's going to be a doozy." He glanced at Bailey's suitcase. "If you're going somewhere, you'll want to get a move on, soon."

"I'm leaving now," Bailey said. She picked up the suitcase. *Thanks a lot, guards. So much for stepping in to save me.* Bailey turned to Allissa. "Can I borrow your yacht?"

"No, no, I don't think so," Allissa said.

"I'll take you," Jake said.

"Over my dead body," Brad said.

"There's a potential buyer captaining the ferry today," the Coast Guard said. "I'm sure he'd take you across." So that was that, Bailey thought. The Coast Guard was definitely not on the side of romance.

"Great," Bailey said. "Can you give him a call and see if he'll pick me up?" Maybe he would say no. Maybe someone besides Brad would try and talk her out of this. The Coast Guard got on his radio and spoke into it quietly.

"He'll pick you up in fifteen minutes," he said.

"Bailey, please," Brad said. "I'm begging you."

"Brad, I just—"

"Let me come with you."

"Not right now."

"Then wait here," Brad said.

"I can't just—"

"Three minutes, Bails. Just three minutes." Brad looked absolutely tortured. Finally, Bailey nodded. He ran out of the room. When he returned, he was carrying a box. He looked at her and answered her unspoken question.

"My journals," he said. "Or diaries, if you prefer." He gave her a sad little smile. "It's the only thing I can give you right now," he said. "Bailey, please." It was so strange to be in this place, a new marital territory, one in which she was pulling away and Brad was the one desperate to pull her back in. She nodded and took the box.

The new captain was having trouble starting the ferry. That was the trouble with ownership. Even ships got used to having one main person to take care of them. Whatever sweet touch Captain Jack had with the ferry, this new guy didn't. He hadn't spent years with her, he didn't know if she needed a little kick or shorter thrusts of the engine, or maybe some kind words whispered before turning the key. He didn't know her capacity, how she performed in storms, how to toot her horn just so. It was just like a marriage. Bailey couldn't understand how married couples were even tempted to cheat. If you were with the right mate to begin with, they were the ones that knew how to get you started, how to keep you humming, how you were going to do when storms hit.

God, listen to her. Panic gripped her. Was she making a mistake she could never take back? Did she really, truly want to leave? No, she just wanted the blinding pain to go away. She

loved the lighthouse, the keeper's house, and she loved Brad
and the life they'd started to make here. Bailey had to admit it,
she even missed Captain Jack. She realized they hadn't even
asked the Coast Guard to arrest Jake or question where Angel
and Jack were. None of it really mattered to Bailey right now.
Bailey sat on one of the benches next to the box of journals.
While the new captain tinkered with the engine, Bailey grabbed
the first notebook and began to leaf through it. At first she
thought she was seeing things.

Bailey has an incredible laugh. I heard her with a customer. Whatever he said struck her as funny, and she
just threw her head back and the sound of her laughter filled our little coffee shop and I looked around and
everyone, everyone was laughing with her. How did I
get so lucky? What if some customer falls madly in
love with her and steals her from me?

Bailey is pissed. I think it's all the traveling, we've
been to Ireland, Scotland, England, France, Italy, and
now Spain. I don't blame her for being grumpy, but I
hate when she's pissed at me. And what's with all the
throwing? What an arm! She should have played baseball.

Bailey thinks she has big hands, but I think they're
beautiful. Especially when they're wrapped around
me. Same goes for her tongue, but if I tell her that she
might stop doing it out of spite.

I don't think Bailey likes California. Neither of us can
surf either. She's getting antsy. It might be time to go
soon.

What was I thinking? Sweaters? Bailey looks fabulous
in them, I think she's allergic.

Bailey put the notebook down and grabbed the next. Again, every entry was about her. What she wore, how she looked, and how she treated him that day. Here were the little moments of their life, their marriage, word by word, sentence by sentence, page by page. Bailey stood up. She was going to go back. She had been through too much with Brad to give up now. Together, they would face this. Brad Jordan loved her. She had never once stopped loving him. Flaws and all, they were meant to be together. Destiny had brought them together, the universe had given her this wonderful gift, this incredible man. What was she doing? The boat's engine suddenly roared to life.

"Got her!" the captain said. But a few seconds later, the engine died again, and they just sat there. Bailey closed her eyes and imagined a dramatic ending. What if there was a massive tugboat behind them, and while trying to back up the ferry he slammed into it with a sickening thud? Bailey would be thrown forward like a weightless rag doll. The captain would hit his head on one of the benches before crumpling to the floor. It would all happen so fast. The ferry would begin to tilt. Everything would roll to the right. Brad's notebooks would careen past her like out-of-control ice skaters.

"Brad." Even though he wouldn't be able to hear her, she would shout his name, then pull herself up to one of the windows and be greeted by the sight of the river filling the windows. She would leap into action.

"We're sinking. Life jackets!" Bailey wouldn't be afraid to die. Wouldn't be afraid to see the light Brad had fallen in love with.

But if anything happened to her now, Brad would be a ruined man. He wouldn't even know that she'd seen the notebooks. He would blame himself for the rest of his life. She would be a hero. Claw her way to the top of the boat, dragging the amateur captain with her. And given that she only had two hands, she would only be able to take one of the notebooks with her. The rest would forever be submerged in an icy grave.

Panic would sober the captain up. They would be forced to

jump. The Coast Guard would rush to the rescue, small life rafts would be positioned below them. In the distance she would hear Brad shouting, his voice almost hoarse. He would be rowing toward her in his leaky little boat—wishing desperately he'd heeded her advice about a Jet Ski. She would want to shout back, but she would have to save all her energy for the jump.

The captain would have no problem. He would jump before she could even say any parting words. He would land perfectly in the life raft, look at her, and give her an encouraging thumbs up. "Jump," the Coast Guard would yell at her, "jump."

The ferry was going to explode. *"Jump,"* she would hear again. This time, it would be Brad. Only then would she jump.

The impact of her body slamming into the freezing water would hit Bailey hard. She would be going too fast to grab onto anything, too fast to stop, and within seconds she would be completely underwater. She would struggle to reverse her direction, swim up, and hit her head on a large, hard object. Pain would soar through her, and she would be pulled under once again. Suddenly, she would able to see underwater. Everything would be calm, her head just slightly buzzing now, and she would be surprised how clear the water was, almost as if a light were shining underneath. Suddenly, a wrinkled hand would reach out for her, and a familiar face would hover above her. "Olivia," Bailey would say, surprised she could talk underwater. And then, everything would go black.

"Um. Hello?" Bailey glanced up. The captain was chewing on a straw. "I think we're out of gas."

"Oh," Bailey said.

"I mean, you can like sit there if you want. But I'm getting off."

"Me too," Bailey said.

She took the box and exited the ferry. She looked at the lighthouse. Smoke was coming out of the chimney. The sky was dark early, and the wind was picking up strength. It had yet to start raining, but in the distance was a rumble of thunder. Bailey walked a few steps, then put the box down and lay down on the rocks. She imagined she were a vessel, before there was a light to warn her away from the shoals, crashed out on the rocks. She didn't know how long she was there before she heard feet crunching on the rocks, coming toward her. She closed her eyes. She felt him lie down beside her.

"Nice night for a nap," he said.

"Yes," she said. She felt his fingertips touch hers.

"Bailey," he said. "This isn't my life." With her other hand, Bailey pawed the ground for a weapon. Broken glass, anything she might use to kill him.

"You wanted to live here. You—"

"No," Brad said. "Those are just the details. You are my life."

"Oh," Bailey said. She stopped searching for something sharp.

"I don't want to lose you," Brad said. "I can't."

"I don't want to go," Bailey said.

"You can't," Brad said. "The ferry is out of gas."

"How do you know that?"

"Because I'm the one who siphoned it out," Brad said.

"You did not."

"Smell me." Brad shoved his hand under her nose.

"Good thing I didn't light up a cigarette," Bailey said.

"You don't smoke."

"I'm thinking of starting."

"Don't you dare. I want you around as long as possible."

"Ah, but I hear the light is the place to be."

"It's overrated."

"Is it now."

Brad rolled over and hovered over her. "Name it," he said. "I'll go anywhere. Do anything."

"Why don't we try sticking it out for a change, Jordan."

"I can do that. I can stick it out." He nuzzled her neck and she wrapped her arms around the back of his head. "I'm afraid to contact him," Brad said. "I'm afraid he'll reject me."

"He might. Then again, he might not."

"I can't get those years back."

"Nope."

"He's going to like you. I just know it."

"I'll make him pancakes."

"You and me," Brad said.

"You and me," Bailey said.

"That's not what I expected you to say."

"Life is full of the unexpected."

"And baby makes three," Brad said.

"Let's take one thing at a time," Bailey said.

"Nothing wrong with that," Brad said. "But I'm not going to be afraid to try."

"Good to know."

He reached over and took her hand. "Hey," he said. "You have nails."

"What?" She curled her fingers in and felt them dig into her palms. "My God," she said. "I never noticed."

"It's a new day," Brad said.

"I like the sound of that."

"While we're on the subject of trying new things . . ."

"Oh God."

"Don't panic. It's something I can do anywhere."

"Are you getting cold? I'm getting kind of cold. And was that thunder? We should get inside before it starts to rain."

"It's not a new idea by any means, but I think I can pull it off." The wind picked up, and the orange cone Bailey had used to mark off the broken part of the dock sailed past them. Thunder rolled again, and then lightning cracked over the river as rain began to fall.

"We'd better get inside," Bailey said.

"I promise you—it's exciting."

"Great."

"You can do it with me."

"We'll see." Bailey wrapped her arms around the back of Brad's head, pulled him into her, and kissed him long and hard, as if trying to kiss all the ideas out of his head. Their foghorn pierced the air, and when the light from the tower swept over them, it seemed to linger, like a spotlight, before going to black. When Bailey finally let go, Brad struggled to his feet and then helped haul Bailey up. Together they braced against the wind and the rain and started walking back to the keeper's house.

"And I know where we're going to spread Olivia's ashes."

"Where?"

"Remember the gambling cruise that goes by every year?"

"Uh-huh."

"We should take it. Play a hand of poker, then set her free, into the Hudson."

"That's actually not a bad idea."

Brad pulled Bailey in closer. "A screenplay!" he shouted over the wind, and the thunder, and the lightning, and the foghorn, and the occulting white light. "I'm going to write a screenplay."

"Uh-huh."

"We'll make tons of money, and you can be my cowriter."

"Wonderful."

"It'll be based on our lives, only way more exciting."

"Good call."

"And screenwriters can live anywhere. And what's more romantic and inspiring for a writer than a lighthouse? Although once in a while I might have to take a meeting in LA." Bailey let go of Brad's arm and broke into a run.

Nails, she thought as her husband chased after her. *I've grown really sharp nails.*

Epilogue

My name is Patrick Jordan, but you can call me 'Trick'. Just kidding. See, gotcha already. Let me show you the ropes. This is a kick ass lighthouse. I'll be your guide and feel free to tip me. It's open year-round as a B&B if you're brave enough to stay. And not because of the so-called ghost, but because of a newborn baby crying almost twenty-four-seven. Julia Jordan. I think I'll call her JJ for short. She's freaking cute except for the crying thing. If you had told me a year ago that I'd get to meet my biological dad, and grandmother, and step-mom, and be an uncle, and live in a freaking lighthouse, I would have thought you'd gone off your meds. But here I am, right? Working hard to educate and entertain you. I've been here for two months now and not once have I had to listen to anyone pressure me about what I want to do with my life. See, where I come from that's kind of like a mortal sin. Or is it moral sin? I can't remember. I just know I'm supposed to be a doctor, or a lawyer, or something ending in "er" only I don't have a clue as to what I want to do. Mostly because I want to do everything. So I changed my major in college like a dozen times until my grandfather said he'd had enough of me and threatened to stop bankrolling my future. Which, you know, I don't blame him. And that's when I get this little notecard, from this lighthouse, from my biological dad. Pretty awesome, right? I thought my old lady was going to freak, but she was actually relieved. Said she's felt guilty keeping us apart all these years.

According to the old step-monster (just joshin', she's great) I'm a lot like my father. She says we're Renaissance men, which is just a fancy way of saying we're good at a lot of things, so we can't just stick to one dream. Some people are just born knowing what they want, others take a while to discover it. In the meantime, I like it here. Sure you've got to take a stupid little rowboat to get anywhere, but I'm building up the biceps which is never a bad thing. And I'm helping Brad (still can't call him "dad" but at least it rhymes!) write a screenplay. It's a mix of horror and romance, like *Amityville Horror* meets *The Notebook*.

We'll start here in the Museum Shop where you can view the original Fresnel Lens. Watch your step, there's baby crap everywhere. Sorry, baby *stuff.* From here we'll tour through the main house, including the spooky attic, then we'll get to climb up to the lighthouse tower, and then back to the house so you can tip me and sign the guest book. Hope you enjoy your tour and come back real soon. If you want to help fund our movie, we'd be much obliged. I've already called shotgun for the starring role (kinda weird to play my dad, but when you're just starting in the biz you can't be too picky), but if you cough up enough dough we might let you be an extra. Especially if you can scream and weep on cue. We've already got the "lights"; now we just need the camera and the action.

Please turn the page for a very special

Q&A with Mary Carter!

Why did you want to write a story about a lighthouse?

Like many people, I've always thought of lighthouses as romantic and mysterious. I would love to live in one myself. I also liked how the metaphor of a light designed to guide you to safety can be used a metaphor for a marriage.

What research did you do?

I've visited lighthouses around the United States in the past. For this book I did a lot of research online, I watched videos, I read books, and I contacted several lighthouse keepers as well as those involved in conservancy groups to save lighthouses that have been decommissioned. I briefly spoke with a few Coast Guard members as well to try and understand their role in the "access to optic" agreements.

Why the Hudson River?

I was surprised to learn that there used to be fourteen lighthouses on the Hudson River. Today there are nine. I needed Bailey to be underwhelmed by the prospect of living in a lighthouse. She says she might have been more excited if it were in Maine, or California, or Scotland. No offense to the location I did choose, but it didn't quite fit her dream of where she wanted to live.

Can you really buy a lighthouse at an auction?

Yes. The Coast Guard does indeed auction off lighthouses. However, the rules and regulations vary from state to state regarding whether or not you are still going to run the light or decommission it. There are a few privately owned lighthouses that are run as an "aid to navigation" in which the Coast Guard is not involved, but I was told that is no longer allowed—some are simply grandfathered in. Most private owners have to either decommission the light or it has to be run by a board or non-profit agency, and in that case, the light is normally automated and the Coast Guard is responsible for the maintenance and regulation of the light.

There are many groups dedicated to preserving lighthouses, and they are disturbed by the thought of private owners turning them into for-profit bed-and-breakfasts and decommissioning the lights. They would prefer to see the lighthouse run by a conservancy group whose aim is to keep the light running and make sure all the money goes back into the preservation and maintenance of the lighthouse.

Is a Fresnel lens really that valuable?

Fresnel lenses come in six orders, or sizes. The largest, or the first-order lens, can be up to twelve feet tall and weigh six thousand pounds. They are made of bronze and crystal, all with concentric "beehive" rings with a magnifying glass in the center. And yes, an original fourth-order Fresnel lens could easily fetch $250,000. Modern-day lights are often a solar-powered battery mounted on a steel pole.

12. Marriage is a give and take. Who does more giving and who does more taking when it comes to the Jordans?

13. Will Brad ever change? Should he change?

14. Does Bailey really put up with too much from Brad? Should she leave him? Would Bailey have been happier selling condos in Manhattan?

15. Brad felt a strong need to save the lighthouse—keep the light running. In order to do so he gave up actual ownership of the lighthouse. Do you agree with his decision? Did this secret damage their marriage the most, or the revelation that he had a son? Do you understand his passion to keep the light running?

16. Is Bailey's attraction to Jake or Brad's to Allissa or Angel any real threat to their marriage? Is it normal for couples to have little crushes on someone outside their marriage? When does it cross a line? Did Bailey or Brad ever cross that line?

17. Muhheakantuck is the name the Indians gave to the Hudson River because its conflicting tides make it flow both ways. Captain Jack calls it "The River That Cannot Make Up Its Mind." Who is most like that river, Bailey or Brad?

18. Is Captain Jack a dangerous criminal or a slighted brother? Were all the strange goings-on in the house due to him, or did Olivia's ghost ever make a real appearance? How did the presence of her ashes affect Bailey?

19. How has Bailey changed at the very end of the story? How has Brad changed? Who has changed the most? The least? Are they ready to be parents? Is their marriage better or worse off than at the beginning? Why is it significant that they are crashed out on the rocks?

A READING GROUP GUIDE

THE THINGS I DO FOR YOU

Mary Carter

ABOUT THIS GUIDE

The suggested questions are included to enhance your group's reading of Mary Carter's
The Things I Do for You.

DISCUSSION QUESTIONS

1. In what ways are Brad and Bailey similar? In what are they different?

2. What role has Bailey played in their past business ures?

3. How have Brad's and Bailey's upbringing affected w they are now?

4. Which guest affects Bailey the most? Brad?

5. Olivia Jordan lived a bit of a double life. Why do yo think she hid that life from Bailey and Brad?

6. What kind of mother would Bailey be? What kind of fa ther would Brad be?

7. Bailey and Brad run into several couples: Allissa and Greg, Angel and Jake, and their French guests, Dean and Rachel. How does each couple affect Brad and Bailey's marriage?

8. Guests all come with their own quirks and set of problems. Which guest affected you the most? The least?

9. Elizabeth Jordan wouldn't be up for Mother of the Year. Has she changed? Would she now make a good grandmother?

10. How has Brad changed from his Near Death Experience? In what ways is he the same?

11. Light and shadow is a theme throughout the book. When the story opens, Bailey is studying shadows while Brad is gravitating toward the light. How is this a metaphor for their marriage? Who has the most power in the marriage? Has it changed throughout their relationship? Does it change during the course of the novel?

THE THINGS I DO FOR YOU

Mary Carter

ABOUT THIS GUIDE

The suggested questions are included to enhance
your group's reading of Mary Carter's
The Things I Do for You.

DISCUSSION QUESTIONS

1. In what ways are Brad and Bailey similar? In what ways are they different?

2. What role has Bailey played in their past business failures?

3. How have Brad's and Bailey's upbringing affected who they are now?

4. Which guest affects Bailey the most? Brad?

5. Olivia Jordan lived a bit of a double life. Why do you think she hid that life from Bailey and Brad?

6. What kind of mother would Bailey be? What kind of father would Brad be?

7. Bailey and Brad run into several couples: Allissa and Greg, Angel and Jake, and their French guests, Dean and Rachel. How does each couple affect Brad and Bailey's marriage?

8. Guests all come with their own quirks and set of problems. Which guest affected you the most? The least?

9. Elizabeth Jordan wouldn't be up for Mother of the Year. Has she changed? Would she now make a good grandmother?

10. How has Brad changed from his Near Death Experience? In what ways is he the same?

11. Light and shadow is a theme throughout the book. When the story opens, Bailey is studying shadows while Brad is gravitating toward the light. How is this a metaphor for their marriage? Who has the most power in the marriage? Has it changed throughout their relationship? Does it change during the course of the novel?

12. Marriage is a give and take. Who does more giving and who does more taking when it comes to the Jordans?

13. Will Brad ever change? Should he change?

14. Does Bailey really put up with too much from Brad? Should she leave him? Would Bailey have been happier selling condos in Manhattan?

15. Brad felt a strong need to save the lighthouse—keep the light running. In order to do so he gave up actual ownership of the lighthouse. Do you agree with his decision? Did this secret damage their marriage the most, or the revelation that he had a son? Do you understand his passion to keep the light running?

16. Is Bailey's attraction to Jake or Brad's to Allissa or Angel any real threat to their marriage? Is it normal for couples to have little crushes on someone outside their marriage? When does it cross a line? Did Bailey or Brad ever cross that line?

17. Muhheakantuck is the name the Indians gave to the Hudson River because its conflicting tides make it flow both ways. Captain Jack calls it "The River That Cannot Make Up Its Mind." Who is most like that river, Bailey or Brad?

18. Is Captain Jack a dangerous criminal or a slighted brother? Were all the strange goings-on in the house due to him, or did Olivia's ghost ever make a real appearance? How did the presence of her ashes affect Bailey?

19. How has Bailey changed at the very end of the story? How has Brad changed? Who has changed the most? The least? Are they ready to be parents? Is their marriage better or worse off than at the beginning? Why is it significant that they are crashed out on the rocks?

20. By the end, Brad says he is ready to dispose of Olivia's ashes. Does this mean he's ready to let go of the past? Will he? Will she? Bailey also says she loves living in the lighthouse and doesn't want to leave. Is this true, or is she just tired of moving around?